SIREN Call

Eastern Shore Swingers #3

Phoebe Alexander

Kaitlyn —
Enjoy Sirena & Jessie's story!
Phoebe Alexander

Copyright © 2018 by Phoebe Alexander
All rights reserved. This book or any portion thereof may not be reproduced or used in any manner whatsoever without the express written permission of the publisher except for the use of brief quotations in a book review.

Printed in the United States of America

First Printing, 2018

ISBN 978-0-9983353-4-6

Mountains Wanted Publishing
P.O. Box 1014
Georgetown, DE 19947
www.mountainswanted.com

Cover Design by Teresa Conner, Wolfsparrow Publishing

DEDICATION

To my beautiful friends Agathe and Dawn Monique,
whose encouragement and support were
vital to the creation of this book.

CONTENTS

Prologue.....................1
One........................4
Two........................21
Three......................36
Four.......................56
Five.......................73
Six........................89
Seven......................105
Eight......................121
Nine.......................138
Ten........................151
Eleven.....................166
Twelve.....................179
Thirteen...................196
Fourteen...................211
Fifteen....................226
Sixteen....................242
Seventeen..................262
Eighteen...................282
Nineteen...................302
Twenty.....................325
Epilogue...................345
Acknowledgments............358
About the Author...........361
Also By....................362

PHOEBE ALEXANDER

PROLOGUE

I think there are two different oceans - the one that plays with you in the summer, and the one that gets so mad in the winter. - Jodi Picoult, Handle with Care

No one forgets their first time.

Though Jessie had been with a few boys when she was in high school and in her early twenties, she considered her real *first time* to be with Victoria. She called herself Tori, and she was on the verge of graduating from college. The whole world stretched before both young women like an oyster poised to reveal its lustrous pearl of promise.

It happened during Jessie's training at the police academy. The days were long; the nights were short. There was very little in the way of time for socialization or fraternization. Up at 5 AM. PT. Breakfast. Class. Lunch. Class. PT again. Dinner. Study. Bed. Her weekdays were endless cycles of the same events, over and over. The weekends were only slightly less regimented, but there were those few glorious, precious hours when one donned their civilian clothes and pretended to have a life.

Jessie had been walking across the college campus where the police academy held its training, returning from a football game with her fellow cadets. Autumn leaves rained down from swaying trees, then danced around her feet. She squinted as the sun landed on a patch of fiery gold across the quad, illuminating a beautiful woman as though heaven itself were shining down on her. She was sitting on a bench reading a book, and she had a glowing mass of curls piled up on top of her head that caught in the light like a million stars exploding.

Jessie wasn't sure what compelled her to approach the young woman. Maybe the Academy had made her bolder, more confident, even as it tore her body down and built it back up. She was being taught how to become superior, molding her body, her intellect, her will. The whole of her being was being forged into a force for good. At least Jessie hoped she would be a force for good.

She introduced herself, and Victoria smiled. "Call me Tori," she'd insisted, patting the bench next to her.

How did Jessie know she liked girls? How did Tori know? It didn't matter. Later that day, after a labyrinth of a discussion about feminism, poverty, and, of all things, religion, they found themselves in the library wandering among floor-to-ceiling stacks of books. It was a fortress of knowledge giving them cover from the judgmental world around them. Jessie thought she might implode if she didn't find out what Tori's soft, strawberry-hued lips felt like against hers. And she didn't intend to wait one more minute.

Throughout the remainder of Jessie's time in the Academy, the two young women shared more deep conversations and intimate moments: stolen kisses in the quad beneath a bare-branched tree, only a few scraggly brown leaves remaining. Warm hands gliding across silken skin. Coffee together on a Sunday morning. A movie curled up together underneath a thick down blanket. And a few times, during a rare hour or two in Tori's apartment, Jessie learned what made her sigh, what made her scream.

When Jessie graduated that winter, Tori was supposed to be cheering her on from the audience at her graduation. She wasn't. Jessie learned later her girlfriend had gone home that weekend to be with her fiancé and plan their spring wedding.

ONE

*Eros, again now, the loosener of limbs troubles me,
Bittersweet, sly, uncontrollable creature... - Sappho*

Another ten-hour shift trying to keep day-drinking tourists in line. Jessie unbuckled her gun belt and carefully lifted it off her ample hips, where it perched as if it were a part of her body, a sort of exoskeleton. She set it down on the chair behind her, feeling like a giant weight had just been lifted. But it was a weight she was born to carry.

Jessie had wanted to be a cop since she was a little girl. She lost track of how many times she'd dressed up like one for Halloween and colored a uniform and badge on a stick figure in crayons when asked to draw what she wanted to be when she grew up. Now she was grown, and she'd been a police officer in Ocean City,

Maryland, for going on ten years.

She'd seen a lot in her thirty-two years, but most of it had been since donning the badge. *To serve and protect.* It wasn't just a cheesy platitude. It was her mantra, her lifeforce. There was nothing she took more seriously than her role as part of the *Thin Blue Line*.

Her parents were proud of her; there was no doubt. But she had little contact with her family. Her brothers had both been on the other side of the law; both had done time. One was an alcoholic; one was in and out of drug rehab. Not to mention the real reason Jessie left home. She cringed every time she thought about how they had disgraced her family.

Jessie left her childhood behind in rural Pennsylvania where she grew up. She preferred being down here, at the beach. And so did many other Pennsylvanians, judging by how many PA tags she saw clogging the inlet and the Route 90 bridges in Ocean City. She wondered how many of those tags would be on the cars parked at The Factory tonight.

First she had to ditch the police uniform for some club-wear. She always thought it was a rather interesting transformation, not unlike Clark Kent changing into Superman. *No, probably more like Bruce Wayne becoming Batman,* she decided as she ransacked her closet for something curve-hugging and black. Cap and Leah Sheldon, the club owners, had asked her to come in early. They needed her help with something.

There were only two cars in the lot when she arrived at The Factory. One was Cap and Leah's, and the other belonged to her friend Paisley Mitchell, who had introduced her to the whole lifestyle scene a couple of years ago. Paisley was the operations manager of the club and was there any time the doors were open. Her husband Calvin was the head of security. The owners, Cap and Leah, took more of a back seat now that they were parents, but still handled all the club's finances and accounts.

She poked her head through the front glass doors, which were heavily tinted so no one could see inside from the parking lot. She checked out her reflection in them before swinging the door open. *Swinging*, she chuckled to herself at her pun. She'd found a simple black cotton sundress that clung to her wide, curvy hips in just the right places, and had braved four inch platform wedge sandals to elevate her petite 5'2" height.

"You know, you really shouldn't leave this door unlocked when the club is closed," she called across the spacious foyer, which was lined with sleek leather couches and decorated with an "eighties meets steampunk" twist. Or at least that was what Paisley called it.

"Sorry, that's my fault," Calvin admitted, coming down the hall from behind the bar. "I was just bringing my extra set of keys to Leah since she apparently misplaced hers."

"Again?" Jessie cocked an eyebrow. "That doesn't sound like her."

"I think she's a bit stressed now that we're officially in season," he suggested.

Ocean City was a tourist haven, especially for swingers. In the summertime, throngs of couples and singles hoping to hook up descended upon the small town which stretched down a narrow strip of land, separated from the mainland by a shallow bay. On the other side, the mighty Atlantic crashed its foamy white waves upon the golden sand beaches. It was a swinger paradise there in the summer, and The Factory was the only lifestyle club in town.

Jessie nodded in understanding and took the stairs to the offices that overlooked the open space of the lounge below. "Hey," she said, peeking into Leah's office. "Is Cap here? He said you guys wanted to talk to me."

"Yeah, let me text him. He took Lincoln out for a walk to try to get him to take a nap," Leah sighed. Jessie spotted the purple half-moons under her eyes, a sure sign she hadn't been getting enough sleep. Leah forced a smile as she pulled out her phone and flew over the keys. Then she brushed her long strawberry blonde hair away from her face, sweeping it into a band that she fashioned into a messy bun.

"He's still not sleeping through the night?" Jessie asked. She couldn't imagine having the energy to keep up with an active toddler while also not getting enough rest at night. Sometimes she thought motherhood made being a cop look easy.

Leah shook her head. "I don't know how we are going to manage another one!" She laughed, her face brightening.

"Whoa, is there something you want to tell me, Leah?" Jessie asked, gripping the edge of the desk. "Number two on the way already?"

"Oh, gosh, not yet! I think we're going to wait a few years before trying for another. Lincoln is a handful. Cap says he's too old for this…stuff. He used a different word though." She giggled.

Leah's parents were conservative evangelical

Christians, and she hardly ever cursed. If she did break out an expletive, then it was a sure sign she had been pushed past her limits. And like all redheads, she could have a nasty temper when she was put to the test.

Jessie heard footsteps bounding up the metal spiral staircase, which echoed through the empty space and rafters of the old fish processing plant that had first been converted into a boat storage facility and then finally to a swing club through the blood, sweat and tears of the Sheldons. It had been backed financially by Cap and a third party, Casey Fontaine, a local realtor who knew the area like the back of her hand, and who now worked for the club part-time.

"Success!" Cap grinned through his beard, his trademark dimples still visible through his silvery scruff as he leaned down to give his wife a peck on the cheek. "He's in the stroller downstairs. Calvin said he'd keep an eye on him, and Paisley will be right back."

Once they were both seated, Jessie folded her hands in her lap and looked from one to the other expectantly. "So what can I do for you?"

Leah cleared her throat before beginning to speak. Jessie knew Leah enjoyed women, but she had never had the pleasure of playing with her. *Too bad*, Jessie thought, her gaze trailing over Leah's engaging green eyes and smooth, porcelain skin. "Have you noticed that blonde woman, Sirena, who has been coming to the club for about a month now?" Leah asked.

Jessie's mind spun through images of all the female members of The Factory. It was a huge photo album filled with beautiful breasts and lush curves. "She comes by herself? Single woman?" she clarified, her brown eyes meeting Leah's.

Cap nodded. "Yes. She's also very active on our group Facebook page. She posts a lot of selfies on there."

Jessie sometimes wished she could have a social media presence, but with her job, it wasn't advisable. "I know who you're talking about," she finally said, her mind still holding up the image of the woman in question, carefully examining it. "It would be almost impossible not to notice her—or to forget her, for that matter."

Leah laughed. "Yeah, I figured you'd know who we were talking about."

"So is there a problem or what?" Jessie asked.

Cap ran his fingers through his beard, then leaned down toward the desk, placing his elbows on the surface. "Yeah, there are a few issues. There've been some catty remarks about her from some of the ladies in the club. I think most of it stems from jealousy, but there seems to be some tension there. You know how cliques can be. Paisley's been trying to keep an eye on her because she gets pretty drunk and seems to go home with a different single man or couple every night she's here. We're not so concerned about the couples. They've all been regulars, and I'm sure they're taking good care of her."

"In more ways than one!" Leah interjected.

"Right," Cap agreed, smiling at his wife. "But some of these single guys... I mean, we have their information and all, but I don't know. Between the mean girl clique and the single guys, we're just worried about a potential liability issue."

Jessie scrunched up her nose and furrowed her brows in thought. "Doesn't everyone sign forms to deny the club's liability? Isn't that part of the application process?"

Paisley had already asked Jessie to look over their member intake forms to see what she thought of them from a legal standpoint. The last thing they wanted was for the cops to get called to the club. Calvin's father was a detective with the Maryland State Police, and he knew of the club from the blackmailing issue Paisley had a year or so ago. Calvin Sr. helped Paisley get to the bottom of the extortion and threats against her—not to mention the fact he likely saved her life and possibly the Sheldons' lives too. Jessie had found the forms to be pretty ironclad. After all, Leah had a background in the hotel industry and Casey Fontaine's was in real estate. They had waded their way through oceans of legal jargon in their time.

"It is," Cap answered. "But who knows? People could provide fake addresses, IDs, anything really. This is a tourist area. A lot of the people who walk through our doors aren't even Maryland residents. Half of our member roster is made up of people from Pennsylvania, Virginia, Delaware, and New Jersey. We've got the whole mid-Atlantic in here most weekends, and it's getting really hard for Calvin to keep track of everyone."

"I can imagine," Jessie agreed. "So why don't you hire more guards? You've got three or four besides Calvin now, don't you?"

Leah nodded. "Yes, but they're all men. They can't go into the women's restrooms or changing areas. And, honestly, we think we need a woman for this job. And we think you're the right woman."

"A job of keeping tabs on some random blonde lady?" Jessie laughed at how preposterous it sounded.

"What, like you want me to be her personal bodyguard?"

"No, no," Cap answered. "That's not what we're asking at all. We don't even want her to know you're keeping an eye on her." His blue eyes flashed to his wife, who nodded in agreement before he continued. "We'd like you to get to know her. Find out a little about her. Why does she come here alone? What is her background? Does she have a drinking problem? A drug problem?"

"You think she's going to cause some sort of problem?"

"You don't follow the group on Facebook, do you?" Leah asked.

Jessie shook her head. "I fucking hate social media. Wouldn't be caught dead on there." It wasn't exactly the truth, but it was her story, and she was sticking to it. Even if she did want a Facebook page, she'd be opening herself up to people from her past, even family members, tracking her down. That was something she wanted to avoid at all costs.

Cap chuckled. "Can't blame you there. Unfortunately, we spend a lot of time monitoring the group on there. One, to keep it from getting shut down by the prudes who work for Zuckerberg, but also to make sure nothing goes down that's going to get the club—or us—into trouble in the real world. Like with the cops, the State, or whatever."

"What kind of things?"

Leah sighed. "Oh, you know, there's just drama. Surely even not being on Facebook you've seen the impact it has on your...ahem...clients, for lack of a better term."

Jessie did know what she meant. She couldn't count how many domestics had started on Facebook with some ex sending a friend request, or someone posting something they shouldn't have. Social media was a festering cesspool of drama, a bubbling cauldron of shit just waiting to go down.

"Is Sirena involved in some of the drama?"

"Well..." Leah looked at her husband before glancing back to Jessie. "She...how do I put this?" She paused for a moment while she searched for the correct words. "She isn't always...careful...about how she presents herself. She walks a fine line."

"How so?"

Jessie delved deep into her memory to replay some of the times she'd watched Sirena at the club. The memories were brief flashes, just snippets of sights and sounds. They ran with slightly different crowds. But she already had a feeling she knew what Leah was going to say.

"She's a bit of an exhibitionist," Cap spoke for his wife. "And not all women take kindly to her. Like I said—there are a few who don't seem to be fans. Some are a bit threatened that she's so uninhibited."

"Ah, okay. So basically what we have here is a unicorn who is exactly what couples are looking for, but exactly the competition—perceived competition, anyway—that women don't want."

"Yeah, that about sums it up," Leah agreed, chuckling under her breath. Cap nodded.

"So you want me to watch her and see what happens. And step in if there's a problem?"

"Not saying there's going to be a problem at all,"

Cap clarified. "We just want to know more about her, that's all. There's something a bit off. We want to know if you can figure it out."

"Well, there's nothing I love more than a good mystery," Jessie answered. "I'll see what I can do."

Jessie had been coming to The Factory for a year now, ever since she met Paisley coming out of the courtroom in Berlin, the county seat. Paisley was leaving an arraignment in tears with Calvin following on her heels, and then *boom*, next thing she knew, they were all sprawled on the floor in a big pile. *Little did I know that was a position Paisley was both used to and felt comfortable in,* Jessie mused.

Jessie felt like such a klutz. She was wearing her uniform, of course. She was at court to testify at the trial of some drunk-ass tourist she'd arrested on the boardwalk for indecent exposure. Ocean City was a "family resort town" and OCPD meant to make an example out of him.

Jessie felt so bad that she'd caused Paisley to trip. She was supposed to be helping people while wearing her uniform, not tripping people up, after all. Paisley felt equally bad about embarrassing Jessie while she donned her blues.

Jessie offered to buy Paisley a drink as it was nearing 5 PM, and the trial had been postponed. She was going off-shift and had a change of clothes in her police cruiser. Paisley and her boyfriend looked Jessie up and down like they were trying to determine if she'd make a suitable filling for a Calvin/Paisley sandwich. *Of course, Paisley's shapely curves and her bright blue eyes had sold me from the get-go,* she remembered.

That drink made history. Jessie learned Paisley and Calvin helped manage a swing club, and Jessie's curiosity was immediately piqued. After the failure that was her last relationship, she wasn't keen on starting anything serious anytime soon. She had avoided men since her early twenties, preferring women both sexually and romantically, but she found it difficult to meet women she was compatible with in her line of work. And though there was a LGBT-friendly community just north of Ocean City in Rehoboth Beach, she'd never felt like she fit in there, either.

She'd never dreamed of herself as a swinger, but something in her just clicked the first time she visited The Factory. She'd always had a high sex drive, higher than many men and certainly higher than any woman she'd ever met. She'd always thought of herself as open to experimentation, and she loved the open-mindedness of the members. She felt accepted there, more so than she'd been anywhere else. And something about playing with women who were married to men felt safe to her. Like her heart was not in jeopardy.

The rhythm of the music pulsated through the club like a heartbeat, and Jessie already felt weary. After her meeting with Cap and Leah, Jessie had run into Paisley, who conned her into helping set up for the new member intake booth that operated every night. Then she stationed Jessie over at the bar to help the new bartender learn how to check in members' booze, which were carried in but stored behind the bar every night along with mixers. The club didn't stock any of its own alcohol, which meant members never had to pay for their drinks. Most considered that a huge plus, even if it did mean carting in their own alcohol. Only drinks poured by the bartender were allowed, so drunk members were cut off before they got out of hand. By that point, security was usually involved and would show the member to the door. After all, swinging and being completely hammered weren't a good combination.

Jessie sat on one of the leather couches lining the dance floor, her eyes peeled for Sirena. It was late already, and she was getting tired. She couldn't believe she'd even come to the club that night when she had to get up the next morning for work. But she would do just about anything for Paisley, Calvin, Casey, Cap and Leah. She thought of the whole staff as family. She hadn't talked to her own parents since Christmas, and they hardly ever ventured down to the beach. She hadn't seen them in years. She found it best to keep them at arm's length, anyway. So, a surrogate family was much appreciated.

Before she could get too lost in her thoughts, a flash of gold infiltrated her senses. She saw Sirena slip into one of the steel dance cages beside the DJ booth. Intertwining her limbs with those of a pale, goth-looking white chick with dark lips and even darker hair, her hips began to gyrate to the beat.

Sirena's body was mesmerizing. She had an hourglass shape, perfect breasts that were neither too large nor too small, and a mouthwatering backside. Tonight she wore a skimpy cropped gold lamé tank top, and every time she raised her arms, the underneath side of her breasts showed. Jessie guessed from the firmness of her breasts and how toned the rest of her body was that Sirena couldn't be much older than herself. Maybe 35 at the most. But she had a maturity about her, a confidence that Jessie rarely saw in women under 40. It was like she knew she had a body to die for and owned it.

She was the type of woman who caused other women to question their own beauty. Not in an overt, in-your-face, rude kind of way. More in a subtle, *holy shit that woman must have the perfect genes and now I feel totally inadequate* kind of way. She had flowing blonde waves that effortlessly cascaded around her tan shoulders as she danced; long, taut limbs with an ideal amount of muscle tone; and the roundest, tightest ass, the kind that drew stares from both sexes. Then there was her torso. Jessie could envision doing shots—if she did shots—off Sirena's beautifully sculpted midsection, which dipped in at her waist and was hollowed out along her obliques with the most scrumptious sandbar in the middle, one Jessie wouldn't mind getting to know intimately with her tongue. Her hip bones protruded ever so slightly as her hips wiggled against the black pleather miniskirt she wore. And on her mile-long legs? Thigh-high black suede boots. She was a feast for sore eyes, and Jessie's eyes were definitely sore.

Thinking about the feel of a nice hard clit under her tongue while looking at Sirena and her dance partner grinding up against each other caused a familiar sensation to pool in between her thighs. It had been a long while since she'd satisfied any urges, either by her own hand or another woman's tongue.

She wasn't sure she was going to be able to handle this assignment from Cap and Leah, not if she was already horny just from watching Sirena across the room. What was going to happen when she got closer to Sirena, close enough to see the sparkle in her eyes and to breathe in her scent? Jessie already had a bad feeling about this, but she didn't think she could tell the management team no. Besides, if they were curious about Sirena's story, she was ten times more curious by this point. And not only because she wanted to have her way with her.

Jessie had only been 10-8 for five minutes before she was called to the west side for a domestic. Her partner beat her there by about thirty seconds. "Hey, what's up?" he asked, giving her a once-over as his brows creased. "You look like shit today. Were you out late last night or something?"

She pursed her lips, then rubbed her hands under her eyes, willing her exhausted look to dissipate. "Thanks. You always look like shit." She tried to keep her poker face but had trouble suppressing her cocky smirk. "At least your statement implies I look good sometimes."

Bart Farris had been on her shift for two years. Everyone knew he was an asshole, but he and Jessie had formed a quick understanding. Once he realized she wasn't going to allow him to treat her differently because she was a woman, their rapport improved dramatically. Jessie was one of the few officers who could tolerate being his partner, but then again, she tended to get along with everyone.

They began to walk up the steps to the house, which had faded aluminum siding and broken shutters. The windows were filthy and the porch strewn with toys that looked like they hadn't been played with for years. Jessie took a deep breath and knocked on the door. There was no doorbell.

A haggard-looking woman with stringy dishwater blonde hair opened the door after a minute or so passed, but not before there was a commotion and the sound of a dog barking. She was holding the dog back by its collar as she opened the door.

"Corporal Farris and Corporal Martinez, Ocean City PD. Did you call 9-1-1?" Bart questioned as his eyes darted past the woman in attempts to survey the interior of the house.

"I-I did...," she said, then hesitated. "But my boyfriend already left." When she opened the door the rest of the way, she revealed a swelling red mark on her cheekbone. Her eyes were watery, her nose red, and a bruise was starting to appear under her left eye.

"Can we come in, Ms...." Jessie glanced down at her little notepad she carried. "Jackson?"

The woman hesitated again, but then stepped back, pulling the door open wide for their passage. She kept the dog, which appeared to be a mixed breed, close to her side. It let out a sharp bark to let the officers know it would totally give them a piece of its mind if it were unleashed.

Jessie glanced around the small, dilapidated house. There was a sink full of dishes. The TV blared from the other room. There was broken glass on the worn, stained linoleum in the kitchen.

"I haven't had a chance to clean up the mess yet,"

Ms. Jackson apologized, stepping over to the kitchen as if she could hide the disarray from the officers.

"Can you tell us what happened?" Officer Farris questioned.

"Oh, same thing that always happens," the woman said, running her fingers through her greasy hair as her eyes darted from Bart's to Jessie's. "Boyfriend got drunk and hit me. Don't you hear this story like fifty times a day?"

Jessie pursed her lips. It wasn't fifty times, but it was far too frequent. *And they never want to press charges, either,* she thought. "Did he hit you with the bottle?"

Ms. Jackson shook her head. "No, he just threw it on the ground when he got pissed, and it shattered everywhere."

They stayed a while longer, trying in vain to convince Ms. Jackson that now was finally the time to have her boyfriend arrested. But because he had taken off, and she claimed not to know where he had gone, it was a moot point. They took down a description of his car and would run the tags, but nothing would come of it. Just like every other domestic. Even if they had arrested him, he'd probably stay in jail for a night or two, then be out on bond. And nothing would change.

Jessie tried to be a realist, to fight her inner urge toward idealism. She felt like it was a battle she would be waging for the rest of her life. People who were supposed to love each other hurting each other instead. She was all too familiar with it. Like a television show she had seen every episode of.

Nine and a half hours later, the shift was done. Bart told her to try to get some rest, and from the concerned look in his pale blue eyes, Jessie knew he really meant it. They weren't any good to each other if either were sleep-deprived.

The truth was that by the time Jessie had gotten home from The Factory the night before, she was exhausted and hyped up all at the same time. She couldn't get the image of Sirena dancing with that other woman out of her mind. She was headed back to the club that night, and she was going to figure out a way to approach her. To talk to her. She wasn't sure how just yet, but she'd find a way. She talked to people for a living. That was what being a cop was all about. This wasn't any different. Or at least that's what she told herself.

TWO

*Every man needs his Siren
To check his courage and strength
When he hears her song
In his travels through the unknown.*
— Dejan Stojanovic

A nap and a cup of caffeine were the perfect antidote to Jessie's weariness. By the time she rolled into the parking lot of The Factory, she could already hear the bass thumping as she approached the front doors. As soon as she checked in at the desk, she was enveloped by a vibrant hum created by the throng of Saturday night members, changing the rhythm of her own heartbeat. It was a steady, driving force that rocked through her as she made her way to the bar.

She wasn't planning to drink. Even off duty, she never did. She was looking for Paisley first, to check in.

When she didn't see her, she headed to the ladies' locker room to change out of her street clothes and into something more...revealing. The prior night she'd kept her black dress on, the same one she'd worn to meet with Cap and Leah. Tonight she was in the mood for something a bit flashier. She opened her bag and pulled out a short satin empire-waist babydoll nightie in a striking jade color that contrasted beautifully against her tawny skin.

She gathered her long, dark brown hair into her fist, pulling it out of the back of the lingerie. She smoothed out the skirt, shaking her head at the way it flounced around her voluptuous hips. She hated being pear-shaped. She wore a 34B on top, but a size 16 on the bottom, which was always a challenge when it came to uniform-fitting time. The tailor who did all the officers' uniforms always complained about having to take Jessie's trousers in at the waist. Otherwise, her waistband got all bunched up with her gun belt, and it was basically a pain in the ass.

But she was generally pleased with how she looked, especially considering her lack of rest. How she could go from no makeup, hair in a bun, and all straight-laced in her uniform to hair down and flowing around her shoulders, dark eyes smoldering in smoky liner and shadow, and all soft and feminine in her jade babydoll chemise was really quite impressive. *At least I think so*, she laughed to herself.

She didn't dress up for anyone but herself. It wasn't to attract the attention of a man, as she had no interest in them. But she did find that couples and women found her more approachable if she looked the part. And she enjoyed the chance to look feminine after wearing her police uniform all day.

"There you are!" Paisley exclaimed as she came through the locker room door. "I thought you'd be here hours ago."

"Sorry, I took a nap," Jessie explained, still staring into the mirror, trying to figure out what was missing from her ensemble.

"Rough day at the office?" Paisley stood behind her, smoothing the back of her skirt over her full, curvy rump.

"Getting a little handsy with me, aren't you?" Jessie giggled. She looked into the mirror again to gauge the reaction in Paisley's blue eyes. Since marrying Calvin, she wasn't actively involved in the lifestyle anymore, but Calvin was more than happy to endorse girl-time with Jessie. It had been a while, though, since the two ladies had found themselves alone and able to play.

"I might wanna get more handsy with you later," Paisley answered with a wink. "Seriously, though, everything okay at work?"

She whispered the word "work" as Jessie didn't like to broadcast to her lifestyle associates that she was a police officer. It was no one's business, and she assumed it would be safer if people didn't know. If anyone asked her what she did for a living, she usually said she was a nanny. She *had* been a nanny when she was younger, but sometimes she didn't feel like her current job was too different. It's just that instead of putting children in timeout, she put adults behind bars.

Jessie nodded to answer Paisley's question. "Is Sirena here yet?"

Paisley's long, dark curly hair rustled around her

shoulders as she shook her head. "If she doesn't show up, this will be the first night in a month she hasn't been here. Who did she go home with last night?"

"She left with Bill and Cindy. They're locals. She was pretty drunk, but I'm sure they took care of her."

"Do you know if they took her home or back to their place?" Paisley questioned.

Jessie shrugged. "What, you want me to follow her after she leaves now too?"

Paisley huffed a sigh of frustration. "I don't want you to have to do this at all, but frankly, something is going on, and we want to get to the bottom of it."

"What do you mean?" Jessie's intuited there was more to this situation than what Cap and Leah had let on.

The doors to the locker room swung open and a group of five ladies entered, all carrying bags with clothes to change into. Their privacy had gone up in smoke. Paisley's brows scrunched as she almost imperceptibly shook her head again, silently relaying that the conversation was now over. "I'll come find you later," she explained and turned to go.

Jessie greeted the ladies who had just entered, then excused herself to go look for Sirena. The beat of the music sucked her in as soon as it hit her eardrums. It was times like this she wished she did drink. Even a single cocktail might be able to take the edge off, to make her forget she always needed to be in control. But no, that ability to let go, even for a moment, was snatched from her long ago. It was stolen from her before she even knew what was happening.

Her eyes darted around the club, from the

bartender pouring drinks into clear plastic cups to the couples gyrating and intertwining on the dance floor, to the ones posed all over the lounge in various suggestive positions. She could almost guess what every interaction was about, just from seeing the body language. That couple over by the stairwell was trying to decide if they were going to play with the single guy who was lurking a few paces behind them. They weren't using words, just their eyes. The wife was apprehensive; the husband seemed gung ho. *He's more into the guy than she is*, Jessie observed.

There were two couples hanging out by the bar ordering drinks. The men were having an easy conversation. One was trying to be funny, but wasn't. It was written all over the other woman's face that he was a clown, and she wasn't having any of it. His wife was embarrassed for him. It was so obvious, Jessie might as well have been reading the scripts they were acting out. She knew what was going to happen before they did. Sure enough, the other couple got their drinks and swiftly made their way back to the lounge.

People are so fucking predictable, she thought. Except for the rare few that weren't. Who were erratic. Inexplicable. She had a feeling Sirena belonged in that category. And no sooner had her name crossed Jessie's synapses did she see the flurry of blonde coming down the stairs from the second level playrooms. Her lips looked a bit swollen, glistening with saliva. She had either been dancing a sophisticated tongue tango or performing oral sex. Jessie could spot it from yards away. She took a deep breath and approached her.

"Hey," she floated the single word on the air as casually as she could. "What are you drinking?"

She preferred her sober, but she knew the reality

was that Sirena was headed to the bar for a drink. If she'd learned anything about her target when she'd observed her the night before, it was that she had a drink after every interaction. Sometimes two.

Many people came to a swinger club and never actually swung. They might hang out with friends or possibly play the role of voyeurs, just flitting from room to room to see who would offer a glimpse into the scene unfolding therein. Some couples might finally, at the end of the night, find a room and just play by themselves, without anyone else. Or they might wait and leave the club with another couple or single to play in a hotel room.

Sirena was a unicorn. A single bi female, which meant she was very much in demand. Not to mention the fact that she was drop dead gorgeous with her alabaster skin; milky smooth, rounded shoulders; and long, tempting legs. As she approached Jessie now, her mesmerizing green eyes came into view, heavily outlined with smoky liner and expertly blended with a shimmering purple shadow that made them pop off her face like two perfect emeralds shaded by a fringe of lashes. Tonight she wore a pink silk halter-top slip, and it appeared as though nothing was underneath. Her breasts formed full mounds on each side of the bodice, held in place by the delicate fabric. Jessie felt a twinge of need as she wondered if the pink color of the fabric matched her nipples. She could see them pressing into the silk, making the most erotic imprint with their firm buds.

It wasn't as though Jessie could actually buy her a drink. It was BYOB, but she would order it for her as soon as Sirena answered her question.

"Orange crush," Sirena revealed, the words sliding

off her tongue like a joke, because afterwards she burst into laughter that sounded like windchimes sparkling in a gentle breeze. It was slow and melodic, hitting every note in the scale with a lilting precision.

Jessie smirked, not sure what to make of Sirena's amusement. She hoped she wasn't already too drunk to carry on a conversation. There was much she wanted to know. She ordered the orange crush, the official drink of Ocean City, and waited for the bartender to make it while Sirena perched herself on the barstool, her eyes intent on a couple across the lounge.

"I'm Jessie," she finally said, offering her the drink once the bartender finished making it.

"Oh, I know," Sirena smiled. "Everyone knows who you are."

Jessie squinted, trying to see if there was truth or deception in those smoldering green eyes. "What makes you say that?"

"You're the pretty Latina cop with the big, sexy ass," Sirena answered nonchalantly, then she took a sip of the orange drink and licked her lips as if it were the punctuation on her sentence.

Jessie tried to keep the scoff she felt trying to eject itself from her throat under wraps. *Do not confirm or deny*, she told herself. She wasn't the one being interviewed here. She needed to bring the focus back to the subject. "You're Sirena, right?"

"My reputation precedes me!" She laughed her windchime laugh again, following it with another sip. Then she sucked her bottom lip underneath her top teeth, chewing tentatively while she waited for Jessie's answer.

"Yeah, you're the smokin' hot blonde with the nice tits," Jessie answered her, giving her a flirty wink. "And the most sought-after unicorn in Maryland. Am I right?"

"In Maryland?!" she exclaimed. "You have to at least give me credit for the whole Eastern seaboard!" She erupted in more laughter, her eyes crinkling in amusement at her own joke.

"Fair enough. Do you live here in OC?"

She nodded. "I do in the summer, anyway. Thinkin' about making it permanent any old time now."

"What do you do?" Jessie pressed, finally feeling like she was getting somewhere.

"Wouldn't you like to know?" Sirena gave a slow, teasing wink.

"Well, since you think you know what I do...it couldn't be any more...sensitive than my job...right?" Jessie put her hand on top of Sirena's hand, which was resting on the countertop. Out of her peripheral vision, she saw Paisley in the corner behind the bar, watching their interaction. Now Jessie wondered what Paisley was about to tell her in the locker room before the clique of women interrupted them.

"Do you want to dance?" The music changed over to a driving rock beat, and her body began to move to the rhythm. Her eyes glimmered so wickedly that Jessie had a hard time finding the word "no" in her vocabulary. Jessie found instead that her body wanted to mirror Sirena's, her feet involuntarily tapping.

Sirena didn't wait for an answer; she pulled Jessie by the hand, dragging her out to the dance floor where the lights were making hypnotic patterns in yellow, green and purple, accented by sparkles from the disco ball suspended from the rafter above. But nothing shone brighter than Sirena's smile when Jessie's hips began to sway in her jade satin babydoll. She didn't say a word, just fixated her gaze on Jessie's body moving to the beat.

Jessie moved close enough to smell notes of jasmine and vanilla wafting from Sirena's silken skin. Waves of golden tresses bounced around her shoulders as she seductively moved, like an enchantress to an ancient tribal beat. She put her arm out to touch Sirena's arm, and she turned around, bending at the waist to present her curvy backside. Jessie didn't hesitate to press her pelvis against the firm globes, barely concealed underneath the pink silk material. The heat from Sirena's flesh penetrated her own in an instant, sending a shock through her system.

It has been too long. Much too long, she thought.

They moved together, their bodies sliding in and out of contact like teeth in a gear, so smoothly, no friction where the two silky fabrics met, and a bit of an electric shock when it was skin on skin. As the song faded out and another one began, Jessie noticed they had been joined by five or six more people. At least two couples and two more ladies forced them apart into a bigger circle. In a heartbeat, one of the ladies captured Sirena's attention, grinding up against her, then whispering something in her ear. In another heartbeat, their lips were crashing into each other, fingers threading through long, flowing hair.

Jessie stepped back from the dance floor, feeling a coolness wrap around her from the loss of her dance partner's heat. But the fiery pit in her core continued to burn.

"So what did you find out?" Leah asked, her eyes pinned to Jessie's as Paisley sat at the desk tallying up stats for the night.

Jessie scoffed. "Well, she says she only stays down here in the summer. She wouldn't tell me what she does for a living."

"That's it?" Paisley laughed, glancing up from the clipboards spread in front of her. "Hope you're not planning to try for detective soon. Maybe my father-in-law could give you some pointers, huh?"

Calvin's father was a detective with the state police. Jessie shot Paisley the finger and returned her gaze to Leah, who looked both frustrated and tired. Jessie wondered why she was even there. Usually Cap came to collect the deposit at the end of the night, and by then, Leah was at home with Lincoln.

"You didn't find out if she's married?" Leah asked.

Jessie shook her head. "Would you please tell me what is going on with this woman? I mean, besides the going home with other members when she's drunk thing. What the hell happened that you're all so obsessed with her?"

Leah glanced at Paisley, who lowered her gaze to the rows of names on the clipboard. She let a sigh escape her lips before she settled herself down in the chair across from Paisley. "So this woman just showed up a month or so ago. We'd never seen her before that. We don't get too many single women joining our club, especially not ones who look like her."

"Uh, what's that supposed to mean?" Jessie scoffed. "I'm a single woman!"

"You know what I mean. She's a unicorn. Every couple's wet dream, right?" Paisley interjected, looking up again. Leah shot her a dirty look. "What are the chances you would have joined if you hadn't met me?"

Jessie pursed her lips. "Fair enough."

"Let me find her paperwork so you can see for yourself," Leah offered, sliding the drawer of the metal filing cabinet in the corner open. She thumbed through several dozen manila file folders until she stopped at one. "Take a look."

Jessie scanned over the documents, paying close attention to the name and address. "I don't think that's a real address. I am pretty sure there's no Palmetto Court in Ocean City."

"You think she made it up?" Leah's eyes widened as she stood over Jessie to look for herself.

"Yeah, I kinda do, actually." Jessie's eyes darted over in time to witness Leah's brows arch higher on her face. "Did someone see her ID? I thought protocol was to make sure the address they give matches what's on their license."

"I would have to check who was processing new member registrations that night," Paisley said. "It wasn't me. I didn't remember seeing her till the following weekend. I think the weekend she joined was when Calvin and I were celebrating our anniversary, so we weren't here."

Leah nodded. "I had the hosts doing registrations that night. I would have to go back and look at the schedule to see who it was." She grabbed a calendar off the wall and flipped back to May. "John and Pam," she read. "I guess we'd have to ask them, but they processed so many registrations that night because it was one of the first big weekends of the season. We had a huge influx of people renewing who hadn't been here all winter, and we always make them update their files."

"But they wouldn't have forgotten her...would they?" Jessie questioned. "A beautiful single woman like her? You already said she was out of the ordinary." She peered down at the documents again, looking at her birthdate. Doing the math in her head, she calculated Sirena would be 38 years old. *A little older than I thought,* Jessie noted. *Six years older than me.*

"Who did she leave with tonight?" Leah asked, changing the subject.

"She was with Steve Benson," Jessie answered. "But I don't know if she went home with him or he just escorted her to her car. Oh, speaking of which, let me get her car and tag number."

She thumbed through the stapled pages of the member intake form until she got to the next document. Members were required to register their car make, model and color along with the tag number if they were going to leave it in the lot. After everything that had happened with Paisley and her stalkers a couple of years prior, Cap and Leah didn't want to take any chances. Most of the members understood the new security procedures and were happy to comply. The very few who were put off by them didn't renew their membership. But everyone knew The Factory had a stellar reputation for keeping information secure, and it was not just the *premier* lifestyle club on the Eastern Shore – it was the *only* club.

Jessie scribbled down the info on Sirena's car as well as the phony address. "I'm going to run these plates and check out 23 Palmetto Court. But I am pretty suspicious." Her dark eyes swept from Leah's to Paisley's as she noticed them silently relaying each other a look.

"What is it you're not telling me?" she demanded, resolving not to let them skirt the question this time. "You know I get paid to read people, right? That's my whole fucking job. And you two are hiding something from me."

Paisley cleared her throat and shot Leah another look. Leah nodded in return before shifting back to face Jessie.

"There are a lot of rumors circulating about Ms. Horne at the moment," Leah revealed. "Some crazy stuff, and to be honest, we think a lot of it is just stemming from cattiness and jealousy. As you may have noticed, some of our female members haven't taken so kindly to her, particularly Jeannette's clique. You know, the ladies who came into the bathroom when you and Paisley were talking tonight."

Jessie's eyes flashed to Paisley, who nodded as if to admit she'd told Leah all about their earlier conversation.

"What kind of rumors?"

Paisley laughed. "You're going to die when you hear some of this stuff. Everything from she's a drug dealer, to she's a spy for a rival club. We've heard she's a porn star and that Sirena Horne is a fake name. Someone even said she used to be a man."

"What?" Jessie's eyes bulged. "There's no way!"

Giggles gurgled up Leah's throat. "I know, it's all pretty crazy. We are a little worried about her safety, given all the...things we've heard...as you can understand. And we don't want to put the club at risk either."

"You can't do anything about the rumors?" Jessie asked.

Leah shrugged. "We just want to find out who she really is, and we'll go from there. That's where you come in."

"Understood," Jessie answered. "I'll do my best to find out."

"Work smarter, not harder," Jessie's father used to say. She wasn't sure how that applied to his job as a truck driver, but she definitely used his mantra in her police work. Before she left the parking lot of The Factory, she had already entered Sirena's address into Google maps. Nothing came up for a Palmetto court in Ocean City, but she did get one in Berlin, a neighboring town not too far from the club.

She put her car into gear and whizzed down the narrow country road, following the directions on the map. She turned right into a trailer park, then down a single lane gravel road on the left. The twisted, bent metal sign read "Palmetto Court" in faded green letters on a white background. It was a pitch black, moonless night, and she could hear water trickling nearby. It was probably one of the tiny tributaries that emptied into Ayres Creek and then into the bay, which was separated from the mighty Atlantic by the tiny strip of land where Ocean City and the Assateague parks lay.

She left her headlights on and pointing straight ahead, illuminating nothing but an empty, marshy lot that gave way to what appeared to be a swamp. The map indicated the address was in this field, but all she saw were clumps of low-lying brush and reeds. She pulled her trusty flashlight out of her car and shone it around the area. On the left hand side, underneath a trio of knotty loblolly pines was a junked-up metal trailer with faded, peeling green paint. It looked abandoned, with weeds growing up all around it and swallowing the decaying wooden porch in their twisted green madness. The railing was broken and some of the floorboards missing. It was clear no one lived there.

She ran the list of the rumors Leah had shared through her head. *Everything from she's a drug dealer, to she's a spy for a rival club. We've heard she's a porn star and Sirena Horne is a fake name. Someone even said she used to be a man.*

"Who the hell are you, Sirena Horne?" she asked aloud into the thick, humid night air. Her words seemed to hang in a cloud over the marsh, until they were absorbed into the symphony of creature noises composed by cicadas, bull frogs, and swooping owls.

THREE

*Come to me once more, and abate my torment;
Take the bitter care from my mind, and give me
All I long for; Lady, in all my battles
Fight as my comrade.*
— *Sappho*

Jessie stretched her arms high above her head as a yawn claimed her mouth. There was nothing better than sleeping in on a weekday, and waking to the sound of waves crashing on the shore below her condo was a definite bonus. She was a practical type of person, her one splurge being on her home. She insisted if she was going to live in a beach town, she was going to actually live on the beach. It seemed so much closer to her roots. Her grandparents still lived in Puerto Rico, as did many of her aunts and uncles, and though she had never lived there herself, living directly on the beach reminded her of the many visits she had made to her ancestral seaside village.

She had left her sliding patio door open so the ocean breezes could gently lull her to sleep, and now they tickled her nose, enticing her to get up and head to the balcony. She gingerly stepped over the pile of clothes she'd been wearing the night before and followed the well-worn path in the carpet to the open door. The cement on the balcony was chilly on her bare feet and immediately woke her up, erasing the last bit of her dream that had seeped into the languid reality of the morning.

Her eyes bolted immediately to a shiny charcoal gray flash in the water yards from shore. A dolphin. Her lips curled up into a smile as another one broke the turquoise surface, followed by another, then yet another. She counted seven in all, merrily somersaulting their way through the waves as they moved south along the coast. *Maybe I'll go down and put my feet in the sand today*, she thought. *You can't go wrong starting your day with a dip in the ocean.*

She was waiting for the hosts who had done Sirena Horne's intake to call her back. She'd left a voicemail on the cell phone in their member file, and she wanted to know if they had actually verified her name and address with her ID. She had a feeling they hadn't. Usually the hosts were warned to be wary of single men trying to gain access to the club. Single men now had to be sponsored by at least one couple who had been members for over a year. They'd had too many issues with single men being creepsters—and a few who had gotten thrown out for fighting, being too drunk, and one for assault. Calvin had managed to take care of that situation without the club coming under fire from the state police, thanks to his connections.

Part of her wanted to forget this whole crazy assignment. It wasn't like she was getting paid for her troubles, nor did she feel she could ask for any compensation. She had half a mind to leave her phone in her condo and spend the day on the beach, frolicking in the surf like those dolphins she'd seen. But the haunting image of Sirena's sexy body gyrating to the beat last night at the club continued to flicker through her mind.

"The car isn't in her name," Jessie revealed. She glanced from Leah to Cap and then to Paisley, who had just arrived and put her purse down on her desk. "It's registered to someone named Joseph Patterson in Chester, PA."

Leah was silent as she turned to lock eyes with her husband. Paisley squeezed her large hips into the desk chair and looked up. "What about the address?"

"Bogus," Jessie answered. "There's no Palmetto Court in Ocean City, but there's one in Berlin, not far from the club, actually. It's at the back of some junky trailer park, and it's basically an empty lot."

"So what do we do now?" Cap asked. "I don't want to kick her out when she hasn't done anything wrong."

"That's not all," Jessie continued. "I finally got Pam McAulty on the phone today, and she said she distinctly remembers the night they processed Sirena's membership application."

"And?" Paisley's eyes widened as she leaned forward, putting her elbows on the surface of the desk.

"She never showed them an ID. She claimed she had forgotten it at home, or it had fallen out of her purse or some bullshit."

"Great!" Cap slammed the stack of files he was holding down on the desk, making Paisley jump. "We can't even trust our hosts to screen people. Paisley, you and Calvin are going to have to start doing it every night again, even if that means it takes two hours to get everyone processed."

Paisley groaned as Leah shook her head hard enough for her strawberry blonde waves to rustle around her shoulders. "Wait, does Casey know anything about this?" Leah asked. "Casey knows everyone on the Eastern Shore. We should really give her a heads up."

"Agreed," Jessie answered. "But one more thing. The night she applied for membership, she came with Susan and Brian King. They vouched for her. That's why John and Pam weren't too insistent about the ID thing. That, and apparently Sirena was on the verge of tears thinking she had lost her license."

"Okay, okay. So talk to Casey and the Kings. Let us know what you find out tomorrow night," Cap instructed.

"I'm gonna go get changed," Jessie said, moving away from the low filing cabinet where she had been perched. "Tonight I'm going to put the moves on Sirena. See what happens."

"Are you sure that's a good idea?" Leah questioned, worry in her forest green eyes.

"I flirted with her at the bar last weekend, then danced with her until someone stole her attention away from me." Jessie licked her lips. "I'm not gonna let that happen tonight."

Sirena appeared like a gift left by Santa Claus under the tree on Christmas morning. Perhaps that analogy struck Jessie because she came out of the locker room wearing a gown of crimson lace with matching stripes of satin encircling it. One stripe was strategically centered over her nipples, the other over her pussy. Now she looked like a present with the best parts concealed under shiny red bows.

She was being tailed by a couple, and Jessie happened to step in their path just in time to pull Sirena into a dark corner. She was clearly caught off guard, her creamy bosoms heaving with surprise. "What do you want?" she gasped, still trembling as Jessie's eyes raked over her.

"I didn't mean to scare you." Jessie trailed her fingers down the smooth, porcelain white skin on her forearm. *How can someone live in Ocean City and still not have a tan this far into the summer?* she wondered. She liked the way her topaz skin contrasted with Sirena's pearly complexion. She'd never considered that combination for jewelry, but now that she saw it in person, she thought it would make a lovely piece.

Sirena let out a tiny giggle and tilted her head. "You look beautiful tonight," she observed, now giving

Jessie a once over. "That's definitely your color. Really looks nice against your tan skin."

Jessie had slipped on a pale aqua-colored cami and shorts set, which was trimmed in buttery yellow lace. Her long dark hair was pulled into a loose braid which hung over her shoulder, and she wore a dusty pink velvet choker around her neck with a pink and ivory cameo in the center. She was going for a soft, feminine look, and she couldn't help but smile when she learned Sirena appreciated her efforts. "Yeah, I can have a girly side when I want to," she answered. "I'm sorry I startled you. I just saw you come out of the locker room, and I remembered that we never got to finish our conversation last week."

Sirena's green eyes narrowed until the memory brightened her face. "Oh, yes, at the bar and then on the dance floor... I remember. When I turned back around you were gone."

That wasn't exactly the way Jessie remembered it, but she wasn't going to go down that path. "So, you're into girls...right?"

Sirena licked her lips. "I think you heard correctly." She giggled her sparkly little laugh again, then lifted her eyes to Jessie's, where they stayed, flickering with their playful brand of mischief. No wonder she was the much-hunted unicorn. No wonder jealous women were gossiping.

"Do you like...showing off in front of a crowd?" Jessie inquired, though she already knew Sirena did. The times she had watched her before, it appeared as though Sirena craved the spotlight as much as any diva.

"I've been known to have a tiny exhibitionist

streak," she admitted, batting her thick, black lashes. Jessie loved the way they fanned out over her sultry green eyes, forming a flirty veil that begged for attention.

"Come with me?" Jessie asked, wrapping her fingers around Sirena's soft, delicate hand. She pulled her toward the hallway in the direction of one of her favorite rooms in the club. Sirena didn't say a word, but she didn't hesitate to follow either. She teetered on her four-inch heels, towering over Jessie as they made their way down the hall to the Oasis room.

It was unoccupied this early in the evening, just as Jessie suspected. The serene blue walls echoed the sky, and the bed was made to look like a boat adrift at sea with plastic palm fronds hanging from every corner and also the ceiling, forming a canopy over the bed. Better yet, a speaker in the corner piped in the sounds of a gentle surf breaking on sandy shores. Jessie once fell asleep in this room after the club closed for the evening, and it felt nearly as peaceful as being in her own bed.

"What did you have in mind?" Sirena asked, locking her eyes onto Jessie as they made their way to the center of the room.

Jessie answered by reaching up on her tip-toes to caress her fingers across Sirena's rose-hued cheek, then she tilted her chin down till she could lift her lips high enough to brush against Sirena's. She wrapped her arms around the curvy blonde beauty, pulling them close enough together that she could feel her body heat mixing with her own. She wasn't sure whose skin was hotter, but she was about to find out.

Her lips were feather-soft, and her vanilla jasmine scent wrapped around Jessie as she urged her lips open with her tongue. With one arm around Sirena's waist, and the other stroking down her neck, she deepened the kiss and felt the exact moment when Sirena surrendered to her. She felt the give in her shoulders, her breasts as they pushed against her. Without breaking their union, Jessie guided her toward the bed, pressing against her until she fell down against it with Jessie on top.

The satin shorts she wore stretched, the curves of her voluptuous ass peeking out as Jessie spread her thighs to straddle the golden nymph beneath her. She stroked her hands down her lush curves, but her lips never strayed, as if she didn't want to take the chance of Sirena noticing anyone or anything else in the room. Jessie felt the eyes appear and bore into her, two by two at the door, in the room, which was left open, a stage that quickly filled with an audience. She felt the energy of their desire permeate the room, their titillation at the sight of two beautiful women writhing in a coiled knot of passion.

The red gown came off; the satin aqua shorts set was discarded. Caramel skin met peaches and cream in a swirl so delectable, everyone in the audience—man and woman alike—wanted a taste. But Jessie was the one who savored the treat, reveling in that first moment the sweetness hit her tongue. She kissed her way down Sirena's statuesque form until she found herself at the crest of her torso, her crown resting upon the union of her thighs. She found her slick with desire, wafting an aroma of pure seduction, spiked with the vanilla jasmine scent Jessie had discovered behind the shell of her ear.

Sirena's back arched, hinged on the moment Jessie's tongue would make contact. But Jessie was in no hurry, moving in slow motion. She loved the showmanship, the expertly crafted moans escaping those kiss-swollen lips. Her eyes rolled back; her cheeks flushed, and the perfect mounds of her breasts decorated with the most exquisitely pert pink nipples, heaving toward the ceiling as she anticipated the touch that would alleviate her need. "Oh, god, please..." she panted, writhing against the sheets.

Jessie pressed a smile against Sirena's swollen-with-desire lips as she slowly, methodically lowered her tongue to her clit. She exhaled, letting her hot breath tease Sirena's pink pearl, then inhaled, letting her enthralling scent fill the deepest recesses of her senses. She was going to enjoy this treat even more than Sirena would, and she had no doubt her name would be torn from Sirena's lips by the end of it. If not before.

It didn't take long for Jessie's wish to come to fruition. A few gentle licks and a nibble were all it took for Sirena to beg for more of Jessie's tongue. Unable to hold back her smile, Jessie wrapped her arms around each of Sirena's perfectly shaped thighs and settled in, dedicated to the task at hand, and ready to ride wave after wave of her partner's pleasure as they crested one after another.

Toward the end of the show, several audience members dragged their companions away...compelled to extinguish their own needs before desire overthrew good sense.

Jessie was pleased to find that Sirena became her shadow after their adventure in the Oasis. She couldn't keep the smug smile off her face every time Sirena gushed about the attention Jessie had lavished upon her. "I've just never had oral like that before!" and "How did you learn to eat pussy like that?"

By the end of the night, they found themselves in a nearly-empty lounge with Sirena nursing a cocktail and Jessie a glass of ice water, but Jessie still hadn't revealed all her secrets. And she had plenty of tricks up her sleeve should they be required. Paisley stopped by to remind them it was last call and ask if they wanted anything else from the bar before it closed.

"No, no," Sirena shook her head, smiling. "I've had enough orgasms tonight that no amount of liquor could make me feel any better than I do right now."

"She's got quite the talented tongue, doesn't she?" Paisley agreed, nodding and winking over at Jessie.

"That she does. How did she learn to eat pussy like that?" Sirena asked again, still seeking answers to her questions. Jessie liked that she had questions, too. It was fun to be the one cloaked in a bit of mystery for a change.

"Lesbians give the best head," Paisley remarked with a grin.

"Oh, you're a—oh, no men at all for you, huh?" Sirena gasped, but more from surprise than judgment. "So you're totally on the other team? You just don't seem like what I think of when I picture a—well, you know..."

Jessie chuckled. "I'm not a big fan of labels, but it's

been a long time since I was with a man."

"Don't you ever miss cock?" she questioned, her eyes wide.

"I know I sure would!" Paisley chimed in. Then the two giggled like school girls, loudly enough that Calvin and Cap both stopped for a moment to smile at them on their way through the lounge, even though they couldn't have possibly had a clue why they were laughing.

"Well, I don't know," Sirena finally said, her voice sounding a little swoony. "With oral like that, I may not need a cock!"

"My work here is done!" Jessie grinned and wrapped her arm around Sirena. She was feeling closer to finding out her secrets. Paisley gave her a knowing glance, then made an excuse about having to get to the office to close out the books.

"Are you going straight home?" Sirena glanced up at Jessie, her eyeliner smudged a bit around her smoky eyes. She looked tired.

"Well, not straight—" Jessie answered, trying to make a joke, but she wasn't sure it registered with Sirena, who looked at her expectantly. "I usually stay and help them clean up," she clarified, gesturing to Cap and Calvin. The two men were talking to the bartender, presumably about how the night had gone. Members were starting to drop by the bar to pick up the liquor they had checked in at the beginning of the night, then they filtered out through the front doors looking tired but happy.

"Oh." Sirena's lips pooched out in a pout.

It dawned on Jessie that Sirena left with someone

every night. And she had been with Jessie all evening, so she hadn't had a chance to capture anyone else's attention and garner an after-hours invitation. *She very well may be asking me to take her back to my place,* she realized. She felt a second wind of energy surge through her at the possibilities it unlocked. *Maybe she doesn't have a place down here at all?* Jessie considered. After all, the address on her membership forms was obviously fake.

"We can go back to my place after that, though, if you want," she offered as casually as possible.

"Mmmm, that would be fun!" Sirena's face brightened. "I would love to return the favor, you know..."

Jessie parked her car in her reserved space in the parking lot at her condo. Sirena had been chatty for the first part of the ride back to Jessie's place, until Jessie turned onto Route 50 and headed north. Once the neon signs from all the restaurants and bars began to bleed into the car, Sirena fell silent, her eyes glued to the passing scenery. There was still a lot of traffic for being two in the morning. Bars were just beginning to close, and people were making their way home. Jessie counted at least four OCPD cruisers at various points along their journey. That's probably what she would be doing too—trying to find a drunk—if she were working that night.

"So this is your place?" Sirena asked, her voice a

bit gravelly and tired from the late hour.

"Yep. Come on, let's go inside. You look tired."

Jessie couldn't help but feel some semblance of victory. How many other club members wanted to have Sirena in their beds that night? Even if nothing happened...she'd still be sleeping next to Jessie.

"Oh, thanks." She shook her head and ran her fingers through her golden waves. Then she rubbed her thumbs under her eyes, attempting to wipe away smudged eyeliner. "I'm sure I'm a mess."

"You can take a shower if you want, and then we can go to bed. No need for anything else if you're not up to it," Jessie offered, wrapping her arm around Sirena's shoulders. Even though she had no proof Sirena was in imminent danger, for some reason, she still felt like she needed to protect her. She just didn't know what from.

"You're such a sweetheart," Sirena sighed as she stepped into the lobby and followed Jessie into the elevator. "I thought female cops were supposed to be real cunts."

Jessie's eyes bulged out. She hadn't been expecting that word to come out of Sirena's pretty lips. "Who told you that?" She tried to laugh it off.

"Oh, you know, trying to be as tough as the guy cops. Just makes them kind of dicks, I guess. Only you don't have a dick. So, I made a little substitution." She slurred the last word a little bit. Jessie was certain she wasn't drunk. She hadn't had hardly anything to drink that night, unlike most of the nights she had observed her at the club.

"Well, I know I'm short, but I seem a lot taller in

uniform." Jessie winked at her as the elevator stopped on the ninth floor.

"Oh, you didn't say you lived on such a high floor..." Sirena grasped onto the railing in the elevator, clutching it for dear life as the door slowly slid open.

"I live on the ninth floor. Is that okay?"

"I'm just not a big fan of heights," she admitted, precariously tiptoeing out of the car and into the wide, carpeted hallway.

"I don't think tiptoeing is going to make you any safer." Jessie laughed as she offered her arm to her companion for support. "You can lean on me. I won't let you fall."

"Just don't go too close to the windows," she urged as she gripped Jessie's arm.

"You aren't going to go out on the balcony with me, then?" Jessie couldn't help but sound a little disappointed. She loved taking dates out on the balcony. They were always mesmerized by the waves crashing on the shore below.

Wait, she stopped herself. *This isn't a date. This is essentially work; I have to get to the bottom of this whole Sirena Horne thing. Shit. I said "get to the bottom of." Well, a girl's gotta do what a girl's gotta do. Right?*

She shushed her inner monologue as she fished her keys out of her pocket. She never carried a purse. It seemed too girly to her. She shoved the door open—it always got a little sticky in the summertime—and ushered her guest inside. She loved that her entire condo smelled of ocean breezes. That's why she left the windows open most of the time and hardly ever bothered with the air conditioning. It just felt more natural to her. *Why live on the beach if you can't hear it and smell it?*

"Did you want to take a shower?" she asked as Sirena looked around. She wasn't sure what she could be looking for. Something personal? Family photos? Jessie didn't have anything like that in her condo. The most personal thing she had was a wooden cross in her bedroom, which her mother had insisted on hanging there. Her mother knew Jessie wasn't a practicing Catholic, but just having that relic in plain sight seemed to make her feel better, that and the St. Michael pendant Jessie wore around her neck when she worked, tucked inside her uniform. St. Michael was the patron saint of police officers, and her mother had bought her a St. Michael necklace the day she graduated from the police academy.

"Sure," Sirena consented, flashing Jessie a tired smile.

Jessie walked down the short hallway off the living room and opened the bathroom door. "Here you go. There are towels in the cabinet in there."

"Perfect." Sirena disappeared into the bathroom as Jessie's gaze was drawn outside to the moonlight dancing on the waves. The peaceful blue that hovered over the water washed over her—even if only metaphorically. She was filled with the sense that things were working out just as they were meant to be.

Sirena popped her head out of the bathroom door, zeroing her eyes on Jessie. "Hey, do you want to join me?" She had a hopeful glint in her voice.

"Do you want me to?"

Sirena nodded, her lips curled into a seductive grin. Jessie couldn't pass up an opportunity to see

Sirena naked again, so she made her way to the bathroom, which was already beginning to fill with steam. She began to undress while Sirena slipped into the shower, letting out a heady moan when the hot water hit her flesh. "Oh my god, that feels so fucking good!" she practically sang, and Jessie couldn't stop a smile from spreading across her face.

Maybe this is my third wind? she questioned as she stepped inside, suddenly feeling re-energized. There was something about Sirena that made her feel more alert, more alive. There was a crackling electricity emanating from the blonde, even though she was so tired during the car ride back that she almost fell asleep. Now she was bright-eyed again, laughing and playing in the water, taking the hose off the shower head and spraying it all over Jessie.

"Turn around," Sirena commanded. She aimed the water at Jessie's well-formed, muscular back, making droplets bounce off her taut tan skin. Then she reached down to grab the sponge and body wash, squirting a dribble and lathering it up. She spread the bubbles all over Jessie's back, then dug her fingers into her flesh, kneading the tight muscles as the hot water ran down Jessie's long, dark hair and on either side of her neck. "You like that?"

Jessie could only grunt in reply. Sirena's fingers were like magic. This was the first time she had touched her first—made the first move. Jessie couldn't help but feel something stir inside, a fullness in her core as she felt her body respond to Sirena's touch, especially when she leaned forward and brushed her soapy tits against her back.

Once she was satisfied that Jessie's back was squeaky clean, Sirena used the hose to wash off all the bubbles, moving the sprayer in long strokes across her body. When she reached Jessie's full, round ass, Jessie's back arched at the tickling sensation of it. It wasn't an uncomfortable, laugh-inducing tickling, but a sensual one. She groaned a bit as she stuck her ass further out and spread her legs.

Sirena moved the sprayer so it angled between Jessie's thighs. When the hot water flowed against her clit, she bit her bottom lip, feeling the pleasure surge through her. Right behind that feeling was a growing need that started in her clit but swelled inside her walls, reaching throughout her pelvis as Sirena used her other hand to stroke down Jessie's thick curves.

When she couldn't take any more, Jessie whipped around, taking Sirena's face into her palms and claiming her lips with her own. Sirena dropped the sprayer, and it landed in the tub, sending water in a three-foot arc against Jessie's backside. She didn't care; all she wanted to feel was Sirena's hot tongue against her, their lips speaking a language entirely devoid of words.

The night was sultry and sweet. Every time Jessie turned over, she felt the lush curves next to her calling her name and caught a whiff of fading perfume. She would inch closer, close enough to press herself against Sirena's backside. There was something so comforting about that soft skin radiating warmth into her own. It had been a long time since Jessie had slept with anyone else—slept-slept, with actual sleeping going on. She hadn't been in a relationship for over a year, and her last girlfriend didn't like to snuggle. Sirena seemed oblivious to it, so dead to the world that she barely stirred when Jessie wrapped her arm around her.

They hadn't done too much talking before succumbing to slumber the night before. Jessie had tried to probe a bit, asking Sirena where she had grown up. She'd said Georgia. Jessie hadn't detected the southern accent in her speech before this revelation, but now that she mentioned it, she definitely heard a tiny tinge. She assumed it was because up until they entered the quiet confines of her condo, they had been at the crowded, noisy club. Sirena's voice had a crystalline quality to it—clear, precise, as though she'd been brought up in an affluent, refined home, and it had the slightest stretch to the vowels, a dignified drawl.

"What brought you up this way?" Jessie had asked.

"What takes anyone anywhere?" Sirena had answered, a wistful far-away sound to her voice. "Love and heartbreak. Those are the two forces that move people."

Then she changed the subject, a bit of vibrancy coming back to her tone. "What about you? Where did you grow up?"

"Outside Philly," Jessie answered. "Southside. Not the good part, that's for sure."

"Oh," Sirena had replied, but it was drawn out, with lots of "h's" beyond the initial "o."

We must come from two different worlds, Jessie realized. She could only imagine that Sirena was trying not to feel sorry for her. Or maybe she wondered if she was born here—in America. She'd been told to go back to Mexico more times than she cared to admit, by "clients," nonetheless. She'd not only been born in the U.S., but her parents had as well. It was her grandparents who were born in Puerto Rico, came to the States in the 1960s, then returned to their motherland when they retired. As many times as Jessie had visited their village on the beautiful island, she knew they definitely made the right decision, even if it meant being far away from those they loved.

Where one lives becomes engrained in a person, like a smoker always has that cigarette smell embedded in his clothes, house and car. If someone comes from the city, there's a toughness that wraps around them like concrete and steel girders, preventing any trespassers, but making them vulnerable to graffiti. In the country, a resourcefulness, a hardiness springs up like the mighty oak that pushes its way past all the competing saplings to reach the sky. A pull toward tradition grows from deep within as each season stakes its claim on the fertile soil, rotating between sun and rain, birth and death. And here, by the water, Jessie internalized the endless cycle of ebb and flow, learning to roll with the punches life never failed to deliver. She never seemed to get a break. And she wasn't likely to. But it was her heritage; she came from a long line of beings forged by the relentless tides.

Jessie moved down here to escape the city, to replace the hard, cold truth of humanity with the heartbeat of the pounding surf. What Sirena said made sense. People move because of love or heartbreak. For Jessie, it had been heartbreak. Not the romantic kind. The kind that had its roots so deeply entrenched around her, the only way to escape was to cut them out.

Why had Sirena abandoned her affluent southern belle upbringing to move to Maryland? Was it love or heartbreak? Jessie intended to find out.

FOUR

Some women can't say the word lesbian... even when their mouth is full of one. - Kate Clinton

Jessie awoke to an empty bed. There was not only no sign of Sirena, but she had left nothing behind, not the clothes she had worn at the club, nor her purse or bag. It was all gone, and there wasn't even a note or any proof she had been there at all. Jessie had to wonder if the whole thing was a figment of her imagination, and she might have been inclined to believe it was, if it weren't for the faint smell of vanilla and jasmine embedded in her pillow and the two wet towels they'd used after their shower the previous night.

She had another day off work. A lot of times when she was off work, she'd find a sub job for someone on vacation or who called out sick. Her sergeant would get frustrated with her, though, if she didn't take at least a couple days off per month. He had been all over her case earlier in the week about her lack of downtime, so she knew better than to try to pick up any extra shifts this weekend.

It was Saturday, and she already had plans to go back to The Factory. She knew Cap, Leah and Paisley would be awaiting news of what had happened the night before. And what exactly did she have to report? Well, she could definitely verify that Sirena had never been a man. And she was originally from Georgia. But did she have any other news? Any other breakthroughs? Sadly, no.

She's skittish, Jessie rationalized. *It's not like I can just pull her aside and interrogate her. She knows I'm a cop.* She knew she had to be gentle, discreet, careful. There was no way this was going to be a quick operation. *Slow and steady wins the race,* she told herself. She remembered when she'd first joined the OCPD five years ago. She had lost out on so much information from suspects when she tried to press too hard, too fast. There was something about gaining trust, getting inside their heads. It led to much more valuable information.

She hadn't gotten inside Sirena's head yet, but she had gotten inside her pants. Did she feel guilty about that? Should she? Jessie shook it off. The whole purpose of a swing club was to have fun. She'd had fun. Sirena seemed to enjoy herself, and best of all, Jessie had kept her from getting overly intoxicated or messed up in any drama. That was a win as far as she was concerned. That was why Cap and Leah had called her in, after all. To protect Sirena. And protect the club.

Speaking of impatience, Jessie's phone was lighting up with Paisley's face, obviously too anxious to wait till the club opened for news. "Hello?"

"What's up, chica?" Paisley's voice came across the line.

Jessie groaned. "You know I hate to be called that," she grumbled.

"Good morning, Madame Jessica Martinez," Paisley corrected herself. "Pray tell, how dost thou fare this fine summer morn?"

She rolled her eyes. "I just woke up."

"With Sirena?" Paisley questioned, and Jessie could practically hear her eyebrows waggling.

"She left," Jessie sighed in defeat. "She left without saying goodbye."

"Is she coming back tonight?"

"No clue."

"Did you get her number?" Paisley asked.

"No, sorry. Don't you have a number for her at the club?"

"I do have a number, but I don't know if it's real or not. Besides, I want her to give it to you herself, you know, to show she trusts you. We can't have her thinking you've gone to the office and stalked her. Besides, our members know we don't give out that kind of information."

"Only to cops you aren't really paying to work for you, right?" Jessie scoffed.

"Don't tell me you didn't enjoy yourself last night," Paisley rebutted. "I caught the 'tail end' of your show, so to speak. You looked like you were lapping it up!" She cracked up laughing at her own bad joke.

"Hardy har har." Jessie cleared her throat again. "So, I haven't investigated this Joseph Patterson person yet or talked to the Kings. I'm going to do that today."

"Okay," Paisley relented. "Keep me *abreast* of any new developments." She giggled again.

"Yeah, yeah."

Jessie threw on a pair of baggy camouflage shorts and a black tank top along with some bright orange flip flops and headed down to her car. She took the stairs, happy to get the blood circulating in her legs again. She almost wished she had time for a jog on the beach, but it was already becoming oppressively hot outside. They were due for a high of 95 degrees that afternoon, and it had to be every bit of 89 already, she guessed. She hadn't meant to sleep in till eleven, *but it is what it is*, she decided.

She drove her car over to headquarters so she could look up the tag number on Sirena's car. She ignored the prying eyes of her colleagues, who were moving about the space like worker bees buzzing around a hive. It was a summer weekend in a tourist town. Of course they were busy. There were drunken shenanigans to investigate, thefts at the outlet mall, and usually some sort of indecent exposure complaint on the boardwalk. Fortunately, Jessie slipped past all of that without attracting much attention.

"Joseph Patterson," she said aloud as she typed the PA tag number into their database. They were always looking up out-of-state licenses, and it wasn't unusual for her to be on the phone with officers in Delaware, Pennsylvania, New Jersey, New York, and Virginia on a regular basis. When she got the hit, his license picture appeared, showing a man in his early fifties with long salt-and-pepper hair that hung over one side of his face in disarray. He had pale, bloodshot blue eyes and a reddish tint to his skin, like maybe he had been a redhead at some point in his life. He didn't look particularly friendly, but he didn't look menacing either. Jessie wondered if he could be Sirena's father? *No, too young.* Brother? *Maybe.* Husband? *Possibly.* In any case, he had owned the car for four years, and the address was in Chester, Pennsylvania. It wasn't too far from where Jessie had grown up outside of Philly.

She couldn't exactly ask Sirena who Joseph Patterson was. She'd have to figure out a creative way to get the information. When she looked up his license, she saw it was suspended. He'd had multiple DUIs. *Great,* she thought. *Guess he's not missing his car too much.*

Jessie stationed herself at the entrance of The Factory so she could ambush the Kings as soon as they arrived. They were regulars and hardly ever missed a Saturday night. She only hoped she could talk to them before Sirena arrived, and she rarely appeared before 9:00. It was 7:00 now, and the club had just opened.

"What did you find out on the car?" Calvin asked. Apparently Leah, Cap, Paisley, Calvin and Casey were all being kept apprised of the investigation. Whenever Jessie relayed one piece of information, the rest seemed to know it within hours. *Apparently the management has a pretty good internal communication system,* she surmised.

Jessie glanced up into Calvin's hypnotic hazel eyes. If she were to ever...*ahem*...swing that way again, Calvin would be just her type. He was tall, lean and muscular, like a basketball player, with eyes and lips to die for. His skin was just a shade darker than hers, the perfect cross between his dark-skinned African American father and his fair red-headed mother. He was just positively scrumptious, even she could admit. Paisley sure was a lucky lady.

"Registered to some older dude near Philly named Joseph Patterson. No idea what his relationship is to Sirena, though."

"And I don't supposed you can just ask her?"

"Oh, you mean like casually?" Jessie chuckled while shaking her head. "I'm pretty sure that would not have the outcome we're looking for."

"Why are women so skittish?" he asked. "I bet if it were a guy, I could figure out a way to ask him. 'Hey, where did you get your car? Why does it have PA tags?'"

"Lots of people down here have PA tags because Maryland is a royal pain in the ass to transfer your registration. You know, with the inspections and all that. So that doesn't seem like that big of a deal. I thought maybe it was her parents' car, but I don't think this dude is old enough to be her dad. He's only 15 years older."

"It's Pennsa-tucky," Calvin laughed. "You never know."

Jessie gave him a playful punch in the arm to stand up for the state she was born in, just as Brian and Susan King breezed through the door. She was wearing a stunning red floral off-the-shoulder dress, and he was decked out in a pair of sleek trousers and a slim-fitting royal blue golf shirt.

"Hey, guys, can I talk to you for a moment?" Jessie had met them before, and even been to a party at their house, but she didn't know them, know them. There were hundreds of club members, and it would have been impossible for her to be well-acquainted with all of them.

They wrinkled their brows with confusion but nevertheless followed Jessie up to the offices overlooking the lounge. Once she had them seated in Leah's office, she folded her hands in her lap and looked at them with a reassuring smile on her face. She felt exactly like she was at work, which was not a welcome feeling. She came to The Factory to escape work, not to feel like she was at work.

"What's up?" Brian questioned, holding his wife's hand protectively in his and pinning his blue eyes on Jessie.

"Oh, you're not in trouble or anything," she clarified, then immediately regretted it. *That sounded like something a cop would say*, she chided herself. She decided to move right on, hoping those words would be forgotten by her next sentence. "I was just wondering how well you know Sirena Horne?"

The Kings looked at each other before a knowing smile crept onto Susan's face. "Oh, we heard you two put on quite the show last night! I heard it was really hot."

Jessie felt a bit of a flush creep from her cheek toward her ears. She was not normally one to blush, and fortunately her tan skin helped hide her fluster. "I was told you were the couple who vouched for Sirena when she put in her membership application here six weeks or so ago."

"Oh, yes, we did," he answered, his face looking open and honest. "We'd met her at Seacrets the weekend before. We're the ones who told her there was a club here. She was unaware, being from out of town and all."

"Out of town?" Jessie's eyebrow rose.

"Yeah, where did she say she was from, honey?" Mrs. King asked, still clutching her husband's arm a bit possessively. *She doesn't have to worry about me*, Jessie thought. *He needs to worry about me more than she does.*

"Uh, Ohio? Pennsylvania? Oh, maybe it was West Virginia. I don't really remember."

"Okay, so you're basically saying that you only met her one weekend before you vouched for her membership?"

They both nodded as if it was slowly dawning on them why that could be a problem. "But we played with her that night we met her. I mean we knew she was legit as far as that is concerned... She's not a wannabe," Brian explained.

"She's not vanilla," Susan clarified, "not by a long shot." A devious grin spread her lips up at the corners.

"Okay. Fair enough," Jessie smiled, rising to pace toward the door. "Thanks for the information."

"Is something wrong? Is there a problem with her?" Brian asked as they also rose from their chairs.

"No, not at all. We're just auditing some member files," Jessie answered.

"Oh, I didn't realize you work here now... I always heard you were a cop," Susan answered.

Jessie felt a strong urge to slap her palm over her face. *Why is it so hard to keep that a secret? Damn it!*

Sirena was distant when she finally arrived. Jessie tried to give her some space—after all, just because they slept together didn't mean—*well, it doesn't mean anything*, Jessie reminded herself. She was racking her brain to come up with a solution for finding out about Sirena's car. She wondered if there was any way she could be the one to walk Sirena to the vehicle in question after the club closed up.

Wait...did she even have her car here last night? Jessie struggled to remember. She didn't recall Sirena saying anything about it. *And she certainly didn't drive it to my place.*

She watched Sirena with her long, graceful limbs sashay to the bar where she smiled at the bartender as she checked in her alcohol. She had one tiny bottle of...Jessie wasn't sure what...*schnapps? Amaretto?* She guessed other people shared their liquor with Sirena as she had never noticed her checking any in before today, and she certainly didn't stop by the bar last night to pick up her bottle when the club closed.

Moments later, Sirena sauntered away from the bar holding a full plastic cup when she seemed to notice Jessie perched against one of the steel columns that supported the second floor of The Factory. She shot Sirena a tiny smile, hoping it was enough to encourage her to approach without being pushy.

"Heya," she drawled. Jessie couldn't believe how much more southern Sirena sounded after she admitted to being from Georgia.

"Long time no see. You didn't say goodbye this morning."

"You were sound asleep, snoring away," Sirena said with a little giggle. She sipped her drink as if that would quell the laughter.

Jessie's cheeks enflamed a bit when she thought of snoring in front of Sirena. "I'm so sorry... I only do that when I'm dead tired. And I was pretty dead tired last night."

Sirena batted her eyelashes as she swirled her drink around in the cup. "I think we wore each other out."

Jessie's blush did nothing but expand, staking out additional territory across her chest this time. She exhaled a deep breath, trying to blow it out of her system. They didn't have sex, though. They fooled around in the shower, but Sirena never did return the oral favor. No, the two had laughed and giggled for another hour about their lifestyle experiences. Jessie hoped Sirena would inadvertently reveal answers to the myriad outstanding questions she had, but it was not to be. They mostly talked about things that happened before they discovered The Factory. And it was all in vague terms. Nothing specific about locations. And Sirena never revealed any actual romantic relationships, just various play partners.

The Kings came up behind Sirena, and Susan

wrapped her arms around her, giving her a kiss on the neck. Jessie watched Sirena swoon into Susan's arms, and a feeling ricocheted through her so fast, she almost felt like she'd been shot.

Jealousy.

That was not a feeling Jessie was accustomed to. In fact, she couldn't remember feeling it since she was in high school and that uber-bitch Melanie Watson had stolen her boyfriend Peter Barnes right out from under her. She wanted to punch Melanie so damn hard in the face it wasn't even funny. But after Peter dumped Melanie, and she and Jessie began to talk, they found solidarity in their roles as the ex-girlfriend. It wasn't long before Jessie realized she had developed a little crush on Melanie. But nothing ever happened on that front. Other things happened instead. Things that made Jessie not want to be with anyone at all, at least not until she met Tori during the time she was at the Academy. It was Tori who made Jessie realize she did have a sexual appetite somewhere in there...buried beneath layers of...

Susan bent to whisper something in Sirena's ear, something that made the blonde shake with laughter. Sirena raised her chin toward Susan, but her sultry green eyes never left Jessie's. She angled her mouth toward Susan's ear and whispered back. Brian and Susan both nodded and flitted away, both laughing and looking pleased with the outcome of whatever their whispered secret was. *A promise to play?*

Sirena downed the rest of her drink and headed toward the bar. "You want something?" she questioned, and Jessie shook her head.

"Okay, I'm going to grab another drink and meet the Kings in the Jungle Room. You wanna come watch?"

Jessie did not want to watch. She didn't want to see anyone else's hands on Sirena, and she knew that was wrong. A: they were in a swing club. That was what went down in such a locale. Partners shared each other. That was what it was all about. B: She wasn't supposed to be feeling anything about this woman she was investigating for Cap *et al*. She was doing the Sheldons and the Mitchells a personal favor; she was doing it to protect the club.

But she went anyway because she wanted to keep an eye on Sirena. Taking a deep breath of resolve, she climbed the staircase that led to the second floor of themed play rooms that hung over the bar. The Jungle Room was the biggest of the upstairs rooms and was done up to resemble an Amazonian rainforest, complete with animal sounds, vines and a canopy of trees. She walked slowly down the corridor, peeking into the other occupied rooms. Some of them had windows. There was a woman on a Sybian in one of them, riding herself to climax after climax as a small crowd cheered her on.

If you ever feel like you need a cheering section to help you get over that hump, Jessie thought to herself, *a swing club is a good place to get one.* She was a bit more private with her orgasms, preferring to share them with one partner in private. Last night's exhibition was out of character for her, but somehow Sirena made it feel like they were the only ones in the room. Once she devoted herself to the task at...tongue...Jessie barely noticed any of the audience members' eyes boring into them, though she was aware that the air hung heavy with lust. And, obviously, word had gotten around about their show. Brian and Susan had not been watching, but they seemed to have heard the highlights from someone else.

Another room had two couples. One man was dominating the two women while the second man watched. They were tied to two flogging benches, their bright red rumps raised high in the air as they received lash after lash from a leather crop. The second man was so turned on, he had taken his cock out of his pants and was slowly stroking it as he watched.

The room right next to the Jungle Room was done in all black and white. It was affectionately known as the Interracial Room, though Jessie was certain that wasn't the theme Casey Fontaine had envisioned when she decorated the club years ago. She always referred to it as the Ebony and Ivory room. Still, it wasn't unusual for interracial couples and groups to congregate there, and tonight was no exception. There was a group of three women, two white and one black, along with two men, one white and one black, in such a confusing mass of limbs, they looked like they were trying to form a pretzel. Jessie couldn't begin to make out who was fucking or licking whom.

By the time she made it to the Jungle Room, the Kings were already making themselves comfortable while they waited for Sirena to join them. Susan was lying on her back with Brian's face buried between her legs. Jessie waited outside the door until Sirena arrived, or they invited her in, whichever came first.

Sirena came flying up the stairs, her flowing pink chiffon babydoll nightie billowing behind her. Jessie noticed she was barefoot. She wasn't sure why, but there was something sexy about her bare feet. It wasn't just her sleek skin looking so smooth, but her actual feet. They weren't small...as Sirena was a tall woman at

5'7" or 5'8". But her feet were beautiful, narrow with high arches, and her tiny toenails were painted a rosy shade that complemented her fair complexion.

"Are you going to watch or play?" she whispered, stopping on a dime right in front of Jessie, who stood leaning against the metal pole of the spiral staircase that descended to the hallway between the lobby and bar.

"I wasn't invited to play," Jessie answered, locking her dark eyes onto Sirena's. She didn't know if she was asking for an invitation or just stating facts. She moved her hands down to her hips absentmindedly, bracing herself for a response.

Sirena took a moment, eyeing her up and down as Jessie smoothed her hands down her short terrycloth shorts. The theme for the evening was Pajama Party. The men were mostly shirtless, clad in pajama bottoms, while the women wore all manners of sexy, frilly, sporty, and comfy nightwear. Jessie had put her long hair into two ponytails that hung on each side of her face and opted for the comfy/sporty look with shorts and a tank top with no bra underneath. She watched Sirena's eyes zero right in on her nipples, which were pressing into the ribbed cotton fabric of her tank top.

"I can ask Brian and Susan if they mind?" she suggested, her eyes snapping back to Jessie's after getting their fill of the hardened nipples.

Jessie looked around the club. It was starting to fill up, and she wondered if this meant Sirena was going to be occupied for the whole night. After she played with this couple, then what? She was trying to gauge whether or not joining in would give her more or less access to Sirena for the rest of the evening.

"I might watch for a while. Maybe we can meet up later?" Jessie asked, making a quick decision.

"Sounds good." Sirena smiled and batted her eyelashes. She sauntered into the room where Brian was still pleasuring his wife. He immediately popped up and gestured for Sirena to take his place. He watched her begin to lick and tease at his wife's clit for approximately a minute before he began to slide a condom onto his cock, which was short and fat.

Jessie sighed. *No foreplay or anything?* Yet another reason she didn't sleep with men anymore. As Brian moved behind Sirena, he stroked his fingers down her back, then squeezed her ass cheeks for a few seconds, all the while rubbing his condom-sheathed cock into her crack.

Oh, I guess that was the foreplay, Jessie thought as he pushed his way inside her. She let out a little yelp at the intrusion and returned her attention to Susan. Brian moved his hands to either side of her hips and gripped her tightly as he rammed himself in and out of her.

Jessie felt that feeling come over her again. She didn't want to watch; she couldn't. And she felt sick to her stomach. She slipped down the stairs, heading straight to the bar to get some ginger ale when she realized only fresh air was going to work for her.

She passed Paisley on her way out of the club, who gave her a bewildered look, but Jessie just shook her head and kept going. She opened the door into the stifling, thick summer night air and gasped for breath as she made her way into the parking lot. She was aiming for the little strip of trees right past where the orange lights illuminated all the cars parked in neat rows outside the club.

What the hell is wrong with me?

She stared off into the woods, which sounded alive with night creatures. It was so loud, it was almost as deafening as the sound inside the club with the music blaring, bass thumping, and the din of the crowd all mingling into a chaotic cacophony. *At least this outdoorsy sound is natural*, she thought, wrapping her arms around her chest as a stray breeze blew right through the thin fabric of her tank top, making her nipples hard all over again. Just like they'd been under Sirena's gaze.

She felt like she was getting nowhere with this investigation. She hadn't seen any signs that Sirena was being mistreated. She hadn't seen any evidence she really was who she said she was, but if she wasn't in danger and wasn't hurting the club, when what did it matter? She wasn't a spy for a rival club. That just made no sense. There weren't any rival clubs. The nearest one was almost 3 hours away. She definitely wasn't a man; that rumor Jessie had personally dispelled. What about the one where she was a porn star? Well, that was possible, but so what? She probably wasn't the only member of The Factory who had been in porn, if not professional, then definitely amateur.

Why does it bother me so much to see a man fucking her?

Sirena wasn't gay. Jessie knew this. She wasn't even sure if Sirena truly liked women, or if she just liked putting on a show. *But the way we made out in the shower last night... No one was there to watch...*

She hated the conflicting feelings welling up inside her. And she hated that the image of Brian King sliding his fat, stubby cock into Sirena's pussy was still flashing in her mind.

FIVE

I wondered if all women did with other women was lie and hug.
— *Sarah Winman,* When God Was A Rabbit

Jessie considered leaving the club. There were parts of her that wanted to spend her Saturday night off from work curled up in bed with a book or going on a Netflix binge. But she'd left her things inside, so if she wanted to leave, she would have to go inside and retrieve them out of her locker first, which meant Paisley or Leah had plenty of time to ambush her and attempt to change her mind.

When she opened the doors to the club, Calvin flashed her a smile. He was stationed by the door along with one of the other security guards. She nodded at them and went off toward the women's changing room. As usual, it was full of a flurry of heavily made-up, perfumed, scantily clad women ranging in age from their twenties to sixties. It was amazing what a diversity of sizes, shapes, and ages The Factory attracted. And colors. Jessie was pleased that even since she had joined the club, many more members of color had followed suit.

Jeannette MacPhail's band of followers surrounded their leader as she contemplated what outfit to change into. Jeannette had won The Factory's first Sexy MILF contest, and she'd been a diva ever since. She always brought multiple changes of clothes—if you could call them clothes—to the club, and she would transform herself multiple times per night. Yet no one actually ever saw her play with or even touch another member. She was there specifically to strut her stuff. And hang out with her ladies, while her husband usually got it on with some less flamboyantly dressed female club member.

Jessie just rolled her eyes. She had no doubt that Jeannette herself was responsible for many of the rumors floating around Sirena. After all, Sirena was a beautiful woman, and it was obvious that Jeannette felt threatened by her. Sirena was younger, prettier, and she didn't need over-the-top outfits to draw attention to herself. Jessie had to laugh at how juvenile the whole thing was. *You'd think we were back in high school instead of 30 and 40-year-old ladies*, Jessie mused.

She hoped to be able to grab her bag out of her locker and head out without drawing any attention from Jeannette's posse, but it was not to be. "Hey, Jessie," Jeannette's best friend Shayla purred as Jessie turned the corner to head out the locker room door.

She nodded her head but didn't say anything, hoping to scoot past. It was strange because if she were in uniform, there's no way a group of ladies would intimidate her. But in her little shorts and tank top ensemble she felt stripped down. Not powerless...just non-confrontational. But it might have been because she was too worried about saying something she'd regret about Sirena—putting Jeannette in her place for spreading gossip that wasn't even true. *Hell, she probably blatantly made up some of that shit,* Jessie rationalized.

"You've been hanging out with that Sirena chick, haven't you?" Shayla asked, her blue eyes wide and eyebrows raised.

When Jessie failed to answer, Jeannette's eyes snapped up to hers from where she was lacing up her black leather boots. Jessie couldn't imagine wearing black thigh-high boots when it was still 90 degrees outside, but apparently Jeannette didn't care about that.

"You know she's a spy and a porn star, right?" Jeannette asked. Her muddy hazel eyes were so thickly lined with eyeliner and mascara, Jessie could barely get a read on them. And reading people was something she excelled at.

Jessie rolled her eyes and simply retorted, "Oh yeah?" She had learned a lot about dealing with people from her years as a cop. One thing was to let them lay their cards on the table first. Let them dig their own grave.

"Yeah, she and her husband are going to build a rival club north of town next year, and they are going to headquarter their porn production business there."

Jessie fought to keep her features from showing a reaction. She swallowed, refusing to give in to the sensationalism Jeannette so desperately craved. "Who told you that?" she answered flatly.

"Oh, I have my sources." Jeannette's eyelashes batted as she gave a smug smirk.

"Well, it's a free country," Jessie observed. "No one is stopping anyone from opening another club in Ocean City."

"No, but don't you think it's wrong for her to spy on The Factory and on Cap and Leah's operation?"

Jessie shrugged. "I think that's the cost of doing business."

She turned to leave, brushing Shayla lightly on her arm as she made her way toward the door.

"Wait a minute," Jeannette said, grabbing her arm.

Jessie balked, ripping her arm out of Jeannette's grasp. "Don't touch me," she instructed curtly. "Do that again, and you're going to regret it."

"Oh, you think just because you're a cop that you're some kind of bad ass?" Jeannette laughed. The other women gathered around fell silent, whereas before they had been quietly murmuring amongst themselves.

The door swung open, and Casey Fontaine pushed her way through it. Her eyes lit up when she saw Jessie. "Hey, I've been looking for you, darling!" she gushed in her smooth, honey-coated voice.

Jessie's face immediately brightened. Casey was the matron of the club, the grand old dame. In her sixties and recently retired, she had started the club with Cap a few years back. Now she worked part-time helping with marketing and outreach. She also organized community charity events, such as a toy drive in the winter and a Veterans appreciation luncheon. She always looked like she stepped off the pages of an old-fashioned pin-up calendar, her hair perfectly coiffed, makeup done to perfection, and no wrinkles daring to muss up her beautifully tailored clothes.

"Casey!" Jessie immediately launched herself toward the older woman for a hug. She'd been away on a trip for the past several weeks, and Jessie had missed her presence around the club and around town. Having been a local realtor for nearly forty years, Casey Fontaine knew practically everyone in Ocean City. She was a great asset to The Factory, and Cap and Leah always credited her for really getting the club off the ground, especially when it came to local zoning ordinances. That is how they ended up so far out in the country between Ocean City and Berlin. Off the beaten path. That way the family-friendly atmosphere of the tourist town was not blemished in any way...though anyone visiting Seacrets on a Saturday night might agree the family-friendly title was already tarnished.

"Mmmm, so good to see you, Baby Girl," Casey purred, hugging Jessie and kissing the top of her hair. "What is this crazy outfit you're wearing? You look like you're attending a slumber party circa 1985. Were you even *born* in 1985?" She chortled with a deep, throaty laugh.

"I was about two," Jessie replied, joining in her laughter. She cast Jeannette a dirty look, then returned her dark eyes to Casey. "Hey, do you have a minute?"

"Of course I do, sugarplum!" She held the door open and gestured for Jessie to follow her.

Jessie's last fierce glance over to Jeannette was meant to remind her of her earlier warning.

"What was going on in there?" Casey asked as she closed the office door behind her. "It looked like you had Jeannette cornered."

Jessie grunted with a single chuckle. She was glad she appeared to be on the offensive rather than defensive, because that was certainly not how she had felt in the moment. *Oh, how looks could be deceiving.* "She was talking shit about Sirena Horne. I just wasn't having it."

"Oh, yes. Leah filled me in about that situation. Something about that woman seems so familiar to me, but I can't put my finger on why," Casey mused. "Do we have any news?"

Apparently Casey had been kept in the loop along with Cap, Leah, Paisley and Calvin. But she had been traveling, and Leah probably didn't want to disturb her vacation with all the details. If anyone deserved to get away from it all, it was Casey. Even firmly in her sixties, the woman didn't seem to know the meaning of the term "slowing down."

"I'm still working on it. Do you think there's any truth to this rival club theory? Did Leah tell you about that?"

Casey sighed and gently touched her neck as if she were overheated. "That rumor has been going around since long before we founded The Factory. Some people thought The Factory was the fulfillment of that rumor, in fact. Did you get the part about the porn company doing business from there?"

Jessie chuckled. "Sure did. So where did that come from?"

"I think it's an urban legend. I don't think we have any reason to believe Sirena is involved."

"She just sort of appeared out of nowhere, from what I understand. No one seems to have known her before she showed up in May. And she's from Georgia originally, though she drives a car registered to someone in Pennsylvania, someone with a different last name. That much I do know."

"I heard the Kings vouched for her. Have you checked with them?" Casey questioned, her brows drawn slightly with concern.

Jessie nodded. "But they only met her the weekend before at Seacrets. So she comes down to Ocean City to scope out the swinger scene one weekend, meets the Kings, and then the next moves down here and joins The Factory? It seems really weird to me."

Casey nodded in agreement. "Does she have a job? Kids? A family? What is she, mid-thirties? It's so strange that she reminds me of someone, but I can't figure out who!"

"Thirty-eight according to her membership application. She wouldn't tell me what she does for a living. Speaking of which, how does everyone know I'm a cop? I've tried really hard to keep that secret. I'm not on Facebook. I've never arrested any of these people. I don't think I've even written a ticket to anyone here."

"You know Jeannette's father is the Worcester

County Sheriff, right? That woman has loose lips...so to speak!" Casey laughed at her own pun. "Maybe that has something to do with everyone knowing you're a cop." She crossed her legs at her ankles and smoothed her flowy navy skirt over her thick thighs. "This is a small town, Jessie. It doesn't take long for word to get around."

I'll have to look into the sheriff thing, Jessie thought, feeling a bit disheartened at the idea of having so few degrees of separation between her work life and private life. "I know that about small towns, but that's exactly why I'm surprised I haven't been able to get to the bottom of this Sirena business. I feel like someone knows her story but isn't telling."

"You'll get to the bottom of it," Casey predicted. "I have no doubt."

Sirena emerged from one of the downstairs playrooms shortly after Jessie left Casey's office. Jessie watched her amble up to the bar, looking a bit disoriented. She studied her for a moment before deciding she better go see what happened. She didn't mean to feel responsible for Sirena, but she did. For some reason she always seemed on the verge of crisis, but Jessie couldn't put her finger on why. There was a vulnerability there, even though she seemed so confident in her body and sexuality. There was something underneath, something concealed, that triggered Jessie's radar.

"How did it go?" Jessie asked as casually as she

could. She didn't want to know, but she asked anyway.

"It was fine. I'm a little sore."

"Sore?"

"Yeah, after I was done with Brian and Susan, I got lured downstairs and had a threesome with two single guys. DP, the whole nine yards. With an audience, of course." She looked both exhausted and proud at the same time.

"DP? Really?" Jessie couldn't help but cringe. She wasn't one to question anyone's sexual preferences—it would be fairly hypocritical of her, after all—but double penetration had never held any allure for her whatsoever. She could no longer stomach the idea of vaginal penetration after some of the sorry excuses for boyfriends she'd had in high school, and the idea of anything up her bum was cringe-worthy even on her most adventurous day.

Sirena shrugged. "Smoke 'em if you got 'em," she quipped, following it up with an arpeggio of her crystalline laugh.

"I guess that's one way to look at it." Jessie was still trying not to appear disgusted. She had no problem with the idea of multiple partners. It wasn't that. She was afraid her face was betraying her as Sirena stared, eyeing Jessie's expression, which was a combination of shocked and perturbed.

After a beat, Jessie asked, "Who were the guys?"

"Uh..." Sirena's eyes darted around the club, from the lounge, to the dance floor, to the area behind the bar where there were two pool tables. "I didn't really get their names. It was loud." She pointed to a tall, stocky man who was racking up the pool balls. "That guy." And then she pointed over to a leather couch on the other side of the dance floor. "And that guy. I think his name was Al."

Sirena didn't know the man playing pool, but she did know Al Purcell. He was an older man, a silver fox whose wife had passed away the year before. He was harmless, and from what she understood, had a really sweet disposition that made him popular with the ladies. And he had that whole widower's thing going for him too. She studied the man playing pool. He looked to be in his late thirties, early forties. With his crew-cut hair, he could have been a cop. Or military. He had that look.

"Well, did you have fun? That's the important thing."

Sirena nodded, her tired but satisfied smile spreading across her cheeks again. "Yes, but I need a drink."

Jessie laughed as Sirena signaled for the bartender. "Got it. Hey...I meant to tell you I had a nice time the other night."

Sirena looked up as if she wasn't expecting the conversation to continue. "Oh, yeah. Me too. Who doesn't love a girls' night?" She winked and returned her attention to the bartender, who was sauntering over to take her order.

"But I didn't get your number," Jessie persisted after the bartender went to get Sirena's liquor out of the fridge.

"Oh," she answered, her lips curling ever so slightly into a frown. Jessie wasn't sure if it meant she didn't want to give her number, or she was upset she had forgotten to.

Jessie tried to keep the flirty smile on her face. "So, could I have it?"

The bartender returned with Sirena's drink just in time for her to evade Jessie's question for a moment longer. Then her face softened after her first sip. "Oh, of course." She waited for Jessie to pull out her phone, then rattled off the number.

"Thanks for that. I appreciate it."

Sirena nodded and fixed her eyes to Jessie's as if she was searching for something. Her face brightened as an idea flashed across it. "You're a really good kisser, you know that?" she offered.

Jessie felt her heart immediately start to thunder against her ribcage. "Well, thanks, I—"

And before she could get any other words out, Sirena leaned in to brush her lips against Jessie's, so softly, like an angel's whisper. Electricity shot through Jessie's body as every nerve-ending cried out for more—more of Sirena's lips, more of her body. She could taste the alcohol on her tongue as she deepened the kiss. It seemed foreign to her, but sweet and intoxicating at the same time, as if she could get drunk on just the taste.

Jessie felt eyes on her, scoping out the kiss. Some were jealous; some were curious, and some were just plain titillated by seeing two women's lips interlocked. The lifestyle was pro-bisexual women. It was expected—nearly demanded—for women to make out, explore each other, and then return to their aroused male partners. It was safe; it was stimulating. No one complained or called out the double standard of being hypocritically anti-bisexual males. Not in public, anyway.

"Hope you enjoy the rest of your night," Sirena whispered into her ear as she broke away from their embrace. Jessie immediately felt the air shift, a cool shadow slipping between them as Sirena stepped away from the bar and toward the dance floor.

She guessed that meant she was done with her for the night.

"Why don't you follow her? See where she goes?' Paisley asked, looking around at Cap, Leah, Calvin and Casey to see if they had any objections or better suggestions.

"I can't believe you of all people are asking me to follow a club member," Jessie scoffed. "Especially after what you went through a couple years ago." Paisley had been blackmailed, not to mention stalked and threatened. It wasn't just Paisley who was threatened, but Casey and the Sheldons too. They were all lucky it didn't have a tragic outcome.

"You're not following her to harass her," Paisley argued, "but to keep her safe. We know there are members here who don't think highly of her."

"You don't seriously think Jeannette and her groupies would try to harm her, do you?" Jessie's eyes were wide with disbelief. Jeannette was too smart to do something so stupid. She was all bark and no bite. *But if her father is the sheriff, maybe she thinks she's above the law*, Jessie considered.

"I just have a bad feeling about all of this," Leah finally said. "Maybe she *is* a spy. I would kind of like to know if she's planning to jeopardize my livelihood. Say what you will about her, but something doesn't add up. She's not completely innocent."

"Fine," Jessie agreed. "It's almost two. We'll be shutting down soon. Let me see if I can find her and discreetly shadow her." She rolled her eyes, not believing she was essentially going to be working on a Saturday night she had off work. Perhaps she would have liked to find something more enjoyable—some actual fun—to fill her time off work, to relax for a change. After all, she wasn't getting paid for this work. It was all *pro bono*.

She left The Factory management in the office area and descended the stairs again to scope the premises for signs of her target. Sure enough, she saw her coming out of the locker room with her bag slung over her shoulder. She met the gaze of the clean-cut guy she'd played with earlier, the other "M" of the threesome with Al. Jessie wished she had gotten his name, but she figured soon enough she'd have his tag number and be able to run it.

She waited a bit for them to exit the front doors and get into his car, then she slinked out the back and around to her car in the parking lot, firing it up as she saw their headlights begin to move toward the road. Lots of people were leaving, so it wasn't going to be suspicious if she pulled around behind them as they waited to exit. She just hoped she wouldn't lose track of them in the traffic.

The guy had Delaware tags, which was no big deal. The state line was only fifteen or twenty minutes away depending on how clogged the highway was through Ocean City. She guessed that meant she would be following them all the way across the state line. Maybe that would be better. Out of state she was just a person following another person. She would be out of her jurisdiction.

Once they got out on the highway, the traffic began to thin out. At 2 AM in the summertime, even Ocean City had to crash at some point. There would be sun and surf enough for the next day, and weary vacationers would turn into bed or pass out from drunkenness. When they made it to Route 50, she stayed in a different lane a few paces behind so as not to attract attention to herself. The mystery man changed lanes a few times, and she wasn't sure if he was trying to lose her tail or if he was drunk. She sincerely hoped not the latter, because she would call him into OCPD faster than he could fail a field test.

They passed the Route 90 bridge, and he was still weaving in and out of traffic. "That's it," Jessie decided, picking up her cell phone and dialing in the non-emergency number for the police department.

"This is Jessica Martinez, #584. I'm following a black Dodge pick-up truck, Delaware tags PC15789. He's changing lanes a lot; he's been left of center a few times. Suspected drunk driver heading north on Ocean Gateway. Is there a unit in the area of 49th?"

She glanced up to the next stoplight and could see her headlights reflecting off the OCPD emblem on the side of a waiting cruiser. In seconds, the flashing red and blue lights came alive, and the unit moved onto the highway right behind the truck. Her lips curled into a smug smile as she whipped into the parking lot across the street to witness the interaction.

She watched the scene unfold, but it wasn't

gratifying at all. If the driver was drunk and got arrested, Sirena was going to be stranded. Then she'd have to show up, rescue her and step into the role of hero. Despite her line of work, the prospect wasn't appealing. But after the OCPD officer ran the tags and returned the driver's license and registration, he allowed them to leave the scene. Apparently the driver hadn't been drunk after all. Jessie rolled her eyes at the other potential causes for him weaving in and out of traffic, like perhaps Sirena's lips were wrapped around his cock and distracting him.

She looked down at her phone, then back to the highway with cars lined up at the light. It would be hard for her to catch up with them now, and she didn't have a lot of desire to drive all the way to Delaware. She had the tag number and could still look up the driver if she wanted to. But in the morning. Right now she was feeling restless, lonely, and horny. It was the perfect recipe for making bad decisions.

Scrolling through the contacts in her phone, she had the fleeting idea of sending a text to Sirena. Maybe she could ask her on a real date. But when she saw Cate's name, she stopped. Cate was a sexy biker chick she'd met during Bike Week the year before. They'd gotten together a few times. They didn't have much in common personality-wise, but she was fun to hang out with. *Maybe she was lonely on a Saturday night too?* Jessie wondered as her thumbs flew over her keyboard.

She began to head north toward her condo, waiting for her phone to buzz with a text back from Cate. *Maybe "Booty call?" wasn't the best thing to say.* Maybe she should have gone for some small talk first, but the night was growing older. Dawn would be creeping up over the water in only a few short hours.

The cloak of darkness—the preferred wardrobe of sinners and sluts—was quickly fading away.

She pulled into the lot at her condo, her phone still black with rejection. Finally it lit up with an incoming text just as she put the car in park. She reached for it, a smile already turning up her lips, when she realized it wasn't from Cate at all.

It was from Sirena: *Damn, I thought you were going to follow us the whole way. I'm sure Steve would have loved to have two girls for the night.*

SIX

*"Do people always fall in love with
things they can't have?'
'Always,' Carol said, smiling, too."*
-Patricia Highsmith, The Price of Salt

The sky opened up to pour just as Jessie and her partner pulled into the parking lot at the outlet mall. Located near the inlet bridge, it was a popular destination for tourists, especially on days that beach-going wasn't ideal. It was so hot, the rain nearly sizzled on the pavement as it struck the black surface, and the smell of the sea hung heavy in the air.

"I don't think our girl is here," Bart said, exhaling a puffy sigh as he turned to look at Jessie.

"Fucking shoplifters," she answered, shaking her head. "How many times a week do we get called out here?"

"Like two dozen?" He surveyed the skies and let out a second sigh. "I say we sit here and take a nap. It's good napping weather."

Jessie laughed at him. "I'm sure Sarge would be real cool with that."

"You're such a goody two-shoes sometimes. No wonder you can't find a hot piece of ass!" He chuckled as he turned the radio up a notch or two.

"What the fuck?" She punched him in the arm playfully. "I can find as many hot pieces of ass as I want. It's the relationship thing I'm not cut out for, and that's all women want. Until they don't, of course." As soon as she said it, she wanted to swallow the words back down. Bart had just gotten divorced over the winter. She had a feeling his complaint was more of a projection than a commentary on her dating skills.

"Yeah, I can definitely relate. I'd settle for a hot piece of ass right now too." He was on his third sigh of the conversation already.

His wife had been cheating on him. Not very many of their colleagues knew that, but he had confided in Jessie. She was honored in a weird way, even though she didn't feel particularly close to him.

"Wish I could help you out," Jessie fired back and watched the smile twist his lips up. They liked to joke around about both liking girls.

"So, you can't find any nice lezzies to shack up with, or what?" he questioned with what seemed to be true curiosity, even if he worded it in a rude way.

"It's not a matter of 'can't;' it's a matter of not wanting to. Not after what happened with Cindy."

"What *did* happen to Cindy? You guys seemed so

hot and heavy when you brought her to the Christmas party last year."

Now she regretted this line of discussion even more. The last thing Jessie wanted to do was dredge up old memories of her last girlfriend, who had turned out not to be a lesbian, as she had professed to be. In fact, she was barely bi; she was just in a man-hating phase. At least until her old boyfriend came around and tried to win her back.

"She got back together with her ex," Jessie explained curtly, hoping he could catch her vibe of not wanting to delve any deeper into it.

Bart seemed to take the hint and didn't press. "Okay, Miss Goody Two-Shoes, let's get the hell out of here. I bet if I ever get a new partner, she'll let me take a nap."

"You know no one else can put up with you, Farris," Jessie retorted. "You're stuck with me."

He gave her a smile, turned the windshield wipers on full blast, and put their cruiser in gear. "Guess it could be worse."

Jessie looked around the table from Cap to Leah to Paisley to Calvin, and then finally to Casey, who was seated at the end. She felt honored to be invited to participate in this special occasion, especially since she wasn't technically an employee of the club. A few of the security guards and hosts were also in attendance.

They were gathered to celebrate the third anniversary of The Factory opening.

Casey and Cap recounted the tale of securing the building, and how it almost didn't come to pass because of the drama between Leah, Cap, and a former member of the Ocean City swinging community, Rhonda. Cap had always had Leah in mind to manage the club, but he had no idea it would grow into a big enough success to warrant hiring Paisley, Calvin and so many security guards. He gave a speech about how much every member of the team meant to him and Leah, and how they wouldn't be able to run the club without their help.

"And on that note," Casey projected over the applause that trickled out across the room following Cap's speech, "I have an announcement to make."

All eyes snapped to her as she struggled to maintain her composure. Jessie had never known Casey to be an emotional person, but she did seem to be having a hard time keeping her tears at bay. She looked down to see that Casey's hands were trembling as she gripped the edge of the table.

"I recently learned," she began, her eyes glistening with moisture as they glanced around the room from face to face, "that I have breast cancer."

There was a collective gasp heard around the room. Jessie felt a pang to her heart as if she'd been stabbed. Casey was one of the strongest, most beautiful, most compelling women she had ever known. She couldn't imagine any adversary, even one as formidable as cancer, being able to bring Ms. Fontaine down. She seemed immortal.

"I'm so sorry," Casey said, wiping her eyes with a

silk handkerchief she pulled out of her perfectly coordinating handbag. "I hoped to be a little more pragmatic about all of this." She chuckled softly as she scanned the shocked faces of her friends. The only people who had known were Cap and Leah, evident from the fact they looked more sad than surprised.

Casey took a deep breath. "I'm going to be leaving my position at The Factory to move to California where my sister lives. She is an oncology nurse, as luck has it, at one of the premier facilities in the country for treating breast cancer. And she's going to take care of me while I go through chemo and radiation."

Paisley covered her mouth with shock as tears began to well in her eyes. Calvin reached down to wrap his hand around his wife's, attempting to provide some comfort through his touch. The hosts were also misty-eyed, and a silence enveloped the room as everyone searched for words of encouragement and hope.

"And due to my leaving, Cap and Leah are going to be hiring a social media and outreach coordinator. So if you know anyone who would be good for the job, don't hesitate to let us know!" She managed to paint a smile on her cherry red lips as she dried the last of her tears on her hanky.

"We'd like to hire somebody who is already a member of the club," Leah added. She stood up and gave Casey a huge bear hug, squeezing her body tightly to the older woman's. "We're going to miss you so much. But we know if anyone can kick cancer's butt, it's YOU!" She gave her a kiss on the cheek.

"Thanks, doll," Casey said, the tears welling up again as she found her seat at the table.

"I know that wasn't a happy announcement," Leah

continued, "but Cap and I do have something happy to share with you all."

Jessie's ears perked up. She had a feeling she knew what they were going to say, but after Casey's announcement caught her off-guard, she was starting to second-guess herself.

"It's probably not going to surprise anyone too much, but Cap and I are expecting baby #2!" she revealed, her smile so bright, all of her teeth were visible. Cap stood next to her with his arm over her shoulder, squeezing her to his side.

What an interesting couple, Jessie thought, not that she hadn't ever thought it before. Cap was several years older than Leah, a tall, broad-shouldered hulk of a man with hair that got more silvery every year and a beard that did little to conceal his dimples. He had the brightest blue eyes Jessie had ever seen. Leah was not a small woman, but she did seem dwarfed by her husband. At 5'9" with a hearty, midwestern build, she'd look sturdy next to any other man, but next to Cap, who was so roughly hewn from decades of work at sea, she seemed delicate with her strawberry blonde waves and piercing green eyes, upturned nose and chiseled cheekbones.

"Congratulations!" the unanimous roar went up toward the ceiling. Everyone seemed to take it as a signal to mingle about the room, giving best wishes to Casey, Cap and Leah. A few people joked that they were ready for an announcement from Paisley and Calvin, but Paisley firmly shook her head and expressed there was no way in hell that was happening.

Jessie looked around the room at all the people The Factory had brought into her life. She understood now more than ever why Paisley had asked her to help out. Casey was leaving, and Cap and Leah were just about to get a whole lot busier—as if their son Lincoln didn't already demand a big chunk of their time. Paisley and Calvin were going to have to keep the club running, and they couldn't afford to have any liabilities lurking in the wings, waiting to sabotage their efforts.

As Jessie walked out to her car that night, she decided to send Sirena a text. It was mid-week, and she likely wouldn't see her until the club re-opened on the weekend. But it didn't seem like Jessie would ever get to the bottom of the mystery of Sirena Horne if she only worked on Fridays and Saturdays. A voice in her head screamed at her not to get involved, especially considering her impossible-to-ignore attraction to Sirena. But the bigger, louder voice drowned it out with the obligation to Paisley and the rest of the management team...not to mention the professional part of her that couldn't resist unraveling a mystery.

Sirena did not text her back. Jessie tried to brush off her disappointment, but a call late that night after the celebratory dinner distracted her with a different surge of emotions.

"Hello?" Jessie had gone to bed early to prepare for her morning shift, and her grogginess was reflected in her gravelly voice.

"Jessie, it's Leah. Sorry to call you so late." She sighed before starting again, as if there was just too much in her head to wrangle the words she needed to explain the purpose of her call. "I just got off the phone with Al—Al from the club, you know?"

Jessie nodded before she realized a verbal answer was required. "Yes?"

"Sirena just left his house, and she's drunk. She showed up there with bruises all over her, but she wouldn't tell him where they came from. He's really worried about her. Is there anything you can do?"

Jessie bolted up in bed, alertness rushing through her like a fast-acting drug. "Do we know what she's driving? The car with Delaware tags?"

"It's a gold Honda, like early 2000s model," Leah answered. "A Civic, Al thought, but wasn't positive. I don't think he mentioned the plates. What can we do?"

Jessie shook her head. The last thing she wanted was for Sirena to get pulled over in Ocean City. Even if she dropped Jessie's name, the outcome would not be good for her. There was a zero tolerance policy for driving drunk, and no connections in the world would get her out of being arrested. "Fuck," she finally said. "I'll go after her."

Leah breathed out a sigh of relief. "Thank you, Jessie. We owe you big time."

"Do we know where she was going?"

"Al said she wouldn't tell him. I'm sorry I don't have more information."

She breathed the word "fuck" out again. *Nothing like being a bodyguard for a person who has no idea you're protecting them*, she thought as she pulled on some shorts, a t-shirt, and her sneakers. She hightailed it to the elevator, then down to her car. *Tomorrow is going to suck donkey balls*, she predicted as she started up the engine.

Ocean City was not exactly a small place. There was the main highway, dotted with hotels, resorts, restaurants and bars, but there were plenty of side streets too. And who knew if she was staying in Ocean City? She could be halfway to the state line by now. It was 10 PM, not exactly late, but just about the time that—if someone were looking for it—trouble could be easily found. Jessie struggled to put herself in Sirena's shoes, or rather behind the wheel of her car. She just didn't know her well enough yet. She reviewed countless snippets of conversations they'd had the night of their sleepover, but nothing was rising to the surface, nothing stood out.

She began to back out of her parking space when she saw a small car whip into the lot off of Route 50. When the car caught in the beam of her headlights, she realized it was gold. *Sirena.*

She waited for the car to come to a stop before approaching her. She had her gun in its holster on her belt, just in case. She wasn't sure why her heart began to pound when she grew nearer to the car. *It's just Sirena, my friend*, she told herself. *It's not like some insane serial murderer is going to jump out.*

She stayed in the shadows as the car door slowly creaked open. Once she saw a wedge-heeled sandal hit the blacktop, she knew for sure it was Sirena, but she waited, not wanting to frighten her. If she was actually drunk, who knows how she would react.

The car door slammed, and Jessie made her way toward the shadow. "Sirena?" Jessie called out, stepping into the streaming blue light from one of the nearby poles. Sirena turned to face her and froze, clutching her chest as though she was afraid.

"I didn't mean to startle you," Jessie apologized, her voice even and smooth. She had perfected her steady, calming voice for dealing with her "clientele."

"Jessie?"

"Yeah, were you looking for me?"

She didn't even get a word out. Instead, she ran to Jessie and threw her arms around her, engulfing Jessie in her spicy vanilla scent. Jessie felt the blonde's lithe body break down into sobs as Sirena squeezed her tightly to her bosom.

She didn't want to stay in the dark parking lot, so she pulled away from her sobbing friend and took her hand instead, guiding her toward the building, then toward the elevator that would carry them to Jessie's floor. Sirena's sobs faded into faint whimpers by the time they arrived at Jessie's door, though from the way her body moved, Jessie could tell she had been drinking. Her balance and depth perception were clearly off. Jessie breathed another sigh of relief that Sirena had been able to drive from Al's house to her condo without any issues—that she knew of. She'd have to get on her case about that when she sobered up.

Once they were seated on the couch under the soft lights of the shell-shaped lamps in her living room, Jessie was able to observe the bruises on Sirena's skin. There were marks around her forearm that looked like they were made by fingers gripping her firmly. There was another bruise on her chest between her collarbones. She winced to think of how that one got there. Possibly a palm shoving her into a wall.

When Sirena's eyes met Jessie's, the tears welled up all over again. Jessie wasn't even sure she was going to be able to talk, especially considering she was still drunk. She contemplated just taking her to bed and letting her sleep it off rather than trying to get to the bottom of it. But before she had a chance to make up her mind, Sirena drew back with a long wail, then asked for a tissue.

Jessie held up a finger and ran into her bedroom for the box of tissues she kept by her bed, the whole time trying to formulate a game plan for getting Sirena to spill her guts about what had happened. She was skittish, Jessie had to remember that. She was like a wild animal caught in a trap. She needed to be approached calmly, gently, slowly. She handed the box of tissues to Sirena and sat back down. She had a feeling she was in for a long night.

Sirena blew her nose, then ran her fingers through her golden waves, which were in disarray. "I suppose you're going to yell at me?" she questioned. She had dark purple circles beneath her eyes and her nose was bright red from crying and blowing it. Her skin looked sallow and dull. Jessie had never seen her look so disheveled. She was wearing a loose tank top and cut off denim shorts, nothing like the sexy dresses and lingerie Jessie was used to seeing her wear. But there was still a pull, still an attraction, which Jessie tried to shake away as she figured out how to answer her question.

"I'm not going to yell at you, but you have to know how irresponsible it is to drive under the influence," Jessie began. "And I'm going to tell you right now that if you got pulled over, dropping my name would not help you one bit."

"Dropping your name?" Sirena scoffed. "I don't even *know* your last name. What am I supposed to say,

'I know this cop chick who belongs to the swinger club I go to?'"

Jessie shook her head. "Fine. I'm telling you for future reference. I'm glad you made it safely, though."

Sirena sniffled again as she brought another tissue to her nose. "Me too."

"So why did you come here?" Jessie asked. It might have been too direct of a question, but her curiosity was greater than her willingness to take it slow.

"You texted me," came the answer.

"To see if you wanted to meet up for coffee sometime." Jessie smirked as she scanned Sirena's face for the true reason.

"No time like the present," Sirena answered, forcing a smile. She looked as if it hurt her to use those muscles. Maybe there were bruises that hadn't even appeared yet.

"What happened to you?" Jessie couldn't handle any more beating around the bush.

"What do you mean?"

Jessie wanted to roll her eyes. *She can't be serious.* "You're covered in bruises. What the hell happened?"

Sirena glanced down at her forearm and then back to Jessie, pressing her green eyes into Jessie's brown. "I just fell down the stairs earlier when I was drinking. I'm not too graceful on a good day, but I'm ten times worse when I'm drunk." She gave a little forced giggle, but it sounded tinny and hollow compared to what Jessie knew was her genuine crystalline laugh.

Jessie took a deep breath. *There is no fucking way in hell she fell down the stairs*, she thought, studying the bruises again. They were finger-shaped, and from a large hand, too. She pinned her eyes on Sirena's and gave her the look, the look she gave every suspect when she wasn't buying their story. She never had to say a word.

"What, you don't believe me?" She furrowed her brows and pursed her lips, looking incredibly indignant. *Not to mention sexy*, but Jessie was trying not to notice that part.

"If you didn't want to tell me what really happened, why did you come here tonight?"

"Another sleepover?" Sirena's eyebrows lifted suggestively, then she stroked her finger down Jessie's cheek.

No, she's still drunk, Jessie immediately thought. *What, she came over here to seduce me? What the actual fuck?* It was amazing how her tears had seemed to dry up, just vanished into thin air. And now she was flirty and suggestive. *What is with this woman?* she wondered. *She is going to be the death of me, I swear.*

"You can stay over if you want," Jessie conceded, "but I have to go to sleep soon. I have work tomorrow."

"So that's it?" Disappointment carved Sirena's lips into a frown.

Jessie didn't feel like playing games. It was late, and yes, there was nothing more she'd like to do than lead Sirena to her bedroom and bury her face between her luscious thighs, but there was no way in hell she was doing it when she was drunk. The having to get up thing was a ploy. Under ordinary conditions, she'd certainly sacrifice sleep for sex.

"You're drunk," Jessie explained. "And bruised.

And we both know you didn't fall down the stairs."

Sirena looked down for a moment as if to gather her thoughts. A gust of wind blew the curtains open, and Jessie felt the cool air whip around her legs. She left the balcony door open, as usual, and a storm was blowing in from the south. She had a feeling they were in for heavy rain and turbulent winds. There was a tropical depression out at sea, moving up the coastline. She definitely didn't want Sirena driving home in that, not drunk, and not bruised.

"So are you going to tell me what really happened?" Jessie scanned her eyes for signs of capitulation.

Sirena sighed. "I just got into a disagreement with someone."

"A man with large hands?" Jessie presumed.

A soft chuckle escaped Sirena's lips as she considered her response. "It's no big deal."

"It is a big deal. He left bruises, Sirena. That's assault."

"You should see the other guy!" she joked, waggling her eyebrows.

"Just tell me it isn't a man from The Factory," Jessie pressed. If so, Cap and Leah would need to know immediately.

Sirena laughed. "No, of course not!"

"This isn't funny, and you know it. I don't know why you're being so evasive." Jessie sighed as she reminded herself to take a gentler approach. She took Sirena's hands, which were silky smooth with long, elegant fingers, into her own and squeezed them. "I'm trying to help you, you know. I'm trying to be your friend."

"Is that what we are?" Sirena asked. She swung her leg up over Jessie's hips and planted herself on Jessie's lap, facing her. She leaned in so far that their lips were nearly close enough to touch. "Just friends?"

Jessie felt her heart try to leap out of her chest at their sudden proximity, her senses filling with the smell of Sirena's fading scent. There was no way she'd ever be able to smell vanilla or jasmine again without the image of Sirena conquering her thoughts. She knew she couldn't give in to Sirena's advances, but the temptation was holding her captive, requiring every ounce of her strength to keep the walls from crumbling.

"What do you want to be?" Jessie rasped as Sirena lowered her mouth to plant a kiss on Jessie's neck.

"Friends with benefits?" came the reply, then a golden-bright, "Lovers?"

Though the wind had stopped gusting through the open patio door, Jessie still felt a coolness swirling around her, contrasting with the heat she felt radiating from Sirena's core onto hers. *Why is it so hard to resist her charms?*

Sirena didn't want a verbal answer. When she looked up into Jessie's chocolate brown eyes, wide and open like a vast sea of truth, it was painted all over her face that words were superfluous. The corner of her lips tilted up, and her wanton simper was not even so much of an invitation as it was a lure, a beckoning that Jessie could not ignore.

Jessie watched Sirena's eyelids flutter shut, her lashes resting like a veil against her cheeks, and she knew there was no turning back once she pressed her lips against the bait. She braced herself for the sweet flood of desire that would surely crash upon her shores the moment their skin met.

And when it happened, she let it wash over her, cleansing her and sinking her down with its weight in the same wave, in the same breath the two women shared between them as Sirena's hands threaded through Jessie's thick, dark hair. She tasted of liquor and what Jessie knew would someday be regret.

SEVEN

It's morning now, and I miss the soft rasp of her voice already. Ugh. I'm in trouble, aren't I?
-*Pat Shand*, Destiny, NY, Volume One:
Who I Used to Be

"So you slept with her?" Casey asked, her eyebrows raised, not in judgment but in disbelief.

Jessie wanted to defend herself, and she didn't even know why. "Yeah, but—"

Casey shook her head and looked over at Leah as if to gauge her reaction and ask a silent *what now?* She turned back to Jessie, taking in the worried expression on the younger woman's face. "I've never seen you look so...run-down before, Jessie. I'm concerned about you."

"Me too," Leah agreed, nodding. "We really didn't mean to put you in a bad position with this. We had no idea it was going to take this much time or effort on your part. We kind of figured you'd discover who Sirena was, where she lived and what she does for a living, and then we'd go on, you know, business as usual."

Jessie shrugged. "I didn't mean for things to get out of hand last night. She had bruises. She was crying. Then when she started to sober up, she came on to me. I—"

"You were thinking with your 'little head?'" Casey joked, trying to lighten the mood. "Oh, come on, we all know women do it too. Our 'little head' is even smaller than a man's. Well, most men." She offered up a boisterous chuckle at her joke.

Jessie wished she could find the humor in it. She felt like she had let them down. But worst of all, she felt like she had let herself down, especially that promise she made after Cindy not to fall for anyone else, especially not a straight girl.

And that's what Sirena was, essentially, right? Straight. *Okay, maybe bi.* But she wasn't gay. And she wasn't the type of bi woman to fall in love with another woman, not in a million years. She was the type of bi girl who liked to put on shows for men. She wasn't going to give up men to be in a relationship with a woman. Not that Jessie would even ask her to do that—would she?

She shook her head, trying to rattle out all of those thoughts and get back to the matter at hand: solving the mystery of Sirena and keeping the club out of trouble. That was her purpose. That is why she'd left work still in uniform to get over to the club before they locked up for the night. During the week, the office only stayed open till 5 PM.

"She said the bruises were not caused by a member of the club," Jessie verified. "But I don't know whether to believe her."

"Do we know yet where she actually lives or who this Joseph Patterson person is?" Casey asked.

Jessie shook her head. "I haven't been able to find out much about him. He has some DUIs on his record; his license is suspended. That's pretty much the extent of it. He's quite a bit older than she is, and I'm still not sure how they're related."

"Jessie, I really think you've done all you can," Casey finally said after seeming to stew about it for a moment. "We can't in good conscience ask you to do any more. You're not on our payroll, and you're busy enough with your own job. It wouldn't be right to expect anything more than you've already done."

"I agree with Casey." Leah nodded as she looked Jessie up and down. "Plus, you look exhausted. Do you have some time off coming up? I know this is the busy season for you guys..."

"It's tourist season. We're all busy," Jessie answered. "It is what it is."

"But you don't even have time for a life between work and this—this is work!" She shook her strawberry blonde hair with an accompanying laugh. "Only you're not getting paid, so it's worse than work."

"I don't mind," Jessie insisted. "I want to get to the bottom of this too..."

"Wait," Casey interrupted. She glanced from Leah back to Jessie again. "You don't have...feelings...for her, do you?" Her eyebrows arched with her scrutiny of Jessie's face for the truth.

A firepit roared to life inside Jessie's stomach, the flames stretching their burning tendrils out to every corner of her body as the heat pressed onto her skin, looking for a place to escape. She knew her dark skin wouldn't betray her with a flush, but she could still feel its effects. And that was when she knew there was no reasoning her way out of this one. Even if she chose to lie now, the truth had staked its claim, planted a flag on her heart.

She found she was too stunned by the realization of this, of this happening before she even had the chance to stamp down the flickering embers, to formulate any words. Casey and Leah continued to stare at her, urging her lips to move. She felt somewhat spared by the fact that Paisley wasn't there, because she knew Jessie well enough to surmise the answer. She would have blurted it out, brazen and bold, just like everything else that came out of her mouth. But Leah and Casey were too genteel, too refined, too knowing of the secrets people must harbor to protect themselves from the truth.

"Jessie?" Casey finally pressed.

"Oh, it's just a little summer fling, I guess," she answered, offering up a tiny, embarrassed smile. "Sirena's not into women...not like that..."

"Maybe not, but that wouldn't necessarily stop you from having feelings for her," Leah answered, as if she knew all about trying to suppress feelings one knows are verboten.

"Yes it would," Jessie insisted. "Trust me, I've been down that road before. It's a pointless trip. But I would be lying if I said I didn't enjoy Sirena's company." She tested Leah and Casey's acceptance of her explanation and found they were convinced. "Look, I understand if you want me to back off from pursuing her for The Factory's sake, but I am interested in learning who she really is for my sake."

The two other woman looked at each other to confirm their agreement. "It's a free country," Casey remarked. "Just be careful, Jessie, okay? Something about her just doesn't sit well with me."

"Or with me," Leah concurred. "Which is why I started this whole mess in the first place."

Jessie thanked the two women and turned to head out to her police cruiser with one thought on her mind: *So Leah's the one I'm going to blame when I get my heart broken.*

Jessie was surprised to find a text from Sirena on her phone when she returned to her car. It was simple, innocent, and Jessie struggled not to read anything into it. *How was your day?*

She didn't reply right away. Tourist traffic was clogging Route 50 by the time she got back into Ocean City, and because she was driving her cruiser, everyone drove that much slower as she tried to pass in the left lane. Several potential replies to Sirena's text bounced around her mind. It was Thursday, and she assumed she would see her again at the club on Friday. How was she going to deal with Sirena wanting to play with other members?

Maybe I shouldn't text back at all, she considered.

She reflected on Casey and Leah's reservations, along with their admonishment to relax and try to take some time for herself. They said she looked "rundown," "stressed." She was 32 years old, and the only thing she had to worry about was her job. Now she added one thing into the mix, and she couldn't handle it? What did that say about her? She'd always thought she was a strong person.

Maybe Sirena makes me too weak. Too vulnerable.

Jessie made it back to her condo and even managed to make herself dinner without replying to Sirena's text. She got a phone call from her parents, but she ignored it. She always did. She hadn't actually spoken to her mother since Christmas, and every time she spoke to the woman, she continued to pretend that Jessie's brothers were anything but lowlife asshole scumbags. And until her mother would acknowledge what they did to her, there was no way she was exchanging anything with her other than the shallowest pleasantries.

No wonder I can't stand to see women hurt by men. No wonder I became a cop. No wonder I'm the first one they ask to respond to domestic situations. I know how it feels.

Late that night when she crawled into bed, the sound of waves crashing on the beach below serenaded her, filling her room with a sense of peace and tranquility. Her mind felt clearer than it had for some time, and she was able to look at the Sirena situation a bit more objectively. She wanted to protect Sirena. She felt a sense of obligation to, in fact. Despite her allure, her appeal, the danger of falling for her—there was an undeniable duty to find out who was hurting her, not to mention to keep the club from suffering any ill consequences.

What if Sirena had lied? What if someone at the club *had* assaulted her? She couldn't run the risk of something like that happening without consequences for the perpetrator.

She grabbed her phone, now gripped with fear that something else had happened. Her innocent *How was your day?* text could have been a call for help. She'd seen this with abuse victims before. They were ashamed of being victims and most weren't willing to shout it from the rooftops. They had subtler means of reaching out.

What's new? Going to the club tomorrow? she texted. All the calm and tranquility she felt when she initially slid into bed vanished. Now she felt nauseated and overly warm. She kicked off her blankets and headed out to the balcony where the moonlight dappled the rolling waves with silver caresses.

What if she doesn't text me back? It's not like I can go check on her.

But she heard her phone ding from where she left it on her bed. Sirena's reply was *wouldn't miss it xoxo*.

Everything else okay? Jessie pressed.

Yup. Just going to bed. Miss you xo

Her heart throbbed in her chest at the words. She replayed the scene of Sirena climbing onto her lap the night before and asking if they were friends with benefits...or lovers. *What was going on?* Jessie fell asleep with so many questions swirling in her head that her dreams were filled with tidal waves crashing upon shores, violently smashing everything in their path to smithereens.

Jessie was late getting to The Factory. She decided to stop sharing the details of her investigation—if that was even the right word—with the management. She knew Paisley would still ask. She hadn't been in on her meeting with Leah and Casey the day before, and well, Paisley didn't like to be in the dark about things. Besides, Paisley was Jessie's best friend, but Jessie didn't feel obligated to share once the club had backed off from the issue.

Sirena was there early, it seemed. Already on the dance floor with a drink her hand, seductively swiveling her hips among a crowd. No one from Jeannette's crew, obviously. Jessie hadn't spotted them yet, but would have bet money they were in the locker room helping Jeannette with a costume change.

Sirena spotted her before she could approach, and her entire face lit up. She had been beautiful the other night, even ravaged by tears and bruises, but now she was positively radiant in a fitted coral dress that made her skin glow. Jessie could still see the remnants of the bruises on her chest and arms, but they had either faded considerably, or they'd been concealed with makeup.

Jessie froze while her eyes raked over the gyrating blonde, until Sirena beckoned her with her finger, silently asking Jessie to join her on the dance floor. Jessie had never considered herself much of a dancer, which she felt somewhat embarrassed about considering her Latin heritage, but she acquiesced. She made her way toward Sirena, feeling the soft chiffon of her pale ivory chemise fluttering against her thighs.

"You look absolutely beautiful," Sirena whispered into her ear as she pulled her tightly against her chest. Jessie felt Sirena's ample breasts smoosh into her, and all she could think about was how responsive Sirena's nipples were when she ran her tongue over them.

"I have plans for us tonight," Sirena continued before Jessie had a chance to respond.

Jessie cocked her brow. "What kind of plans?"

"Will you play with me and a friend?" she asked, her eyes wide and hopeful.

Jessie exhaled a long, deep breath. "Who?"

Sirena pointed across the room. "See that guy with the beard? That's Tom. He's new here."

Jessie narrowed her eyes as she scoped out the man, who was leaning back in a chair, tipping a beer bottle up to his mouth. He was wearing stonewashed blue jeans, even in the summer heat, and a black button-down shirt with the sleeves rolled to his elbows. He was giving off a biker vibe with his black boots.

She was surprised to see a new single male as she thought Paisley had capped off single male memberships for the month. Not to mention that the jeans weren't following dress code. They typically didn't allow them unless they were really dressy jeans. Jessie had the feeling this guy knew Cap or Calvin—maybe Paisley—otherwise he wouldn't have been admitted.

Single men were always the pariahs at lifestyle

clubs. Often between partners, many were just looking for an easy piece of ass and didn't understand all the nuances of swinger etiquette. Or they were creepy guys who weren't adept with women at all, and they came to leer at all the naked and half-naked female members. The first type were overly pushy, not liking to take no for an answer. The second type were too shy to make a move, so they just lurked about soaking up the scene. Every once in a while, there'd be a clean, polite, respectful single man who was more than happy to help couples out with a threesome. Jessie got the impression this man was the rare third type, though she wasn't sure how respectful he would be.

"What do you think?" Sirena asked, sensing Jessie's hesitation.

It was true, her internal debate team was firing off round after round of pros versus cons. *Pro: it means getting to be with Sirena again. Con: It means having to watch Sirena get fucked by a guy.*

"Okay," she finally said, though she was sure she would regret it. She was finding herself anticipating regret after many interactions with Sirena. Yet she couldn't seem to say no.

Sirena turned to Tom, who met her gaze with a dark, intense look. After she mouthed something, the tiniest smear of victory wiped itself across his face. He set his beer bottle down, stood up from the table and seemed to adjust his cock, which had already grown into a bulge in his pants. As tight as they were across his pelvis, it was pretty much impossible to ignore his huge endowment.

Jessie held on to Sirena's arms, noting that she was vibrating with anticipation. Tom headed toward the dance floor, but didn't stop as he passed, apparently expecting the two women to follow his lead. Jessie rolled her eyes. She already didn't like where this was going. If there was one category of men she hated the most, it was fake alpha men. These were men who thought they needed to put up some bullshit cocky front just to look tougher, when it was, in fact, a cover for a serious lack of confidence. Her partner Bart had been that way when she first met him. That's why a lot of their colleagues disliked him, male and female alike. Once Jessie made it known she wasn't buying it, he let his guard down. Jessie liked the real Bart so much better, even though he was still an asshole at times.

They followed Tom to the Oasis room, the same room where Jessie and Sirena had had their first encounter. Jessie felt a pang of disappointment; she didn't like the idea of the room being defiled with the memory of Sirena being fucked by some cocky asshole, but at this point she figured it was too late to call things off. Besides, if she left, it wasn't like it would stop Sirena from playing with him. At least this way, Jessie could make sure Sirena would be safe.

They entered the room, and Sirena whipped off her coral dress in a heartbeat. Tom began to make a move toward her as he unbuckled the thick black belt holding up his jeans. *Harley Davidson belt buckle*, she observed. That was exactly what she expected to see.

"Hey, let me get one thing straight before we get going," Jessie stopped him, standing between him and Sirena.

His eyes jerked up to hers with an instant cloud of annoyance. She even thought he might swat her away, but her voice was commanding. Her work voice. She waited for him to respond.

"What?" finally came his gruff reply.

"I don't fuck guys," Jessie answered. "I'm only here to play with Sirena."

"Whatever," he growled. In seconds, his lips were on Sirena's neck, biting, nibbling his way down to her perfect breasts. Just watching him tease her nipples into tight, hard buds made Jessie jealous. She wanted to be the owner of the mouth doing that. He guided Sirena toward the bed, leaning her back until she was horizontal, splayed across the surface.

As he finished undoing his pants and pulling them off, Jessie slid onto the sheets, resting on her side parallel to Sirena, her body stretched alongside hers. Sirena's skin was so warm, it sent little rivets of heat radiating through her body, pooling in her core. She really wanted to get her tongue on Sirena's clit before Tom had a chance to have his way with her.

Tom seemed agreeable to that plan. He stood, stroking his cock, which was really quite a sight to behold...*if you're into that sort of thing*, Jessie thought with a sarcastic laugh. She decided to ignore him and pretend like he wasn't there. She bent down close to Sirena's ear and whispered, "What do you want me to do to you, baby?"

A shiver raced through Jessie's body as Sirena's lips formed the words, "Use your magic tongue on me."

Jessie couldn't help the sly smile that crept onto her face. She'd never had her tongue called magic before, but she liked it. It tingled with excitement, just knowing the delicious feast that awaited. But first...teasing. The body lying beside her needed to be prepared, curated, cultivated into such a state of desperation that her very ability to breathe depended on Jessie's lips pressed against her pussy.

She threw her leg over Sirena to straddle her, then lowered her mouth to her lush, coral lips. She was anxious to cover up the kisses Tom left with her own, so she wasted no time delving her tongue into Sirena's mouth, tasting her, preparing her for what was to come... a little preview. Once she heard Sirena's sigh escape into her own mouth, she took it as a signal to work her way down her body to those pert breasts heaving in the air. She couldn't get over how lovely they were, creamy mounds of splendor, begging for her attention. She cupped one in her hands, admiring the contrast of the peachy pink skin against her own tan flesh and the way her blue veins crisscrossed underneath. The tip of her tongue jutted out to test the firmness of her nipples, and when she felt how hard they were, a jolt of need shook her core like an electric shock.

Sirena gasped as Jessie raked her teeth over the swollen bud, then gently bit down before sucking it into her mouth. Her skin was sweet with her familiar vanilla jasmine smell, and it permeated Jessie's senses as she worked Sirena's nipple into a wanton frenzy, so expertly that in seconds, Sirena's body was bucking against hers, seeking pressure against her enflamed core. The words, "Please, baby," slipped past her parted lips as Tom made his way over to the bed, climbing onto the mattress to press his cock against her mouth.

Sirena eagerly lapped at his stiff rod, swirling her tongue up and down it until he finally took her blonde head into his palm, threading his fingers through her golden waves, then slid himself deep into her throat. She was immediately silenced, her mouth full of his manhood, and Jessie was disappointed to lose the beautiful moans of desperation escaping her lips.

She had a feeling she could break Sirena's concentration on Tom's cock by moving her magic tongue down to where it really counted, down to her epicenter of pleasure. Now she felt like the cocky one—rightfully so, because she was confident in her ability to bring waves of ecstasy crashing down on the beautiful blonde writhing beneath her.

She tapped Sirena's long, lithe thighs, commanding them to spread so she could situate herself between them on the bed. Stroking her fingertips down the smooth skin of her abdomen, she watched as Sirena engulfed Tom's cock deep into her throat. Jessie wondered how much teasing it would take for her to forget all about the cock and for all of her attention to be diverted to her own impending orgasm.

She started with soft kisses planted on the fleshy parts of Sirena's inner thighs, working her way toward her glistening pink slit. She was completely bare, the usual for women in the lifestyle. Jessie preferred a bit of hair, maybe a landing strip, but it was obvious Sirena kept up with regular Brazilians because it was far smoother than a razor could ever achieve.

There was a deep moan, garbled by the cock in her occupied mouth, as Jessie spread Sirena's lips with the tip of her tongue, running them from her clit down to her perineum in one long stroke. She felt Tom's eyes on her and knew the sight made him even harder. *Good, he would have to wait, too.* But she felt other eyes on them as well; an audience had gathered. Wherever two women were, a crowd was sure to follow. Jessie didn't understand the hetero obsession with girl-on-girl action, but it was rampant, like an infestation. A pandemic.

Not all bad though, she reflected as she sucked one of Sirena's honey-coated lips into her mouth, nibbling her way up to just shy of her clit. After all, this obsession had allowed her to meet more women in the past year of her club membership than she had ever been able to before in her life, and it was all no-strings-attached. It was like a balm to her heart while it healed from her horrible breakup with Cindy.

Sirena's back arched, silently begging for Jessie to pay careful attention to her aching clit. She found it with her tongue: swollen, throbbing. Jessie scooped her hands under Sirena's ass, bringing her pelvis closer to her face and humming against her as her body began to buck from the intensity. Tom was making more of an effort now, commanding her mouth on him, pushing her down faster and further onto his cock as she gasped for air.

It wouldn't be long now. She sucked Sirena's clit into her mouth, knowing just the pressure, just the rhythm required to make her explode. This was her...what? Third time doing this? It didn't take Jessie long to know all the secret buttons to push, the long, complex code required to open the floodgates. Yes, more pressure here, less pressure there, a finger here, a lash of the tongue there. It was an intricate dance, and Jessie was the ultimate dance partner, an aficionado. It was a role she relished, one she prided herself upon. If cunnilingus were an Olympic sport, she had no doubt she'd bring home the gold every damn time.

And just like that, Sirena's mouth opened, Tom's cock forcefully spit out. Her voice broke like dawn over the Atlantic with a mighty roar. "Oh my god, Jessie! Oh fuck, don't stop!" she bellowed. Every ear in that damn building was perked to the sound, which directed all blood flow to the audience's nether regions like the Pied Piper.

Tom knew better than to interrupt. Grasping his cock in one hand and her head in his other, he leaned down to cradle her while she journeyed to the moon and back on wave after wave of orgasmic bliss. Jessie felt the power of Sirena's explosion rocket through her, surging out from her core as the walls of her pussy contracted so hard against Jessie's fingers, she was momentarily prevented from thrusting them in and out of her.

And all the while, a smug smile perched upon Jessie's lips. Victory was hers.

EIGHT

I found you in the clarity of the moon, not the rigor of the sun. Not in the light, where it's easier to see, But when the world is blind and love's eyes are free.
- Malika E Nura

Jessie woke up with Sirena in her arms. She was sure they hadn't fallen asleep that way, both exhausted after a late night at The Factory, but sleep brought out the subconscious. Sirena's head was propped in the space between her armpit and breast, Jessie's arm wrapped protectively around her. It was the physical embodiment of Jessie's instinct to give Sirena shelter, to keep her from harm.

Jessie felt Sirena's body awaken, her muscles stretching, jostling Jessie into a state of semi-alertness. Sirena sighed, a beautiful sound to crack the silence of the encroaching dawn. The pink rays had crept past the blinds and were striping the thin quilt with shadows and bands of light. Jessie popped one eye open, glancing down at the mass of blonde hair that fell over her shoulder and draped onto the sheet. Sensing Sirena was trapped in that blissful half-dreamlike state before the harsh reality of the world crashed down onto her, she pulled her closer, aligning her body with hers, feeling how her long limbs molded to hers.

Then, finally, "You awake?"

Jessie's mouth cracked into a smile before she could answer. *Why does this feel so comfortable? So right?* she questioned before confirming Sirena's assumption.

"What are you doing today?" Sirena asked, lifting herself up on her elbow to peer down into Jessie's sleep-ravaged face.

I probably look like shit, she worried, glancing up into the green eyes reflecting back at her. *How is it she still looks utterly gorgeous even after a night of drinking, dancing and fucking?*

She let out a breath as she contemplated her agenda. "I've gotta go in to work for a bit and check some warrants I had issued. I have a court case on Monday, and I need to go over the video and reports."

"What kind of court case?"

"Oh, this dumbass local guy got into a fight with a tourist at the Purple Moose a couple months ago. Knocked him out cold. Fighting over some chick." She rolled her eyes at the absurdity of it. But this was a pretty common occurrence. Alcohol made people do stupid things, which is why she abstained. She wished she could convince Sirena to do the same. She'd certainly feel a lot more comfortable if she did.

"Oh, fun. I wonder what the woman thought of that," Sirena answered, yawning.

"Who cares? I don't even remember her, to be honest. I had to interview the victim at Atlantic General. He was pretty fucked up."

"You don't think having two men fight over you would be...flattering?" she asked, then realized her mistake. "Oh, I suppose you wouldn't."

"Women are not objects to be fought over," Jessie corrected her. "Women do not belong to a man, or to anyone. We belong to ourselves."

Sirena shrugged, unconvinced, as she sat up cross-legged facing Jessie. "Did I ever tell you I hate cops?"

Jessie scoffed. "Not in so many words, but gee, thanks."

"I just haven't had too good of experiences with them," Sirena explained. "They can be real jerks, you know? Especially ones in the lifestyle."

Jessie sighed and nodded. She did know, unfortunately. Asshole cops gave good cops a bad name. The reputations of those kinds of cops made things more difficult and more dangerous every time she went on duty.

"Are you like a total bitch at work?" Sirena questioned. "Or are you like this?"

"Like what?" Jessie asked, chuckling.

"You know, like sweet and caring. Protective." Sirena reached out to touch Jessie's thighs, then glanced up to meet her gaze.

"I try to be just me all the time. But I'm human. I make mistakes sometimes." Jessie could think of a few instances where her anger had gotten the better of her. Every time some asshole gave her a hard time because she was a woman or Latina...it was really hard not to fight back, even if it meant locking the handcuffs a little tighter, or shoving them into the back of her cruiser with a little more force than was necessary. Not enough to hurt them. Not enough to face disciplinary action. But just that extra oomph the adrenaline of anger produced.

"I bet you're a really good cop. I bet you're fair," Sirena decided. She bent down to give Jessie a kiss on the cheek. "I'm sure you are, in fact."

"You going to the club tonight?" Jessie asked, changing the subject.

"Yeah, of course." She fluttered her eyelashes and looked so beautiful that Jessie had to stop the urge to take her again, to make her writhe under her tongue once more. Sirena had yet to reciprocate, but Jessie didn't even care. She hadn't asked her to, and she didn't care that she hadn't. At this point, she just wanted to bestow orgasm after orgasm upon this exquisite creature. Watching her caught up in rapture was the most beautiful sight Jessie had ever seen.

Jessie wondered if there would ever be a time that she and Sirena would show up at the club together, like a couple, instead of just running into each other at the bar or on the dance floor like they had the past few weeks. *Like acquaintances. Afterthoughts.* Then she wanted to smack herself for even thinking such a ridiculous thing. She ran into Paisley on her way in, as she and Calvin were processing new member registrations, but she didn't say anything at all about Sirena. Though Paisley winked at her and guessed that "someone got laid!"

So it was written all over her face. *So what?* Jessie shrugged off her best friend's assessment and went to find Leah and Casey. After finding out Leah was pregnant and Casey had breast cancer, she felt protective of them too. *Why do I think I'm responsible for saving everyone?* she asked herself as she knocked on the office door.

She heard a muffled, "Come in," but wasn't expecting the sight that awaited her.

Leah and Casey were clutching each other, their bodies heaving together in giant sobs.

She wasn't sure if she should stay or go, but Leah turned her head just before she began to walk away. "Hey," was all she said.

"What's going on?" Jessie asked, but she knew the answer.

She had never seen Casey look so distraught. Even at the Factory anniversary party when she got a little sniffly and teary-eyed making her announcement, she was still perfectly coiffed and made up. Her clothes were still impeccably tailored and devoid of wrinkles. But tonight she looked—her age. And like a cancer patient. Though she was still a larger woman, there was something about her that, for the first time ever, appeared frail. Delicate.

She was not wearing a speck of makeup, and her skin was sallow. Her normally sparkling eyes were rimmed with red and tear-marks made stripes down her cheeks. She was wearing a pair of elastic-waist jogging pants and a baggy long-sleeve t-shirt. And as if that weren't bad enough, her hair was flat and seemingly unwashed, matted to her scalp and held back with two small tortoiseshell combs.

"Leah just told me they're throwing me a huge going away party in two weekends," Casey said, her body still shaking with sobs. "I told her all that fuss wasn't necessary, but she insists." A smile peeked through her tears like the sun emerging after a thundershower.

Jessie just nodded, unable to produce any words because she too was choked up. She wasn't the type to get emotional, but these women, including Paisley, were the first women she'd ever really bonded with that she wasn't dating. Most of her close friends had been men and girlfriends until she met Paisley and joined The Factory. Non-lifestyle women were petty, catty, and quick to stab anyone who pissed them off in the back. But these three...they were in a league of their own. Secure. Generous. Loving.

She wondered if it was because the three women she spoke of were all bisexual. She wondered if that was the difference, or if they were really cut from another cloth entirely. Whatever the explanation was, Jessie was going to miss Casey fiercely. She was a mother figure to her and had been more supportive than her own mother had ever been.

"Of course we're throwing you a party," Leah argued. "Like we are really going to let the co-founder of The Factory move across the country without some sort of fanfare!"

"I just don't think you should close down the club

and lose out on that revenue just for little old me!" Casey explained.

"Cap and I have already agreed. In two weeks, we're having Casey Fontaine night. We're all dressing to the nines and keeping it classy all night long."

"I think that's a fabulous idea!" Jessie agreed, moving to put her arm around Casey. "I'm supposed to work, but I am going to see if I can take the night off. I don't think I can stand missing it!"

"Oh, you are too sweet!" Casey gushed, squeezing Jessie to her ample bosom.

"Cap is going to make an announcement later tonight. And we're going to put away all the kinky stuff like the Sybian and swings, so feel free to invite anyone you'd like," Leah offered.

Casey sighed. "I really don't have anyone in my life anymore except you, Cap and the gang. Everyone else I used to work with or be close to has either moved away, or we've just grown apart. That's why I had no hesitation to leave...with the exception of you all."

"Well, everyone here loves you," Jessie declared. "This is your family. I know I've come to feel that way about this place too."

"Where are you from, Jessie?" Leah asked. "I've never heard you talk about your family at all."

Jessie shrugged. She never brought them up. Never. "I grew up near Philly. My family isn't worth talking about."

Leah seemed to sense that was all she was going to get out of her friend, at least at the moment. "Now, I've left a message with the chef at The Pearl, Xander Vincent. He owes me big time from when I used to work there, so I know he'll be willing to cater, even on short notice."

Casey's lips spread into a smile, which brightened her whole face. "Just don't go to too much trouble—or too much expense. Really, Leah. I know how you and Paisley are with your backgrounds in hospitality and event management. Just simple and sweet is fine with me if you insist on doing this!"

Leah's eyes grew misty again as she drew Casey in for another hug. "I shouldn't have even told her," she said to Jessie, speaking over Casey's shoulder. "But she would have hated being surprised. She hates surprises as much as I do!"

"I'm still here, you know," Casey protested, even though she was laughing. Jessie was relieved to see she was keeping her sense of humor. How else could someone be expected to survive something as horrific as cancer?

She shook off the dark thoughts encroaching her and excused herself to find Sirena. She wondered if she would agree to being her date for the special going away party. *Date? Why do I keep going down that road?* she asked herself. *It's pointless for me to get so attached to her. She's a hot piece of ass. A summer fling. And that's it.*

Sirena was MIA for most of the night, and when Jessie finally found her, she was getting her things from the locker room to leave with a couple. If Jessie hadn't been walking past the locker room door at that exact moment, she would have missed her entirely. And it was obvious she would have left without so much as saying goodbye.

How can I have her in my bed one night, and then the next she won't even speak to me? Jessie wondered with growing frustration.

The couple who had captivated Sirena's attention for the night was new to the club, visiting from North Carolina. *Don't they have their own damn clubs down there?* Jessie wondered as she saw the giddy expression painted on the man's face. They stunk of money. She could tell by looking at them that they were about to take Sirena out to their Mercedes or maybe it was a Lexus or BMW. Just from their clothes and the wife's jewelry, she knew they were filthy rich. Her whole job was discerning things like this, to surmise a person's background even before they uttered a single word.

Jessie grabbed Sirena's arm as she was exiting the locker room, then instantly regretted it. How was that any different than what some asshole guy had done to her a week or so before? She didn't mean to hurt her, but Sirena jerked her arm away as if she had. Guilt stabbed into her as she flashed Sirena an apology with her wide brown eyes.

"Where are you going?" It came out more demanding and possessive than she intended.

"Why do you care?" Sirena asked in return, her voice on the border between flirty and defiant.

"I just want to make sure you're safe, that's all." Jessie folded her arms across her chest and waited for Sirena to argue against that logic.

"You know I'm a grown woman, right?" Sirena snapped. "I don't need you following me around like some sort of bodyguard all the time. I can take care of myself."

Jessie scoffed as her body flooded with every manner of defense mechanism. "Right. Which is why you showed up at my house drunk and bruised the other night."

She watched the rage in Sirena's eyes enflame like a fire doused with gasoline. "I knew coming over there was a mistake."

She turned to go without another word. The music pumping out of the speakers was deafening, but Jessie called after her. "Wait! You aren't going to say goodbye?"

But just like that, she was gone.

Jessie made the decision in a flash, just like she did at work every day. She didn't know if it was because of her duty to keep Sirena safe—though she claimed she didn't need it—or rampant curiosity, but she felt compelled to follow her nonetheless. She waited for enough time to elapse that they wouldn't notice her leaving the club at the same moment, but not long enough to lose them. Sure enough, she watched the male half of the couple tucking his two female passengers into the back seat of his Mercedes.

"Fuck, am I good, or am I good?" Jessie muttered

under her breath as she made her way to her own car. There were some other people in the parking lot too, but she could slip by them undetected. Sirena was drunk, or at least tipsy, anyway, Jessie had gathered from their brief encounter. Her southern accent was always more pronounced when she was working a good buzz. It was like a precursor to slurring her words.

Jessie cranked up the air conditioning in her car as she realized she was burning up with...something...rage? Jealousy? Disappointment? She knew it was a tornado of all those things combined, and it had settled over her, violently tossing her in its vortex of emotion.

As she maintained a stealthy distance from the Mercedes, she remembered what Sirena had told her about growing up in Georgia. She had come from a wealthy family. She always spoke of her childhood as if it was so long ago—a bygone era, when Jessie knew from her membership forms she was only six years older than Jessie. She assumed it was because she had grown up in the slums of Philly, while Sirena's idyllic southern belle upbringing was more traditional—a throwback to a kinder, gentler time. Even after all the talking they'd done during their two sleepovers, she had never revealed the real reason she left Georgia, though Jessie assumed it was for a man.

She followed the car onto Route 50 as it headed north toward the bigger resorts. It came as no surprise when the Mercedes turned into The Pearl, the same resort where Leah Sheldon had been assistant general manager when she first met Cap. She'd heard their love story a million times over, about how the good Christian girl from Wahoo, Nebraska, fell under the spell of the rugged, charming charter fishing captain who just happened to be a swinger.

Another couple from entirely different worlds, Jessie reflected as she parked her car and waited to see where Sirena and her companions would go. *Except we're not a couple. And never will be.*

She wished she were in uniform so she could prowl about the complex and not raise any eyebrows, but she was dressed a bit inappropriately to be traipsing about such an upscale venue. As she watched them walk across the parking lot toward the entrance, she grew twice as angry as she had been when she left The Factory. But not with Sirena. With herself.

How many times am I going to make the mistake of chasing straight girls? Jessie wondered. *How many fucking times?* Sirena had said it herself. *She doesn't need me looking after her. She's a grown woman.*

She threw her car into reverse and squealed out of the parking space before bolting toward her condo a few blocks up from The Pearl. She was done with this stupid project. It was pointless. Sirena didn't want to be understood, and she sure as hell didn't want to be loved.

Jessie wasn't used to being alone on the job. They almost always worked in pairs, but the holiday weekend meant extra crowds and extra work for the OCPD. Bart took a disturbing the peace and public intoxication complaint down on the boardwalk, while Jessie got called to a suspicious person report a motorist called in at an apartment complex farther north. The description came across her radio as a white man, 20-30 years of age, brown hair, average height, average build, wearing jeans and a black t-shirt. In other words, it could be anyone.

She parked in one of the empty spaces at the apartment complex, which was one of the most rundown in the city. They had been called to several complaints here in the past, mostly drug issues. They even shut down a meth lab here a year or two back. Jessie hadn't been part of that investigation, but apparently the police raid at 2 AM didn't do much to deter other dealers.

A woman stood on a ground floor patio with a toddler wearing only a diaper and sucking on a dirty-looking bottle. Her eyes followed Jessie's as she moved toward the building where the report originated. It was the building nearest to the street where the motorist had witnessed the suspicious person.

Why is he suspicious? Jessie wondered. Even though it had only taken her five minutes to reach the place, even a person on foot could cover a lot of ground in that amount of time. Who knew if he was still there?

"Are you looking for Robbie?" the lady on the patio called after her.

Not wanting to shout back, Jessie turned and headed toward her. "Officer Martinez, Ocean City PD. Who is Robbie? I got a call about a suspicious person."

"Yeah, probably Robbie Butler," she answered, rolling her eyes.

"What's he look like?"

"White guy. Brown hair. Total jackass," she answered, popping the gum in her mouth for emphasis.

"How old?" Jessie locked her eyes on the lady's, which were a dull gray. Everything about this place was dingy and gray, like the colors had faded out in the oppressive summer sun.

"I don't know...early twenties?" she guessed. "He was living with my neighbor Mariah, but she kicked him out last week for hitting her son."

Now we are getting somewhere, Jessie surmised. "Where does Mariah live?"

"She's in the next building over, 5400." She pointed to the building near the street where the suspicious person was spotted. "She got a restraining order, but we all know that does no damn good for some of these guys."

Jessie nodded, less of an agreement than a confirmation she'd processed the information. "Do you know which apartment is Mariah's?"

"Fifty-four twenty-nine," the woman answered.

"And what's your name?" She was scribbling the info down on her little notepad as the lady spoke.

"I'm Ashley Dorsey."

"Okay, thanks, Ms. Dorsey."

Jessie headed to the 5400 building with Ashley's eyes still glued to her back. She opened the door on the side and walked down the hall, noting the odd numbers were on her left and the even on her right. They stopped at 5420, so she entered the stairwell and made her way up the stairs. She briefly thought about calling Bart from her cell to see if he was done at his scene yet. She wouldn't mind the reassurance that backup was on its way.

A scream coming from down the hall shrilled through her ears, and then she knew beyond a shadow of a doubt she should call for backup. She radioed it in as she approached apartment #5429. She took in a deep gulp of air and pounded on the thin, paint-peeling wood door. "Ocean City Police, open the door."

There was no answer, so she repeated the process.

It had been a while since she had kicked open a door, but she had done it before, and she would do it again. Once another scream pierced the air, she readied herself. Being short, it wasn't going to be easy. She needed to aim right below the lock, but she knew those thick, muscular thighs of hers would help. She brought her leg back and kicked forward, the brunt of the impact on her heel. When she heard a crack in response, she knew she was on the right track. It took two more kicks, but she was able to break through.

She drew her gun and proceeded through the tiny foyer, her head swiveling slowly left and right as she searched for the occupants. One more scream, and she knew she needed to head down the hall toward the bedrooms. There were two: one on the left and one on the right. The scream had come from the one on the right, and the door was open. She was at least momentarily relieved not to have to kick down another door, though an interior door would be a lot easier.

She spotted the brown-haired man with the black t-shirt and jeans first. "Hands in the air, now!" she yelled authoritatively. She was always surprised at how stern her voice could come out when she wanted it to.

It was like all of her training kicked in and wrapped itself around her vocal cords, just like it was supposed to do.

A woman, whom she presumed was Mariah, was crying and shaking, tears streaming down her reddened face as the man reluctantly lifted his arms in the air. He got them about halfway up before he turned to face her, a smug grin creeping across his face as he surveyed Jessie's small stature.

"Oh, what do we have here?" he sneered in a raspy voice, one that sounded drunk or high, or both. Jessie lifted her gun to point right at him, her eyes narrowed into thin slits as she waited for him to comply.

"Hands on the wall!" she shouted back at him, but he just stood there with his ridiculous, silly expression, his facial features slack with the effects of whatever substance he was on.

"Did you hear me?" Jessie repeated. "Hands on the wall."

He shrugged and spun around, almost in slow motion. Jessie struggled to tamp down her frustration as he muttered under his breath something about her being a "stupid fucking Mexican" and "ruining our country." The woman moved over to the bed and collapsed upon it, holding her stomach and bawling her eyes out with long, piercing wails.

Just as she began to pat him down, he whipped around and pinned her to the wall, pressing his body against hers so he was right in her face. She swiftly brought her knee up, making sharp contact with his groin, and sent him reeling back toward the bed. As soon as he regained his breath, he yelled, "Fucking Mexican cunt!" as he hunched over on the mattress, holding his crotch in his hands and turning green with the pain. She'd scored a pretty direct hit, and she wasn't the least bit sorry.

At that exact moment, she heard footsteps pounding up the stairs and down the hall. Her finger didn't even tremble as she moved to the trigger, shouting at the man to get on the floor with his hands on his head. *Fucking asshole*, she added inside her head.

"You okay?" Bart asked as he and another officer slipped inside. Jessie nodded, her aim never leaving the suspect's head.

"I have a restraining order!" the woman yelled, her sharp wails finally subsiding. "He tried to rape me!" She pointed to her t-shirt, which was ripped at the collar. Bart moved directly to the suspect, who was finally on the floor. He quickly got him in cuffs, then dragged him upright.

Jessie motioned for the woman to follow her as Bart and the other officer began to escort their prisoner out the door. As soon as Bart finished rattling off his rights, she called after him, "And by the way, I'm Puerto Rican, not Mexican, you fucking racist scum!" She said the last part under her breath. He wasn't worth it.

There's only one thing I hate more than men, she reminded herself as she walked the woman down to her cruiser. *Racist men.*

NINE

*Amazing how eye and skin color come in many shades
yet many think sexuality is just gay or straight.*
-DaShanne Stokes

Friday night came and went at The Factory, and Sirena was nowhere to be found. Jessie brushed off her concern, but Paisley remarked, "Hey, have you heard from Sirena? This is the first night she's not been here in almost two months."

Jessie shrugged. "No, we don't really talk anymore."

Paisley's eyebrows shot up. "Why not?"

Another shrug. "She doesn't want to be understood. She doesn't want anyone close to her."

Paisley seemed to know better than to push, so she changed the subject to Jeannette's latest outlandish outfit. She was wearing a retro disco-type dress with white patent leather lace-up platform boots that hit her at mid-thigh. "She should have saved that for 70s night," Paisley laughed, rolling her eyes.

Jessie wished she could get out of her own head. In the past week, her thoughts oscillated between the scene at the apartment when that douchebag assaulted her and how she could have handled it better...and Sirena—and how she could have handled it better. *Basically it all comes down to my own incompetence*, she decided. And she hadn't been able to forgive herself for fucking everything up.

She wondered if maybe she was just a low-life good-for-nothing waste of oxygen like her brothers were.

"You okay?" Paisley asked, noticing Jessie didn't react to her observation about Jeannette.

Jessie couldn't force her dark eyes to meet Paisley's blue. She couldn't believe her confidence, her moxie had been stripped away. She felt naked. Worthless. This was not a feeling she had felt since...another time, another place. One she didn't care to revisit.

"I'm worried about you," Paisley said, wrapping her arm around her friend, who was almost a head shorter. She squeezed Jessie into her 42DDD bosom until she nearly suffocated. Then Calvin came by and flashed his smile, causing Paisley to lose her grip.

"I think you just saved my life," Jessie sputtered at Calvin, then forced her lips into a smirk. She didn't need to worry Paisley. Her friend already had enough on her plate with worrying about Casey leaving and trying to make sure Leah didn't over-exert herself in the heat of summer. Leah had already called out for the weekend due to excessive morning sickness. Cap agreed his wife had no business working and had even arranged for one of his adult daughters to take their son Lincoln for a couple of days.

"Hey, I love rescuing beautiful women," Calvin answered, his grin still brightly carved onto his glowing bronze skin. "You okay? Where's Sirena?"

Calvin, Cap, and Bart were three men—the only three men—Jessie tolerated, and the first two she adored, but they could all be overly clueless at times. Jessie gave a combination of a shrug and head-shake, then excused herself from the conversation. This was yet another time she wished she drank. It would be a relief to drown her sorrows at the bottom of a bottle, but it was just not in her nature. Not after the last time she had been drunk.

She made it as far as the changing room, her bag still slung over her shoulder with a green silk teddy waiting to make its first appearance at the club, before she changed her mind. She marched right back toward the lounge where Paisley and Calvin were still making googly eyes at each other like schoolyard crushes. That pierced Jessie's heart even more sharply. *I'll never have that*, she told herself. *I don't deserve it.*

"Where are you going?" Calvin questioned as she passed them.

She whipped back around, her long brown hair flying over her shoulder like a dark, silky waterfall. "I have to get up early for work tomorrow. I think I am just going to go to bed early. I'm pretty tired."

Paisley stepped toward her to wrap her arms around Jessie again. *Another squish to the boobs*, Jessie sighed as Paisley's womanly curves pressed against her cheeks. She was so soft and smelled amazing, but it wasn't the vanilla jasmine scent Jessie had grown so fond of in the past month. "Take care of yourself," Paisley whispered in her ear, her voice full of concern.

Jessie nodded, a lump in her throat preventing a reply. As she headed out to the parking lot to find her car, she glanced down at her phone in her hand and wondered if she should text Sirena. Then she reminded herself she was done.

Saturday's shift at work was grueling. They were doing a special seatbelt enforcement initiative with the state police, and she'd been out near the highway on the outskirts of town pulling over violators, along with drivers on their cell phones. She had probably written a thousand tickets, given the same spiel a thousand times, and hadn't felt generous enough to give any warnings, not even to the 78-year-old woman who reminded her a little of what Casey might look like in another 15 years. *If she makes it to that age*, the dark thought crossed Jessie's mind.

She was wrestling with her decision to go to the club that night. Weekends were like a record. Friday nights were Side A, Saturday nights, Side B. She wasn't sure she wanted to hear the flip side song this weekend. *Maybe I'm better off alone,* she considered.

When was the last time I had a vacation? she wondered. She honestly couldn't remember. She had taken time off last winter from work, but she'd spent it at The Factory helping repaint the lounge area and some of the play rooms. She was always picking up extra shifts. It's like she didn't know the meaning of time off. And it was chipping away at her, like the sun chips away paint as it relentlessly beats down upon the earth season after season.

Fine, I'll go, she told herself as she walked in the door of her condo after work. *It's either that or sit here alone being a total recluse.* Or texting some ex of hers, hoping for a booty call. She didn't think she could fuck another woman right now anyway. All she would be able to think of was Sirena. She tossed some clothes into her bag and headed out the door.

She always arrived at the club well after opening when it was a work weekend. She mouthed the word "Hi" to Paisley as she took down information from a new member, who looked a bit daunted by all the paperwork. Paisley locked eyes with Jessie, seeming to ask if she was okay. Jessie nodded, even though she didn't feel particularly "okay."

She parked herself near the dance floor and waited. Even when she was invited to dance, she still waited. Finally another couple sidled up to her and asked if she wanted to play. By that time, it was eleven, and she knew there was no chance of Sirena showing up. She knew she should either say yes or go home to bed. After all, she had another shift in the morning.

This was a couple she knew, Becky and Warren, and they were friendly and low-pressure. Warren didn't mind that Jessie didn't want anything to do with him; he was more into watching anyway. And Becky liked Jessie because she knew there would never be any drama or jealousy. Jessie was a safe choice for couples looking for girl-on-girl action. Maybe she should just embrace her "safe" label and play.

She followed them upstairs, momentarily frozen in her stride by a flash of golden waves flitting down the staircase on the other end. But it wasn't Sirena; it was just some other lady with blonde hair. "Everything okay?" Becky asked, turning around to see why Jessie wasn't one pace behind anymore.

"Absolutely," Jessie lied, affixing a smile to her face. If nothing else, she could hope this would serve as a distraction. Maybe she could get through it without thinking of Sirena. After all, Becky was a short, plump redhead with pouty lips and big, doe-brown eyes. It helped that she had nothing in common with Jessie's golden goddess, who was seemingly MIA.

Becky patted the bed. "You look like you need to get off," she said to Jessie with a knowing smile on her face.

Jessie scoffed. *How could she tell?* It had been a long time since Jessie had allowed another woman to bring her to orgasm. She didn't even remember, as a matter of fact. She guessed it must have been her ex-girlfriend. *Why not let Becky try?* She was so used to pillow princesses who wouldn't reciprocate, it was a nice change of pace to be on the receiving end of a tongue-lashing.

Jessie glanced at Warren, and he was practically drooling as he took a seat in the chair across the room. He didn't even actively participate in girl time. He liked to sit far enough away that he could observe the whole scene, all while stroking his stubby little cock. Jessie didn't mind. It was better for her if he stayed off the bed anyway. Most of the husbands liked to get right up close so they could get in on the action, a slap on the ass here, a finger inserted there. Sometimes they liked to kiss their wife and taste Jessie on her lips. Warren would do that, when he was close to orgasm. That was usually what pushed him over the edge.

Becky stroked her fingers through Jessie's hair and then across her cheek, tilting Jessie's mouth toward hers. She pressed her lips softly against Jessie's as a moan escaped, the sound from which vibrated right through Jessie's jaw. She swallowed it down as she licked the seam of Becky's mouth, nudging it open. Becky obliged and repeated the action, swirling her own tongue into Jessie's mouth. There was something so intoxicating about kissing a woman. Before Jessie did it for the first time—with Tori on that beautiful fall afternoon—she'd only known the roughness, the impatience of men. She'd only experienced the scratchy stubble against her silken skin, and the urgency that broke their kiss way too fast, their attention diverted to other parts, to whatever action put their dicks in closer proximity to her mouth or pussy.

With women, it was a gentle graze. There was nothing set in stone; it started as just a promise of maybe, possibly more to come. It was a faraway light that gradually intensified, heating up a tiny bit more with every breath exchanged, every sigh elicited. Sometimes it might end at a kiss, with nothing more. But if the pot heated up enough, if the water began to boil, then a raging inferno might be spawned, powerful enough to incinerate everything in its path.

It was like that tonight. Becky was so soft, but her need began to grow, and Jessie could feel it in the way the pressure of her tongue and hands increased, by the way her nipples hardened as they pressed against Jessie's curves. And finally, when Jessie drew her hand down to swipe her finger between Becky's pussy lips, she found them soaked with desire, with need. Just feeling that, what Jessie had done to this woman's body, turned her on. She felt a heaviness grow inside her, a flame that became a fire, a hungry one at that.

Becky moved down her body, sliding down the satin gown she wore like it was a slip and slide. She wore a wicked grin on her face as she prepared to taste the gift that waited for her between Jessie's legs: a perfect pink pearl, coiled tight with desire. Her tongue flicked out, and Jessie nearly came unglued, it had been so long since she'd been touched there by anyone's tongue.

As the pressure of Becky's lips against her most intimate parts increased, the flames of need reached up into Jessie's breasts, her cheeks. Sensing it, Becky reached her hand up to cup one of Jessie's small, perky breasts, gently squeezing it until a moan escaped Jessie's lips. Then she took her light brown nipple between her thumb and forefinger and tweaked it, just on the edge of pain but still very clearly on the spectrum of pleasure. Jessie grunted, unable to control what was coming out of her mouth.

Her back arched as her control continued to slip away. As soon as her mind took a long enough break to recognize her body seemed to be responding on cue, she froze. Visions of Sirena exploded like fireworks in front of her eyes: her lithe body writhing under Jessie's tongue, her blonde tresses falling into her face. The way she looked propped up on one elbow in the morning, sleep crusted in her eyes. The way she pursed her lips, and the sound of that southern accent rolling off her tongue...all of it came rushing back. Jessie shuddered—not from her impending orgasm, but from the panic of seeing fragments of that beauty blow up in front of her eyes, clouding reality from her vision.

She sprang up in the bed, clutching the sheets around her mostly nude body. Her breasts had been pulled out of her gown and rested on top of the satin. She lifted the straps so they fell back inside and arranged the skirt over her legs, covering up her mound and upper thighs.

"What's wrong?" Becky shrieked, jerking her head up to lock eyes with Jessie. Warren stopped jerking his cock and stood up from the chair. "Did I hurt you?"

Jessie shook her head. "No, no, I'm fine, I—"

"Do you need to stop?" came Warren's booming voice from across the room as he approached the bed.

She nodded. Closing her eyes, she pursed her lips in disappointment. Not in Becky, but in herself. "I'm so sorry."

Becky touched her leg with her warm hand. "Don't be sorry. I just want to make sure you're okay."

Jessie's eyes fluttered open and darted between the two of them. "I will be," she promised them. "I've gotta go."

She grabbed her panties from the floor and headed out of the room, turning back to offer Becky and Warren a small, reassuring smile. She knew what she had to do.

She didn't even make it down the staircase before Cap pulled her into his second floor office. Being grabbed automatically put her on the defensive, and Cap was lucky she figured out it was him before she hauled off and decked him square in the nose. Or worse, the balls. "I'm sorry; I'm sorry," he apologized, realizing he shouldn't have touched her like that.

"What do you need?" she huffed, trying to calm down her racing heart.

"I just want to talk to you," he said, flashing his dimples and his ocean-blue eyes.

"Okay," she acquiesced, taking a seat on the small leather loveseat that was crammed in his office along with a half-dozen filing cabinets and an oversized desk. The ladies' offices were always immaculate; Cap's not so much. She was surprised, too, because she thought boat captains would want to have everything spic and span. And maybe he did, on his boat. Just not here at the club.

"I haven't told Leah this yet," he shared, "but I wanted to let you know."

Cap told Leah everything, and vice versa. So just the fact he would preface his statement with that fact set Jessie on edge. It meant whatever he was going to tell her was something Leah wouldn't like.

"I've been doing my own digging on Sirena," he revealed. "And that's not even her real name."

Her eyebrows flew up her forehead. She wished she'd had more time to dig into Sirena's background, but without going to Pennsylvania and finding out who Joseph Patterson was, she wasn't sure where to start. She had searched some records in Georgia, but Horne was too common of a name, and she had no idea if it was her birth name or not. She was always so busy working, she barely had time to think about anything else. And the rest of her spare time was spent here, at The Factory.

"Well?" She pursed her lips, waiting. "Are you going to tell me or what?"

"Her name is Anna Patterson, and she's married to that Joseph Patterson who owns the car she drives."

Jessica shook her head. "But he's so old!" She realized it was an irrational thought. May-December romances were a thing. She wondered how long they'd been together, if he'd stolen her innocence when she was a young woman in Georgia.

Cap shrugged. "Well, she's not thirty-eight. That's what she put on her membership application, but according to my source, she's forty-eight."

"What?" Jessica's lungs deflated as she struggled to suck back in a breath. "No, that can't be. There's no way she's forty-eight."

"Good genes, I guess," Cap said, handing her a black and white document. It looked like a scan of her driver's license. Sure enough, it said Anna K. Patterson and her birthdate was ten years different from the one on her club membership form. Now it made more sense about her and Joseph—they were at least not that far apart in age.

"How did you get this?" she questioned.

"I own some property in Pennsylvania, and a buddy of mine is a state trooper. He was able to do some digging for me."

Shit, Jessie thought. *Digging that I should have been able to do myself.*

"She hasn't been here this weekend, right?" Cap verified.

She shook her head. "No one's seen her. I asked around."

"What do you think we should do?" He scratched his beard as if he was trying to answer his own question as much as asking for Jessie's opinion. "Technically, falsifying your membership information is grounds for being banned from the club, but I can't understand why she would do it, unless one of the rumors is true about her."

Jessie scoffed. "Like which one? I've heard she's a drug dealer, a porn star, and that's she's trying to open a rival club."

"It could be any of those," Cap said with a sigh. "Or all three."

Jessie stood up. "Fuck this. I'm going to PA." She was already planning to do that when she left the Oasis, where she'd been with Warren and Becky. And now she was even more determined to get to the bottom of this. She had a feeling the fake name was just the tip of the iceberg.

"Are you sure that's a good idea?" Cap questioned. "I know Leah and Casey thought you should back off for now. We didn't want you pursuing your investigation any longer, not for the club, in any case."

"I want to know what's going on as much as you do," Jessie explained. "Besides, Casey is leaving, and Leah has her hands full. So does Paisley, for that matter, just trying to keep Leah from doing too much. If Anna or Sirena, or whoever the hell she is, has plans to harm the club, I intend to put a stop to it."

She realized as she said the words that her hands were trembling. She wasn't sure if it was the adrenaline coursing through her veins, pumping her full of the courage to go hunt Sirena down—or if it was the heartbreak of finding out she wasn't who she professed to be. She accepted it was some combination thereof and fought a tear stinging at the corner of her eye.

Cap took her hand and pulled her in for a hug. It had been a while since she'd been touched by a man—well, except that stupid fuck the other day at the apartment complex—but there was something comforting in a big brother kind of way about Cap's heavy limbs enveloping her. Not like any big brother she had, though. Like a big brother she wished she'd had.

"Okay, I'm going to go," she told him, closing her eyes just in time to vanquish the tear. She managed to force it down her throat and swallow it harshly. It tasted bitter, like the regret that had been building about her feelings for Sirena.

"Wait, Jessie," he called out after her once she'd slipped away from his arms. She turned back and locked her chocolate brown eyes with his and saw that he knew. He knew she had fallen in love with her. He didn't confirm it, but it was written all over his face and even peppered his last words to her, "Be careful, okay?"

TEN

All I can tell you is this. Some hearts break from grief, some from joy. Some even break from love. But hearts break because they are too small to contain the gifts life gives us. Your task will be to let your heart grow large enough not to break. -Catherine M. Wilsonson

The idea of going to Pennsylvania had to be kept separate from the mission to find Sirena. If Jessie could simply compartmentalize them, then she might be able to keep herself from driving her car off the Inlet Bridge just north of Ocean City, over the state line in neighboring Delaware. Pennsylvania held nothing but horrific memories for her, and she hadn't been back for a long time, even though her hometown was only a few hours away.

When her parents had last made the drive down to visit, she'd told them in no uncertain terms that she'd never be back. Her mother had stood glaring at her, then muttered something under her breath in

Spanish, something that sounded like "ungrateful, spoiled brat." Jessie shook off that memory from the last time she had seen her parents in person. *It had been...what? Three years now*, she thought, and there had only been maybe two or three times as many phone conversations since. And not even one of those for six months.

Her mother lived in some sort of magical fantasyland where nothing bad ever happened. The memories Jessie fought off daily simply failed to exist in her mother's narrative. And her father played the big dumb guy, too stupid to know what was going on with his own family. She shrugged it off, just like she always did, pushing it deeper below the surface where the light of day would never illuminate it.

Sirena. That was who this trip was about. She took a page out of her mother's book and pretended she was going somewhere other than the place she'd grown up, where her innocence had been destroyed. She could use denial as a tool, too.

She blasted the radio as she drove, the grunge rock she remembered from her junior high days filling the cozy space of her car. She'd called Sarge that morning before she left and told him she was sick. It was not a lie. She sent a text to Bart to tell him the same thing. They were both incredulous. Jessica Martinez had never called in sick, not in however many years she'd been on the force. Never. *It doesn't matter*, she thought. *It's still not a lie. I'm sick with dread that something is wrong, and I'm not going to be able to work with a clear mind until I know for sure.*

The sound of the tires turning over and over on the pavement numbed her, kept the fears from taking the steering wheel from her grasp. She had the address from Sirena's driver's license scrawled on the back of a scrap of paper Cap had handed her from his office the night before. She'd taken one last look at the photocopy of her real license, knowing just from the outline of her face that it was truly her. Her slim, graceful neck, high cheekbones and her delicate nose were unmistakable. Anna, though? Why not just come to The Factory and be Anna? What did she have to hide that would prevent her from using her real name?

Jessie should have checked to see how Sirena paid for her membership. She'd forgotten to ask that. *A credit card? Cash?* If the former, didn't they notice it wasn't her name? *These are questions cops think to ask, not managers*, she told herself. And besides, it was too late now. The only way to get to the bottom of this was to keep her eyes on the road as she sped north.

Three hours later on the nose, Jessie pulled into the town printed on Anna Patterson's driver's license. It was tiny. There was a derelict gas station on one corner at a flashing yellow light, and the other corner had a boarded-up restaurant. A half-mile further revealed a little town square with only a few shops that appeared open, one of which was a crumbling brick post office. There was also a grocery store with a full parking lot and a faded "Double Coupons Honored Here" banner flying in the breeze; it was probably the only grocery store for miles.

It was hard to believe little towns like this still existed when just twenty minutes away the skyscrapers of Philadelphia loomed into the skyline like steel and glass giants. Jessie's own neighborhood wasn't too far from this, but it was closer to the city, a dirty, forgotten finger that had been cut off from the gentrification of other nearby slums. This wasn't the hardened, graffiti-rampaged, litter-strewn ghetto where she was from. It was a faded, rusty attempt at suburbia way back when. A failed attempt. People had abandoned this place for city high-rises or the nicer suburbs with their brick-faced brownstones and townhouses, or their squat little starter homes shit out by some fly-by-night construction company promising great value for the money.

The houses lining the street here were stately great dames, built in an era where quality and craftsmanship really mattered. But nothing stays pristine if no one is there to take care of it. Berlin, one of the smaller towns near Ocean City had houses like these, but they had all been refurbished, repainted, and were lovely, helping to earn Berlin many accolades like "Best Small Town in America." This little shit town was probably on the worst small towns list.

Jessie glanced down at her phone. She had sent Sirena a text that morning when she left, just simply asking if she was home, which she figured would strike Sirena as odd, because to Sirena's knowledge, Jessie had no idea where her "home" was. It certainly wasn't at 23 Palmetto Court, wherever the hell that was supposed to be.

She'd been planning this speech in her head the whole drive up, trying to decide if she should lead in with, "Hey, why did you lie about your name?" or with "Where the hell have you been?" She threw both of those options away almost immediately because, once again, Sirena would have that whole deer-in-the-headlights thing going on. Her fight or flight response only had one mode, and it was going to be the latter. Every. Single. Time.

Her GPS directed her to turn left on a narrow

street ahead. It was lined with more dilapidated two-story houses, but as the street widened out, the houses grew farther apart and became smaller. They were still derelict and lacking any of the Victorian charm of the ones closer to the center of town. There was a boxy stone structure with broken windows and a rusted out pickup manufactured circa 1974 in the driveway. And beyond that were the trailers. They were probably the newest of the buildings in this god-forsaken town, but they were also the most depressing.

She saw Sirena's gold Honda in the driveway at the end of the street, which stopped abruptly in a bare field with brown grass. Fifty yards away there was a stand of trees, and at least those looked healthy and thriving. Everything else around her looked scorched, even though nothing had been burned. *Maybe it's wishful thinking on the town's part*, Jessie considered.

Fortified with a deep breath filling her lungs with the thick summer air, she got out of her car after grabbing her phone off the seat. Still nothing from Sirena. *She's probably still asleep*, Jessie guessed as she plodded down the stone pathway, which was surprisingly intact. Blue shutters were falling off from the front window, and the slip-shod porch erected to elevate guests to the front door was decaying. There was a plastic bin full of beer bottles that stood in greeting right outside the dented metal door. She briefly remembered the flimsy apartment door she'd kicked in the week before. She wondered what her luck would be with one of the metal variety, should the attempt be warranted.

Speaking of warrants, she did feel an awful lot like she was at work. It was common to approach some of the most rundown buildings in Worcester County, either responding to a domestic or throwing out an evicted tenant. For a split second she forgot what was at stake.

She knocked, and at first only silence echoed back at her. Sirena's car was there. She had every reason to believe she was home. The next time, she pounded on the door and used her cop voice to demand it be opened, even though she had no jurisdiction or right to do so.

When all else fails, turn the doorknob, she chided herself. She jiggled it, and sure enough, the metal door creaked open. The stench that hit her nostrils consumed her with its foulness. "Sirena?" she called, stepping through what seemed to be mounds of dog shit and trash, not to mention clumps of dirty clothes. "What the fuck?" she murmured aloud until she stopped dead in her tracks.

There was a ratty, threadbare recliner near the window, parked in front of a muted TV. It was some dumb gameshow playing, *The Price is Right* or something. A man with greasy gray hair was sprawled out in it, still clutching the remote in his hands. He appeared to be asleep, and for good measure, she focused on his chest for a few moments to make sure it was rising and falling. She didn't have to go any nearer to know this was the elusive Joseph Patterson, to whom the gold Honda was registered.

"Sirena?" she called again, more softly this time. She didn't want to wake the old man, who had a line of slobber trailing down his chin and onto his chest, which was matted with thick gray hair. He was wearing only boxers, and it was not a sight Jessie ever wanted to remember. She hoped it wouldn't freeze up in her mental archives.

If he didn't wake up from me pounding on the door, he's not likely to wake up from me calling out her name, she reflected. She had her hand on her gun, which was holstered to the belt in her shorts. She had debated long and hard about whether or not to arm herself on this adventure, but all she could hear was Bart's or even Paisley's voice admonishing her if she failed to protect herself. It wasn't her OCPD-issued service weapon, of course, but her own hand gun.

"Sirena?" she asked again, pushing open the last door in the hallway. The first two yielded nothing. One was a bathroom, and the other, a bedroom so tiny a bed could barely fit inside, but both were empty in any case.

She had wondered where the dog was that had left the steaming piles of shit all over the house, but she found it curled up on the bed, an ugly brown mutt, but one slumbering peacefully nevertheless. And right beyond the dog was the form of a woman in a fetal position. *Sirena.*

Jessie made her way across the floor, hoping she wasn't stepping in anything except dirty laundry. She bent over the golden-haired figure, who appeared even more passed-out than her husband in the falling-apart recliner. "Sirena?" she questioned again, her voice barely louder than a hoarse whisper. She still wasn't brave enough to take in a full breath of air in this disgusting sleaze-pit of a trailer.

How the fuck do people live like this? she asked herself. It was a question she asked a million times per shift, almost any time she had to make a home visit. The house she grew up in wasn't nice or new, but her mother at least kept it clean.

Not surprisingly, Sirena didn't stir. Jessie reached

down to grasp her by the shoulder, shaking her gently and all the while wondering for the *nth* time why she was here and what the hell she was doing. *This is a woman masquerading as someone else. Even after spending the night with me and knowing I'm a fucking cop, she still didn't come clean about who she really is— or the fact she lives in Pennsylvania. She said she was living in Ocean City, at least for the summer.*

Still, I drove all this way. Fuck. Why can't I just leave well enough alone? It's not my job to save this woman.

After receiving absolutely no response to her pokes and prods, Jessie pushed her body firmly at the torso, flipping her over onto her back. She gasped as her eyes raked over Sirena's body. Deep purple bruises spotted her from head to toe. There were even finger-shaped bruises around her neck.

"Holy fuck." The words spilled out loud enough to rouse the dog, who was asleep nearby. He let out two short barks, and even then, Sirena did not stir. Her lip was swollen, and Jessie began to wonder if she was having trouble breathing. Her chest was barely rising with each breath.

She didn't bother to do any other assessments. She picked up her phone and dialed 9-1-1.

Paramedics arrived in about fifteen minutes. Because she wasn't family, Jessie was not allowed to ride with them to the hospital, but she followed closely behind in her car. During the entire drive, all she could think about was how she had come all that way and now had even more questions than she'd brought with her.

She left her gun in her car and hurried up to the ER check-in station to ask for Anna Patterson. That was the name she gave the paramedics when they arrived. Jessie hadn't been able to find any identification in her house, nor a purse or handbag of any kind. And nothing for the old guy. She was told to wait in the waiting room.

It felt like hours slipped by. She got a text from Paisley asking if she was okay. She couldn't tell from the tone of it if Cap had told her where she went or not, but she pretended as though Paisley didn't know. *Yeah, just have a bad summer cold*, she answered.

Do you want me to bring you some chicken soup? Paisley asked, always thinking of others, as was her nature.

No, thank you. I'll be fine, Jessie texted back, hoping beyond hope that Paisley didn't show up at her condo only to discover she wasn't there.

Not long after that, a petite African American female doctor came out to the waiting room to look for her. "Are you Jessica Martinez?" she asked, looking down at her clipboard.

Jessie nodded. "Yes, can I come back?"

"I want to talk to you first," she answered, her brows scrunched in a worried look. She smoothed her crisp white jacket and ushered Jessie behind the double doors into the bowels of the emergency room. She showed her inside an empty exam room. During a weekday in summer, the hospital was not particularly busy, but there was a constant hum of activity. Orderlies passed by pushing patients in wheelchairs; nurses scurried toward curtained-off rooms where loud beeps wailed. Doctors' dress shoes squeaked against the shiny, recently disinfected floor tiles. The hospital was old, but it was well-maintained, and Jessie was surprised it was only fifteen minutes or so from the rundown trailer where she'd found them.

"Mr. Patterson is a frequent flyer here at St. Vincent's," the doctor told Jessie as soon as she flipped on the light in the room.

"I don't really know him," Jessie answered, looking down at the doctor's name badge. It was some African name she couldn't pronounce. "I know his wife... Uh...we're friends. I came up here to check on her because she usually stays in Ocean City every weekend. But she didn't come down this past weekend, and she wouldn't answer my calls or texts."

"I see," Dr. Whatever-Her-Name said. She flipped through the chart again. "We can't seem to find a next-of-kin other than Mrs. Patterson. Do you know of someone else we could contact?"

Jessie shook her head. "What's wrong with him?"

"I'm sorry. HIPAA," she answered.

"I'm only trying to help," Jessie defended herself. "I'm a cop. Not here, but I mean, I'm not exactly a threat to either of the Pattersons. I'm simply concerned and want to help. I hadn't been up here before, but their trailer is almost uninhabitable. I don't know what kind of resources might be available to them, but knowing his condition would help me ascertain that."

She sighed. "It's not that I don't want to help. You

can talk to the police when they show up."

Jessie's brows quirked. "Police?"

"Yes, your friend has severe contusions and—well, when they arrive, they can tell you, if they choose to."

"Can I see her?" Jessie knew she was just trying to do her job, but her curt manner was lacking in compassion. *Isn't it obvious I care about her?* she wondered.

"Yes, but be advised that Officer Grayson will be here soon to take your statement."

Jessie thanked the doctor for her time, even if she was less-than-impressed with the amount of information she revealed. Then she paced into the next room where the doctor had pointed.

Jessie barely had time to survey Sirena's form lying in the bed, her skin looking sallow and washed-out, except where the darkness of her bruises contrasted against the white sheets. Two uniformed officers stepped inside the room, and from the looks of them, they were Pennsylvania state troopers. Jessie reached her hand out in greeting. "I'm Corporal Jessica Martinez, Ocean City Police Department, Maryland," she added.

They seemed a bit taken aback, but then the older of the two men began to speak. "I'm Corporal Grayson, and this is Trooper Smith. We understand you're the friend who called 9-1-1 this afternoon?"

She nodded. "I did, but I had just gotten to their house a few minutes before I called. There was no answer, and the door was unlocked, so I let myself in. Mr. Patterson was asleep in the recliner, and I found...um, Anna curled up in a fetal position in the bedroom. She wasn't responsive, but was breathing."

Grayson nodded as his partner began to take notes in a little notebook. "Do you know how she got the bruises?"

Jessie shook her head. "No, but it's not the first time I've seen her with bruises."

"What is the nature of your relationship?" he asked, and Trooper Smith's head jerked up to listen to the answer.

Fuck, Jessie thought. She didn't want to tell them she and Sirena were lovers. "We're friends. I know her from Ocean City. We have mutual friends, and she generally spends the weekends down there." She left out the part about it being a swinger club or the fact that Cap had called in a favor from a state trooper buddy to provide her real name and address, though she did think about how strange it would be if one of these two troopers was his buddy. "She didn't show up last weekend, so I decided to come up here and check on her. I just had a feeling something wasn't right."

"Sounds like those suspicions were confirmed," Corporal Grayson said, nodding at Jessie and then at his partner. "How well do you know Mrs. Patterson?"

"I just met her a few weeks ago, but—" This is where she needed to decide if she should come clean. "But we've spent some time together. It's not the first time I've seen her with bruises." Jessie couldn't force herself to say Sirena was using a different name. Who knew what kind of trouble she might be in? Jessie still felt obligated to protect her, even after she lied about her identity.

"Did she tell you how she got them?" He was asking all the same questions she would have asked if the roles were reversed, but she had a feeling neither of them were going to get the answers they needed.

Jessie shook her head. "She was pretty evasive about it. Said she fell or something, even though it was clear someone had grabbed her arm. And now it looks like she's been beat up. Maybe choked."

"We suspect it was her husband," Grayson said, leaning in close as if Jessie were privileged to hear this theory. She wanted to retort, *no shit, Sherlock*, but she restrained herself. "You're sure you never met him before?"

"Nope. Still haven't, in fact. He was passed out when I got to their house."

Corporal Grayson glanced at his partner, who nodded as he finished scribbling on his notepad. "Okay," said the younger man, "here's my card. Can you call us when she wakes up?"

Jessie said yes and took the card, but she knew it would depend on what Sirena had to say for herself when she came to. Jessie had an overwhelming urge to take her, just remove her from this ugly world where someone as beautiful as she was clearly did not belong. But she had so many questions, more questions she had a feeling would be difficult to discover the answers to.

After the state troopers left, she sat in the uncomfortable plastic chair at Sirena's bedside and waited. And waited. A nurse came in a couple times and asked if there had been any changes. Jessie shook her head solemnly, still not understanding what had happened. And no one would tell her. *They probably don't know either*, she rationalized. *And her tox screen may not have come back yet.*

What if she is an addict? Jessie wondered. *In addition to almost certainly being an alcoholic. Then what?* She knew she should run far away from that kind of mess. She dealt with addicts all the time in her line of work, and it was a horrific circumstance, one she wouldn't wish on her worst enemy. But she had a feeling Sirena didn't have anyone else to help her. *If she did, wouldn't they be here with her right now instead of me?*

As the sun shifted across the sky, the room grew brighter, warming to an eye-popping tangerine shade. The light made a stripe right across Sirena's face, and the parts of her hair illuminated in it looked like spun gold. She was so still, like a doll, and then finally, a grimace clutched her features, and there was the tiniest restless movement.

Jessie reached out and took the blonde's hand into hers, admiring how long and elegant her fingers were and the smoothness of her skin. *Especially for 48*, she sighed, wondering how on earth this exquisite creature was really that old. Her eyes traveled up Sirena's arm, which began to shake under the weight of her stare, especially when her gaze fell upon the deep, purple bruises that marred her perfectly creamy complexion.

Her eyes opened into thin slits as the light filled them, and Jessie nearly held her breath as she gained lucidity. She shook her head as if trying to clear her blurry vision, then glanced down at the IV in her arm. "What's going on?" she finally mumbled, her words all slushed together.

"Hey, lady," Jessie said with a smile, wanting to reassure her before she freaked out about being in a hospital bed.

"Where's Joe?" were her next words.

Jessie assumed she meant her husband. "I don't know. In another room, I guess."

"He's dying," she murmured, then closed her eyes.

"Dying?" Jessie squeezed her hand, bringing her to life again. "Dying of what?"

"Liver cancer," she answered, her eyelids fluttering open, then closing once more. "I have to take care of him." She said the last words with her eyes shut tightly, but her voice was full of resolution.

"Even though he beats you?"

She didn't answer. Her eyelids were sealed shut, hiding her brilliant green eyes. Jessie sighed. *Fuck. Now what?*

ELEVEN

The truth will set you free, but first it will piss you off.
— Joe Klaas

The problem with someone lying is that after you catch them in their lie, you're not sure if you can trust anything that comes out of their mouth ever again, Jessie reflected as she helped Sirena get her things ready to drive back down to Ocean City.

One thing was for certain: Sirena did not want to leave her husband. The hospital was moving him to hospice, even though Sirena protested that he didn't want that and there was no way they could afford it. He had Medicaid and a disability check, but that was all their income. Jessie was floored. With all of the nice clothes Sirena flaunted every weekend at the club, she was still having trouble reconciling that she and Anna were the same person, especially after seeing Joe and the dump they lived in.

There were so many times that Jessie questioned why she was letting herself get caught up in this drama, in this crazy chaotic circus. But then she saw the bruised and battered woman lying in the hospital bed, who just wanted to take care of her dying husband and didn't have anyone else to help. What was left was not only Jessie's strong vocational responsibility pulling her toward Sirena, but her own personal compassion for the woman as well.

"I want to help you, okay?" Jessie tenderly brushed some wayward strands of golden hair out of Sirena's eyes. "But you have *got* to be honest with me, do you understand?"

"Why are you treating me like a child?" she argued. "I'm almost old enough to be your mother, for Christ's sake!"

She had a point. Now that Jessie knew her true age, she realized Sirena wasn't that much younger than her mother, only by four years. Maria Martinez had gotten married at 18 when she became pregnant with Jessie's oldest brother Antonio, and it was only a year later that her brother Phillip came along. Jessie was born two years after that. *No wonder she was tired all the time,* Jessie thought. Three kids in four years. And her father was always working two jobs, never home to help out.

Why did life have to be so fucking hard? Jessie had it tough growing up. She had fought for everything she had, especially since she left home at seventeen to get her own job. She was lucky to already have her high school diploma—she'd been bright and graduated a semester early—but that was almost all she had when she ventured out on her own. She'd thought things had been different for Sirena, though.

She had conjured up an image of Sirena's life that was so far from reality, it seemed like a fantasy now. Her well-bred accent and statuesque posture made her seem like a wealthy high society lady. She imagined Sirena had inherited a pretty penny from her father, or perhaps she was the widow of a wealthy gent several decades her senior. Though Sirena had never made her living arrangements known, Jessie would have never guessed in a million years that she lived in a rusty, dilapidated trailer in Shit Town, Pennsylvania, with a violent, alcoholic cancer patient who beat her.

"I can't leave Joe here," she finally said as Jessie put the last of her things in her car.

"Why not? You aren't leaving him forever." Jessie tried to soften her expression and appeal to Sirena's fun, adventurous side, the side she's known in Ocean City. "Just come spend the week with me and get your head on straight."

"I can't leave the dog here either," Sirena insisted, turning to face to Jessie with her wide, sad eyes.

Jessie sighed. "Fine, bring the dog, whatever. But you can't stay here. I feel like I should drop a match in there before we leave. After dousing it with a good amount of lighter fluid."

Sirena didn't respond to that statement. She went inside and came back carrying the dog, which was a fuck-knows-what breed. It was medium-sized and brown with a white patch on its belly. It had sad brown eyes and a long pink tongue that never stayed in its mouth long. "What's its name?" Jessie asked as she got it settled in the back seat.

"It's Georgia, and it's a she," Sirena answered as if the poor mutt was the most dignified creature on earth.

"Of course it is." Jessie shut her door. "You got everything?"

"I do now," Sirena answered with a hint of resignation in her voice. As Jessie pulled out of the driveway, Sirena kept her eyes glued to the tiny beat-up trailer for as long as she could.

Why the hell would she be attached to this place? Jessie wondered, failing to find any rational reason for it. She had never pushed Sirena into giving answers, but now that she was opening up her home to her for an extended period of time, she felt she had a right to know certain things, to at least get an opportunity to understand.

She waited until she got on the main road to start her interrogation. She hoped to make it more like a dialogue, but she knew it was going to come out one-sided. "How long has Joe had cancer?" she started.

"He was diagnosed last summer and given six months to live," she answered. "The doctors weren't too optimistic beings as his liver was already beat up from all the drinking. But he has always been one to defy odds, so here we are."

"Did he do chemo and all that?"

She nodded. "Yeah, and was basically laid up till winter. But in the spring we learned the cancer had metastasized anyway, so there wasn't much we could do. And he didn't want to do any more treatment or hospice or any of that. We'd already sunk so much money into trying to fix him. He had horrible insurance, and the bills were piling up. He just wanted to go at home, peacefully."

"Did he start beating you before or after he got cancer?"

The question just hung there in the small space between them in Jessie's car. Unanswered. But Jessie knew Sirena had heard because she instantly turned her head to stare back out the window at the passing fields, all green with corn and soybeans and the occasional strip of trees.

"I'm sorry." Jessie broke the silence and reached her hand out to rest against Sirena's knee. "I shouldn't have said it like that." Jessie wasn't expecting her to flinch, but she did. She realized it was the first time she had touched Sirena since she was released from the hospital that morning. Jessie was in work mode, taking care of business mode. She'd nearly forgotten the gentleness she needed when it came to the woman next to her.

Sirena sighed. "Joe and I go back a long way. I make him angry. He gets drunk; he hits me. It's just what we do."

Jessie shook her head. "That doesn't make it alright. Why would you think it's okay for him to do that?"

Sirena scrubbed her hands across her face as though trying to ward off a headache. "Don't ask me questions you don't want to hear the answers to," she said. "I'm not a good person, Jessie. I don't even know why you're helping me."

Jessie wanted to answer that she didn't know why either, but she bit her lip. She decided to go for the low-hanging fruit. "Why did you come to Ocean City every weekend?"

Sirena scoffed. "Isn't it obvious? I needed a break. I needed to get the hell out of Dodge."

"Fair enough. But why the fake name?"

"Fuck, Jessie, you're not at work, okay? I'm not some suspect, and you're not taking me to jail. There are no simple answers to any of your questions."

Was this woman mentally ill? Jessie had her suspicions, but she was still not sure how to proceed. The first step was making her feel safe. Trust is a two-way street, and Jessie knew Sirena would never trust her if she thought she was being judged.

She let a long swath of silence pass between them as they worked their way through northern Delaware. The gentle rolling hills of Pennsylvania had disappeared, and now the highway was a long, straight silver ribbon extending toward the horizon. The sun beat down on the car, and even with the air conditioner blasting, a patch of sunlight burned into Jessie's temple. Then Georgia began to whine from the back seat.

"We should stop and let her pee," Sirena suggested. "And get her some water."

Jessie nodded, at least relieved that Sirena hadn't totally given up on speaking to her. She pulled off at the next exit. They were making good time and would be back in Ocean City before dinner. *Maybe Georgia would like a walk on the beach?* she wondered.

Something changed in Sirena when she came back from the restroom. Jessie had been handling the dog, giving her a few treats they'd packed, and she learned Georgia knew some tricks like staying and catching a treat in the air when she tossed it up. She was smart, that much was certain. Sirena had a huge smile on her face, watching Jessie play with Georgia. It was a wistful smile, one of undisclosed fantasies filling her blonde head.

She got into the car and fastened her seatbelt, and Jessie noticed she was still smiling.

"What are you thinking about?" Jessie questioned as she fastened her own seatbelt.

"I was thinking about road trips my parents used to take us on when we were little. We went to Florida all the time, to this beautiful place called Siesta Key. The sand is like powdered sugar there, so much whiter and finer than the sand in Ocean City. And it's on the Gulf side, so the sun would set right over the water, exploding like a big red bomb, turning the water all scarlet, then black as the sun slipped down past the horizon.

"We went there almost every fall when my dad could take a vacation. And my sister and I would collect a million shells and build the most beautiful sand castles ever. Then the next morning when we'd go back down, the tide would be letting out, and it had always taken our castles with it, toppling them into a couple of small hills. It used to make Elizabeth so sad. She was four years younger than me, and such a sensitive soul. You'd probably never believe it, but I was the tough one. Back then, anyway."

She stared out the window now, but her eyes were full of memories. She didn't seem to notice the tall buildings of Wilmington rising up ahead of them. Jessie wished she could crawl into her mind and have a look around. Maybe then she'd understand what the hell was going on.

Jessie got a text from Paisley asking how she was feeling around the time she crossed the state line into Maryland. She was still driving, so she didn't bother to reply. She still hadn't decided what to do about Sirena. She almost felt like she was harboring a fugitive, and she had a feeling Paisley and the rest of the management of The Factory would disapprove, even though Cap had all but asked that she go check on her.

When she pulled into the parking lot at her condo, she gently shook Sirena awake from her nap. Even the minimal conversation they'd had during the drive had wiped her out. She was still recovering from her blackout, and it still wasn't evident to Jessie if it was due to alcohol, being assaulted, or some other substance she'd taken. She wondered if she should have Sirena evaluated by her own doctor, one of the best on the Eastern Shore.

Sirena was groggy as Jessie pulled her and Georgia out of the car. "Let me get you settled upstairs, and then I'll come back for your things, okay?"

Sirena could barely manage a nod, and Jessie had to drag them both up to the condo building, the dog because she was really more interested in being outside. Thankfully she did her business before they reached the doors.

As she walked back down to retrieve Sirena's things, Jessie's head throbbed with all she needed to do. She'd need to call in sick for her shift again. She knew she couldn't just take time off because it was their busy season, and there was no vacation time to be granted. On the other hand, she couldn't tell Sarge what was really going on either. She was stuck between a rock and a hard place, and tomorrow was really the last day she could take off work without getting a doctor's note. She hated playing the system like that, but she truly felt like she had no other options.

When she made it back to her condo, Sirena was already back asleep on the couch. Meanwhile Jessie's phone buzzed with another text, this time from Bart. *What's going on with you? You're never sick.*

She texted back: *I have some shit I have to take care of. Sick friend. I'll be back the day after tomorrow. Thanks for checking on me.*

Then returned Paisley's text: *I brought Sirena down here. Things are a bit of a mess. I'll try to call when I can.*

There, that's as much as I can do for now, she decided. She looked over at Georgia's sad eyes. She felt exactly how the dog looked. "Let's go for a walk on the beach, girl." Her voice instantly made the dog's ears perk up. "We'll both feel better after a little time with our toes in the sand. Or paws in your case."

She clipped the leash she'd just taken off Georgia back on and guided her down the hallway to the elevator. She wasn't technically supposed to have a dog in her apartment that wasn't part of her lease, but hopefully her landlord would understand it was a temporary thing. She sure wished dogs could talk, because she had a feeling she could get a lot of information out of Georgia if only she were able to share it.

"Why haven't you touched me?" came a soft voice when Jessie led the dog through the door.

Apparently she's awake, Jessie thought, glancing over at the couch where Sirena sat propped up with what looked like a half-dozen pillows. She bought herself some time to answer the question by unleashing the dog and going to fill up a bowl of water for her. The dog was so thirsty, she made a loud show of lapping up the water before Jessie joined Sirena in the living room.

"Nice to see your eyes again," Jessie said, a small smile creeping across her face as she looked over to Sirena. Her right eyelid was still purple, but the bruises around her neck had faded a little, taking on a greenish hue.

Sirena set her lips in a thin, firm line.

"What's with all the pillows?" Jessie questioned, still ignoring her previous question, or pretending she hadn't heard it.

"You didn't answer my question," Sirena insisted. "Why should I answer yours?"

Jessie narrowed her dark eyes and crossed her leg over so her ankle rested on her knee. She always found her legs were too short and thick to do a proper ladylike leg-crossing. She reached out to gently place her hand on Sirena's thigh. She barely touched the woman, but she winced anyway.

"That's why I have all the pillows," Sirena

answered, her face still twisted with pain. "My whole damn body hurts. I feel like I got hit by a bus or something."

"Well, your husband looked like a pretty big guy," Jessie retorted. "You practically *did* get hit by a bus. Can I get you something for the pain? Do you want any of your pills?"

She vehemently shook her head. "I don't know what they pumped me full of in the hospital, but I can't take that shit. Vicodin makes me sick. I'd rather just suffer than feel like that."

Okay, so she's not an opioid addict, Jessie thought. *That's a good thing.* "Are you really forty-eight?"

A sly smirk curled Sirena's lips. "Who told you that? The hospital?"

"I can't reveal my sources. But I know your name is Anna. And I know you're ten years older than you stated on your membership application at The Factory."

"I can pass for being in my thirties though, right?" She giggled a vain little laugh that sounded like a waterfall gurgling into a pond.

Jessie sighed. "Look, I don't know why you feel the need to be this international woman of mystery around me, but if you want me to help you, I really need to know the truth about who you are and what your situation is."

"I never asked you for help," Sirena fired back. "As a matter of fact, I specifically told you I could take care of myself! I've been telling you that all along." She glared at Jessie with her green eyes blazing as though they were lit from within.

"So you're saying you think I should have left you in Pennsylvania in that dump with a man who drinks and beats you?"

Sirena rolled her eyes. "I asked you why you haven't touched me."

Jessie let the breath she was holding escape, and it almost sounded like a hiss. She was accustomed to dealing with people in crisis; it's just that she normally had some sort of power. She could lock them up or institutionalize them or something. She had a course of action. With Sirena, she could merely suggest, but she couldn't enforce compliance. She had no idea it would be so frustrating.

"I don't want to hurt you," Jessie sighed, bending toward Sirena. She meant that both literally and figuratively.

"I thought you were just interested in me...physically...at first," Sirena admitted. She wrapped a thick lock of her golden hair around her index finger as she spoke. "You know, those nights I spent here and we cuddled and made out. You didn't really contact me afterward..."

Jessie felt her heart leap as she processed Sirena's words. She had no idea what to say. "I didn't think you—"

Sirena's eyes were full of tears, her fingers trembling. *Fuck, what did I do?* Jessie wondered. *Fuck, fuck, fuck.*

"Just tell me what you need, Sirena. I want to be here for you." She locked her dark eyes with Sirena's and pressed her hand into her own, trying not to squeeze too tightly as she had a bruise just above her wrist.

"I just want to be held. I want to be needed," she whimpered.

Jessie wondered if she stayed to take care of her abusive husband because she wanted to be needed. He probably would have died months ago if it weren't for her taking care of him. But what did she do with him when she was in Ocean City? Jessie was too afraid to open up that can of worms and start interrogating Sirena again. Instead, she just gathered the sobbing woman up into her arms and held her against her chest.

She still wasn't sure exactly who this woman was, nor did she understand her entire situation, but it was clear she was not only in physical pain, but emotional anguish as well. And if there was one thing Jessie hated seeing, it was people in pain. Before going to Pennsylvania, Jessie thought she could just walk away from Sirena because she'd never be interested in Jessie the way she might want her to be, but now she realized how badly Sirena needed a friend. Jessie just hoped she could be the friend Sirena needed without wanting more.

TWELVE

I know the odds are against us. I know she's a siren. I know she's eaten people. I know she's five thousand years older than me. But I really like her.
— *Simon Rich,* The Last Girlfriend on Earth: And Other Love Stories

"You seem really...distracted," Bart observed, his eyes bouncing between Jessie's as she settled herself in her seat. They'd just grabbed food from the sandwich shop they liked to frequent on their shift and were beginning to dig in. "What's going on?"

While it was true Jessie had found most men to be almost laughably oblivious to the emotional anguish of others, cops did have a leg up, even male cops. Their whole job was to read people, so it would be almost impossible for Jessie to cover up the fact that her mind was spinning with too many thoughts, too many unanswered questions.

She shot Bart a look that said *don't mess with me*, but she knew it wasn't like him to heed that warning. She braced herself for some dumb-ass comment to spew out of his mouth.

"Lady troubles again?" he teased her. "It's that hot Latina blood you got flowing through your veins." He laughed as he took a swig from his bottle of soda.

Her eyes narrowed as she decided to take a chance on actually being able to relate to Bart on a semi-human level. "Can I ask you a question?" She decided to ignore his little remark about her ethnic heritage as she usually did.

"Okay," he agreed, popping a handful of potato chips into his mouth and making obnoxious crunching sounds as if he got paid to lighten the mood.

Probably a completely worthless endeavor, she decided, but then asked anyway, "If you were interested in someone and then found out they had been lying about their identity...what would you do? Run the other way? Or stick it out?"

His brows stitched together as if he hadn't expected such a complex question. He chewed thoughtfully for a moment, then tossed back, "I guess it would depend on why they lied. Were they in danger or something?"

She shrugged. "Maybe. Maybe you don't understand why they lied, but it wasn't just to you, it was to a whole bunch of people. Basically, you found out they were portraying themselves as someone very different than who they actually are."

"Yeah, I don't know about that," he answered. "Like I said, context is a big thing. If it was to protect themselves, I guess I can understand. Are you writing a movie script or something?" He laughed again as he crumpled up the wrapper his sandwich had come from. Jessie had no idea how he'd managed to eat it so quickly. It was like he inhaled it.

"I wish I were writing a movie script," she replied. "That seems a whole hell of a lot easier..."

Jessie stopped by The Factory in uniform before going home. She didn't like going there in uniform, but it made more sense than going all the way home, changing and coming back. And if she did that, she'd have to tell Sirena where she was going, and she didn't want to.

She saw Cap first. "Hey, is Paisley here?"

"Yeah, she's upstairs."

Cap took a closer look at her, his blue eyes scanning her much like Bart's had done earlier in the day. *Leave it to me to know all these observant males after a lifetime of men who didn't give one shit about me*, she thought. *I must have heartache written all over my face or something.*

Before she could make it to the stairs, Cap asked, "What's going on?"

She sighed. She might as well gather the troops and just tell everyone at the same time. It wasn't as if they weren't all going to know at some point eventually anyway. There were no secrets among the tight-knit staff of The Factory. "Come up with me?" she questioned, and he nodded as he moved toward her.

The whole crew was upstairs, so it was easy to assemble everyone in Leah's office, which was the largest of all the offices in the building. Jessie waited until everyone had taken their seats. "I feel like I'm giving a press conference or something," she joked as she looked around the room at Cap, Leah, Casey, Paisley and Calvin.

"So you went to Pennsylvania, right?" Paisley started off the questioning.

Jessie nodded. "As you know, last weekend Sirena was a no-show, which was the first weekend in about two months she hadn't been here at the club. No one I spoke to had heard from her, and she didn't return my calls or texts. Though, I will admit, I didn't try to contact her too many times. I was trying to ignore the whole situation, but then my 'spidey senses'—"

Calvin burst out laughing. "'Spidey senses?' Isn't that trademarked?"

Jessie shook her head. "Would you prefer 'my womanly intuition?'"

He scoffed. "No, I definitely prefer spidey." He looked around the room at the faces of those growing annoyed with him for interrupting. "Sorry, I'll let you talk."

"I felt like something was wrong, and then when Cap told me his cop buddy in PA came back with a different name and age for her, I panicked. I just felt like I needed to get up there and check things out."

"So, what *is* her real name?" Casey asked. "Maybe I do know her from somewhere after all? I always thought she looked familiar."

"It's Anna Patterson, and her husband is the one who owns the car she drives, Joseph Patterson. She's actually forty-eight years old, can you believe it?"

Casey's mouth gaped open. "What? That can't be right! And no, that name doesn't ring a bell either."

Leah nodded. "I know, when Cap told me her age, I was absolutely floored. I want to know what kind of products she uses on her skin."

"No kidding!" Paisley agreed.

"So I got to the address Cap had given me, and guys, it was a total disaster. Beat-up metal trailer, looked like it was made in the '50s or something. Beer cans and bottles everywhere. Dog shit throughout the house, which must have been because they weren't taking the dog out, because she's a sweetheart and totally housebroken."

"And Sirena?" Leah questioned.

"Well, first I saw her husband passed out in this old junky recliner. I thought he might be dead at first, that's how out of it he was. He didn't even hear me come in. Their door was unlocked, and I'd almost beaten it down knocking before I went inside. I went down the hallway—god, this place totally reeked—I'm just glad I finally got the smell out of my nose. And I found Sirena curled up on her bed, also passed out. She was covered head to toe in bruises, including a black eye."

Casey gasped and covered her mouth immediately. Leah and Paisley had similarly surprised and concerned expressions on their faces. Cap and Calvin were on the edges of their seats as if they were waiting for the ending to a ghost story.

"So what did you do?" Calvin asked.

"I called 9-1-1; what else could I do?" Jessie was trembling as she relived the details, her heart pounding as the memories filled her mind and formed themselves into words. "So the ambulance came and took both of them, but they wouldn't let me ride with them, of course. And when I got to the hospital, they didn't want to tell me anything. Then the cops came and asked me a ton of questions, none of which I could answer."

"So what happened to her?" Leah queried, her green eyes still wide and round.

"Long story short, her husband has liver cancer and was given six months to live almost a year ago now. They lost all their savings and their home trying to pay for his treatments, that's why they were in that nasty trailer. He gets drunk and beats the shit out of her. That's why she had bruises a few weeks ago when she was here, though all she would tell me was it wasn't one of our club members who gave them to her. I was hoping it was some sort of sexy thing—you know, a BDSM thing, even though she's never indicated she's into that. I was just hoping—"

It was Cap's turn to pose a question. "So what happened to her husband?"

"They took him to a hospice facility," Jessie answered. "Even though Sirena didn't want them to. They say he doesn't have much time left. His body is shutting down."

"And she doesn't want to be there when he passes?" Casey was struggling to understand it all. The word "cancer" had already caused a dark shadow to grip her features.

"She didn't want to come with me, but I didn't give her much of a choice. She couldn't stay in that fucking pigsty. I don't know what she's going to do. She has called every day to check up on him since she's been down here with me."

"He fucking beats her!" Cap roared. "Why does she feel obligated to take care of him?"

Jessie shook her head. "That's what I've tried to understand, but she simply won't answer those questions. She refuses. She's hardly said a word about him. I don't even understand who took care of him when she was down here every weekend, but I do understand why she needed to come down here to unwind, or she'd have gone mad by now."

"So maybe the fake name was just so she could be someone else on the weekends? A way to completely escape?" Paisley wondered. She was no stranger to using aliases. She had used one when she fled a horrible situation in her hometown in Kentucky when she was barely eighteen, a situation that had come back to haunt her. Jessie couldn't even remember what her friend's real name was, but she'd had it legally changed to Paisley Parker at some point, and now to Paisley Mitchell after she and Calvin had tied the knot.

"I don't know," Jessie said, and she felt like she had been saying that a lot lately. "I better get home to her. I just wanted you guys to know what's going on."

"So what is your plan?" Leah asked. She always wanted to know the plan. Not one of her most endearing qualities, but it was one of the most pragmatic.

"I don't have one, really. I guess we're waiting for

news about her husband. We might have to go back up there."

"Aren't you from Pennsylvania too?" Paisley's eyebrows shot up as if she was just making the connection.

Jessie gave her a curt nod. She didn't want to make this about her. She couldn't explain how much her skin crawled just being back in the state.

"Do you think you'll be at my party next Saturday?" Casey asked. "I'm flying out that next afternoon...so if not...then..."

"I will do everything in my power to be there," Jessie reassured the older lady, walking over to put her arm around her. "I still haven't come to terms with the fact that you're going."

"I'll be back to visit," Casey promised. "I still have property here. I'm sure I can't stay away from this place too long."

Jessie tried to swallow down the lump that was stuck in her throat when she thought about saying goodbye to the woman who had been more of a mother figure to her than her own mother ever dreamed of being. She gave her a soft kiss on her cheek. "I'm sure I'll be here for your party."

"Let us know if there is anything we can do to help," Leah said. "Like a fundraiser or something? How is she going to pay for her husband's care? What about her horrible living conditions?"

"I don't know," Jessie said again. "But, yeah, we're going to have to figure something out." She could already see Leah's wheels turning as she bid everyone farewell.

It was amazing what a few days of rest and recuperation near the ocean could do for a body. Jessie could easily survey every inch of Sirena's skin because she was standing naked on the balcony when she got home from work, silhouetted against the late afternoon sun. Apparently she had gotten over her fear of heights and found the incredible view could cure a host of maladies. Her bruises were fading into a greenish-gray, and her skin tone had already deepened from the effects of lying on the beach. She had a healthy glow about her which only made her even more beautiful.

Jessie discarded her gun belt on the glass-topped table in her dining area, taking care to set it down lightly and not disturb Sirena's reverie. Georgia was standing right beside her, ears perked as she tracked some seagulls gliding across the sky. When Jessie cleared her throat, Sirena whipped around, her face instantly warming with a smile.

Jessie had to be careful not to let her jaw hit the floor when Sirena's nude body came into full view. Her perfect breasts fell against her ribcage with their gentle curves, topped off with two hard, delectable pink nipples. The graceful swell of her hips as she made her way toward Jessie elicited all sorts of potent chemicals to fire throughout Jessie's body. What surprised her, though, was how intent Sirena was on staring back, seemingly pleased by what she saw.

"What?" Jessie questioned, feeling a warmth bloom on her cheeks and hoping it was concealed by her coloring.

"I guess I haven't really looked at you in your uniform before," Sirena admitted, her eyes traveling up and down Jessie's body with total captivation.

"You're the one naked," Jessie joked, suddenly feeling a little shy. She was used to lavishing attention on women, not having the tables turned on her.

"That uniform is very becoming on you," Sirena noted, her southern accent peeking out amongst the words. "You look strong and sexy...and serious... I like that." She moved close enough to run her fingers down the front of Jessie's uniform. "Wow, is that your vest? It's so...hard."

Jessie chuckled. "Yeah, and not the most comfortable thing to wear, either. But it's not like I have a choice."

"You still have some damn fine curves, even though that uniform is trying its damnedest to cover them up!" Sirena smiled as she traced Jessie's womanly figure from her breasts to her thighs, dipping in at her small waist and flaring out considerably as her uniform stretched to accommodate her ample hips and ass. "And I like the bun too," she offered. "Though I kind of have this insane desire to pull it out..."

"No one's stopping you," Jessie goaded her, waiting to see if she'd take the bait.

With a wicked grin on her face, Sirena reached toward Jessie's hair and took hold of the perfectly sculpted bun at the back of her head. Jessie's hair was so long and thick that, when coiled into a round shape, the resulting bun stretched from her crown almost to the nape of her neck. It was held in place with only a few pins, which came out when Sirena pulled. The dark tresses flew out into a long waterfall of a ponytail, which flowed down Jessie's back. "Do you want me to take it all down?"

"Yes," Sirena murmured, moving closer still. As Jessie reached up to pull the ponytail holder out of her hair, Sirena leaned down to brush her lips on Jessie's neck, just below her ear.

Jessie felt her knees nearly buckle as desire shot through her like a cannonball. Her hair cascaded around her until Sirena gathered it up in her fist and pulled Jessie's lips toward her. Jessie had always thought Sirena was more of a submissive partner, not in a BDSM-type way, but preferring her partner to make the moves. She had always thought of her as a Pillow Princess, a woman who enjoys receiving pleasure from a partner who enjoys giving it. But the way Sirena's lips were attacking hers as her nude body pressed against the stiff fabric of Jessie's uniform was swaying her opinion.

As their tongues danced together, Sirena made quick work of the button and zipper on Jessie's uniform shirt, peeling it away to expose her undershirt and vest. It didn't take her long to figure out how the vest attached, and she pulled the velcro strips holding it in place and lifted it over Jessie's head until it was free to be discarded on the floor. Then she did the same with Jessie's plain white tank top, lifting it off and tossing it aside until Jessie was standing before her in nothing but a white lace bra and her uniform pants.

But Sirena didn't stop there. She reached down and squeezed Jessie's body to hers, aligning their hips until sparks shot through Jessie's core. She had no idea what to expect next, what Sirena had in mind, but she had to admit that having her in control was sending her need spiraling to the point of no return. Sirena moved her hands toward the front of Jessie's body, fumbling with the button and zipper on her pants. Jessie's hips were wide, so she had to help work her tight-fitting pants down her thighs until she could step out of them. Then she was down to her white lace bra and lime green and white polka dot boy shorts.

"Those are cute," Sirena said, stepping back a bit to get a look. "You have a really lovely shape, you know that?"

Jessie felt the heat on her cheeks again. She'd always been a little self-conscious of her pear shape, especially since her hips were so much wider than her shoulders. She had perky, taut little breasts, which she liked, but her thighs reminded her of tree trunks before they narrowed into shapely calves and delicate ankles and feet. At 5'2", she did have pretty little feet and wore a size 6 shoe.

But when Sirena's long, elegant fingers trailed down her sides and hips, she didn't feel unwieldy or out of proportion at all. She felt lush and feminine, two qualities she always appreciated in other woman's bodies, but never felt like she could claim for herself. Something was different about Sirena's touch, though, something about her raw sexuality, the way her touch felt hungry and needy.

"Come on," Sirena whispered in her ear, following it up with another hot, steamy kiss right below it. Jessie didn't even ask where they were going, just let Sirena guide her into the bedroom where she led her to the bed and pushed her down on top of it. There was no way Jessie was going to protest, not when Sirena's silky smooth body came to rest on top of hers, and she felt the heat of her skin disperse across her.

"You're so fucking beautiful," Jessie murmured as Sirena's mouth found her neck again. She turned her head and captured Sirena's lips with her own, claiming them with her tongue and teeth. As she kissed her, Sirena's hands wandered to Jessie's heaving breasts cupping their small, firm mounds in her palms and squeezing them gently.

"So lovely," Sirena said, her voice a soft sigh soaking into Jessie's skin. She stretched the tip of her tongue out to tease Jessie's nipple, coaxing it to a stiff peak in no time at all. Jessie gasped as Sirena took it into her mouth, raking her teeth over the areola and feeling her nipple harden even more. Her back arched with pleasure, and Sirena dwelled there, giving each nipple adequate attention as her hands explored Jessie's lush curves.

Jessie hadn't been this aroused in so long, and though she loved to please her partner, she felt like she might explode if she didn't have her own orgasm this time. Jessie reached behind Sirena, stroking her hands down her back, feeling how soft her skin was as her fingers trailed over it. She found the globes of Sirena's remarkably firm, supple ass and gave them a squeeze, pressing her down onto her own pelvis, attempting to relieve a bit of the pressure. But it only made things worse.

As if sensing her growing desperation, Sirena wrestled free from her grip and slithered down Jessie's body, stopping every so often to paint her tawny skin with a stroke of her lips, on her soft abdomen, at her hip and across her mound of springy curls. She came to rest between Jessie's voluptuous thighs and propped her chin on her hand as she gazed up into Jessie's lusty, smoldering eyes.

"You probably should let me take a shower first...if you're planning to go down on me," Jessie warned her. "I—"

"Shhhh," Sirena said, letting her hot breath fall against Jessie's pulsating core. "I want to make you come for a change."

"That's sweet, but really—"

"No," Sirena said firmly, taking the tip of her tongue and using it to gently part Jessie's swollen-with-lust folds. She inhaled a deep breath, absorbing Jessie's scent into her system, her desire so pungent it amplified within her and mingled with her own to create a powerful perfume of feminine arousal. "I could bottle this scent up and sell it for millions," she purred, the words humming into Jessie's core.

"You think so?" Jessie gasped as Sirena's tongue delved ever so slightly into her, lightly lashing her clit.

"Mmmmmm..." Her throat vibrated the words as tangibly as if she'd taken one of her fingers and stroked it down Jessie's slit. "You are so. Damn. Wet. Jessie..." She was clearly enjoying the way her words were causing Jessie to squirm beneath her.

"Such a fucking tease," Jessie complained. "I should have known."

"What fun is it if I can't tease you just a little?" she protested. "You've done it to me. And turnabout is fair play."

Jessie chuckled before the sound transformed into another gasp as Sirena lightly sucked her clit into her mouth. She suckled for just the briefest moment and then popped back up to look at Jessie.

Jessie's skin had started to slick with sweat, and

her chest was heaving up and down. She hadn't been this on edge for a long, long time. She'd gotten used to pleasuring herself, usually with a little vibrating bullet, and she'd gotten "getting off" down to a science. It only took her 2 minutes. Max. So to put the fate of her orgasm in another's hands was really a challenge for her. It was taking everything she had not to just reach down and finish the job. Her thighs were trembling, her breaths shaky as she waited for Sirena to speak. And she *knew* she was about to speak; she could almost see the words dangling off her tongue, which she wished was back on her clit with a ferocity she didn't recall ever desiring.

"No penetration?" she asked, a knowing expression on her face.

Jessie shook her head. "No, please...just your mouth...god...please?" Even her words were quivering, right alongside the rest of her nerves, which were strung to the very edge of sanity as she awaited that blessed contact with her pussy.

"Just checking!" Sirena quirked her lips into a devilish smile and made a show of slowly, seductively lowering her head back to the matter at hand. She made another long stroke up Jessie's slit with her tongue, causing Jessie to nearly leap off the bed. She braced herself, holding Jessie's thighs down with her forearms, leaning in to put her whole body into the act.

Jessie had never been overly impressed with the way that bi girls—and especially not the straight ones masquerading as bi—ate pussy. But Sirena had this teasing thing down pat. She could teach a class on teasing, in fact. She had licked and nibbled at every square inch of Jessie's lady parts without concentrating too long in any one spot and without establishing any type of rhythm. It was enough to make Jessie mad, especially since she was used to the constant vibration of her bullet. She groaned as Sirena made her way back to her clit again, the pressure building up so tightly inside her that she fisted the sheets, squeezing them tightly as she tried to control Sirena's tongue, willing it to do what she needed it to do to bring her to climax.

But Sirena refused. She was a butterfly flitting about from flower to flower, only giving sporadic attention to the tight rosebud that needed her sweet touch more than any other plant in the garden. "Fuck, Sirena, you're killing me!" Jessie moaned, her hips bucking against Sirena as she continued her long, masterful torture session.

"Settle down," Sirena murmured, the sound vibrating right through Jessie's clit, almost as strongly as her bullet. It was almost enough...it had taken her right to the brink and left her hanging on the cliff. She felt herself suspended, dangling there as she awaited her fate.

Sirena reached up and cupped Jessie's pert B-cup breast in her hand, squeezing ever so gently as Jessie writhed beneath her. Jessie sighed as Sirena's thumb and forefinger trapped her taut, needy nipple between them and pinched it hard enough to make her squeal. At that precise moment, Sirena's lips enclosed over Jessie's clit, sucking it with the perfect rhythm to seduce her body into freefall.

And Jessie tumbled, falling head over heels through a thick dust cloud of shimmering sparks, all raining down on her, the universe swallowing her up into a galaxy of never-ending stars. Her body shook violently as it rolled through her like a summer storm, so strong and so powerful, she lost all sense of reality as she rode wave after wave of pleasure.

Sirena never relaxed her grip, seeing her through all the way. Until at the end, when Jessie was reduced to a mass of goo, intermittent, pulsating spasms still afflicting her. Her voice had been stolen, and her lungs struggled to take their first breaths of earthly air since returning from the depths of space.

Sirena crawled up Jessie's body, wrapping her arms around the quivering puddle into which Jessie had been rendered, and hugged her tightly to her body. She rocked her gently as Jessie fully returned to earth, still too shocked to utter a word. Sirena didn't seem to mind, she just kissed Jessie softly on the scalp and said, "I think you needed that."

THIRTEEN

Grief is like the ocean; it comes on waves ebbing and flowing. Sometimes the water is calm, and sometimes it is overwhelming. All we can do is learn to swim.
–Vicki Harrison

The call came that night, late, as these types of calls do. Sirena had been in and out of sleep, mumbling and restless ever since Jessie had returned the favor. She hadn't even wanted to eat dinner. Her body was still healing. *Her mind may never heal*, Jessie realized.

Jessie jerked awake at the sound of the ringtone, but the form lying next to her twisted up in the sheets barely stirred. She scrambled for Sirena's phone, hoping all of the activity would jostle her awake. Finally, she was able to shove the phone into a groggy Sirena's hand and help lift it to her ear.

Jessie couldn't make out the words on the other end, but she did notice how swiftly Sirena's eyes flashed open. She mumbled a few words back and then threw the phone onto the bed. Her tired eyes met Jessie's. "We have to go now."

Shit. Jessie wasn't sure how she was going to miss work again. She'd have to figure out what to do. She glanced at the clock, and it was only 1 AM. There was a chance she could drive the three hours up to Pennsylvania, leave Sirena there, and still make it back in time for her shift. *Well, maybe. If I drive like a bat out of hell.*

She jumped out of bed, the adrenaline surging through her. She expected Sirena to be every bit as wired, but she was still groggy and moving slowly. Jessie did everything she could to hurry her along. *Fuck, what should I do with Georgia?* she thought as she noticed the dog curled up at the end of their bed, completely oblivious to all the commotion. *I'll have to call Paisley or Leah. Fuck.*

She had no idea how long Sirena would need to be away, so she just threw a bunch of shorts, shirts and dresses into a duffle bag and pulled Sirena out of the shower after it had already been ten minutes.

"Why are you rushing? He's either going to make it or he's not. It's not like we have any choice in the matter," she noted with more stoicism than Jessie expected.

"I've got to be back for work at eight." She felt selfish telling her, but it had to be said.

"Just give me your car, and I'll go by myself," Sirena offered, drying herself with the towel Jessie had handed her.

"No, you're not going by yourself," Jessie answered firmly. There was no way she was going to budge on that.

Sirena let out a long sigh. "You know I'm a grown woman, right? And almost old enough to be your mom?"

"Come on, just get dressed, and let's get out of here. It's all going to work out."

Another ten minutes after that, they were riding the elevator down to the parking lot. Jessie packed down the car and squealed out of the lot. She had never gotten a speeding ticket, no matter how fast she drove. As soon as she pulled out her wallet, which had space for her badge and police ID on one side and her driver's license on the other side, any cop who pulled her over simply waved and said, "Drive safely." It was professional courtesy. She did the same thing for any fellow officers she pulled over in her jurisdiction.

She scrambled for the state line, flying up Route 1 at 85 miles per hour. It was late on a weekday, and there were hardly any cars on the road. She passed into Delaware and surged over the Inlet Bridge. Even in the busy tourist town of Rehoboth Beach, there weren't too many people out at this hour. She kept expecting to see flashing lights, but didn't.

She hit Dover and then Wilmington, in awe of the incredible time they were making. *It won't be much longer now*, she thought, as she instructed Sirena to put the address for the hospice facility into her GPS. She complied, and the smooth woman's voice told them they'd reach their destination in forty-five minutes. *Not bad*, she thought, silently congratulating herself on being able to make the trip so fast.

It wasn't long after they passed into Pennsylvania that her rearview mirror lit up with flashing red and blue lights. "Motherfucker!" she shouted, slamming on her brakes and pulling over to the shoulder. Sirena shot her a worried look, but Jessie shrugged it off. "It'll be okay. I got this."

Jessie's heart started to flutter a bit as she watched the officer approaching with his flashlight illuminating his path. She got her wallet with her OCPD ID, badge and license ready to hand to him and rolled her window down. His footsteps grew closer; she could hear his boots crunching in the loose gravel at the side of the road.

He shined the flashlight right into her eyes, temporarily blinding her. The first thing she heard after he took her license was a deep chuckle, right before her eyes regained sight. *What the fuck?* she wondered, trailing her eyes up his body. The officer was so tall that when he was standing up, she couldn't see his face. Then he bent back down into view.

It was Officer Grayson whom she'd met during Sirena's stay in the hospital. And Sirena had never called him back. She refused to. *Shit.*

"OCPD, right. I remember you," he said, handing her back the wallet. "And this is Mrs. Patterson, right?"

Sirena nodded, but her face had drained of color; Jessie could tell that much in the harsh white beam of the flashlight.

"Did you just get out of the hospital?" he asked. Apparently he wasn't going to address the true reason for the stop.

Sirena nodded hesitantly, then squeaked out, "We spent a couple days in Ocean City, but now my husband is dying, and I am trying to get to the hospice care place before he does." Her voice grew stronger and more defensive with every word.

Officer Grayson's eyes darted between the two ladies while he contemplated what to do. Then he simply said, "Drive carefully," and headed back to his cruiser. In seconds, he'd turned the lights off and slowly pulled onto the highway.

Jessie let out a breath as she reached for the gearshift. "Small world, huh?"

"I didn't call him back like you told me to. I thought he was going to—"

"Don't worry about it," Jessie cut her off. "You have enough on your plate at the moment."

They pulled into the parking lot at the hospice care facility less than three hours after they left Ocean City. Dawn had yet to break but was flirting with the horizon, warming it up in the far eastern skies as a few clouds hung low over the tree line in the west, hoping to sleep in. The two women were silent as they stepped out of Jessie's car and made their way inside. No words came at all until Sirena approached the information desk in the lobby and simply asked for Joseph Patterson. She didn't even look back at Jessie as the large wooden double doors opened, swallowing her down a long, gleaming white hallway.

Jessie stood frozen for a moment until the

receptionist gently asked if she would like to take a seat. She gave a slight nod and turned to find the nearest chair. It felt like hours as her eyes burned holes into the wall on the opposite side of the building. She had learned everything she could about the waiting room: the dreary blue drapes; the soft, bucolic farm scenes in the paintings on the wall; and the few people waiting alongside her. She wished she felt some sort of camaraderie with them, a solidarity. But they were simply strangers living out their own tragic stories. She couldn't get a read on any of them like she usually could. She liked to invent little stories in her mind about each character she encountered, and she had a feeling she was right more often than she was wrong. But today those faces were blank. Their stories were untold.

She finally looked at the clock and saw it was nearly 5 AM. She was going to be late for work if she didn't leave right that minute. The two choices pulled at her, stretching her limbs to their absolute limits; she nearly felt herself rip down the middle. Every time she questioned her obligation to Sirena, she found her heart crying out about compassion and duty. And every time she questioned her obligation to work, she found her mind arguing about her future and priorities.

In the end, she stood up and sent Sirena a text that said *I have to work today. But I'll be back tonight.*

There is no way I can keep driving back and forth, she thought as she headed south. She wondered how long Sirena would need to stay in Pennsylvania. She still wasn't sure why she felt obligated to be part of this mess, but she knew Sirena had no business staying in that horrible trailer that truthfully needed to be condemned. *I've got to get her down to Ocean City permanently*, Jessie thought. *So she can start a new life. Just like I did.*

Jessie wasn't expecting her sergeant to call her that afternoon and ask her to meet him at the substation on the boardwalk. Bart gave her an *uh oh, you're in trouble* look before sending her down south without him. He was going to a complaint.

Jessie found Sgt. Grimes in the office, his eyes engrossed on the screen of the desktop monitor. She cleared her throat, and his gray eyes immediately rocketed to hers. She knew she'd be able to tell his mood from what his mouth did, and it immediately spread into a smile. Just the fact that the corners of his mouth turned up made her release the breath she was holding.

"What's up, Sarge?"

"Martinez," he said, still smiling. "Have a seat."

Her brows scrunched together as she sat down, her mind rambling over a million different things that could warrant being called to the principal's office. At least that's what it felt like. Like the time in high school when the principal's car was literally flipped over in the parking lot—a senior prank. And Jessie's brothers were suspected of being involved. Jessie was called to the principal's office and interrogated regarding their whereabouts because they hadn't bothered to show up for school that day. Not only were they playing hooky, but they'd also roped some friends of theirs into helping with the car.

"Farris told me he was concerned about you," Sgt. Grimes explained, folding his hands together on top of his desk and piercing her with his gray eyes.

"What?" Jessie scoffed. "What do you mean 'concerned?'"

"He said you were having some family issues."

She tried to stop a little gasp that made its way out of her mouth. She was going to have to beat Bart's ass the next time she saw him. *Which would probably be in about fifteen minutes*, she reckoned, clenching her hands into fists.

"Well, is it true?" he pressed.

Her mind felt like scrambled eggs as she tried to find the right words. "It's not affecting my ability to perform my job," she settled on.

He laughed. "I know that, Martinez. But after what happened to you a couple weeks ago when you responded to that suspicious person report, and now hearing you have some personal stuff going on...I took the liberty of checking your records. Other than the couple of days you took off when you were sick last week, you haven't had a full week off in the last six months. That's against department policy, Martinez. And it's my fault for letting it slip through the cracks."

"But I—"

"No buts. You need to take some time before the Chief finds out and rips me a new asshole." He chuckled as he held up what she presumed to be her personnel file. "You aren't to report back until the sixteenth."

"Sixteenth? But that's more than a week," she protested. "And it's tourist season. I can't—"

"Martinez." He folded his arms across his chest and shook his head. "Why are you arguing with me? Any other officer would be jumping for joy if they were given paid leave."

She just stared at him, dumbfounded. "I'm sorry, Sir," she finally managed.

"That's more like it. Now get out of here. I don't want to see you again until the sixteenth, you hear?"

"Yes, Sarge," she answered, trying to suppress a grin. She walked out of the substation not knowing whether she was going to kill Bart or give him a high five.

When Jessie arrived back at her condo, Georgia was so excited to see her, she nearly knocked her down. "I missed you too, girl!" she said, patting the panting, tail-wagging furry beast. She immediately fell to the ground and rolled onto her back, exposing her belly for additional rubbing and petting. Jessie couldn't believe how much the dog had grown on her in a short time.

Now the question was, what was she going to do with this dog while she figured out the Sirena thing? She obviously needed to go back to Pennsylvania, but she had no idea how she was going to deal with the dog. She was just getting ready to call Sirena to check on her when her phone rang.

"Hello?" She had no idea why Leah would be calling her. She hadn't gotten a call from Leah since the day she'd been summoned to The Factory and asked to shadow Sirena.

"Hey, is this a bad time?" Leah asked.

"Uh," Jessie hesitated, looking into Georgia's pitiful brown eyes. *If she could speak, she would be begging to go outside,* Jessie noted. She headed to retrieve the leash off the kitchen counter and the dog's ears immediately perked. Then she let out an excited bark.

"Is that a dog?" Leah questioned. "I didn't know you had a dog!"

"Oh, it's not mine." She had nearly forgotten that Leah and Cap were dog owners, but the unmistakable sound of canine love in Leah's voice served as a reminder. "I'm just dog-sitting for Sirena."

"Oh. I was going to ask if you two wanted to come help decorate for Casey's party this weekend. But it sounds like you are busy," Leah explained.

"I would love to," Jessie answered, "but things are a bit crazy here right now. I took Sirena back up to PA this morning; the hospice people called and said it wouldn't be long."

"Wow, I'm so sorry, Jessie. Is she okay?"

"I don't know. I had to leave her up there and then come back and work a shift. And I had left the dog down here too. I'm not sure what to do now, though. I have some time off work, but if I go back up there, it's not like I have a place to stay—"

"That's right; you said her place was uninhabitable, right?"

"Yeah. Might have to get a hotel up there. I have no idea how long we'll be gone, but Sirena is going to have to figure out what she's going to do."

"And she doesn't have any other family up there?"

"Not that I know of."

"Let me take the dog," Leah offered. "Then there's at least one thing you don't have to worry about."

"I can't let you do that, Leah," Jessie protested. "You have Lincoln, plus Casey's party to worry about, not to mention your little bun in the oven."

"No, really, please let me help, okay? Cap's daughter is here this week. We have extra hands on deck," she insisted. "It's the least I can do... I feel responsible for getting you involved in this whole mess."

That's right, Leah is who I'm supposed to blame when I get my heart broken, a little thought flashed through Jessie's mind. "Are you absolutely sure?"

"Yes. Let me text you our address, and you can come drop him off right now." Jessie could hear the smile in her voice. "And I will be praying for Sirena too," she added.

"Thank you so much, Leah. It would be a big help. It's a 'she,' by the way. Are you sure she'll get along okay with your other dogs?"

"Oh, yes. Keeper and Glory are always happy to have canine company!"

Jessie laughed. "Okay. We'll be right there." She clipped the leash to Georgia's collar and led her out of the condo. *I'll have to come back for some stuff on my way out of town*, she realized. She didn't want to make Georgia wait any longer to do her business.

The dog was so excited to have the fresh air on her face after Jessie coaxed her into the car with a treat she had hiding in her pocket. Georgia rode with her long tongue flapping in the wind the entire way to Berlin, where Cap and Leah lived on Ayres Creek, not far from the fake address for Sirena that Jessie had scoped out weeks ago now. She briefly thought about how mysterious the golden goddess still was, even after all she had learned in the time she'd known her. *I feel like I could spend every day with her and still not understand her*, she thought.

When Leah answered the door, she had a toddler clinging to her leg. "Well, hello, Lincoln!" Jessie beamed at the adorable blue-eyed boy. He had strawberry blonde hair like his mom, but his eyes and dimples were carbon copies of his father's.

Georgia was so excited to see a little person, she nearly knocked him over. And in a flash, Keeper, Cap's chocolate lab, and Glory, Leah's beagle, were on the scene to check out the commotion and greet their visitors. Naturally, a lot of butt-sniffing ensued. None of the dogs growled or barked at each other, so Jessie considered that a minor victory.

"Her name's Georgia," Jessie said, handing over the leash to Leah.

"Doggie!" Lincoln exclaimed, heading back over to give the new dog a pat on the head. She sniffed him rather thoroughly and was seemingly pleased with the results.

"I wish I knew more," Jessie apologized. "But I'll keep you in the loop."

"Thanks." Leah gave her a reassuring smile. "I hope you will be able to make it back for Casey's party. She would really hate missing you."

"I know." The idea of missing it caused a sharp pang of sadness to shoot through her heart. "Thanks again for doing this, Leah. You have absolutely no idea how much it means to me."

"Like I said, it's the least I can do." She reached out and gave Jessie a hug. "I know I said I would pray for Sirena earlier. But I'm going to be praying for you too, okay?"

Jessie's lips turned up into a smile. "Thanks. I have a feeling I'm going to need it."

Jessie sent Sirena a text before leaving Ocean City, but she heard nothing back. She rolled into the parking lot of the hospice facility, where she had dropped Sirena off a mere twelve hours earlier. She couldn't believe she had spent 9 of the last 24 hours in her car. More than that if she counted the time she'd been in her patrol car at work.

She asked for Sirena at the desk, and the receptionist said that she left earlier in the day. And, naturally, due to HIPAA, she couldn't get any more information. "Thanks a lot," Jessie said in return, but she didn't mean it nearly as friendly as it came out.

Her legs balked at the idea of getting back in her car, but what choice did she have? She drove twenty minutes to Sirena's depressing trailer, but no lights were on, and her gold Honda was gone. She took out her phone and tried to call, but it went straight to voicemail.

Perfect. I'm in fucking Pennsylvania for this crazy chick who is MIA. Pretty much the last place in the world I want to be, and yet here I am. She beat her fists against her steering wheel until she could feel her heartbeat throbbing through her hands.

She thought about everything she had done for this woman. *Drove three hours in the middle of the night. Drove three hours back to Ocean City to work. Got called to the sergeant's office. Took care of her dog, dumping her with a pregnant lady who needs another thing to stress about as badly as a fish needs a bicycle. Then I got all my stuff together and drove another three fucking hours only for her to be gone without a trace. That's just awesome.*

She'd had no sleep, hardly anything to eat, and her head was pounding just as hard as she'd pounded her fists against the steering wheel. She leaned her seat back and closed her eyes before the tears stinging at them had a chance to fall. She was beyond the point of exhaustion. Beyond the point of pretty much any feelings at all, except her eyes hadn't apparently gotten that memo.

She didn't notice the sun slipping down into the pocket of trees in the distance, burning its orange goodbye into the bark as it lost its battle to the moon rising in the east. She was beginning to settle into a dream of walking Georgia along the shoreline, right in that space where the waves intermittently reach just far enough to splash over feet and whisk away footprints, sending them out to sea. A knock on her window jolted her eyes open and jumpstarted her heart to the point she thought it might crack her ribs.

She felt her breath begin to return when she realized it was Sirena. She had knocked then walked away from the car. Jessie saw her form silhouetted against the very last remnants of the sunset. She forced her bleary eyes to focus and made her way out of the car. "Sirena?" she called as she stepped toward the woman, who stood facing her home with her arms crossed and her blonde hair flying like a cape behind her in the dusky breeze.

Just as Jessie reached her, she whipped around. Her eyes met Jessie's and told the story before she could utter a word. They were cracked with red streaks, evidence of all the tears that had been shed, her eyelids swollen and painful-looking. And when words came to her lips, which were dry and colorless, they only moved just enough to say, "He's gone."

Jessie couldn't begin to understand the heartache this woman felt for a man who, in her estimation, had only caused her anguish and pain, but she wrapped her in her arms nonetheless. Who was she to question her grief?

FOURTEEN

But pain's like water. It finds a way to push through any seal. There's no way to stop it. Sometimes you have to let yourself sink inside of it before you can learn how to swim to the surface. — Katie Kacvinsky

There are only so many ways you can comfort someone who is grieving. Platitudes are not helpful. Telling someone their loved one is free of pain and is finally at peace is hardly reassuring. It can't possibly soothe the gaping hole that is left. But comforting the grieving widow of a man who was addicted and abusive is even worse. Jessie was at a loss. She settled for silence and the eternal truth of "actions speak louder than words."

Sirena was numb. Getting people who are numb to make decisions, to spur them to action, is no small challenge. It felt like trying to move a mountain. Jessie called funeral homes. Jessie made appointments. Jessie wrote checks from an account she wasn't even sure had the funds needed. All while Sirena became a ghost.

But on the third day, she seemed to snap out of it. Like a miracle was touching down on an angel's wings, she looked at Jessie and asked, "We're going to Casey's party on Saturday, right?"

Jessie's brows flew up her forehead. "What?"

"Isn't Casey's going away party on Saturday at The Factory?" Her eyelashes fluttered as the tiniest of smiles curled the corners of her lips upward.

"I didn't think—" Jessie started, searching her lover's face for signs of anguish. The hollow look Sirena had worn to bed the night before was gone. Vanished. Poof.

Sirena's shoulders lifted into a shrug. "I don't think it's fair for you to miss a party just because I've had a rough week."

"Rough week?" Jessie repeated. "I'd say it's more than a rough week."

"Now that we're just waiting for Joe's remains to be ready, there's no reason for us to stay here. Besides, I don't like the idea of you paying for this hotel room anyway. I think I'm ready for a distraction!" She laughed in spite of herself. It sounded like bells chiming in a far-away tower, bells that hadn't been rung in centuries.

"I don't even know what to say. I just didn't think you'd be up for a party." Jessie folded her arms across her chest as she continued to study Sirena's face. It was smooth and clear. No makeup, just her pure, unblemished porcelain skin. Her straight nose. High cheekbones. And mesmerizing green eyes. All framed by golden waves of silky blonde hair.

She was a goddess. One who looked as though she'd been resurrected. But Jessie didn't understand what had changed. They were still in Pennsylvania waiting for Sirena to be able to pick up Joe's remains and to take care of paperwork. She didn't want to have any type of memorial service. She just wanted to take the ashes back down to Ocean City for a burial at sea.

"Why?" Jessie asked, surprised Sirena would want to take her husband's remains to her place of refuge from him.

"He loved the water. He loved Ocean City. We went there on our honeymoon." It was the first time Jessie saw any evidence of happiness, a sign there had been a tiny glimmer of joy in their marriage, even if the joy was short-lived. She still didn't understand how they'd gotten from point A to point B. She assumed Sirena would tell her someday—if she wanted to. And if not? Then clearly it would remain as murky as a muddy swamp.

"So we'll have to come back up here...when? Next week? Don't you have other things you need to take care of? What about the trailer?"

Sirena lost the far-away misty look she'd gotten thinking of her honeymoon as her lips set into a thin line of reality. "Nothing that can't wait until we come back. I'm not sure what to do with everything."

"We'll figure it out," Jessie assured her.

"Aren't you from this area?" Sirena questioned as though she were eager to change the subject.

Jessie let out a sigh. If Sirena wanted to put off the reality of getting her affairs in order until the following week, then she understood completely. Jessie wanted to put off sharing the details of her past indefinitely.

She'd never told anyone. Except Tori, the first girl she'd ever been with. And obviously that didn't turn out so well.

Sirena seemed to understand that she shouldn't press. "So yes to the party at The Factory, then?" Her lips spread into a beautiful smile, and Jessie wanted nothing more than to kiss it right off her. The past few days she'd tried to be the strong shoulder Sirena needed. The bulk of their physical closeness had been Jessie holding Sirena every time she broke down into tears. Jessie had so many questions about who this man was, what their marriage was about, why they didn't have any children. Why and how a million other things. All she'd gotten in the way of answers were tears. A deluge of tears. But it seemed as though they had finally run dry.

Jessie wasn't sure who was more happy to see Georgia: her or Sirena. If a dog's happiness could be measured, this mutt's was definitely off the charts. Her tail wagged as though battery-powered and her whole face lit up with a wide grin.

"Thank you so much for watching him while we were away," Sirena said to Leah and Cap. Jessie thought this might have been the first time they had ever been formally introduced. She wasn't sure why, but it was important to her that they all liked each other. She hoped that Leah and Cap could see that Sirena wasn't a problem after all, and that she'd been unfairly targeted by the rumors. She was clearly just a woman who needed a break from reality, a break she found at The Factory. Jessie had a feeling the Sheldons now understood that.

"I'm so sorry to hear about your husband passing," Leah offered.

Sirena glanced down at her feet, unable to meet Leah's gaze. Jessie watched her to see what would happen next. She hadn't mentioned Joe since they'd left Pennsylvania that morning.

"If there's anything we can do to help, please let us know," Cap added, waiting for Sirena to make eye contact with him. His dimples showed his sincerity; his ocean blue eyes radiated warmth.

"Thank you both so much," Sirena finally said, forcing a smile. Her eyes still reflected her sadness though. Her brokenness. "I'm really not sure what the next step is for me."

"Well, we'd be happy to have you here in Ocean City," Leah said. "There are always jobs in the hospitality industry, and I have a lot of connections from my time at The Pearl."

"We'll cross that bridge when we come to it," Jessie said, wrapping her arm around Sirena's shoulder and pulling her close to her body. She still felt the need to protect her, even though it seemed like the real person she needed protection from was now gone.

"You guys coming to the party tomorrow night?" Cap asked, sensing another change of topic was needed.

"Wouldn't miss it," Sirena said. This time her smile was genuine. "Thanks again for watching

Georgia. No wonder Jessie thinks so highly of you. You're such a lovely couple."

The way she said it made Jessie think Sirena wondered what the Sheldons might be like in bed. She knew Sirena had a penchant for couples, for fulfilling dreams of unicorns. For some reason, it made a little stabbing feeling in her heart to think of Sirena sleeping with Leah and Cap, even though she knew it was ridiculous for her to feel that way.

"I know Casey will be so glad you're both there," Leah said. "You're coming too, right, Jess? You're off work?"

Jessie nodded. She hadn't been called "Jess" in a long time. And she only went by Jessica at work, though it was almost always "Martinez" or "Officer Martinez." She shook off her uncomfortable feelings about that nickname as well as the ones about Sirena playing and walked over to give Leah a hug. She followed it up with one for Cap as well.

She needed to get over this sudden sensitivity that Sirena brought out of her. She wanted to stuff it back down deep inside her, to bury it in the sand. She didn't have time for anything but strength. Strength, resilience, and independence. They were the cornerstones of her entire existence. It was how she kept going. It was how she needed to keep going.

Sitting in her living room with Sirena surfing

Facebook and Georgia curled up on the ottoman, Jessie felt something domestic...even familial. She'd lived alone for so long, she wasn't used to having people or pets around. She had thought having company for so long would drive her crazy, but it was beginning to feel normal. Even nice.

"Do you have a Facebook account?" Sirena asked from her cross-legged position on the end of the sofa.

The thoughts she'd had popped like bubbles, vanishing into thin air but leaving behind that iridescent residue like soap does. "No, no," Jessie answered. "No social media."

"Ah, why not? I wanted to tag you in this photo I took of us with Georgia on the beach this morning." Her lips curled down into a little pout as she looked up from the computer screen.

"It's not advisable for police to have social media accounts," Jessie explained. "It's just not a good idea."

"Oh, so that means you've never been in The Factory's group on Facebook then?"

Jessie shook her head. "No, why?"

Sirena shrugged. "No reason. Everyone is talking about tonight's party. Complaining there won't be playtime."

Jessie's face brightened with amusement. "Oh, that's right. Leah wanted it to be 'classy.'" She glanced over toward the computer screen. "That might be a stretch for a few people at the club."

Sirena laughed. "No doubt. I need to figure out what to wear. I hope I have something."

"Do you want to go shopping? We could hit the

outlets if you want. It'll be a madhouse on a Saturday, but it's worth a shot. I don't know what I'll wear either."

"It's been a long time since I've been shopping with a girlfriend," Sirena observed. "Too long. That sounds fun. Maybe lunch too?"

"So you don't have...uh...girlfriends you hang out with regularly?" She had been meaning to ask, but the time had never seemed right.

Sirena scoffed. "You know the way Jeannette and the other ladies at The Factory look at me? There's only been a couple of females in my life I've ever been able to hang out with, and one of those was my sister."

"I've heard you mention your sister a couple times now. Are you two close? Where does she live?"

The smile faded from Sirena's face. "It's a long story. Let's go shopping, okay?"

Jessie also lacked platonic female friends, the type to go shopping and have lunch with—except Paisley, Leah, and Casey, of course. She had sort of assumed that straight women had lots of girlfriends. She hadn't considered Sirena wouldn't be like that.

She probably thinks of me that way. Like a straight girlfriend. Not a lover, Jessie thought as she and Sirena made their way toward the outlets. Other than the aforementioned women, Jessie didn't have much experience with straight girlfriends—not since high school, and they had all turned out to be two-faced bitches. Most of her girlfriends, the ones she'd had romantic relationships with, had not been the girly types. They didn't like to go shopping. They weren't into hair and makeup. They were low maintenance. Jessie thought of herself as low-maintenance too, but she was high maintenance compared to some of the women she'd dated.

Sirena was one of those women who seemed born with the innate knowledge of how to make her hair wavy and bouncy and how to create the perfect smoky eye. It was effortless for her. Jessie hadn't noticed her taking hours to get ready in the bathroom. She simply spent five minutes on her hair and face and voila, perfection. *Must be nice*, Jessie mused.

Looking so much younger than her true age, Sirena could get away with wearing trendy clothes. She didn't think twice about stepping into a shop even Jessie felt somewhat out of place in. "Isn't this for...like...twenty-somethings?" Jessie had asked, glancing around at the two salesladies who didn't look a day over 21.

Sirena shrugged. "Who the hell cares what they think?" she asked, loud enough for the salesladies to hear her. She ran her hand over a strapless jade-green dress. "What do you think of that?"

"It's...uh...wow," Jessie said. "You know I can't fit into anything in here, right?"

"Oh, I bet you can," Sirena argued. "What size are you?"

"Sixteen? Eighteen? I have a big fucking ass."

"I love your big fucking ass!" Her lips curled into a

smile as she found another dress on a different rack and held it up for Jessie to see. "What about this one?" It was fire engine red and also clingy and strapless.

"For you, right?" Jessie asked.

"No, silly woman. For you!"

"You've got to be kidding me." She shook her head, trying to suppress the laugher. There was no way her curvy ass was fitting into that garment.

"Will you just try it on?" Sirena asked. "I bet you oral that it looks great on you!"

Jessie felt heat creep up her neck just from the mention of the word. "Let me get this straight," she confirmed, her lip twisting up into a wicked smirk. "You're going to go down on me if this dress fits me."

"Not only will it fit you, but it will look amazing. Trust me on this," Sirena promised, crossing her fingers in an invisible x over her heart.

Jessie rolled her eyes. "Alrighty then. You're on."

Sirena giggled and pulled her toward the dressing room at the back of the store. The saleslady gave them a look of disapproval, but Sirena obviously didn't care.

"You go first," Jessie insisted.

"We're sharing a room," Sirena decided, and she pulled Jessie's arm, whipping her inside the handicapped stall at the end of the hall.

Jessie plopped down on the bench opposite the full-length mirror and crossed her arms over her chest. "Fine. But you try on your dress first."

Sirena said nothing, just smiled as she shimmied out of the tiny denim shorts she was wearing. All that remained on her bottom was a white cotton thong with tiny purple and pink flowers. Jessie couldn't take her eyes off Sirena's beautiful body, which soon became fully on display as Sirena pulled her loose, flowing floral sleeveless blouse up over her head, leaving her in a white lace bra. She giggled for a moment as if she were embarrassed to have Jessie's eyes plastered to her.

Jessie took the jade-colored dress off its hanger and handed it to Sirena, who kept her gaze pinned to Jessie as she unzipped and stepped into the garment. She slid the smooth material up her thighs and hips and pulled the bodice up around her breasts. "Guess I can't wear a bra with this, huh?" she questioned, still staring at Jessie.

"Damn. That's a shame," Jessie teased, biting her lower lip.

"Quit looking so fucking sexy and get over here to help me with this zipper," Sirena directed in a low voice.

Jessie flashed her a wicked grin and stood up to reach the zipper. She glided it up Sirena's back with absolutely no resistance. The dress couldn't possibly have fit better. It was like a glove designed especially for Sirena's stunning figure.

Sirena spun around, her hands on her hips. "Well, what do you think?"

Jessie couldn't begin to force a word out of her mouth; any semblance of speech she might produce was hopelessly stuck down her throat. She just stared, enraptured, at the beautiful creature in front of her. Even if she didn't win the bet, there was no way she was going to be able to keep her hands off Sirena. She wanted her so badly that desire began to pool between her thighs, and she could feel the hot, moist heat radiating from her core.

"Too much?" Sirena questioned, her eyes darting back and forth between Jessie's.

"Uh," Jessie managed. She reached out with both of her hands to smooth them down the sides of the dress, tracing Sirena's perfect curves. "Just the right amount." She pulled Sirena's body to hers and pressed her lips softly against her collarbone.

"Is it classy enough, though?" Sirena asked, ignoring the kiss and spinning around to check her reflection in the mirror. She pulled the skirt down, which hit at mid-thigh. She had a lot of leg showing. But the cut of the dress and the way it hugged her figure was anything but trashy. She still looked sophisticated. *She just happens to also look like sex on a stick*, Jessie noted. *And she can't even help it.*

"I love it," Jessie assured her. "The color. The cut. The way it hugs your luscious curves. It's beautiful...just like you."

Sirena's eyes rocketed from the mirror to Jessie's, where they rested for a moment before she spun back around. "You're too kind," she said, grinning. "Okay, you talked me into it. Now it's your turn." She left the jade dress on, and took Jessie's seat on the bench, leaving Jessie standing in the middle of the dressing room wishing she had stolen another kiss while she had the chance.

She slipped her own shorts off, as well as her t-shirt, leaving herself in her plain gray cotton sports bra and matching boy shorts. She suddenly wished she'd put on something sexier, but she didn't own a lot of girly lingerie. Most of what she had she reserved for wearing at The Factory when she visited.

"This is going to be a disaster, by the way," she said, pulling the red dress off its hanger and holding it up to look at it with skepticism. "No way it's going to fit over my ass."

"Just wait and see," Sirena insisted again. "It's very stretchy material."

"Here goes nothing," Jessie said, gritting her teeth. She was used to always putting dresses over her head and pulling them down rather than struggling to yank them up past her ample thighs and hips, not to mention her derriere, which stuck out like she had a built-in bustle. She always wondered what it would have been like to live in the era of bustled dresses. She would have fit right in.

She stretched the material over her breasts, then pulled it down her torso to her hips. She was surprised at how forgiving the fabric was. It was thick, but stretchy, and sort of sucked everything in, holding it in place. She tugged it down onto her thighs, pulling the material out a bit so it would fit over her backside. Once it was in place, she was almost afraid to look in the mirror, especially when she heard Sirena gasp.

Her eyes darted to Sirena's before she braved looking at her reflection. The expression on the blonde's face was one of surprise and...Jessie tried to interpret it...appreciation? Lust?

Jessie directed her eyes toward the mirror and drank in the image reflecting back at her. Yes, the gray sports bra was terribly out of place, but if she looked past that, she saw a body that looked like it belonged to someone else—not herself. Instead of looking pear-shaped or out-of-proportion, her shoulders looked strong and round, her breasts pert and curvaceous, and her waist sleek and trim. Her hips and thighs swelled out in a perfect wave of silky red, and the color contrasted beautifully against her tawny skin. She thought she'd been speechless when she'd seen Sirena in her dress, but she'd expected Sirena to look amazing. She never thought SHE would be capable of pulling off something like this.

"Jessie." Sirena lifted herself off the bench and paced toward her. She didn't get any other words out of her mouth before her lips captured Jessie's with an overwhelming and sudden need. She took Jessie into her arms, pressing their bodies against each other as they rode the waves of passion that consumed them whole.

The dresses both flew off in a flash, panties, bras, too. Jessie felt how hot Sirena's pussy was as it pressed against her, desperate for attention. Sirena's hands threaded through Jessie's thick, dark hair as she presented a masterclass in kissing. Jessie thought they might generate enough heat to melt the polar ice caps as Sirena forced her against the wall and slid down her body with her tongue leading the way.

"Here, sit on the bench," Sirena managed, her voice a low rasp. She didn't even give Jessie a chance to respond, just pushed her down and fell to her knees between Jessie's legs.

"We can't do this—"

"Shhh," Sirena said, pressing a kiss to Jessie's inner thighs as she spread them with the palms of her hands. "I'm going to make good on my bet."

"Wait, I thought I was getting oral if you were

wrong?" Jessie stopped her. "I mean, if the dress didn't fit."

"Whatever, you were getting oral either way," Sirena laughed and swiped her tongue between Jessie's lips. She moaned as Jessie's sweet honey juices infiltrated her taste buds. Reaching up Jessie's heaving chest, she captured one of her nipples between her thumb and forefinger as she sucked Jessie's clit into her mouth.

"Fuck," Jessie breathed out, hoping she could keep her volume down. She gripped the edges of the bench as it became apparent that Sirena was hell-bent on making her come. There was no way they were leaving this dressing room until Sirena had lapped up every last drop of Jessie's orgasm.

She felt the pressure inside her swell. The noises Sirena made while licking her pussy were unbelievably sexy. She couldn't believe the saleslady hadn't come to check on them. Or maybe she had, and the sounds of unabashed slurping had sent her running back to the sales floor. Or maybe they turned her on too? Maybe she was standing outside the dressing room, her own desire beginning to drip down onto her panties. Maybe she was contemplating inviting herself to join in.

Thinking about the saleslady getting off on watching them soon sent Jessie flying over the cliff, and as her body succumbed to ecstasy, she felt her whole core seize up before bursting into orgasmic bliss, drowning Sirena in a rolling sea of her pleasure.

FIFTEEN

Vulnerability is the essence of romance. It's the art of being uncalculated, the willingness to look foolish, the courage to say, 'This is me, and I'm interested in you enough to show you my flaws with the hope that you may embrace me for all that I am but, more important, all that I am not.' -Ashton Kutcher

Jessie was sure she saw Paisley and Calvin's jaws both drop when she and Sirena came through the doors of The Factory wearing their new dresses. Paisley's mouth spread into a grin as she gave Calvin a look that said *I told you so*. He shrugged, then grinned too.

"Oh, you guys look amazing!" Leah said coming down the stairs from the offices. "Thanks for coming early too to set up. I've been going over applications all day, and I didn't realize it was getting so late."

"Applications?" Jessie's eyebrows drew together.

"For the social media and outreach coordinator position," Paisley answered for Leah. "We are going to hold interviews next week."

"Oh, right!" Jessie nodded. "I almost forgot about that."

"Yeah, we're just sorry we didn't get our act together in time for Casey to sit in on the interviews. She flies out tomorrow." Leah frowned. It was written all over her face how much she was going to miss her mentor and friend.

"Speaking of the Woman of the Hour," Sirena chimed in, "where is she?"

"She should be here any minute," Calvin answered. "I think the caterers just pulled up, Leah. I'm going to go see if they need help."

"Have them pull around to the back bar entrance," Leah instructed, rubbing her lower abdomen. Her eyebrows furrowed for a moment, then a momentary flash of discomfort evaporated from her face.

"You okay?" Jessie didn't like what she just saw. *Leah is overdoing it*, she worried.

"Yeah, just a little growing pain. My doctor says it's normal to have more of those with a second pregnancy since the muscles are all stretched out."

"Is Cap with Lincoln?"

"Yeah, back at the house until he gets up from his nap. Then his big sister is taking over for the night."

Must be strange to have a little brother more than twenty years your junior, Jessie considered. She wondered if Cap's daughters would be having babies someday soon. They would end up around the same age as their uncle and soon-to-arrive aunt or uncle.

She glanced up and noticed Paisley was still

staring at her and Sirena. "What's wrong with you?"

"I just can't stop looking at you two," Paisley answered, awe in her voice. "You make quite a striking couple."

Jessie laughed. "Well, I don't know about couple..."

"Thank you," Sirena answered, and she flashed Jessie a smile as if she agreed. Jessie wasn't sure if it was with the striking part or the couple part of Paisley's statement.

"I'm so glad you both made it tonight," Leah said, gripping a clipboard with her checklist for the night's festivities. She was the most organized, focused person Jessie had ever met, and she had no doubt this party would run like clockwork. "Now, I have some assignments for you."

"I knew that was coming," Jessie joked, rolling her eyes. At that moment, the caterers' voices filled the back of the club, and she could hear Calvin giving them directions on where to put everything.

"Are either of you good with graphics or designing stuff?" Leah questioned with a hopeful look on her face. "I need little cards printed out for the buffet table and the drink specials, et cetera."

Jessie began to shake her head as she looked at Sirena, whose face brightened. "I can do stuff like that," she said excitedly.

"You can?" Jessie had a little flashing memory of Sirena sitting on her sofa, her eyes glued to the laptop screen as she cruised Facebook. She had no idea what kind of professional skills Sirena had—she didn't even know if she had a degree or career or anything. All she knew about was her taking care of Joe the past few months.

"Before my husband got sick, I worked in marketing and did all the social media for a chain of restaurants in Philly," Sirena answered. Jessie could hear the pride in her voice.

But what was most interesting was the expression that appeared on Leah's face. "Girl, you've been holding out on us. Why didn't YOU apply for the social media and outreach coordinator job?"

Sirena shrugged. "I didn't know about it."

"Let me take you up to the office and show you what I need," Leah answered, but Jessie could already see her wheels turning with ideas that went way beyond Casey's going away party.

She watched the two women walk up the steps to the office. Paisley was watching as well. "So, what's going on?" she asked Jessie as soon as the two were out of earshot. "And where did you get that dress? It is fucking fabulous!"

Jessie laughed. "I know, none of you are used to seeing me in stuff like this."

Calvin finished with his supervision of the caterers and joined their little huddle. "Hey, what's going on with Sirena?"

"That seems to be the question of the hour," Paisley answered, putting her arm around her husband.

"Everything is kind of weird right now," Jessie explained. "She's been on a roller coaster the past four days. And we're going to have to go back to PA next week to take care of some stuff. I really don't know what is going to happen, but for right now, she's staying with me."

"Are you guys...like...together, though?" Paisley whispered, even though there was no way Sirena was going to hear from upstairs.

Jessie shrugged. "I don't think so...though we did get it on in a dressing room today!" She chuckled, then felt a wave of heat rock through her when images of their encounter flashed before her eyes.

"Fuck, that's hot," Calvin noted. "Wish I'd had seen that."

"Just be careful, okay?" Paisley warned her. "It still seems like something is a bit off with her. Like she's hiding something else."

"Something else?" Jessie laughed. "She was hiding a husband who hit her and her real name, age, and address. I think that's probably all, don't you?"

Paisley's blue eyes were still as they locked onto Jessie's. "I'm just worried about you is all," she admitted. "I don't want to see you get hurt again."

By eight o'clock The Factory was throbbing with people, all wanting to give Casey Fontaine the send-off to California she deserved. As they had envisioned, the joint was classed up. Leah, as always, had done an incredible job of bringing together the right people, music, food, and decorations to do the occasion justice.

At 8:15, Leah stepped up onto the stage where the steel dance cages that normally swung on either side of the DJ both had been removed. The space had been draped with a waterfall of tiny twinkling LED lights which glowed from beneath a curtain of soft, flowing tulle. She took the microphone from the DJ and waited in the center of the stage while the song playing faded out. Once it was over, the DJ started another song and turned the volume down low to serve as background music.

"I thought about having him play 'Wind Beneath My Wings,' but that would be too much, wouldn't it?" she joked and the crowd roared in agreement. As the laughter died down, Leah reached out with her other hand and pointed at Casey. "Well, come up here, woman! We can't exactly give you a send-off without a speech."

The woman of honor was dressed to the nines, even more spectacularly than normal. She was wearing a glittering midnight blue evening gown that exposed her milky white shoulders. Her copper hair was set in soft curls that framed her face, and as usual, her makeup was completely flawless, showing off her beautiful porcelain skin which hardly looked like it had taken sixty-plus trips around the sun. Her beaming smile radiated all around the room as she made a slow, dignified walk toward the stage.

Jessie was so glad to see Casey looking more like herself, all made up and outfitted to perfection. The last few times she'd seen her, she looked tired, closer to her age, and was wearing loose-fitting clothes. But tonight, she looked like the radiant star she was, and her adoring fans couldn't get enough of it. There had to be three hundred people crammed into the lobby and dance floor of The Factory. Jessie was sure the OCFD would be...*alarmed...pardon the pun*...if they knew this size of crowd was assembled in such a small space. And it wasn't even a small space. There were just that many people.

Once Casey made it over to stand next to Leah, Leah didn't hand the microphone over right away. Instead, she swallowed hard, obviously overcome with emotion. Then she held the microphone to her lips as she wrapped one arm around Casey's shoulders. "This woman right here," Leah began, "Casey Fontaine, is an absolute legend in Ocean City. I will never ever forget in a million years the first time I met her. It was when she was hosting a party at The Pearl, where I used to work as the assistant general manager. I wanted so badly to impress this woman! As soon as I met her, I knew I was dealing with the utmost integrity and exquisite taste, and I wanted nothing more than to make sure her party was perfection. So much so, that I even ended up bartending it myself. I met Cap that night at the party she hosted, so I can say beyond a shadow of a doubt that my life changed forever as a result of meeting Casey Fontaine.

"She has been my business partner, my mentor, and most importantly, my friend. And I know she would do absolutely anything for me. I can't tell you how badly my heart is ripped in two knowing Casey is going off to California to fight for her life. I'm just absolutely shattered that I won't be seeing her every day like I do now. But I know she is going to fight the good fight, and she'll be the woman of honor at a victory party right here at The Factory very soon. I love you, Casey. Thank you for being you and helping mold me into the woman I am today."

Leah threw her arms around Casey and squeezed her so tightly that some feedback screeched through the PA system. With tears streaming down her cheeks, she pulled back and handed the microphone to a very misty-eyed Casey. The two women locked eyes with each other, and the whole crowd exploded into applause. Casey gave Leah a kiss on the cheek, then raised the microphone to her lips.

She paused for a moment to stare out at the crowd. The spotlight illuminating her meant that the crowd stood in the shadows, but she seemed to make eye contact with many of the people standing there, including Jessie.

"This is going to date me quite a bit," she said, her smooth voice echoing across the silent room, "but my father was a Marine who served in WWII. He was a tough old dude, no doubt about it. Besides being a vet, he also served in the U.S. Congress. He passed away about two years ago now, but one thing I remember him always telling me when I was growing up was to never stop fighting for what I believed in. He never stopped fighting as a Marine or for his constituents.

"I was a real estate agent here in Ocean City for just about thirty years, and I always fought to get my clients the best houses at the best prices, a work ethic I learned from my daddy. And when Cap and I decided to build this club, I fought to make it work. There was a time The Factory almost didn't come to fruition because of some gossip and misunderstandings, and I still fought with Cap to convince him to keep pursuing our dream. Once Leah was confirmed to come on board, the three of us fought to get this place up and running. Do you have any idea how bad it smelled in here when we first started out?"

There was laughter in the crowd. Casey's eyes flashed over to Leah, and she mouthed the words "thank you" before taking a deep breath and continuing her speech.

"And I have fought some other things too. I've had some personal battles. I've had my heart broken a time or two. I wanted to go out saying I don't have any regrets, but if I died tomorrow, that just wouldn't be true. I have a ton of regrets. But I've *never* regretted how hard I fought for the things and the people I believed in. Now it's time for me to focus that fighting spirit on myself.

"When I got the cancer diagnosis a few weeks ago, I kept it to myself at first. I am not sure if you've noticed, but I'm not exactly the type of person who feels comfortable asking for help. I'm independent. I've lived alone for the last twenty years of my life. I'm not too proud to admit I've even pushed away a few people who tried to get too close to me because I didn't want to have to rely on anyone.

"But I realized pretty quickly that cancer is not a battle you can fight alone. You need your own strength, to be certain, but you also need the strength of everyone around you: your doctors, your family, your friends. So I am pretty damn happy I have aligned myself with such amazing people. Because I know as hard as I plan to fight this thing myself, that all of you are going to be right alongside me fighting just as hard. And even if I'm in California and you're here, 3000 miles away, I know I'm going to feel your strength inside me. Thank you all for your love and support, and I promise this is not a forever goodbye. I'll be back before you know it!"

With that, a thunderous cheer went up from the

crowd and everyone raised their glasses to Casey, who raised hers high in the air. Jessie looked to Sirena and saw her eyes were glassy with tears. "You okay?" She wrapped her arm around the blonde's waist and pulled her body closer.

"Yeah, it's just so touching," Sirena whispered into Jessie's ear. "And I don't think there is one person in this room who doesn't think Casey will beat this thing. Casey versus cancer? Come on! My money is on Casey!"

Jessie laughed and nodded as Sirena pulled out her phone. "I should get some pictures before anyone gets too drunk," she said.

Jessie raised an eyebrow. They didn't typically allow photos to be taken during parties at The Factory, but she supposed since this was a vanilla event, it didn't matter. She thought Leah had hired a photographer. "Why do you need photos?" She was more curious as to why Sirena wanted them. She hardly even knew Casey.

"If I'm going to be the new social media coordinator, I'll need stuff to post on their accounts," she answered just as the DJ turned the music back up. The sound swallowed up Sirena's voice.

"What?" Jessie's eyes bulged out at this new information. She didn't wait for Sirena to answer because she knew she wouldn't be able to hear. Instead, she pulled Sirena down the hall into one of the empty play rooms. There wasn't supposed to be any playing, and they were greeted by a sign on the door that Sirena had apparently designed when she was upstairs helping Leah. It had the word PLAY in big letters with a circle around it and a big red slash, the universal sign for NO.

"We aren't supposed to be in here," Sirena protested as Jessie pulled the door closed.

"Since when are you such a rule follower? You certainly didn't care about rules in the dressing room earlier today!" Jessie teased her. "Now, what's this about a job?"

Sirena's face was beaming. "Leah wants to talk to Cap and Paisley first, but she thinks I'd be perfect for the social media and outreach coordinator position they're hiring."

"Wow, really?" Jessie wasn't sure if she was more surprised about the prospect of Sirena working at The Factory or her staying in Ocean City. They hadn't discussed what was going to happen after she settled her late husband's estate.

"Yeah, really," Sirena said, her face still glowing with pride. "I'm going to have to start over somewhere, and I thought..." The blonde's voice trailed off as she studied Jessie's eyes, trying to read the messages she was broadcasting from them.

Jessie's heart began pounding with the realization that this was it: the moment their relationship was delineated from its murky mess. Her nerves spiked with anxiety as a wave of intense dread passed over her. She hadn't realized until that moment her body flooded with panic how much her own happiness hinged on Sirena's future plans. And it seemed like it was all on the line right at this moment. Sirena would tell Jessie that her hospitality had been appreciated, but it was time to part ways. Jessie had been coasting along hoping to delay this conversation for as long as possible, but now it was staring her in the face. Sirena didn't need her anymore.

"So, you'll be getting a place down here then?" Jessie questioned, afraid to hope for the answer she longed to hear, as much as she had tried to deny it.

The smile melted from Sirena's face. In an instant, all traces of pride were gone, and a raging storm began to brew in her eyes.

"What?" Jessie's eyes darted back and forth between Sirena's, wondering why her face had suddenly become a tempest. She didn't understand why Sirena would be upset about Jessie questioning her decision to move to Ocean City. Unless, of course, she didn't think it was any of Jessie's business. Her heart felt as though it might explode at any moment as she awaited the truth.

"I, uh—" Sirena began, her gaze pinned to Jessie with the same intensity. Her stormy eyes began to fill with tears as though her hopes and plans were all being trampled upon, and she was powerless to stop it. Jessie could pinpoint the exact moment she gave up. When her heart retreated. "Never mind," she said, the words coming out on the heels of a sob. "Just never mind."

Jessie shook her head with bewilderment. "I don't understand, Sirena, wait!" She watched her body pivot to leave and instinctively reached out to grab her arm. "Please don't go. Maybe I'm being dense, but I don't understand what I said that was wrong."

Sirena's eyes were glowing bright green with tears as she slowly turned back to face Jessie. Her chest heaved as she fought off the deep, heart-wrenching sobs that seemed to be stuck in her throat. Jessie reached out again, pulling her body against hers and feeling her warmth soak into her skin. Sirena went limp like a rag doll in Jessie's arms, her body melding to Jessie's.

"I thought you wanted me to stay with you," Sirena finally managed, her words punctuated with soft whimpers.

Jessie felt a surge of heat bolt through her body as she scrambled to make sense of what was happening. "Of course, I want you to stay with me while you get back on your feet," she answered. "But I—" The whole time she had told herself it was temporary. She'd locked up any hope for more and thrown away the key.

"You what?" Sirena's head shot up from Jessie's shoulder, and her eyes snapped to Jessie's.

"We haven't talked about anything long-term...I mean as far as being roommates is concerned." Surely Sirena didn't think—she couldn't imagine that she had misread the situation. Jessie was the savior, the comforter...she had no delusions that it wouldn't all be over once Sirena got on her feet again.

"Jessie," she said, her voice clearing.

Jessie felt her heart begin to pound against her ribcage again. She saw the look in Sirena's eyes, and it made her tremble, afraid to hope for what she thought it meant. She stroked a finger down Sirena's cheek, smoothing away a few strands of her golden blonde hair that had fallen out of place due to her tears.

Sirena had a sudden look of courage wash over her face. She took a deep breath and stated, "I thought you got involved with me because you care about me." She cleared her throat of her remaining tears. "Because you...like me..." She let the words trail off.

Jessie's face flushed when she recognized the vulnerability painted on Sirena's face. "Of course I like you, Sirena. And of course I care about you. But I never thought a relationship was on the table...if that's what you're asking."

Her heart was thundering so fast now, she couldn't have slowed it down if she tried. Not even a deep breath helped. It was so intense, she could feel her heartbeat in her fingers, in her toes. Her whole body was pulsing with something between butterflies and fear of heartbreak.

Jessie swallowed hard as she gathered the courage to lay her cards on the table. "Is that what you're asking?"

"Why not?" Sirena questioned. "We slept together. Many times." She gave a little nervous laugh as though she was just as afraid of being rejected as Jessie was.

"Because I didn't think you were into girls that way. I thought it was just a fun sexual thing for you...you know, a lifestyle thing."

"I thought so at first," Sirena admitted, suggesting the reality had surprised her just as much as it was shocking Jessie.

Jessie's jaw hurt from forbidding a smile to crack on her lips. "But...now you feel differently?"

Biting her lower lip, Sirena reached down and took Jessie's hand into her own. She took a deep breath and closed her eyes for a moment as if she were gathering the courage to let the words on her heart flow through her mouth. "I'm pretty sure I'm falling in love with you."

Jessie's eyes stayed locked with Sirena's as she processed her words, what they meant, and how she could possibly respond when her heart was beating a million miles an hour and her brain was buzzing with more thoughts than a hive has bees. She had too many questions, but she knew she couldn't delay answering. The longer she waited, the faster the hope was dissolving from Sirena's eyes.

"God, Sirena," she managed. She pulled the woman into her arms, breathing in her delicious vanilla jasmine scent, letting it fill her lungs as though she wanted it to be permanently soaked into her cells. Her lips crashed against Sirena's, all tongue and fingers threaded through hair, bodies seeking heat, hands seeking flesh. It was all she could do to keep herself from throwing Sirena down on the bed and taking her right then and there in the off-limits playroom.

"Jessie," she whispered, "you know we can't here..."

Jessie let out a deep, frustrated sigh and gently pulled away. The part of her mind that wasn't concentrating on Sirena focused on whether or not it was a good idea to travel down this path. She still had a feeling she was being strung along, despite the sincerity she saw in Sirena's eyes.

She wanted to trust Sirena. She really did. But her brain was trying to reason with her in a loud, shrill voice about what a mistake she could be making. About the heartbreak she could be walking right into. And it wasn't just the fear Sirena could be using Jessie, but knowing she'd been on an emotional roller coaster with her husband's death and everything that went with it. She wasn't exactly in a good position for starting a new relationship. So why couldn't Jessie just tell her that? Refute her claims that she was falling in love?

Her heart took over, softening her features into a hopeful smile. "So, what, you want to be my girlfriend or something?" Sirena's chest was still heaving from their intense kiss.

She giggled, her face brightening. "Something like that?"

Jessie fought to keep a grin from fully spreading her lips. "And you're going to move in with me?"

Sirena's brows furrowed again with confusion. "I kind of already did...right?"

"Yes, I suppose you did...I just didn't know—"

Sirena pressed a finger to Jessie's lips. "Here's what I know, okay? I have nothing and no one in Pennsylvania. The Factory may be offering me a job. And I really like being with you, Jessie. You are so good for me."

"I am?" The thundering heartbeat was back...maybe twice as bad now.

"You are. I hope I can prove how good I can be for you too..." her voice trailed off in a sultry slur.

Jessie trailed her finger down Sirena's cheek again. She didn't say a word, but she hoped the same. *Hell, at this point, I'll settle for just not getting hurt.*

SIXTEEN

The best way to find out if you can trust somebody is to trust them. –Ernest Hemingway

Looking over at Sirena sleeping next to her, Jessie couldn't help but feel a mix of emotions. There was pride: *how is this beautiful creature in my bed?* There was contentment: *coming home to her after a long day of work is so rewarding.* There was fear: *all signs point to this being real, but what if she's using me?*

It had been a week since Casey's going away party. That night, Sirena and Jessie left arm and arm and returned to Jessie's condo where they made love all night. There was something different about their time together than previous times, a sense of investment, of establishment. Jessie fell asleep with Sirena's name on her lips, wondering if it was all too good to be true, but telling herself that only time would tell. And now, a week later, she was still waiting for time to render its verdict.

She gently shook Sirena's shoulder, urging her awake. "Baby, I've got to go back to work today," she whispered in her ear, reveling in the way Sirena's body shivered in response to Jessie's warm breath caressing her.

She stirred a bit, then stretched her long, lithe limbs. "But it's so early," she mumbled.

"Early bird catches the criminal," Jessie joked. She'd been lying awake for twenty minutes already, just reviewing everything that had happened in the last week she'd been off work. She didn't want to go back; she would much rather stay in bed with her girlfriend. But she also felt a deep sense of guilt for being away from work so long during the busy tourist season. Bart had even texted her the night before, saying he was looking forward to her return. *That's because he got stuck with Adamson the last two weeks, who is a notorious asshat,* she thought, yawning.

"What time will you be home?" Sirena asked.

"Hopefully by four." She stroked her fingertips down Sirena's cheeks, which were warm from sleep. She could just barely perceive the faded scent of her vanilla jasmine perfume.

"Is it okay for me to use your car?" Her tired eyes gained a sparkle of hope as she continued with her appeal. "I am supposed to report for duty today at The Factory."

"Yes, of course. We still need to go up and get your car. I keep forgetting about that."

"There's all sorts of unfinished business we need to take care of up there," Sirena answered. Jessie smiled at the way she used "we." "But I'm still waiting on the call that we can pick Joe up. I have no idea what is taking so long."

"Maybe next week. I am off Monday and Tuesday." Jessie forced a smile even though the idea of returning to Pennsylvania made her skin crawl. "My keys are on the kitchen counter. Good luck on your first day, honey." She pressed a soft kiss to Sirena's cheek.

"You can do better than that," Sirena said, pulling Jessie down on top of her. She brushed her lips against Jessie's, letting out a tiny sigh when their skin met.

"Welcome back, Martinez," was the first thing out of Sarge's mouth as the shift assembled for their beginning-of-the-week meeting.

Jessie just nodded. Bart gave her a little shove with his elbow, and she shot him a glare. Then he cracked a smile as though he was just teasing. They got their assignments and headed out to their cruisers to drive up north to look for a robbery suspect.

"What was that about?" Jessie questioned as soon as they were alone.

"What? The elbow?" Bart questioned, giving Jessie an unapologetic grin. "I'm just giving you a hard time. I missed you, that's all. How's married life?"

"What the fuck are you talking about?" Jessie's eyes narrowed. "I'm not fucking married, and you know it."

"Gotta live-in though, right?" He waggled his

brows and made a lewd gesture with his fingers and tongue.

Jessie pushed a sigh out of her mouth and rolled her eyes. "What difference does it make?"

Bart shrugged. "Hey, I'm happy for you. Is that okay? You know Simpson lives in your complex, right? He saw you a few times with your girlfriend."

"Fine, thank you. I'm glad you're happy for me," Jessie apologized.

"Happy and a little jealous," he admitted. "And a little...uh...curious."

She pursed her lips. "Curious about what?"

"What you two do together?"

She rolled her eyes for the second time and unlocked the door to her cruiser, hoping to end the conversation at that point. If there was one thing that annoyed her, it was men who were obsessed with girl-on-girl sex. She just didn't get it.

"It's really none of your business," she finally fired back when she noticed he was still standing there expecting a reply.

A broad grin stretched across his face. "I figured you'd say that. But you know, if you ever feel like—"

"I'm leaving now," Jessie stated. "Either get in and shut up or drive up there yourself."

"Fine, fine," he said, still grinning. "Can't blame a guy for trying."

Jessie ended up home a little later than she'd predicted. *That's what happens when I have to arrest a motherfucker for drunk driving in the middle of the fucking day*, she thought as she headed up the elevator to her floor. A storm seemed to be brewing to the south, but the skies to the north were golden and radiant. She hoped she and Sirena would be able to take Georgia for a walk before it rained.

She could faintly smell cooking from outside the door to her condo, and when she opened it, a delicious aroma greeted her with notes of garlic and onion. "Wow, what's going on in here?"

Sirena was standing in the kitchen wearing absolutely nothing but Jessie's burgundy and black striped apron. The top of it barely contained her breasts, which spilled out the sides and when she turned back toward the stove, her bare ass catching Jessie by surprise. "I'm making you dinner!" she revealed, though it was pretty obvious.

"To what do I owe this honor?" Jessie asked. "You're the one who had her first day of work. I should be cooking for you!" She reached up to give Sirena a kiss on the cheek.

"You work so hard," Sirena answered. "Just look at you, all sexy in that uniform. I can barely keep my hands off you."

"No one says you have to," Jessie fired back with a glint in her dark eyes. She pulled the ponytail holder out and shook her long, brown hair out around her shoulders.

"Hope you like fettucine alfredo," Sirena said, her mouth watering. Jessie wasn't sure if it was due to the dinner she was cooking or Jessie herself.

"It smells amazing. If it tastes half as good, I'll be in heaven." Jessie smiled and glanced around the kitchen. "What can I do to help?"

"Just showing up is all you needed to do. So glad you aren't much later! It's ready to go now!" Sirena gestured toward the table between the kitchen and sofa in the open-concept condo. "Go sit down, and I'll bring you your plate."

"I feel so spoiled," Jessie remarked, doing as Sirena asked. She couldn't remember the last time someone had cooked for her, not in a romantic context anyway. It always seemed like she was the one cooking for her girlfriends. It was definitely a nice change of pace.

Sirena came in carrying the plates, then went back for wine glasses. "I know you don't drink," she said, setting the wine down. "But this is very fruity and light. It's a moscato. I hope you will at least try it. If you don't like it, I'll get you something else."

"That's sweet of you," Jessie said. "I'll try it." Wine wasn't as big of an issue as beer or hard liquor. That's what she had been drinking before when she had issues.

"Now, the big question: should I take off this apron or leave it on while we eat?" She gave Jessie a naughty smirk.

"You better leave it on if you want me to be able to eat the food and not you," Jessie quipped. As Sirena sat down across from her, she had a moment where she felt as though she were floating. She hadn't felt this happy and settled for a long time, and she was trying her hardest to bask in it and not let the niggling worries settle in.

But as soon as she gave any thought to those concerns at all, they flooded over her full-force. She took a sip of the wine, hoping it would alleviate the pressure weighing down on her. She still had so many unanswered questions. Unanswered questions were the bane of her existence. They were antithetical to her whole job.

"What's wrong?" Worry flashed in Sirena's green eyes as she set her fork down on the plate.

Jessie took another sip of wine. "This is actually pretty good," she said, trying to disguise the unease she was sure had seeped out onto her face.

"No, really," Sirena insisted. "What happened at work today? Did you have a bad day?"

"No, just routine stuff. I was hauling some drunk off to jail; that's why I was late," she explained. "I was wondering about your name, though."

"My name? What do you mean?"

Jessie cleared her throat, a little hesitant to open this can of worms, but it had been eating at her for weeks now. "Uh, your name isn't Sirena. It's Anna. After knowing you as Sirena, I really couldn't get used to calling you anything else."

"I know. I like it that way," she answered, a smile flirting with her lips. "It's so much more...romantic, don't you think?"

"I just wondered why you didn't use your real name at The Factory?" Jessie questioned. "I know we've talked about it before, but I am still trying to make sense of everything."

Sirena was quiet for a moment, pausing to take her own sip of wine. Jessie had finished her first glass and paced to the kitchen to grab the bottle off the counter. For some reason she thought it was the perfect night to break her abstinence from alcohol.

"I understand." Sirena finished her first glass too and moved it toward Jessie so she could refill both glasses at the same time. "I haven't really been ready to talk about everything, and maybe I'm still not but—" She accepted the now-full glass and took another gulp of it before proceeding. "I, honestly, I am afraid of telling you the whole story."

"Why?"

"Well, I'm sure you can guess there are some skeletons in my closet. Joe is one of them. There's more. But I haven't used my real name for a long time. Anna actually isn't my real name either."

Jessie tried to ignore the sirens and flashing lights inside her mind. *What the hell is she talking about? How many fake identities can one person have?*

One was understandable. After all, Jessie knew Paisley's story. She totally understood why Paisley had changed her name. She understood why she ran away from home, and what was at stake, and why she couldn't ever go back to her birth name. Her mother sitting in jail was complete evidence of why that could and would never be.

But for a person to use more than one fake name, well, Jessie had a label for those people she'd grown familiar with in the line of duty: *con artists*. Her heart was pounding hard against her ribcage as she waited for Sirena to sort this out, to explain to her why Anna wasn't her real name either.

"Do you trust me?" Sirena simply asked after a few beats had passed.

Jessie sighed. "What kind of question is that? You are here, living in my home, are you not?"

Sirena nodded. "I know, and I appreciate that." She took a look around the condo. "Jessie, you are young. You have a great career. You have your head screwed on straight. You may have had some family issues in the past, but you obviously had the good sense to leave all that behind. And now here you are, and everything is smooth sailing for you from here on out."

Jessie shook her head. She didn't like having her past minimized. She didn't like the patronizing tone in Sirena's voice, but she tried to listen. She tried to understand. *But she doesn't have a fucking clue what I've been through,* a voice kept ringing in her head.

"Things haven't always been so easy or cut and dried for me," she continued. "I grew up in Georgia in a different time. I didn't have a lot of choices because of my family or my gender. I know it's hard for you to understand. I did some things I'm not proud of. I let a lot of people down. And when I left that town, I decided never to look back. Joe is who rescued me from that mess."

"And now I've rescued you from Joe," Jessie interjected. She didn't mean to, but the words just fell out of her mouth before she had a chance to scoop them up and shove them back down her throat.

She thought Sirena would be angry by that statement, but she just gave a resigned look. "Maybe. Maybe you did. But if you think my life was a mess when you found me, I can assure you it was only half as messy as it was when Joe found me."

Jessie still didn't understand. Where was her

strength? Where was her resolve? Why did she need to be rescued in the first place? Jessie had rescued herself. She didn't want to give anyone else the credit for saving her. She was her own heroine.

"So what *is* your real name?" Jessie questioned, trying to get back to the original conversation.

"It's actually Theresa Anne," she answered. "Hence, Anna. And don't ask me where Sirena came from. I just liked it. And it sounded sexy and mysterious, which is what I was going for when I joined The Factory. I haven't been called Theresa or Terri since I was a little girl, and I have no desire to ever hear that name again."

"Fine," Jessie answered. "You know, you're not the only one who has had bad shit happen to them. You're not the only one who has had to start over again. I have too. But I didn't change my name. And I didn't need someone to rescue me."

Sirena's eyes shot down to the floor. Jessie could tell she was trying to suppress her tears. "Well, it's not like you've been particularly forthcoming about your past either," Sirena finally said, the words coming out in a strangled garble.

"Fair enough." Jessie hated seeing her cry. Seeing her cry that night she came over with the bruises had pretty much set them down this path, solidifying their roles as rescuer and rescue-ee. "My middle name is Marie," she admitted, the corners of her mouth just slightly tilting up. She remembered that Sirena had made her dinner, and they should be enjoying it, not interrogating each other.

"Jessica Marie," Sirena repeated. "Now that is a beautiful name for a beautiful woman."

"You think so?" Jessie asked before shoving a forkful of pasta in her mouth.

"I absolutely do." She took her own bite and swallowed. "Now, let's finish this up and take that poor doggie out for a walk." Upon the mention of the word "doggie," Georgia let out a sharp little bark of recognition.

"Sounds good. It's about to storm."

The rain pattered against the roof of the building, and though she couldn't hear it from the bedroom, she could hear it from the balcony, where she stood, watching the white crests crash onto the beach, the only part she could see of the angry, churning sea. She had made a habit of going out to the balcony to collect her thoughts. It wasn't actually a new thing since Sirena arrived, but it seemed like the most logical place to do it since Sirena mostly avoided being out there on account of her fear of heights. She had nearly overcome it, but she definitely didn't venture out onto the balcony at night.

Sirena had taken Georgia out for one last walk before bed. Jessie had to be up again early in the morning, and Sirena had her second day of work at The Factory. Jessie had asked how the first day went, and Sirena's face filled with a sheepish grin. "I've got a lot to learn," she answered, "but I think it will be a lot of fun. And Leah and Paisley are awesome."

Leah and Paisley are *awesome,* Jessie thought as she heard the door close and the bounding gait of Georgia coming out to greet her. She gave the dog an affectionate pat on her head as she wondered how Casey was getting on in California. She hoped Leah and Paisley would have an update when she went to the club later in the week.

"Are you about ready for bed?" Sirena called from the living room.

"Yes, be right there." Jessie took one last look at the turbulent waters, predicting that by morning the only signs of the storm would be debris along the beach. You never knew what might wash up on the shore after a storm rolled through. All manner of trash and oftentimes fish and other creatures. She liked going for a walk on the beach early in the morning after a storm, before the city had a chance to drive their huge trash-eating machines along the coastline.

She still felt a little dizzy and loose after two glasses of wine. *My body clearly isn't used to drinking,* she thought as she slid back into the well-lit living room. Sirena had already made her way to the bedroom, so Jessie turned out the lights and headed off to join her. She found her lover propped up on two pillows reading something on her phone.

"Anything good?" Jessie questioned.

"They gave me admin rights to the Facebook page today," Sirena answered with a prideful grin.

Before Leah and Cap had finalized their decision to hire Sirena, they'd asked Jessie for her opinion on the matter. It seemed like they were asking for her blessing, almost like the point of the marriage ceremony where the officiant says *if anyone knows any reason not to join this couple in holy matrimony, he should speak up now or forever hold his peace.* They wanted to know if Jessie would throw up a red flag or try to advise them against hiring Sirena, knowing she would have access to social media accounts and possibly other sensitive documents.

"I don't think Sirena is out to get anyone," Jessie had confirmed. "She's just had a rough year or two and needs a fresh start. I really appreciate you guys giving her one."

"That's what we thought too," Leah had agreed. "Jeannette applied for the job too, you know."

"Oh, yeah?" Jessie had shaken her head. "She's going to be pretty butthurt if she doesn't get it."

Cap had nodded. "That woman has always rubbed me the wrong way, but honestly, I don't think she'd be a good fit on our team."

"No, probably not," Jessie had agreed. "Paisley hates her, for one thing." Paisley could spot disingenuous folks from a million miles away, and she had no patience whatsoever for them.

Leah had thrown her head back and laughed. "Yeah, there is definitely no love lost between those two, and technically the position reports to Paisley.

No wonder Leah had wanted to recruit Sirena, Jessie thought as she slid into bed next to her girlfriend. They needed to hire from within the club membership, so their options were limited. She was thrilled it had all worked out, especially in her favor. She wasn't used to things working out in her favor, not when they were in the hands of Fate.

"Tired?" Sirena asked, leaning toward Jessie and

raising her eyes up over her half-glasses. Jessie was surprised to learn that Sirena wore reading glasses, but then she remembered she was in her late forties. She always forgot she was that much older.

"A little," Jessie answered with a sigh. She trailed her fingers down Sirena's arms and watched the goosebumps rise on her skin. She loved that she had that effect on her.

"Hey, I've been meaning to ask you something," Sirena said, putting her phone down on the nightstand next to her side of the bed.

"Yes?" Jessie's ears perked. She hoped they weren't headed in the direction of their awkward conversation about Sirena's real name that they'd slogged through over dinner.

Sirena took her glasses off and laid them next to her phone on the table as if she was trying to delay broaching whatever subject was on her mind. Then she let out a tentative, "Well..."

"Well, what?" Jessie gave her a curious smirk. "You know you can ask me anything, right?"

A bashful smile crept across her face. "Well, I know you don't like penetration..." she began hesitantly, "but I wondered what you thought of...using a toy on me or something?"

Jessie felt a little bullet slice through her. Not because Sirena was asking for penetration or to use toys in their lovemaking—not that at all. It was the rebirth of her fears that Sirena was actually closer to straight than bi, and Jessie would never be able to fulfill her needs.

But she didn't ask for a man, Jessie considered,

trying to reassure herself. *She asked for a toy.* She bit back the instinct to toss back a snarky retort. Instead, she smiled and placed her hand on top of Sirena's. "What did you have in mind exactly?"

Sirena pursed her lips, trying to put her request into words. "Have you ever used a *strap-on* with one of your girlfriends?"

Jessie fought the urge to giggle at how the words came out of Sirena's mouth, as though they were too naughty for full volume. "Yes, I have. My first girlfriend loved it." An image of Tori on her hands and knees begging for Jessie to give it to her harder flashed into her mind.

"Really?" Sirena questioned, her eyes lighting up with excitement. "And you don't mind doing it?"

Jessie shook her head. "Not if that's what you want, babe."

Sirena smiled for a second, then her brows furrowed. "Jessie?"

"Yes?"

"Can I ask you something else?"

"Of course. Anything," Jessie assured her.

"Have you ever been with a man?" Sirena's eyes were huge with curiosity and a tinge of sheepishness.

Jessie had prepared herself for that question, but it was more of a challenge to know what answer to give. She nodded. "Yes. It's been a long time, though."

"So you weren't always into just girls?"

Jessie filled her lungs with air as she considered her response. "I've always preferred girls. But it took me a while to admit it. My times with a man...they aren't memories I like to revisit."

"So you didn't like it? Being with a man?" The questions were coming out faster now, and Jessie had a feeling Sirena had been harboring this curiosity for quite some time.

"Uh..." Jessie stammered. She took another deep breath.

Seeing that she was struggling, Sirena sat up and leaned forward to face Jessie. "You don't have to answer if it's too uncomfortable. I'm sorry to ask so many questions."

Jessie considered the fact that she hadn't been forthright with Sirena about her history. *Maybe if I share my past with her, she will open up about hers*, she considered. Before she could change her mind, she blurted out, "I was raped."

Sirena was visibly taken aback, her mouth gaping open and her brows pulling together with concern. "Oh, god, Jessie...I—" She reached out to take Jessie's hand into her own. "I had no idea. I'm so very sorry."

Jessie squeezed her hand and forced a smile. "It was a long time ago. I liked girls way before it happened, so it didn't have anything to do with that, but I haven't been with a man since then. And it's why I am opposed to any penetration...for myself."

"I can understand," Sirena pushed out, still breathless from Jessie's confession. "I'm so very sorry. If you don't want to tell me what happened, I understand."

Jessie could hear the curiosity laced in her words. "It's okay. It's probably something you should know about me, anyway. I just don't talk about it, and have only shared it with one or two people ever in my whole life."

Sirena's eyes grew as she processed Jessie's last statement.

"When I was twenty, I was a nanny. I worked long hours, from five in the morning till ten at night, usually. And I lived with the family I nannied for in a ritzy part of Philly. One weekend I'd had a particularly bad week as I was taking care of twins who were teething, and the mom really couldn't be bothered to help in any way. That whole family—the woman, the man, the grandparents, they were all a bunch of racist assholes." Jessie laughed as she pulled up an image of them in her mind, something she hadn't done for a long time. "The grandmother used to come over and whisper about me as if I didn't speak English. She called me 'That little Mexican girl'—and you can imagine how I felt about that.

"Anyway, so after that really rough week, a girlfriend invited me to go club-hopping in Philly, and I thought that sounded like a pretty good way to unwind after the whole teething twin thing. So we went out and were drinking and dancing, and all that. Then my brother called, and he was at a party and wanted to know if I'd like to stop by. He said, 'Hey, bring your friend.'"

"So did you go?" Sirena asked, still leaning forward, hanging on each of Jessie's words.

Jessie nodded. "Yes. And that's where I learned about a little thing called rohypnol."

Now her eyes bulged from their sockets. "You mean the date rape drug?"

"Yeah. Apparently one of my brothers' friends used it in my drink and dragged me off to the bedroom along with one of their other friends. I only remember bits and pieces of it, but I—" She stopped suddenly as she tried to slam the door closed on the deluge of memories rushing back to her.

"Say no more," Sirena whispered, her eyes filling with tears. She pulled Jessie into her arms protectively. "I'm so sorry that happened to you, honey."

Jessie jerked back as her voice filled with a new strength and resolve. "My brothers were there and knew what was happening. They could have stopped it, but they didn't."

"What the fuck? Are you serious?"

Jessie nodded. Her head began to pound from the thousands of fleeting images, suppressed feelings and locked-away memories that were being unleashed within it.

"Did you press charges? What happened?"

"My friend found me and called 9-1-1. This was all at my brothers' friend's apartment. When they found out the cops had been called, they fucking disappeared—they were totally MIA. My friend saw them leave. They knew I had been raped and was completely incapacitated and they fled."

"Then what happened?"

"The police took me to the ER for a rape kit. I will never forget the cop who stayed with me the whole time. She was amazing. I always knew I wanted to be a cop, but she was the first female officer I ever met. She was in her mid-forties, probably, this white lady with blonde hair and a real take-no-shit attitude. I can still see her face...she was so kind to me." Jessie saw the image of Officer Nelson in her head, and a tear stung at her eye—more because of the woman's kindness than because of the horror of what she was going through.

"So what happened to the guys who did it?"

Jessie sighed. "It took a while for the trial, but they were eventually convicted. One served like four years, I think, and the other around eighteen months."

"Wow, that's hardly any time at all! Why didn't they get longer sentences?"

Jessie shrugged. "They did; both were released early. But they were young with no priors. The second one, they didn't have his DNA on me like the other guy, and he also gave his buddy up to the prosecution. So he pled down. It sucks, but it is what it is."

"It makes me so angry that you went through that, Jessie," Sirena said, her voice cracking with emotion.

"I think I am more angry at my parents than at the guys who raped me," she admitted. There was a certain power in saying those words out loud. She'd never verbalized it so clearly.

"Why?"

"I told them what happened. They knew my brothers were there but didn't put a stop to it, then fled the scene when the cops showed up. My parents took Antonio and Phillip's side."

"What the actual fuck?" Sirena's voice trembled with disbelief.

"That's why I don't really talk to my parents anymore." She hung the words in the air to dry. Even though she tried not to set them on fire with defensiveness, the slight twinge was there nonetheless, as though she needed to explain why she protected herself from the toxicity that was her family.

"I know what it's like to be victimized by your own family," Sirena offered.

"No," Jessie said, her jaw set tightly. "I'm not a victim. I refuse to see myself that way." Her eyes pinned onto Sirena's as she felt her body flood with resolve. "I'm a survivor."

SEVENTEEN

A bridge of silver wings stretches from the dead ashes of an unforgiving nightmare to the jeweled vision of a life started anew. — <u>Aberjhani</u>, Journey through the Power of the Rainbow: Quotations from a Life Made Out of Poetry

Walking through the doors with Sirena on her arm for the first time made Jessie beam with pride. She caught Paisley staring out of the corner of her eye from the reception desk, and she gave a wink of approval. Jessie had asked if Paisley and Calvin needed any help because Leah's long-time vanilla girlfriend Aimee was in town and they were doing mom things with their kids. And Cap was busy with charters. July was always his busiest month. But Paisley insisted they could manage. So Jessie was excited to arrive right at the peak of the night when everyone could witness she and Sirena showing up as a couple.

They had talked about their intentions on the drive over. Jessie asked Sirena what she wanted to get into that night, and Sirena had responded with a devilish laugh. "Do you think it would be fun to find another girl for us to play with?"

The air rushed out of Jessie's lungs as she considered that scenario. Her imagination went to work envisioning how the scene would play out as she cast her gaze over the line of trees silhouetted against the setting sun to the west. It was a beautiful summer evening. Not as humid as it had been. In another hour, the fields on the other side of the road would be flickering with the bright glow of fireflies.

"Well?" Sirena pressed, a bit more insistently this time.

"I don't mind finding a man," Jessie answered. She was absolutely certain that sharing Sirena with a man would be easier than sharing her with another woman. "I know you've gotta be missing the cock."

Sirena giggled at her girlfriend's assessment. "I am a little, but I also know our strap-on will be here any day. I can't wait for you to use it on me." She laid her hand on Jessie's thigh, and Jessie turned to see the excited look gleaming in her eyes.

"You know a strap-on never gets spent...like a man...right?" Jessie questioned, waggling her eyebrows.

"What are you saying?"

"I'm saying you might want to get a warm-up session in tonight, because I'm not going to go easy on you. And the one you chose looks pretty damn big to me."

Now Sirena was laughing hysterically. "I see your point!" she finally managed between chuckles. "Okay, let's find a guy."

"I wonder if Paisley would let us borrow Calvin?" Jessie asked. She obviously didn't want to fuck him, but if she were to fuck a man, Calvin would probably be first on her list.

As soon as they walked through the door and Paisley caught her eye, she knew Calvin couldn't be too far away. She would have asked him first, but she knew the best course of action would be to ask them together. "We'll wait until after registration dies down," Jessie said. Another plus for coming later. Less time to wait. "Let's go get changed."

Sirena nodded and followed Jessie into the women's locker room, which was empty, surprisingly enough. Jessie unzipped their bag and pulled out the lovely peach-colored silk gown they'd brought for Sirena to wear. It made her look like a veritable goddess with a slit that went all the way up her creamy thigh.

"You're changing, too, right?" she asked as she pulled the delicate garment over her head.

Jessie nodded and rummaged around in the bag for her tap pants and cami. They were a vibrant royal blue edged with black lace. She began to unbutton her pants and slide them down her thighs.

"Good, 'cause your ass looks fantastic in those," Sirena said with a wink. She glanced at her reflection in the mirror and seemed satisfied. For as beautiful and well-put together as she always appeared, she wasn't vain and didn't go overboard with primping. She swiped some lip gloss over her full, pink lips and said,

"Let's go find Paisley and Calvin."

Jessie smiled and led the way out of the locker room just as Jeannette and her clique burst their way through. Jeannette gave them both a nasty look, then pranced over to the wooden bench with her nose in the air. Jessie stared straight ahead, refusing to react, and guided Sirena out into the hallway and up the stairs to the offices. "They're probably up here now, watching the cameras."

Sure enough, they were in Leah's office. Paisley sat at the desk with her long, curvy legs propped on top, and Calvin was leaning against the edge, his eyes bouncing from camera to camera. "Getting a nice show?" Jessie asked, peeking her head through the door.

"Well, look at the two of you!" Calvin exclaimed. "Absolute beauty!"

"What's up, ladies?" Paisley said, her blue eyes flashing away from the screens. She was a summer goddess with a long, stretchy maxi dress clinging to her ample curves with a black background and a blue paisley swirl. And, naturally, her cleavage was absolutely mouthwatering. Jessie thought about perhaps asking Paisley to join them as well. *The more the merrier*, she mused.

"We were wondering if you two would like to play with us before the night gets too busy," Jessie asked. Her eyes snapped to Sirena, whose face bore a look of confusion because they'd only discussed Calvin.

"Oh," Paisley laughed, sounding sparkly and surprised. "Cap and Leah aren't here, so I have to hold down the fort. But you can borrow Calvin if you'd like. If he's...uh...up for it, I mean."

Then, naturally, all three women's eyes rocketed to Calvin, who seemed a little taken aback at suddenly being the center of attention. But once he realized what was being asked of him, a smooth smile spread across his face, one of flattery.

"Oh, I'm definitely up for that!" He grinned, and rose to his full height, something in the six-foot range. All Jessie knew was that he was more than a head taller than she was. He had beautiful bronze skin stretched over perfectly sculpted muscles and the most haunting, piercing hazel eyes she'd ever seen. They practically seemed to glow. Sirena nearly looked to be drooling over him as she imagined those strong, lean limbs entangled with hers.

"Sure you don't want to watch?" Jessie asked Paisley.

"Which room are you going to play in?"

"The Oasis," Sirena answered. It was her favorite room.

"I have some paperwork to finish, and then I'll peek in after bit. Have fun, you guys!"

Calvin followed the two ladies out of the office and over to the Oasis room, which was, thankfully, empty. Once in the room together, the three glanced around until Jessie broke the silence. "Calvin, you're way overdressed for the occasion."

He chuckled, glancing down at his button-down shirt and dress pants that flattered his tall, athletic frame. "Is that so?" His eyebrows rose as his eyes darted between the two women. "So what are the rules here?"

Wise man, Jessie thought. *Paisley has trained him*

well. "This is all about Sirena. You can do whatever you'd like to her. I'm out of bounds."

"Oh, that's disappointing," he sighed. "But understood."

"Trust me, if I were going to fuck a man, it would have to be you or Cap," Jessie said, laughing. "Consider that a compliment."

"Oh, I do; I do." He slowly unbuckled his charcoal gray dress pants, which were baggy everywhere but his fine, round ass. Jessie watched Sirena's eyes as he lifted his shirt over his head. The man had a body on him, that was for sure. Muscles rippled down his chest and abs, and he had just the right amount of bulge in his biceps and triceps to where he wasn't overly bulky. He had the body of an athlete, and there was no doubt Sirena was a fan.

"Can I touch you?" she asked, lunging toward him as if she couldn't wait another moment.

"Mmmhmmm," he nodded. He had thrown the shirt across the room and was now standing with his pants unfastened but clinging to his hips. The V of his abdominal muscles was just visible at the top of his boxer briefs.

She glided her fingertips down his chiseled chest, running her hands right down to his shorts. "I can help you off with these." Her voice came out in a purr, and Jessie recognized it as her bedroom voice. It was sultry, seductive, and spiked with that sweet Southern accent.

He stepped out of his pants and stood before them in only his boxers, the bulge of his manhood pressing insistently against the fabric, desperately awaiting unleashing. Calvin wrapped his arms around Sirena and bent to press his lips against hers, so softly and delicately, as if she were a piece of fine china. She moaned in response, urging him for more as she opened her mouth to him. Jessie stepped closer to the intertwined figures until the front of her body was pressed up against Sirena's backside. She could feel the heat Calvin had stirred in her girlfriend's skin rising to the surface and radiating out into her own pores.

As Calvin's tongue stroked deep in Sirena's mouth, Jessie pressed soft kisses along the back of Sirena's neck and down her spine. She knew attention to that area always sent tingles flying up and down her back. "Mmm...you guys just made a Sirena sandwich," she moaned breathily.

"Quite a tasty sandwich," Calvin answered, breaking their kiss long enough to utter the words and then his lips were back on Sirena's. It didn't bother Jessie that Calvin was kissing her girl. She trailed her fingers down Sirena's back and over the firm globes of her ass until she was at that lovely space at the bottom of her ass crack. She slid her hand into her thigh gap and angled one of her fingers up until it brushed against Sirena's slit, which was, as she suspected, slick with desire. She pushed her fingertip inside, and it was instantly coated with juices. She loved the way Sirena's body was responding to Calvin's touch.

Jessie broke away and took Sirena by the wrist. "Come here, darling," she said, gesturing toward the bed. She guided Sirena over and pushed her down on it, with none of the gentleness Calvin had displayed. "Calvin, lose the drawers," she said, taking charge. "Baby, you're gonna suck his cock now, okay?"

Sirena murmured yes as she watched Calvin begin to slide his boxer briefs down his legs. It was only a moment before his long, thick cock unfurled. She stared at the magnificent sight as Jessie positioned herself between Sirena's creamy white thighs. "Hungry?" Calvin asked as he approached the bed with his hand wrapped around his pulsating manhood.

Sirena nodded just as Jessie striped her slit with her tongue, forcing a whimper out of Sirena's mouth. "I'm hungry too," Jessie remarked. "Looks like cock and pussy is on the menu tonight."

It was incredible how wet Sirena was, even with hardly being touched down there. Jessie took a deep breath in of her aroused scent, filling her senses with it. Nothing turned her on more than seeing Sirena chase her next orgasm. Sometimes she seemed to need that release as much as she needed her next breath. Jessie only wished she could always be the one to give them to her...forever. She realized just how much she wished that as she began to lap at Sirena's clit.

Meanwhile, she didn't have to see what was happening between Sirena and Calvin to visualize it. She had seen Sirena take a hard cock into her mouth plenty of times before. Jessie couldn't believe how turned on she was watching her girlfriend enjoy the fine art of cocksucking and the moans of pleasure elicited from the men when they realized how talented she was.

Jessie glanced up just in time to see Calvin's dark, veiny cock slide into Sirena's hungry mouth and his eyes roll back as a gasp emitted from his lips. Before she could watch any more of the action, Sirena threaded her fingers through Jessie's hair and pushed her face into her pussy, bucking her hips up so the two entities crashed together. *Damn*, Jessie thought, her lips curling into a smile. *Guess she wants my mouth on her clit!*

"Fuck," Calvin's voice punctured the air. Jessie had a feeling Sirena had just deepthroated him. She obviously had no gag reflex, and Jessie had watched her suck cock enough to wonder if she'd been trained by a sword swallower. That's how impressive her abilities were. Calvin's enjoyment only seemed to spur her on more; from the rhythm of her hips grinding into Jessie's face, she could tell she was on the threshold of her first climax. With enough devotion, Jessie could usually coax three or four out of her before her body collapsed limply in her arms, completely spent.

Jessie did not divert her attention from her girlfriend's clit, but she could feel the presence of others watching. They'd left the door open, and this early in the evening, theirs was sure to be the only show in town. There was the occasional murmur and gasp from their enthralled audience, completely titillated by watching live porn unfolding before their very eyes.

"Hey, baby," Calvin moaned, indicating Paisley had made her way down to the Oasis to check in, just as she'd promised.

"Enjoying Sirena's mouth on your cock?" Paisley asked, her sparkling voice ringing through the heated air.

Calvin wasn't even able to articulate a response. If Jessie had to guess, she imagined Sirena had just taken him deep down her throat again and was using her other hand to stroke his balls as she swallowed him down.

"Do you want to fuck her, baby?" Paisley asked, and Jessie could feel her moving onto the bed. From the way the mattress shifted, it seemed she had positioned herself behind Calvin. "Do you want to slide that throbbing cock of yours into her tight, wet pussy?"

Jessie could have sworn she heard Calvin gulp, but the sound was swallowed up by Sirena's mouth abandoning her grip on his cock and a scream at decibel level 1000 tearing out of her throat. "Oh my god!" she shouted, her voice laced with a combination of frenzy and desperation. "Oh my god!"

There was no time to lose now. Jessie pushed two fingers in and out of Sirena's pussy like pistons and suckled on her clit as though her life depended on it. She felt a huge gush meet her fingers just as a primal screen erupted from Sirena's mouth. "Oh my god; oh my god; oh my god," she repeated over and over again as Jessie lapped up all the juices that came squirting out. She kept her fingers still so she could feel the walls of Sirena's pussy clench her tightly as each spasm rocked through her core.

Jessie finally looked up when the spasms seemed to diminish, and Calvin was slowly stroking his cock as he watched Sirena come down from her orgasmic bliss. "I hope it's my turn to fuck you now," he said, looking at Sirena as her eyes fluttered open at last. "I'm about to fucking explode just from watching you."

Sirena could barely manage a nod, which made Calvin and Jessie alike smile. He went to retrieve a condom while Jessie slid up the bed until she was face to face with her girlfriend. "How was that, beautiful?" she asked, even though she knew damn well it was spectacular.

"I think you know," Sirena answered, still breathless. Her chest was flushed and heaving up and down as she watched Calvin approach the bed again unrolling a condom onto his shaft. "How do you want me?" she asked.

"Get on your knees so you can take care of Jessie," he directed. Paisley had given him a kiss and told him to have fun, then she'd left to take care of club business. Sweat glistened on Calvin's brow under the lights as he moved back onto the bed.

None of them made any eye contact with their audience, almost as if they were on stage and a fourth wall plainly existed between them and the voyeurs. Jessie rolled to her back, wiggled out of her tap shorts, and slid the cami over her head. "Can't believe I was still dressed," she chided herself, receiving a big grin from Calvin.

"Woman, it's a damn shame you're not into men because you have one hell of a body. I love that big round booty of yours!" he complimented her. Jessie couldn't help but smile. She always thought most men were attracted to more conventional body shapes, such as Sirena's, but it was true that some men preferred women on the softer and curvier side. Knowing Paisley was a beautiful plus-sized woman, Jessie wasn't surprised Calvin was just as into her body type as he was Sirena's.

"Quit flirting with my girlfriend and slide that cock into me," Sirena said from her position on all fours.

Jessie laughed and moved down so her pelvis was aligned with Sirena's face. Calvin pressed his cock against Sirena's ass. "You mean this cock?" he teased her.

"Fuck yes," she breathed out, arching her back.

"What a little cumslut! You just came, and you're already ready for more!"

"Damn right," Sirena said, just barely flicking out

her tongue to make contact with Jessie's pussy. Jessie wasn't expecting it, and the slightest touch sent shivers racing up and down her body.

Then Calvin pressed the tip of his cock against Sirena's dripping wet entrance, just barely rubbing it between her pussy lips. "Fuuuuuuck," she let out in one long moan.

"I want to see you lick your girlfriend's pussy," he answered. "Do a good job, and then I'll give you my cock."

Obediently, Sirena returned her mouth to Jessie's clit, which she stroked ever so lightly again before licking down along her slit all the way to her perineum. Then she flattened her tongue and made another broad pass between her lips, collecting the desire that had been pooling since they first began their play.

"Mmmmm," Sirena moaned, her voice vibrating against Jessie's sex. She felt it all the way through her body, from her clit to her ass. Sirena had done this enough times that she knew all of Jessie's signals, how she liked her clit lightly and intermittently stroked until she got closer to climax, and then she liked the whole thing sucked rhythmically.

"What do you think, Jessie?" Calvin asked as he stroked his cock and waited until Sirena had fulfilled her assignment. "Do you think I should fuck your girlfriend?"

"Yes," Jessie sighed as Sirena attacked her clit again. The word came out much sharper than she had anticipated, like a hiss. "Yes I do."

"I think that can be arranged." He pressed the crown against her again and let her have half an inch or two. Jessie felt her body rock from the sensation, then Sirena pushed back against him, trying to take more of him inside her. But he burrowed his fingers into her hips on either side, strictly controlling the depth. He slowly thrusted just those few inches back and forth, easing the passage of her tight hole as her tongue began to respond by furiously licking up and down Jessie's slit.

"Do you think I should give her a few more inches?" Calvin asked, clearly enjoying the response he was getting from Sirena, whose hips were bucking wildly against him, firmly controlled by his tight grip.

"Maybe one or two more," Jessie replied, enjoying the tease just as much as he was.

"You both are killing me," Sirena said, popping her head up to glare into Jessie's chocolate brown eyes. "Please? Just fuck me, Calvin. Please?"

Jessie grabbed Sirena's blonde head and pulled it back down to her pussy. She kept her fingers threaded through Sirena's golden locks, forcing her to keep her attention on her clit while Calvin took a deep breath and plunged himself balls deep inside of her. The piercing cry Sirena let out was perfectly muffled in the folds of Jessie's sex.

"Holy fuck," Calvin managed. His eyes popped open and snapped to Jessie's. "Fuck, your girlfriend's pussy is fucking tight. I might have to go back to the few inches thing or I'm going to drain my balls in the next three pumps."

"Just think about baseball or whatever it is you guys do," Jessie said, giggling. She heard a few people in their assembled crowd laugh at her comment. She was sorry she'd allowed herself to become distracted by them. She had difficulty achieving orgasm while she had an audience as it was typically a much more intimate event for her. She pinned her gaze on Calvin, though; watching the way his face reacted to his cock being submerged inside her girlfriend would help her focus.

The expressions on his face are almost sexy enough to turn a gay girl straight, Jessie noted as she watched his eyes loll back, his mouth part, and his jaw clench. His fingers were gripping Sirena's hips so tightly they were nearly white. He was desperately trying to control himself, and something about that struggle was so overwhelmingly stimulating that Jessie began to feel her core coil up with that familiar need to release. She felt herself balance on that line, growing ever closer to losing control, same as Calvin. Then his eyes popped open to connect with hers, and they seemed to be sharing something, something deeper even than sharing a love for Sirena's body.

And Sirena too, was responding in a way that only urged them both on. Jessie could feel her deep guttural groans vibrating against her clit with every thrust Calvin made. Her body seemed to be twisting up tight with need. One of her hands was spreading Jessie's lips open, creating a succulent feast for her mouth to devour. The other went from tweaking Jessie's nipple to fisting the sheets of the bed, trying to stabilize herself against Calvin's mighty pounding.

"Fuck, I'm gonna come," Calvin finally wailed, his deep voice booming throughout the room. Just that blatant admittance, the fact he could no longer maintain control set off a chain reaction. Jessie felt that voice rip through Sirena's body and into her own, stringing them all along one thread that was being pulled tight enough to snap at any moment.

And within mere seconds, snap it did, forcing wave after wave of ecstasy to wash over all three of them. Jessie watched Calvin's body jerk with his release, sending a jolt through Sirena's body that went right to her core. When her own damn broke, she knew she gushed all over her girlfriend's face, and she sputtered and fought to keep filling her lungs with breath as her pussy exploded around Calvin's still oozing cock.

The three stayed suspended in their purple bliss for nearly a minute. If their audience had cheered or been silent, none of them would have known. They were swallowed up by another world at that moment, taken to heaven and back, and it took several seconds for the Oasis to reappear before all of their eyes.

"Holy shit," Calvin broke the silence again. "That was fucking hot."

"I think that may be the understatement of the year," called one of the audience members. And then, the entire room erupted in applause.

Jessie and Sirena headed for the bar after playtime. Jessie's skin was still hot from her orgasm, and Sirena's was still visibly flushed. Their hair was a bit disheveled, but otherwise neither were worse for the wear. Jessie loved the knowing smiles flickering on Sirena's face every time she made eye contact. They had just shared something special, their first threesome as a couple. It felt so different than the other times they had played with other partners, and it was the first time Jessie had experienced the difference between playing as a couple and as a single female.

Sirena was swirling her drink before bringing it to her mouth for a sip when a stomp of high heels approached from the dance floor. Jessie's head whipped around just in time to see Jeannette knock the cup right out of Sirena's hands, sending the liquid flying all over Sirena, the bar, and the floor.

"What the fuck?" Jessie shouted, wiping the splatter from her arm. She was off her barstool in a flash, whirling around to meet the glare of Jeannette and her girl gang.

Calvin also arrived on the scene in a heartbeat. "What's going on here, ladies?" he asked with his usual affable demeanor. One of the things that made him so good at handling security issues was that he had a definite knack for diplomacy.

"Bitch took my job," Jeannette mumbled under her breath. "Sorry, Calvin, I didn't mean to make such a mess." She batted her eyelashes at him innocently.

"Oh, please," Jessie shot back. She looked over to her girlfriend to make sure she was okay and found her busy sopping up the alcohol from her peach nightgown with a towel the bartender had handed her. "What do you think is going to happen when you knock someone's drink out of her hand?"

"Ladies, let's take this up to my office, okay?" Calvin asked, but it was more of a statement than a question.

"Sirena didn't do anything to Jeannette. Sirena was the one hired. It's none of Jeannette's business," Jessie argued.

"Fuck you," Jeannette seethed, her eyes darting between Jessie's and Calvin's. "Of course Sirena is going to have her dyke girlfriend fight her battles for her. And that's probably how she got the job too. Everyone knows Jessie works for this shithole."

"That's enough!" Calvin's voice thundered so loudly through the bar area, it was heard even over the blaring music.

Jessie's body was flooded with enough endorphins to take Jeannette out in a single punch, but she bit her tongue and fought with every fiber of her being to keep her arm from swinging into her face. *I want nothing more at this moment than to see that raging cunt go down*, she thought. *But there's no way in hell I'm risking my job for a waste of oxygen like her.*

"Well, it's all true," Jeannette said, crossing her arms over her chest.

"I'm going to have to ask you to leave," Calvin stated firmly. From his stance, it was obvious he was not backing down. His arms were folded, fists clenched, and his feet spread to shoulder width. His jaw was set, and his eyes pinned Jeannette's in place. "Right now. You're out of here."

"I just spilled her drink," Jeannette whined. "Big fucking deal!" She looked around at her posse of girlfriends as if she expected them to back her up, to say something in her defense. But their mouths were all zipped.

"This place is all about favorites and who's sucking Cap's dick. I hope you rot in hell!" she screamed at Sirena, who had just finished drying herself off. She refused to make eye contact and instead reached for Jessie's hand.

"I'm going to send you a bill for Sirena's silk gown you just ruined," Jessie seethed.

Jeannette didn't utter another word. Calvin took her by the elbow and began guiding her to the front door. Surprisingly, she didn't fight against him. Within seconds, the girls in her entourage scattered like dust in the wind.

Calvin returned to the bar as soon as his task was complete. "You okay, Sirena?" he asked, looking her up and down for signs of injury or distress.

"I'm fine, but I'm going to have to change," she said, with a sad sigh. "Thanks for your help, Calvin." She squeezed Jessie's hand and flashed a half-hearted smile at Calvin.

Paisley joined Jessie and Calvin at the bar wearing a concerned expression. "I think I just saw you escorting Jeannette off the premises?" she asked her husband.

He nodded. "Yeah, she just caused quite a scene, making Sirena spill her drink and calling her all kinds of names because she got the job she wanted."

"Fuck that," Paisley said, scrunching up her nose in distaste. "I don't care if her daddy is the sheriff. I mean, seriously! I won't be voting for that asshat."

Sheriff, Jessie thought. *Fuck, that's right.* She'd momentarily forgotten how that fact could complicate matters.

"Well, she's not coming back," Paisley stated. "There is no way Cap and Leah will allow it."

"Not even if she threatens to tell her daddy?" Calvin argued. "Oh, and you should hear what she said about Cap."

"Oh, Cap will hear tomorrow when we both give him a full report. And I don't think her daddy knows she spends every weekend prancing around a swinger club being a cock tease. There's no fucking way she is going to use that as leverage. From what I understand, Sheriff Abrahms is a deeply religious man. I don't believe that is going to go over well for his re-election—or at his church, for that matter."

"Fair enough," Calvin noted. "Guess we'll see what Cap says tomorrow, then."

"Abrahms?" Sirena asked, glancing up. She had a puzzled expression on her face as though the name rang a bell.

Paisley nodded. "Yeah, he's been the sheriff for several years now."

"Let's go get you changed," Jessie said to Sirena. "Sure you're okay?"

The confused look on Sirena's face dissipated. "I'm fine," she insisted, this time emphatically. She followed Jessie to the locker room.

"Maybe we should just go home?" she questioned, rifling through her bag. "We already played, after all. It's not like we're going to play again."

"Are you sure?" Jessie studied her girlfriend's eyes for signs she was saying one thing while actually meaning another. *You know, woman code,* Jessie laughed to herself.

"No, darlin', I just want to go home and curl up in bed with you. Besides, you have to be at work early tomorrow, and I want you to be well-rested." Sirena's eyes were clear and honest, and she took Jessie's hand into hers, squeezing it affectionately.

Jessie nearly let the words *I love you* slip from her lips, but she held them back. It wasn't yet time to say them. She hoped Sirena would say them first, even though she had alluded to it when she admitted she thought she was falling in love. Those words were dancing on the tip of Jessie's tongue, just waiting for their chance to be in the world, to be known.

EIGHTEEN

When wounds are healed by love, the scars are beautiful. — <u>David Bowles, Shattering and Bricolage</u>

Sirena and Jessie were halfway to Pennsylvania to retrieve Sirena's car and husband's ashes when Jessie's phone rang. Cap's face illuminated the screen, and just the sight of it spurred an uneasy feeling in Jessie's stomach. "Hello?"

"Hey, Jessie?" Cap asked. "Are you working today?"

"Uh...no?" Jessie answered. He exhaled loudly into the phone, and by the slight tremble in his voice, she assumed he was about to ask a favor.

"Great. Any way you can come help Paisley today?"

"Is something wrong?"

"Leah just got back from the doctor. She's been having some cramping and spotting, and they want her to take it easy for the rest of the week," he explained.

"Oh, no! Cap, that doesn't sound good," Jessie answered, and right away Sirena's hand flew to her knee. She had taken the phone call through her car's Bluetooth, so Sirena could hear the entire conversation unfolding.

"No, it's not," he agreed. There was a beat as if he were swallowing down the emotion that was caught in his throat. "Are you able to help out? I need to stay home with Lincoln so she isn't running after him."

"God, Cap, I'm so sorry, but I'm taking Sirena up to Pennsylvania for a couple days to take care of some unfinished business. I thought Paisley would have told you; she knew Sirena wouldn't be in today or tomorrow."

"Oh, I see. I've not actually been into the office yet. I guess I'm going to have to take Lincoln with me today. Paisley will love that!" He chuckled, but it seemed like he was trying to cover up his disappointment.

"Just drop me off," Sirena said loud enough that Cap would be able to hear too. "I'll get my car, and there's no reason for you to wait around for me up there."

"But," Jessie protested, "I didn't want you to have to worry about handling things on your own. I wanted to be there for you."

"Tsk," she said, laughing. "I'm not a little girl. How many times have we been over this?" Sirena asked.

You're not a little girl, but every time you seem to

be confronted by something emotional or difficult, you seem to freeze, Jessie thought, but tamped it down low enough to not come out in words. *If you don't freeze, then you drink until you're removed from reality.* Since Sirena had moved in with her, Jessie noticed she drank far less than what she seemed to be drinking before. She only had a glass of wine with dinner. And that was it. She seemed so much more even-keeled with Jessie there to stabilize her.

"Cap, let me call you back in a few," Jessie said, shooting Sirena a glare that warned her to be quiet. "Give Leah my best and tell her to keep her butt in bed!"

She pressed end on the call and turned to Sirena. The sun was just beginning to heat up as it rose to the top of the sky. They expected to arrive at Sirena's place around 11 AM. If Jessie dropped her off, she could be back in Ocean City around 2 PM.

"What is it you're planning to do?" Jessie interrogated her. They hadn't formulated an exact plan because Sirena kept saying they would figure it out when they got there. It smacked of her not really wanting to face the monumental tasks of cleaning the rest of her things out of the trailer, retrieving Joe's ashes, and getting the ball rolling to settle his estate.

She watched the crease between Sirena's brows tighten as she considered what she should say. "I'm going to get some stuff out of my trailer and pack up my car. Then I am going to go see the lawyer with the death certificate. And then tomorrow I'll pick up Joe's ashes on my way home." She said it matter-of-factly, as if that had been the plan all along.

Jessie decided to cut to the chase. "Where are you going to stay tonight?"

"What difference does that make?" Sirena asked with an air of defiance in her voice.

Jessie sighed and somehow stopped herself from rolling her eyes. "You're not staying in the trailer," she stated. "So where are you staying?"

"I may go see an old friend," she answered, her voice smaller and more hesitant.

"What kind of 'old friend?'" Jessie pushed. She didn't like the sound of it, not one bit. Her instincts immediately told her that leaving Sirena in Pennsylvania alone was not a good idea.

"You clearly don't trust me." Sirena folded her arms across her chest and snapped her eyes to the road.

"I don't want to fight with you, Sirena, but as your girlfriend, I think I have the right to know what your plans are. Especially if your plans involve being in the company of someone else....sexually." She spat the word out, unhappy with the suspicion riding on the word, but unable to correct it before hitting Sirena's ears.

"Oh, right. I am gonna just go whore it up all over southeastern PA," she fired back. "For fuck's sake, Jessie."

"It has nothing to do with me not trusting you, and everything to do with me being concerned about you. You remember what your life was like a month ago, right? When you were being beat up by your husband and drinking yourself into a coma almost every night? Then coming down to OC where you spent every weekend hammered with total strangers looking out for you. Do you even remember that?"

"Fuck you for saying that," Sirena seethed under her breath. "I thought you really cared about me. Really enjoyed being with me. I'm just some sort of project to you, aren't I?"

Jessie considered whether or not she should pull over so they could talk face to face, eye to eye. She always seemed to get through to Sirena a lot better when their eyes were locked together. She took another deep breath, not wanting to hurl back anything she might regret.

"I can't believe you would say that," Jessie finally said, willing her voice to remain calm. "I have had feelings for you for way longer than I care to admit. I tried to deny them from the first day I met you. I have taken you into my home, helped you find a job, and held your hand through this entire ordeal with your husband. And you won't even tell me how you got messed up with an asshole like that in the first place! Trust me, if you were just a 'project,' as you put it, I would have given up on you a long damn time ago!"

As soon as she said the last part, she knew Sirena was done with the conversation. She remained with her fists clenched and her eyes staring straight ahead. Her mouth was set in a firm line, and there was no way any words were going to budge past her lips. The bright, leafy green of summertime whizzed past them as Jessie sped across the state line. There would only be silence now until they reached their destination.

There weren't a whole lot more words spoken when they arrived at Sirena's place either. Jessie stood with her hands on her hips, the July sun blazing down on her as she squinted at Sirena. She didn't want to put her sunglasses back on and cover up her eyes. She wanted Sirena to see the emotion radiating from them.

But Sirena had been pushed past the point of reconciliation. Her stance was completely closed off. She couldn't even bring her eyes to look straight at Jessie; it was though Jessie were the sun itself, and staring might burn a hole in her retinas.

"So that's it, then?" Jessie asked. "You're sure you don't want me to stay."

"Go help Cap," Sirena insisted. "I'll be fine." Her words were short, each ending in a sharp barb.

"Are you coming back to Ocean City?" As soon as the words left her mouth, Jessie realized she should have asked "when," not "if."

"I don't know," Sirena answered.

Jessie was filled with anger all over again. The lack of gratitude was infuriating. *After all I've done for this woman!* she raged inside her head. *The fucking sense of entitlement is beyond ridiculous.* She wanted to say something hurtful, something that would really punch Sirena in the gut just as hard as she felt at that moment. She settled on, "Well, if you're not going to show up at your job later this week, you better let Paisley know."

And that was it. Sirena just gave a curt nod and stood like a statue while she waited for Jessie to get in her car. Jessie wanted to apologize, to throw her arms around Sirena's shoulders, beg to start the day over and forget the nasty things they'd said. But she couldn't. Sheer stubbornness, or maybe anger at herself for entrusting her heart to this woman, stood like a walled fort around her. She curled into her car, started up the engine, and with one last glance back at Sirena, she backed down the driveway. Sirena didn't even watch her go. She turned on her heel and disappeared inside the trailer.

When Rod Stewart's "Maggie May" came on the radio, she knew she couldn't listen. She dialed Cap's number and let the Bluetooth carry away the melody too painful to hear.

"Hello?"

"Still need help? I'm on my way now."

"Great! I'll tell Paisley to expect you in a few hours," he said, his deep voice full of relief. "Everything okay with Sirena?"

"As okay as it's going to be," Jessie answered. And then she tried to believe it.

Jessie's entire drive back to Ocean City was one huge scolding session. She was sick of the voice in her own head by the time she arrived at The Factory. How many different ways could she chide herself for fucking things up? For falling in love with a straight girl? For wanting to rescue someone who didn't need or want rescuing?

When she arrived, she was glad to see Paisley and

Cap, and to hear someone else's voice. She needed a break from herself.

"Everything okay?" Paisley asked as soon as she saw Jessie walk through the doors.

Jessie sighed but forced a smile onto her face. "Yep. Sirena's taking care of her shit."

"Oh, you left her up there?" Paisley's brow cocked as she searched her friend's face for a clue as to what was really going on.

"Yeah, she said she didn't need me and that I should get down here to help you guys out. So what's going on?"

Cap walked down the stairs to join the two ladies in the lobby. He carried his son on his shoulders, and Lincoln beamed as if he were the king of the world. Jessie couldn't help but smile at how adorable the little redheaded boy looked with his bright blue eyes and dimples that matched his father's. "Hey, Lincoln," she called, and the little boy bashfully hid behind Cap's head.

"I just finished watching the video footage from Saturday night," Cap said, lifting Lincoln down to the floor. He handed him a small canvas bag which the toddler immediately opened and dumped out on the carpet. There were four or five small plastic cars and trucks and a simple wooden puzzle, the pieces of which went flying across the floor.

"And?" Jessie pressed.

"So Sirena was totally unprovoked?" he questioned.

Jessie nodded. "She was minding her own business, about to take a sip of her orange crush when

Jeannette knocked the glass clean out of her hand. It went everywhere, not unlike the contents of that bag just did!" She laughed and pointed to the floor where Lincoln was making a road and lining his vehicles up.

"Jeannette's been a member here for a long time," Cap said. "And she's never had any issues like that before. I don't understand why she hates Sirena so much. I've been trying to figure it out."

"Oh, you know how women are, Cap!" Paisley prompted him. "Catty. Jealous. Sometimes irrational." She popped her hand over her mouth, giggling. "Oops, did I just say that?"

"We've had plenty of real stunners here at the club, and Jeannette has never had an issue with them. She usually just recruits them into her little clique. I don't understand why Sirena is different." Cap pulled on the ends of his beard as if in deep contemplation. "In any case, I don't know how well it's going to go over to ban her."

"What do you mean?" Jessie fired back. "It's not just what she did to Sirena, but the nasty stuff she said too. Everything she did is a clear violation of club policy. If you don't kick her out, what kind of example does that set for other members?"

"We know," Paisley interjected. "But her dad is the Worcester County Sheriff. We don't want any issues with them since we're in their jurisdiction."

"So, what, you're not kicking her out?" Jessie stood with her arms folded over her chest. She wasn't sure she wanted to come back if Jeannette was going to continue to be welcomed there.

"We haven't decided yet," Cap said. "That's why we're talking about it now. We need to make a decision."

"What does Calvin think?" Jessie asked. "He's the one who witnessed the whole thing."

"He thinks she should be kicked out. For sure. I do too, but Cap is the one on the fence. I think Leah is in favor of kicking her out, too," Paisley answered, glancing over at Cap to toss the ball in his court.

"None of you guys are originally from here," he argued. "Trust me when I say this place is every single stereotype you've ever heard about a small town. Gossip. Back stabbing. Rumors. They're all going to run rampant. They already have about Sirena, and I still haven't figured out why. Jessie, what you uncovered about her husband and his cancer still doesn't really explain it."

"I know," Jessie answered. "There's more she isn't telling me, but I don't know if I will ever get to the bottom of it."

"Aren't you two like...together now?" Paisley asked as she crossed the room to retrieve Lincoln, who was trying to wander into the bar area.

"I don't know," Jessie mumbled. She really didn't want to talk about it. "We were, but she still wasn't particularly forthcoming. There's definitely more to her past, and for some reason, she's too ashamed to tell me. But she did confess that she did some bad shit when she was younger; I just don't know what."

"Has anyone asked Casey what she thinks?" Cap suddenly questioned. "She's from here too, so she gets that whole aspect. And she knows the sheriff personally as well. Maybe we should get her take on it before making a decision."

"I haven't wanted to bug her since she left for California," Paisley answered. "But I think Leah has been in touch. She told me last week that she was settling in well and adjusting to chemo. She was in the process of losing her hair."

"Oh, man, that sucks," Jessie interjected, her heart squeezing for Casey.

Paisley nodded. "Okay, Cap, we still have time before Friday night's party. Let's let Leah talk to Casey and make a decision before then. I don't want to drag this out any longer than we have to, and if we're going to ban her, we need to do it swiftly."

"You're sure Sirena is okay, right, Jessie?" Cap confirmed. This time he took the job of chasing Lincoln down the hall, but his voice carried through the big open space of the lounge.

"I think she's okay as far as what happened on Saturday night," Jessie answered. "As for being okay in every other way? I can't say for sure."

Jessie was trying to recover from a fitful night's sleep after hearing nothing but radio silence from Sirena. She was just as stubborn, refusing to be the first one to make contact, and then feeling guilty because she didn't want Sirena to think she didn't care. She filled up a travel mug with extra-strong coffee, knowing even all that caffeine wasn't going to make a dent in her need for alertness.

"Hey, partner," Bart called to her from the back steps of the police department. "We riding together today?"

Jessie felt her phone buzz in her front pocket, so she held up her finger to tell Bart to wait a moment. She pulled out the phone, swiped the screen, and saw a text from Sarge: *don't leave with Farris before coming to talk to me.*

"Fuck, I have to talk to Sarge first," she answered, looking up at Bart. "That dumb fuck who assaulted me goes to court next week. Sarge probably wants to go over the report before I talk to the AG about it."

Bart nodded. "Yeah. Do you want me to wait?"

She shook her head. "No. This could take a while." She patted him on the shoulder affectionately. "Sorry, buddy."

He rolled his eyes. "Oh, please. I think I'll be just fine on my own." Then he laughed. "Good luck with Sarge. Better you than me!"

She returned his eyeroll and made her way up the steps, then wove down the hallway to Sarge's office. After a sharp knock on his doorframe, she peeked her head in. "You wanted to see me, Sir?"

He motioned for her to come in. "Please shut the door."

Uh, oh. Those four words had always stricken fear in her heart. She tried to shake it off. *Probably just because of the details of the case,* she reasoned. She took a seat in one of the blue leather chairs opposite his desk as her heart thrashed wildly against her ribcage.

"What's up?" she managed as he finished up

whatever he was doing on his computer.

"Martinez, I have a strange question for you," he said, pinning his gaze on Jessie and folding his hands together on top of his desk.

She didn't think it was possible for her heart to beat faster or more erratically, but it was anyway. "What kind of question?"

"Do you belong to a swinger's club?" he asked bluntly.

She didn't perceive a look of disgust or disapproval on his face. His expression was simply open and nonjudgmental. Her brain ran through a million different scenarios based on whether she lied or told the truth.

"Uh, is it a problem if I do?" she asked, her voice coming out small and apologetic.

He laughed. "I don't know. I got a strange call from the sheriff today about some woman he said you were involved with..." He looked down at a scribbled-on post-it note stuck to the surface of his desk. "An Anna Patterson?"

Jessie's eyes bulged out of their sockets. She wouldn't have been surprised to hear him to say "Sirena Horne," but hearing her legal name—even if it wasn't her birth name—was even more disconcerting.

"Why?" Jessie asked, unwilling to admit to anything more until she understood what was going on.

"I guess there were some complaints about her at the local swing club, the one out in Berlin. And some witnesses say you were there too. The sheriff has done some investigating, and it sounds like she had a warrant out for her under another name when she was younger. And I guess she uses a third name here in Ocean City. Kind of a convoluted thing, but supposedly she's an employee there at the club, and there's been some issues. Possibly prostitution."

"Prostitution?" Jessie spouted. "Uh, okay, yeah, I know her. She goes by Sirena Horne, and she's not a prostitute." She bit her tongue when she started to say that the problem was that the sheriff's daughter had it out for Sirena. She assumed the warrant from Sirena's youth was part of the dark history she refused to share.

"Do you know her well?" he pressed.

She nibbled on her lower lip. "Yes."

"So you are a member at the club?"

The air squeezed out of her lungs. "Yes."

She could hear her heartbeat in her ears as he squinted and read the screen again. Maybe it was an email. She couldn't be sure. Maybe he was just trying to figure out what to do with the knowledge she'd given him. Either way, she felt like she was about to explode.

"Do you know her real name or the charges that were pending against her in Georgia?"

She shook her head. She couldn't remember the real name, or at least her head was so full of panic that it wasn't allowing the name to be retrieved at the moment. "I don't think Sirena has done anything wrong. What makes you think she's involved in prostitution? And what kind of charges in Georgia?" She swallowed down her fear and did her best to appear confident and relaxed.

"Apparently the charge from Georgia was for

kidnapping. I don't know what kind of evidence they have for the prostitution thing, but I wouldn't be surprised if you got a call from the Sheriff's office. I'm just going to tell him what you told me."

"Great," Jessie said before she was able to keep the word from slipping out. "Is there anything else you need from me?" *Kidnapping and prostitution?* Those words kept echoing over and over again in her mind.

"Do you know Mrs. Patterson's whereabouts now?" His brows were still pushed together when he glanced from the computer screen back to Jessie.

"Yes, she's in Pennsylvania trying to settle her late husband's estate. He passed away a couple of weeks ago," she answered truthfully. She hoped it would at least buy Sirena some sympathy from Sarge, if not from the Sheriff's Department itself.

"When is she coming back?" he asked, his expression not any softer than it was moments before.

"I wish I could tell you that," Jessie answered. "I have no clue."

And that wasn't a lie, either. Her mother always told her that the truth would prevail in the end. She wished she believed it. It had never quite seemed to work that way for her.

Jessie was relieved to be home after her shift ended. Sirena was not there, as she'd hoped, but

Georgia had the excitement of a dozen people all packed into the space of her tongue-wagging, tail-slapping body. "Hey, Girl!" Jessie called to the dog as she began to take off her uniform. "I gotta leave you there till I change clothes. I don't want you to do your business on my carpet, okay, girl?" Georgia answered with a high-pitched squeal.

"I know, you miss your mom. I wish I knew what was going on with her." *I'll have to text her tonight*, she silently added. *She needs to know what's going on with Jeannette.* She was still trying to work out how Sirena could have been charged with kidnapping when she was younger. *Obviously that's going to need some discussion, as well as the whole prostitution thing.*

Jessie dumped her gun belt on her bed and shimmied out of her work pants, then started undoing the buttons on her uniform shirt. "I'm hurrying!" she promised the dog, whose tail was thumping rhythmically against the floor of her kennel.

She grabbed the leash off its hook before unlatching the cage door. Georgia nearly bowled her over with her unbridled affection, going straight for licks on the face. "Settle down, Girl! How can I get your leash on you with your ass moving around like that?" She laughed, grateful to have some creature happy to have her home after a long day at work. It did relieve a bit of the sting from not having Sirena around.

"Let's go take a short run on the beach, and then we'll rustle up some grub; how about that?" Georgia seemed to agree, so Jessie clipped her leash and headed for the door. She glanced back at her phone, but decided she needed a break from connectivity. She just wanted the peace of the sinking sun and the waves lapping along the shore, so she left it where it laid on the kitchen counter.

Once her feet hit the sand, she felt like she was home all over again. The sun was sinking toward the horizon on the bayside, and the eastern skies over the water were softening to a deeper, huskier hue. The deepest parts of the ocean looked so blue, it nearly hurt to stare for fear one might drown in their depths, even from the shore. There were a few flat, low-slung clouds just hanging over the water as if they too were drawn by its magnetic force. But the best part were the cool, white-tipped, foamy tendrils that rippled along the shoreline. Jessie ditched her flipflops on a sand dune and let the water shock her with its frigid temperatures. "Fucking ice cold, even in fucking July. How do you like that, Girl?" she asked her companion, who charged right into the surf without answering.

She started a slow, gentle jog down the shoreline, letting the waves continue to splash up against her as the tide rushed in. In another hour, the part of the beach where she was running would be under feet of water. It was amazing how that worked, how the earth rhythmically bared and hid itself all day long, as it played peekaboo with the waves.

Jessie couldn't tell who was enjoying this beautiful taste of freedom more: her or Georgia. She reached down to give the wet mutt a pat on the rump. "I bet you're going to just smell lovely when I get you inside." But how could she be mad when Georgia was so abundantly happy? *I bet Sirena won't come and get her*, came a sudden thought, stinging at her lungs as they gasped for air after her sprint toward her condo. *I bet I'm stuck with her forever*. She pursed her lips, trying to imagine if she'd ever received anything better than a dog in the wake of a breakup. She was fairly certain she hadn't.

She dragged Georgia off the sand and up the steps to the bank of elevators in the parking level of her building. The dog panted with her tongue hanging out the entire ride to Jessie's floor. "You need some water, don't you, sweetie?" Jessie scratched behind her ears as she waited for the car to stop and ding its way open.

Georgia pulled her down the hallway to her door and waited semi-patiently for Jessie unlock it. Once they were inside, unsurprisingly, the dog bolted for her water dish. Jessie followed behind, then reached into the kitchen cabinet to retrieve her bag of food. "There you go, Girl," she said, patting her head again.

She grabbed her phone and took it into the living room to collapse on the sofa, where she figured she would scroll through some recipes on her phone until something caught her eye for dinner. *Or Chinese delivery is always an option*, she reminded herself. How could she have so many nights of meals for one, then have a few weeks of constant company, and now eating alone seemed like the worst fate imaginable?

She glanced down at her phone and noticed she had a missed call from Cap, one from Paisley, and one from an unknown number. In addition to that, there were multiple new texts. *What the fucking hell?* she wondered as she scrambled to prioritize the messages. She listened to her voicemail, and the first one was from Cap, who asked her to call as soon as she received the message.

"What's going on?" she asked him, breathless from panic.

"We got a call this afternoon from the sheriff," he revealed. "He's trying to get to the bottom of this

'Sirena Horne' thing, as he called it. Supposedly someone is saying she's running a prostitution ring from The Factory and that she's had warrants out for her arrest in Georgia for years. Obviously because she is an employee here, that is a very big problem."

"What the fuck?!" Jessie shouted, though after what Sgt. Grimes told her earlier that day, she wasn't the least bit surprised. "Does Sheriff Daddy Dearest know that his darling daughter is a MEMBER at said club and had her panties in a bunch because she didn't get Sirena's job?"

Cap let out a long, frustrated exhalation. "I don't really know. We've always had a good relationship with the sheriff, and I'm not allowed to out a member...though technically she's no longer a member now."

"Oh, you decided to kick her out?"

"Yeah, Leah talked to Casey, and she was pretty appalled by what happened. She had never liked Jeannette and her stupid little clique anyway."

"So this is her retribution, and she figures you can't tell her daddy that she used to be a member."

"Yep. See, this is exactly what I was afraid of!"

Her head instantly began throbbing with a headache, not just the normal beginning sequence where the first phase is an annoying niggle, but an all-out throbbing spike of pain hitting her temple. "Cap, I am going to have to think about this for a second. Maybe Calvin can talk to his dad and see what he thinks? I don't know. I just don't understand how this has gotten so blown out of proportion."

"Me either. I still think something must have

happened between Sirena and Jeannette that no one is saying. Can you talk to Sirena? When is she coming back? If we at least knew that, we could figure out how to deal with the sheriff. He's talking about shutting down the whole fucking club!"

"Okay, okay. I'll just fucking call her. I'll let you know what's going on as soon as I can." Jessie hung up the phone and scrolled to Sirena's picture in her contacts. *Okay, fine, I'll fucking call. But I'm getting some Advil first.*

A few moments later, her heart picked up its pace as she pressed the button to call Sirena. "Please pick up," she murmured under her breath. "Please pick up, baby."

With each ring of the phone, Jessie's heart began to flutter faster. Finally, it clicked over to voicemail, and she felt her heart sink into her stomach. She waited for the outgoing message to stop before saying as calmly as she was able, "Look, I'm really sorry about what happened yesterday. I shouldn't have treated you that way. You're not a project, and I care very deeply about you."

She took a deep breath, then added: "And, stuff has come up here. I really need you to come back, Sirena. Georgia needs you too. We both do. So, please...please come home, baby."

NINETEEN

Love recognizes no barriers. It jumps hurdles, leaps fences, penetrates walls to arrive at its destination full of hope. -Maya Angelou

For it still being early in the day, there were certainly a lot of shadows on the wall. Jessie was trying to enjoy her mid-week day off work, but the silence was consuming, chewing her up and spitting her out as she tried to wrap her head around her next move. Distancing herself from Sirena and the club seemed like the only options. Paisley, Calvin, Cap and Leah were her surrogate family. She hated to think she had to abandon her family for her career.

At least with Sirena, it seemed the choice was made for her. She hadn't returned Jessie's call. She hadn't communicated at all since Jessie left her standing outside her trailer in the blazing July sun, a move which Jessie now deeply regretted. *This woman just lost her husband,* Jessie reminded herself. *And I was completely insensitive to it, even if he was a worthless prick.* There must have been something endearing about him at one point in time for her to fall in love with him and want to marry him. Or at least she hoped so.

Guilt and trepidation in equal parts mixed together were a brutal cocktail. She hadn't been able to get out of bed except for the brief walk she took Georgia on when dawn broke over the Atlantic. Now the clouds and shadows had crept in. Georgia had curled up for a nap in front of the patio doors, and Jessie had flung herself back into her sea of pillows and sheets, looking for some comfort, a respite from the storm she was caught up in.

She glanced over at her dresser. On top was a ripped-open package from the online sex toy store, and inside that package was the strap-on Sirena had ordered just before their trip to Pennsylvania. Jessie had only looked at it long enough to determine what it was. *I should probably put that away*, she thought. *Having it staring at me only makes me feel shittier*.

She heard her phone buzzing from the other room. She'd forgotten to bring it back to the bedroom with her. Lamenting about the necessity of getting out of bed to retrieve the phone, she took a deep breath and plodded to the living room. Her heart lurched for her ribcage as soon as she saw it was Sirena calling.

She scrambled for the accept call button and managed to say hello. Her heart pounded as she waited to hear Sirena's sultry southern accent.

"Jessie? You home?"

Just those three words, and Jessie was awash in a combination of relief, hope, and love. Images of the last night she'd been with Sirena danced in front of her eyes, colorful pulses of limbs and lips and moans. "I'm home," she said and waited for more.

"I'm here. Down in the parking lot, but I wanted to make sure you were there before I come up."

"Of course, of course," Jessie said, struggling to control her breathing and tone. Now she just had to control her racing heart and mind until she figured what in the hell Sirena wanted to do.

The commotion woke Georgia up, who started pacing back and forth as if she were in a cage. It was almost as though she sensed her human was coming back. *Maybe she heard Sirena's voice on the phone?* Jessie guessed. She went over to try to calm the poor thing down, hoping it would have a calming effect on her as well.

She saw the front doorknob twist and braced herself for it to open. Finally, there appeared the tall, statuesque figure of her golden goddess, her beautiful locks rippling around her shoulders, her eyes bright and heavily lashed, and her long limbs exposed in a barely-there floral romper. Jessie had seen outfits like that in the store and wondered who could possibly pull them off. Now she knew. Sirena could. She looked absolutely divine.

She wasn't expecting for Sirena to take flight and race into her arms, nearly bowling her over with her passionate embrace. "I missed you so much," she sobbed, and Jessie felt her tears splash onto her shoulder. For a moment she just stood there holding her, feeling their heartbeats synchronize to the same beat.

Jessie pulled away just enough to tell Sirena, "I

missed you too. But we need to talk."

Sirena's face filled with disappointment, and she tilted Jessie's chin toward her, then leaned down to press a kiss against her lips. "Let's talk later. I want to show you how much I missed you."

Jessie felt her spine tingle, a sensation that traveled all the way down to her core when Sirena's warm breath fanned across her neck. *This woman*, she thought, *she is going to be the death of me*. She knew it wasn't the first time she'd made that prediction either. She allowed Sirena to steer her directly into the bedroom, where the first thing she laid eyes on was, naturally, the strap-on sitting on Jessie's dresser.

"Oh, is that what I think it is?" Jessie could hear the wicked thoughts abounding in Sirena's tone. She walked over and picked up the package, removing the black harness and long, thick dildo that attached to it. Her eyes lit up like a child on Christmas morning viewing her presents under the tree.

Jessie simply nodded and waited to see what she would do next. Sirena handed it to her with a look of expectation.

"What?" Jessie asked.

"Let's try it!" Sirena laughed, as if her gesture perfectly expressed her desires.

"Right now?" Jessie's brows drew together in confusion. *Didn't they have shit to work out before they could think about fucking again*? she wondered.

"Yes, right now. I am horny. And I want to be fucked. Now, please," she added. She threw herself on the bed, sinking into its softness and spreading her arms out behind her head.

"Sirena, I think we should—"

"Nonsense. I don't have a problem with you. I'm totally over it. We'll talk about what I learned in PA as soon as we both get a couple orgasms under our belts." She winked and began stripping off the floral romper. It turned out that she wasn't wearing one stitch underneath it. So there she laid, in all her goddessy glory, stretched out on Jessie's bed just waiting to be ravished.

Jessie sighed. *How can I no to that?* She pulled off her own shorts and t-shirt, under which she was also naked. Then she started for the bed.

"Aren't you going to put the harness on?" Sirena stopped Jessie in her tracks.

"Don't you want a little foreplay first?" Jessie giggled a bit nervously as she examined Sirena's face for answers. She shook her head and gave a naughty smirk. "So you want this cock inside you right now?"

Sirena nodded. "Yes, but if you wanted to lick it before you stick it, I'd be open to that too." She laughed.

Jessie shook her head, trying to keep her smile from widening any further, then worked the harness up over her hips and locked the dildo in place. She made a big show of stroking her hands down the shaft, knowing Sirena's eyes would widen with lust, and they did. "You sure you're going to be able to handle all this?" she questioned.

"Guess we'll find out!" Sirena winked again.

Jessie climbed onto the bed on all fours, feeling unwieldy with the dildo jutting out in front of her. She was short and not far off the mattress, so the long, hard phallus brushed against the sheets a couple times on her way to her perch between Sirena's legs. She let her hot breath flow out over Sirena's clit, "So let's see how wet you are already..."

Before she could even touch her, Sirena let out a moan and spread her thighs a little wider to accommodate Jessie. Jessie placed her fingertip between Sirena's folds, gently working her way inside. "Fuck," was all she could breathe out as she felt the moisture immediately soak into her skin. She followed up the motion of her fingertip with the tip of her tongue, swiping it gently up Sirena's slit until her back bowed off the bed. "You like that?"

"Uh huh," Sirena groaned as she gathered up the sheets, clenching them in her fists as she desperately awaited more contact, more attention.

"You're going to come so hard, aren't you?" Jessie predicted. "When I let you..." She didn't plan on letting her off the hook too easily. She might not have wanted foreplay, but she wasn't the one wearing the strap-on, either.

She just barely glided her tongue across Sirena's clit, basking in the way it caused her to jolt with need for more. Then she trailed it, light as a feather, all the way down to the bed. Sirena's hips rose, seeking more pressure, but Jessie resisted. She teased the hell out of her slit until she let the tip of her tongue rest right on her dripping hole. Sirena was squirming against her by this point. Then she plunged her tongue in as deep as it would go, withdrew it, and thrusted it in again. She loved the way Sirena's hips bucked against her. She glanced up to see her mouth gaped open, gasping for breath.

"No, you're not ready yet," Jessie decided, rather

enjoying the sadistic role she had adopted. She leisurely returned her lips to Sirena's sex, brushing them lightly against her folds again, shocked by how saturated with desire they were. Then she slid a single finger inside her again, curling it against her g-spot until Sirena cried out with pleasure. "Oh, fuck, Jessie, don't stop!" she cried out.

Jessie didn't stop, but she didn't move her finger again either. She simply left it there, feeling the walls of Sirena's pussy lightly spasming against it, begging to release the pent-up ocean of passion held beyond her tightly clenched muscles. Then she sucked her clit into her mouth and held it there too before stroking it with feather-like pressure until she thought Sirena may come unglued. The sounds sliding out of her throat now were nearly primal in nature: deep, guttural, animalistic. If she'd had any walls, they were all torn down, and what remained was a writhing mass of nerves, each one connected to that button in Jessie's mouth, just waiting for detonation.

But that was not going to be the means. She paused, taking time to trail her eyes over Sirena's face, which was contorted into an agonized grimace, desperate for release. Then she took the firm, silicone phallus into her hand and waited for Sirena's eyes to capture her long, sure strokes up and down the shaft. "Are you ready?" she asked, and Sirena was too far gone to respond with words. Her eyes answered for her.

Jessie bent, lowering herself toward Sirena's body, aiming the dildo so she could guide it into place. There was some resistance at the entry, and she felt Sirena's body tense up before the simplest plea appeared on her lips: "Please." Jessie pushed and felt the resistance free up, and she slid all eight inches of the dildo inside Sirena's waiting sex, then surveyed Sirena's reaction. She was already bucking her hips against Jessie, wanting more, wanting movement.

Jessie braced herself on her hands, holding her body above Sirena's, then slowly sliding herself back down. Sirena cried out with a sound that sounded caught along the tightrope between pain and pleasure. "Too deep?" she asked, and Sirena shook her head, then grabbed Jessie's hips and pulled her down so the dildo could penetrate even deeper inside her.

"Just hold still," she said, the words coming between clenched teeth. Her fingernails dug into Jessie's flesh as she began to rhythmically press her pelvis up, impaling herself again and again on the fake cock. "Fuck, Jessie!" she screamed as her pace picked up, and soon she was bucking against Jessie so wildly, she thought she might go flying across the room. She did her best to brace herself against the bed and absorb Sirena's forceful thrusts.

"Oh my god, oh my god," she shouted as she threw her head back into the pillows behind her. Her grip on Jessie's hips tightened momentarily as her body was ravaged by her thundering climax, so forceful, it seemed as though it might make the very walls crumble down around them. Then slowly, so slowly, her grip loosened, until she felt more like a puddle of goo beneath Jessie's body. Jessie balanced herself on her knees and carefully withdrew the dildo from Sirena's sex, noticing immediately that it was dripping wet with her juices.

"Fuck, baby, you must have come hard," Jessie marveled as she began to unhook the harness.

"And now it's your turn," Sirena managed, her

voice still raspy as she continued floating back down to earth.

"Where do you want me?" Jessie questioned, laying the harness and dildo aside. She moved much more naturally to lay beside her lover, glad to no longer be unencumbered by the faux manhood. She did love the reaction it garnered from Sirena, but it wasn't something she wanted to do all the time. She much preferred tasting Sirena as she came all over her tongue.

"Lie back," Sirena directed as she slowly lifted herself to her knees and positioned her body between Jessie's legs. She stroked her fingers down Jessie's naked body. "Damn, I missed these curves," she sighed. She lowered her mouth to Jessie's breast and encircled her nipple with her tongue.

Jessie's nipple hardened immediately under the tutelage of Sirena's tongue, and then she teased it further by raking her teeth over it. She cupped both of Jessie's breasts together, squeezing and kneading them. "So beautiful," she breathed out, gently placing a kiss on each of them, then pressing her lips against Jessie's mouth, which had drifted open during the attention to her breasts.

"Thank you for fucking me with that thing," Sirena said between soft kisses planted on Jessie's neck and collarbone area. "I know you were reticent, but it felt amazing. And I know you don't want to do it all the time, which is fine, but—"

She's talking like we are together, Jessie realized, her heart swelling up with conflicting emotions. She wanted to be with Sirena—there was no doubt of that—but she wanted it to be reciprocal. She wanted Sirena to love her as deeply as Jessie loved her. And she needed her walls to be completely torn down. She didn't want to have any more secrets between them...ever. Those were the only terms she could and would agree to.

"Can I lick your pussy now?" Sirena asked, bringing her eyes back to meet Jessie's. There was a sincerity there, an eagerness to please that seemed so genuine, so caring. The look radiating from those gorgeous emerald green irises was one that looked like love. But Jessie knew Sirena was a chameleon. She'd operated under so many identities, how did Jessie know the woman with her in bed right at that moment was the one true, real Sirena?

Jessie nodded, because despite all of the confusion swirling between her ears, she did have a massive well of desire percolating in her core. She craved Sirena's touch and tongue more than she had ever craved anyone else's, and it was a reality she was tired of fighting against. Sirena slid down her body wearing a victorious smile, stopping with her mouth just south of Jessie's hot spot, very close to her right thigh.

She painted a kiss onto the soft flesh of Jessie's inner thigh, then trailed a dozen more kisses a bit farther north so they landed near her aching flesh. Ever since Sirena had walked through those doors that morning, Jessie had wanted her, had needed her. Ever since she'd first seen her at The Factory all those months ago now, she wanted to know every deep, dark secret, from the ones stored between Sirena's eyes to the ones stored between her thighs.

"Your pussy is so pretty," Sirena said, gently brushing her fingers down Jessie's mound. She kept herself trimmed, not fully shaved, which she knew was not customary in the lifestyle, but she found her dark, thick hair too much trouble to tame. And it wasn't the first time Sirena had commented on liking a more natural look. "And so delicious," she remarked, running her tongue between the slit where her lips met.

Pleasure electrified Jessie's body as she felt nerves she'd tried to suppress for a few days now begin to revive, to feel again. A few strokes of Sirena's tongue, and they were all awakened, beginning to sing in unison as they anticipated Sirena's next move. She had perfected the art of making Jessie come, and Jessie did not in any way deny that it was an art. Many of her past girlfriends never bothered to truly study it, and a fair number of them had simply been pillow princesses who wouldn't even attempt to return the favor. She was so relieved Sirena was not that way.

She felt her body begin to tense as the pressure built inside her. That percolating in her core had grown into a wildly bubbling cauldron, and the need for release was mounting. Sirena had applied all of the necessary strokes to the canvas to form the background image, and now it was time to get down to the main event. She attacked Jessie's clit with so much vigor that Jessie nearly shot off the bed and into the ceiling. The sensations rocked through her like an earthquake, and she desperately tried to wrangle her heart into submission before it overworked itself. She was being whipped into a frenzy, every breath hinging on Sirena's attention, the very fibers of her core feeling as though they might shred if her release did not come soon. She fisted the sheets, rocked her hips against Sirena's face until finally, finally the dam burst forth and ecstasy rocketed through her with enough force to propel her to the moon and back.

She lay quivering for minutes afterwards, and didn't even realize she had grasped Sirena's head in her hands, holding her in place until the waves of pleasure subsided. Sirena didn't protest; she just rode out the hurricane until Jessie's body settled on the shore. Then she slid back up the sheets and gathered her lover into her arms, whispering softly, "I love you, Jessie," before they both drifted to sleep, depleted of all energy.

It was, naturally, Georgia who served as a wake-up call. The sun had returned to the Delmarva Peninsula at some point during their nap, and now it was slipping further and further toward the bay. When Jessie awoke, startled by the wet nose in her face and the warm tongue that licked her cheek, she saw the orange glow of the impending sunset heating up the skies outside her bedroom window. "Fuck, Sirena, how long did we sleep?"

"Orgasms are the best sleep aid," she mumbled, yawning and raising her arms into the air to stretch. Georgia took her open position as an invitation and leapt into her momma's arms, covering her face with soggy kisses.

Sirena sputtered as she tried to direct Georgia away from her face. "Hi, Girl! I know, I missed you too!" She gave the creature a hug around the neck, and then Georgia bounded off the bed and into the living room where she sat next to her leash and whimpered.

"Sounds like someone wants to go out," Jessie

surmised, pulling on her shorts and t-shirt that had been strewn on the carpet beside the bed. "Wanna come down to the beach?"

Sirena nodded. "Yes, and you are probably going to die when you see how loaded down with shit my car is." She shook her head with a hint of embarrassment.

"Okay, let's take care of Georgia, then we can work on your stuff. I think maintenance has a wheeled cart we might be able to borrow."

Sirena reached out to grab Jessie's hand before she slid out of bed. "I meant what I said earlier," she said, pinning her gaze on Jessie's.

"Okay?" Jessie questioned, unsure what she was referring to.

Sirena's eyes widened. "I'm really sorry about what happened in Pennsylvania. And you're right that I have been evasive and secretive with you. So I want to come clean."

Jessie's eyebrows shot up. Was this the appropriate time to ask if she was a prostitute? Or tell her what was going on at The Factory and with Jeannette's father? No. That would have to wait. She simply nodded and ambled into the living room to clip Georgia's leash on her collar. Sirena followed closely behind, not saying a word. Jessie assumed she was saving her confession for the beach. *The beach probably is the best place for a confession*, Jessie rationalized. *I mean, even if it's awful and hurtful and shocking, then at least you're at the beach.*

She even waited until their feet pressed into the wet sand near the shoreline. Jessie looked at Sirena expectantly, noticing how serious her expression had grown. Gone were the laugh lines around her lips and eyes, and instead she saw reflected there a host of painful memories, almost as if they'd been painted on between exiting Jessie's door and arriving on the beach.

"Are you sure you want to do this?" Jessie asked, taking her hand while Georgia pulled on her leash so she could frolic in the waves crashing on the shore.

Sirena nodded. "You deserve the truth. Especially after you were honest with me about what happened to you. I just want you to know that I always tried to do the right thing, even if it seems like it ended up going all wrong."

"Okay." Jessie squeezed her hand.

Sirena laughed. "I never thought I'd be confessing this to a cop." She shook her head. "As a matter of fact, I've spent my whole adult life trying to *avoid* confessing this to a cop."

No wonder she didn't want to tell me, then, Jessie thought. "Think of me as your girlfriend, not as a cop, alright?"

Sirena forced a smile, and the two proceeded down the shore, headed south. Jessie wondered if it would be easier for her to share her story if they walked along using the pounding waves and crying gulls as their soundtrack. If they didn't have to make eye contact.

"I don't think I told you that my father passed away when I was a teenager," she began, and Jessie shook her head, then squeezed her hand tightly. "He had cancer." She laughed a little, nervously, then shook her head again. "Imagine that, right?" They took a few more steps.

"My mother didn't take it very well, as you might imagine, and she became somewhat of a ghost to my sister, Elizabeth, and me. I was four years older, and did my best to take care of her. But four years older still didn't make me that old; I was fourteen, and she was ten. Then, when I was sixteen, my mother got remarried. Her new husband had a son who was about my age."

Jessie already didn't like where this story was headed, but she gripped Sirena's hand and braced herself for something bad.

"For a very brief time, things seemed okay. We were doing better financially. My father had made good money, but he worked for himself. He was an entrepreneur, and he didn't have good health insurance. We spent a lot of his savings on his treatment. And a lot of his life insurance went into some account that I wasn't supposed to be able to touch until I was eighteen. We had been fairly affluent before his death, and I'd gone to a private school. But in those two years before my mom married Paul, we ended up having to sell our house, and I had to start going to a different school. It really sucked.

"But once Paul came along, at least our mom seemed happy again. For a little while. Then Paul's son, who was also named Paul, by the way, started coming into my room at night. He'd tell me I needed to take off my clothes and let him do whatever he wanted to me, and if I didn't, he'd tell my mom and his dad, and then his dad would leave and we'd be homeless and penniless again. I thought I was doing it for my mom. To keep the peace. What I didn't know is that Paul, Sr., my stepdad, was raping my sister the whole time too."

"What?!" Jessie stopped walking, and Sirena

whipped around to face her. "Oh my god, Sirena, that's awful."

She nodded. "I know. I didn't know it was happening until I moved out. And I felt so horrible, because I was so caught up in my own abuse that I never recognized the symptoms that my sister was going through the same thing. And she was so much younger than me, and our stepdad was so disgusting. I felt so guilty that what she went through was so much worse than what I endured."

"You can't feel any blame for what happened to your sister, Sirena. You were both just kids. You both went through a complete nightmare." Jessie's eyes began to tear up as she thought about the two girls, desperate and afraid of the men who were supposed to be their new family. "How did you find out about your sister?"

"I went away to college, and one summer when I had a summer job as a waitress, I met Joe. He was in Atlanta for the summer doing some contract work at some big hospital that was going up. He was an electrician, by the way. He used to come in the restaurant where I worked almost every night, and eventually he'd hang out until I got off work and buy me a drink, and then we'd go back to his hotel room and fuck."

"Okay?"

"So I got a phone call from my sister one night, and she was freaking out. I couldn't even understand her, she was crying so hard. But eventually I worked out that she was knocked up. And that she was pretty sure it was our stepdad's. And I wish I could say I was surprised, but knowing what I had gone through with his son—who fortunately left home when he turned eighteen and never came back— I really wasn't."

"Oh, God!" Jessie clamped her hand over her gaping mouth. "What the fuck? And your mom didn't know this was going on?"

"Apparently she had tried to tell our mom, but she didn't believe her. Said she was making shit up, and all that. So that is why Lizzie turned to me. She didn't have anyone else. My mom didn't really have any family. My dad did, but after my mom got remarried, we really never saw our dad's family much."

"So what did you do?"

"Joe and I went and picked her up, and I took her for an abortion in the next county over, where no one knew any of us. But they told us they could only do the abortion if a parent accompanied her since she was a minor."

"Oh...." Jessie's voice trailed off until it was swallowed up by the sound of crashing waves.

"So we went to my mother, and I told her if she didn't take Elizabeth to get the abortion, then I was calling CPS on her ass," Sirena explained.

"And then she did?"

"Nope. Instead she went and told her dumb-ass husband. Paul said if Joe and I didn't leave town immediately, he was going to kill us both. And he had a whole arsenal of guns; it's not like I didn't believe him. But I was even more scared he was going to kill my mom or Lizzie."

Jessie's eyes grew wide. "So what did you do?"

"Joe took me back to Atlanta and said he would take care of Lizzie. He wouldn't let me go with him, though. He just said he'd be back in a few days. And of course, we didn't have cell phones back then, so I was just holed up in this hotel waiting for him to get back. I'd lost my job at the restaurant when I went back home to try to sort this stuff out 'cause I'd missed a shift or two. I was so fucking scared, Jessie. I had nowhere to go. I just sat there for however many days it took, holding myself in a fetal position and crying about the mess I'd caused."

For the first time in the conversation, Jessie noticed she had tears streaming down her red cheeks. The memories were fresh in her eyes, and the horrors of what she endured were evident. But Jessie had a feeling the story was going to get worse.

"I didn't know Joe had a friend in Atlanta who could create driver's licenses and other official documents. He could basically invent whole new identities for people for the right price. Joe kidnapped Lizzie—I still to this day have no idea how—then took her to his friend. They both got new identities and she got a birth certificate that listed him as her father. He wasn't really quite old enough to be her dad, but with his beard and everything, he could pass for a little older than he was. He was eight years older than me, so twelve years older than Lizzie, but they made him twenty years older."

"Wow." Jessie really couldn't formulate any other words. This all sounded like something from a movie, not something from real life. She had always thought her own story was unbelievable, but this was on a whole other level.

"Joe took Lizzie for her abortion and got her set up with some friends of his in Atlanta. Then he came back and got me. He thought I should get a new identity too, and we should get the hell out of town. All of the sudden, I became Anna Patterson."

"What happened to your sister after that?" Jessie asked.

That was when Sirena's face clouded up with even more hurt and anger. She paused for a moment while a violet sob rocked through her body. Jessie pulled her close, wrapping her arms around her while still holding Georgia's leash. "It's okay, sweetheart. You don't have to finish the story if you don't want to. I've heard enough."

"I didn't know how to get in contact with her. And Joe wouldn't tell me her new name."

"I don't understand. Why couldn't he tell you?" Jessie put her hands on Sirena's shoulders, searching her eyes for answers.

"Because the day after he kidnapped my sister, my mother shot herself. And Lizzie knew. She found out right after the abortion, when Joe was still in Atlanta with her. It was on the news because they arrested Paul for her murder, and something like that happening in our small town was pretty newsworthy. Joe said she blamed me. We followed the story even after we left Atlanta and headed north. There were warrants out for kidnapping Elizabeth, so we had to get out of there. And Joe was afraid Paul was going to come after us as soon as they ruled my mother's death a suicide and released him from jail. We had to get away." She collapsed against Jessie again, as if she were completely spent.

"My god," Jessie sighed, not having the words she needed to wrap the woman she loved in comfort. They were old wounds, to be sure, but so much about Sirena suddenly crystallized. She understood her loyalty to Joe, and why she felt she had done something terribly wrong.

"So, Joe, then...you felt like you owed him..."

She nodded. Jessie used her finger to wipe away a stray tear from Sirena's eye. "He saved my sister's life and mine. I just wish I hadn't lost my mother and sister in the process. I still feel guilty. Like maybe there was another way—a way we could have prevented that whole mess and gotten my sister the justice she deserved instead of having to lose her entire family."

Sirena sniffled a bit as her eyes scanned the horizon, then drifted back to Jessie. "I guess Lizzie's still out there somewhere. But who knows where? I wouldn't even begin to know how to look for her, and I begged Joe to tell me, even on his death bed, what her name was, but he wouldn't. He refused."

"Did he always beat you? Was he always an alcoholic?" Jessie couldn't help but let the questions that had been pent up for so long fly out.

Sirena smiled wearily, her cheeks stained by her tears. "No, no, not at all. At first he was loving and kind. He wanted a big family, and he spoiled me at first. He didn't want me to work. He wanted me to be the doting housewife and all that. I wanted to give him children so badly, but our first baby was stillborn. And then we had a miscarriage after that. I couldn't try again. I was absolutely heartbroken. That's when we both started drinking. He just wasn't as in control of it as I was. And he'd go on long benders and be so angry...and—"

Sirena paused to look around, first toward the ocean and then toward the bay. "Wow, it's getting dark. Should we go back?"

"So he didn't start hitting you till you'd been married a while?" Jessie called for Georgia, who had run out into the water as far as her leash could reach, and when she came running to shore, they turned toward the boardwalk leading to Jessie's building.

"No. I'll be honest with you, Jessie. I wanted to get help. I wanted to leave him. But he had always told me that no one else would want me or take care of me. I always thought about what happened when I tried to hold my stepfather accountable for his actions—my sister ended up estranged from me, and my mother ended up committing suicide. I felt like something bad would happen if I told anyone how it was between me and Joe. In some ways, I felt like dealing with Joe was what I deserved for not being able to take care of my sister."

"Oh, sweetheart, how could you ever feel you deserved to be treated like that?' Jessie asked, stopping to look into Sirena's sad eyes.

Her face brightened just a bit as though a memory was illuminating her from the inside out. "I had one bright thing in my life, though."

"What was that?"

She smiled. "A girlfriend."

Jessie's eyes bulged. "Really?"

"Joe's brother and his wife were swingers—that's how we got introduced to the lifestyle, believe it or not. And we started going to clubs in Philly, and then later came down to Ocean City. And so I realized pretty quickly that I had been missing out on being with women my whole life.

"I know you've never really believed that I was bisexual. I know you thought I just liked the attention I get from men when I play with women, but Jessie, I've always been bisexual. I didn't realize it till I was in my thirties, but it has always been there. And it's not just a sexual thing. I've had romantic relationships with women, the longest of which was with a woman named Gloria who moved to California last year. I was devastated. I had been with her for five years at that point."

"Did Joe know?"

"Joe didn't care about that. But in the last few years, he lost his job—he just couldn't work anymore, then we got the cancer diagnosis, and we lost our house and savings. And—"

"And what?"

"And Gloria wasn't here anymore. She was gone. I'd always been able to deal with Joe's shit because of her. She helped me be strong."

"Why did she leave?" Jessie wondered out loud. They had nearly reached the building by now, and behind them the sky hung in layers of mauve and indigo, hovering over the silky waves.

"She met a man," Sirena admitted. "A man who took her to California."

"What takes anyone anywhere?" Jessie asked, quoting something she remembered Sirena saying when they first met.

"Love and heartbreak," Sirena finished the quote. "Love took her to California, and heartbreak took me back to Ocean City." She pulled Jessie into her arms and rested her head against her shoulder.

"And what did you hope to find in Ocean City?" Jessie asked. "You just wanted to escape what was going on with Joe and be in the swinger community again?"

"Yes, definitely those things," Sirena agreed. "But I hoped to find something else too. And I realized I was probably looking in the wrong place for it, but I still had hope."

"What was that?" Jessie asked.

Sirena pulled back and met Jessie's gaze. Even in the faint light she could see a silvery shimmer in her dark eyes. "Love," she answered.

Jessie felt her eyes well with tears knowing all she had hoped to hear and feel was about to be bestowed upon her, all of the dreams she hadn't dared to dream were about to come true. She felt a lump grow in her throat, but she managed to choke out, "And did you find it?"

A grin as bright as a full moon spread across Sirena's face. "I did." She wrapped her arms around Jessie's neck and pressed herself against her body. "I love you, Jessie."

Jessie squeezed her back, then took Sirena's hand into her own, pulling it to her lips to press a soft kiss against her skin. "I love you too, Sirena."

TWENTY

A wise woman wishes to be no one's enemy; a wise woman refuses to be anyone's victim. -Maya Angelou

"I told Cap you were back in town," Jessie said as she breezed past Sirena to get to the kitchen. "I think he's expecting you today."

"I texted Paisley last night too," Sirena answered. "So, yes, I'm planning to go in. I feel bad for being gone longer than I anticipated."

"The main thing is that you accomplished what you set out to do." She reached for two mugs of coffee and filled them both up. "I've gotta go back to work today too."

"I did accomplish what I set out to do. I met with the lawyer to start the ball rolling on the estate; I picked up Joe's remains... I am going to have a memorial service at the beach at some point. I need to ask his brother and his wife when they can come down here."

Jessie's nose scrunched at the mention of Sirena's brother-in-law. "I'm just curious: if Joe had a brother nearby, why didn't he help you out when Joe was sick?"

"He did. Who do you think looked in on him on the weekends I was down here?" she answered. "And by the way, that is who I went to see...the old friend."

Jessie rolled her eyes. "Why didn't you just tell me that, then?" She lifted the steamy mug to her mouth to take a sip. It was still too hot.

Sirena shrugged as a sheepish look crept onto her face. "I don't know. Apparently I like being difficult sometimes." She chuckled and poured a teaspoon of sugar into her mug, then swirled it with a teaspoon.

"It's a good thing you're so sexy," Jessie shot back with a wink. "Did Paisley tell you any of the stuff going down at the club?"

Sirena nodded. "Just a bit. That they banned Jeannette, and she's raising a stink. And something about me being a prostitute and having an arrest warrant for kidnapping. All the charges involving my sister were later dropped, by the way. I know that much. Joe had connections. He could make things disappear."

Jessie frowned. "No wonder you were afraid to cross him. I hate that you went through all of that...and especially that you lost your sister."

"That is really my biggest regret. My mother was never the same after my dad died, not really. I feel like we lost her the day he passed. Lizzie and I were close, though, and I miss her. Every single day. I am always trying to imagine what her life is like now, and if she ever thinks of me."

"I wonder if she would get in touch if she knew how?"

Sirena shrugged. "I feel like she will always blame me for what happened to Mom. I thought about changing my name back to what's on my birth certificate, but I think that ship has already sailed."

"No, you need to move forward. You need to be Sirena Horne, and live out the rest of your days with no one abusing you or trying to control you."

"Amen to that!" she exclaimed, her face brightening.

Jessie started to tell her about getting called into Sarge's office, but decided against it. She was hoping that had all blown over. She hadn't heard any more from Sarge, and Cap hadn't said anything either.

"Well, guess I better go get dressed." Jessie sighed, then drained the rest of her coffee. "Oh, can you take Georgia out before you leave?"

Sirena nodded. "You better not hang out too long after you get your uniform on, or I might be tempted to jump your bones!" A wicked grin played on her lips as her eyes looked Jessie's pajama-clad body up and down.

Jessie felt a wave of heat flush over her as she remembered the time Sirena had done just that. She couldn't be late for work today, though. She had to make an appearance in court for some DUI arrest she'd made a few months back.

Georgia wandered in from the bedroom, sat down next to her leash, then let out a pitiful whimper. "Okay, okay, I'll take you out now," Sirena promised. "Just let me put something on." She returned from the bedroom seconds later wearing a soft floral cotton robe that tied around her waist.

"Give me a kiss now, babe. I may be gone when you get back up," Jessie said, knowing how Georgia liked to linger on the beach during her morning walk.

Sirena pressed her lips against Jessie's mouth. "Have a great day, darling, and don't worry. I have some ideas about how to take care of the Jeannette situation."

Jessie pulled back from the kiss, her brows furrowed. "What do you mean?"

"Don't worry," Sirena said with a wink. "I've got this."

"What now?" Bart questioned as they sat outside the courthouse. "You're awfully distracted today. You sure you're going to be okay on the stand?"

"I just got a text from Sarge telling me to wait here after the trial is over," Jessie explained. "Fuck. What now?" She took a deep breath, trying to clear all of the tension from her body, but she could feel it tightening the muscles in her neck.

Bart shrugged. "I haven't heard anything."

She pursed her lips. "You never hear a damn thing, Farris. You're like the last one to know anything around here." She laughed, which did help to soothe the pressure she felt, and before she could move on to her next thought, she received another text. This time it was from Cap.

You've got a great woman there, Jessie. Don't ever let her go.

That was all it said. But before she could text back, Bart reminded her they better get inside. Jessie nodded and turned off her phone. She rubbed her sweaty hands down her pants, thankful the dark material would hide the moisture, and followed Bart into the courthouse. Her mind was still boggled by Cap's text. *I didn't even know he realized Sirena and I were a couple*, she thought.

She was too absorbed in thinking about the situation with Sirena to get nervous about choking on the stand. She always compiled meticulous reports. She didn't believe in making bad arrests, and she knew in this case, the evidence would speak for itself. She'd pulled over a young lady cruising up Coastal Highway at 80 miles per hour, and she failed her field tests. There wasn't even a point in having a trial, and Jessie couldn't believe she had to drag herself to court when the woman would be much better off taking a plea. But this was the way defense attorneys worked; they always gave their clients that tiny little spark of hope.

While they were waiting for the court to readjourn after their lunch break, Jessie was told the woman took a plea at the last moment. "For fuck's sake," she said as she approached Bart, who was sitting on the hard wooden bench with his knees spread watching the people filter past. She sat down next to him. "I guess I gotta go see what Sarge wants now."

"Plea deal?" Bart confirmed, and Jessie nodded her head. "Do you want me to stick around?"

"Yeah, if you don't mind. Let me text Sarge real quick." Her heart pounded just waiting for the reply.

Bart folded his arms and scanned the hallway, his eyes zeroing in on a curvy blonde waiting outside one of the courtrooms. "Think she's into cops?"

"All women are into cops," Jessie said, winking at him. Her phone buzzed again, and she looked down. This time it was from Sirena.

Don't let the sheriff leave before I get there.

"What?" Jessie uttered the word aloud before she realized it. She squinted at the text again. *What the hell was she talking about?*

"What did he say?" Bart asked, his eyes still glued to the blonde.

"That was my girlfriend. I don't know why, but I have this crazy feeling I'm about to lose my job."

"What?" Now she had Bart's attention. He flashed a concerned look at her. "What the fuck do you mean?"

Jessie exhaled a deep breath, blowing it out until her lungs were completely empty. Then she saw Sarge pacing toward her. "Wish me luck," she muttered as she stood up. He gestured toward a door at the end of the hallway that Jessie knew to be a conference room. She took one last glance at Bart, who had a confused expression painted on his face, complete with furrowed brows and gaping lips.

She felt as if she were death-marching into the room. Sgt. Grimes wore a scowl on his face, and she could only imagine what the sheriff was going to look like if he were indeed in the room. It only took her a split second to ascertain that he was. He was a portly man in his early sixties with a fading auburn comb-over and a thick strawberry blond mustache. Jessie felt the blood in her veins turn to ice as Sgt. Grimes motioned toward a seat at the end of the table across from where the sheriff was sitting.

"Sheriff Abrahms," she offered, forcing a smile and holding out her hand to shake, "it's nice to meet you." He took her hand into his as if it were a fish he was trying to strangle. She thought perhaps her fingers were all broken after he finished squeezing them into his palm. She covered up the pain with a smile and placed both of her hands on the table in front of her, looking up at the sheriff with as pleasant an expression as she could muster.

"Corporal Martinez," he finally addressed her. "I'm going to cut to the chase. I need to know what the hell is going on with this alleged girlfriend of yours, Sirena Horne A.K.A. Anna Patterson A.K.A. Theresa Hornbeck."

Jessie's lungs squeezed out all the air they'd collected from her last breath, pushing it into the stuffy room. The Sheriff's department had obviously done quite a bit of research on Sirena. Jessie hadn't even known Sirena's birth name was Hornbeck, but it certainly made sense given her choice of "Horne" as an alias.

"What is it you'd like to know, sir?" she questioned, struggling to keep her demeanor as calm as humanly possible.

Jessie realized Cap and the other employees of The Factory could not mention Jeannette's membership due to their own policies of non-disclosure, but there was no reason Jessie couldn't let the cat out of the bag. Except for the fact that doing so would imply her own membership. *Damn it*, she thought. *But I will; I will just tell him*, Jessie decided. *I may risk my job, but it will protect Sirena.*

"We have every reason to believe that Ms. Patterson is operating out of a local swinger club as a prostitute," Sheriff Abrahms said firmly, shoving a manila file folder into her hands.

"What is this?" she asked, her heart pounding even more recklessly than it had when she first arrived in the conference room.

"Evidence," he answered gruffly. "Go on, look at it."

She opened the file folder with trembling fingers, running her eyes over the documents at breakneck speed. There were some grainy surveillance photos which did seem to show Sirena with a few unidentifiable male figures. Of course, that proved nothing. There was one of her coming out of what looked like The Factory, and Jessie wondered how they'd wrangled that footage away from Cap and Calvin. There was a copy of an arrest warrant from Georgia that was decades old, and such a poor facsimile that the old typewriter ink was nearly illegible. There was a hotel receipt from someone named—*oh*, she realized, *Brian King, as in Brian and Susan King from The Factory*. There was also a canceled check from Brian King in the amount of $500.00 and two more in the amounts of $250.00 each. Jessie's eyes continued to bulge as she saw more canceled checks, each with names of a male member of The Factory. *What the fuck is going on?* she wondered, feeling her stomach churn with nausea.

"I didn't know about any of this," Jessie said, spitting the words out of her mouth. "But I do know that Sirena's husband was very ill, and she was having a hard time making ends meet. He passed away recently, and I know she's had a lot of expenses."

"Did she ever offer to exchange sex with you for money?" he demanded.

"What?!" Jessie shrieked, unable to control her pitch. "No, why in the world would you ask that?"

"You two are sexually intimate, aren't you?" Sheriff Abrahms inquired.

"That is absolutely none of your business, but it is true that she is living with me."

"Oh," he said, rolling his eyes. "Housing in exchange for sex. Looks like I was right about this con artist, and if we can prove you knew her background, I'm pretty sure you'll be relieved of your duties."

She couldn't even formulate a reply, and she felt so absolutely disgusted, she thought she might hurl her lunch all over the conference room table. Her mind flashed with images of Sirena on the beach the night before, glimpses of the sincerity in her eyes. *The way she looked when she told me she loved me,* Jessie remembered. *Even the best con artist couldn't fake that look.*

"With all due respect, Sheriff Abrahms," she choked out, "I don't understand what the checks are for, but I can verify that Sirena is a member of The Factory because I am too." She took a deep breath and gained a little more courage before continuing. "And do you know who else is a member of The Factory?"

He appeared quite surprised that her voice had suddenly turned more challenging. "Who is that, Corporal Martinez?"

"Your daughter, Jeannette," Jessie revealed, hoping

to deliver the news matter-of-factly and with no traces of malice, though every bone in her body wanted to slap that jealous bitch across the face.

Sheriff Abrahms chuckled. "Oh, please, I don't think so. Her mother and I raised her better than that. She's in church every Sunday morning!" He scoffed again as he continued to spear Jessie with his pale gray-blue eyes.

"I can't produce the member roster or surveillance footage right now," Jessie answered, "but I do know the management at The Factory quite well, and I know that evidence exists." She watched the sheriff's face cloud over with confusion. "Your daughter Jeannette has had a beef with Sirena for months, and has been circulating horrible rumors about her—false rumors, I might add—the entire time. I have no idea why she has such a vendetta against Sirena, but the final straw was last weekend when she learned Sirena got the job Jeannette had applied for at The Factory—"

"Jeannette doesn't work outside the home," he insisted. "She doesn't have to."

"I don't know why she applied, but I do know how she treated Sirena, and it was bad enough behavior to get her kicked out of The Factory—permanently."

The door handle twisted, and the door creaked on its hinges as it was pushed open. Jessie's eyes flashed across the room just in time to witness Sirena entering in a professional-looking pantsuit with a red and navy printed scarf artfully tied around her neck. It almost looked like she'd raided Casey Fontaine's closet.

"Sheriff Abrahms," she said in a more self-assured voice than Jessie had ever heard, "I'm Sirena Horne, and I would like to address the allegations you've put forth about me."

"You're not under arrest, Ms. Horne, or whatever your name is," he replied. "Not yet, anyway. We're still gathering the facts."

"Well, I can give you all of the facts, sir. Please listen," she said, standing at the edge of the table. Sgt. Grimes, who had been completely silent and motionless up until now, used his foot to push the chair opposite of him away from the table, then gestured for her to sit down.

The sheriff didn't say anything as Sirena settled herself into the chair. He wore an expression of boredom, as if he couldn't believe he was getting involved with such nonsense.

"I've been coming to Ocean City for years and years," she began, her eyes darting between Sgt. Grimes and Sheriff Abrahms. "I've used many different aliases and identities throughout my time here because I've learned the hard way that people aren't always trustworthy. I've even changed my look a time or two. I've been a blonde, redhead, and brunette, for example, but there have been some other changes in my looks throughout the years too.

"Many people who knew me and my late husband Joe wanted to help when they found out he had cancer. So, when I first started coming back down here a few months ago, when he was in really bad shape, I had several offers to help us pay for some of his treatments and care. One of those people was Brian King. The other checks you have copies of and illegally obtained from my checking account—because I am almost positive you didn't have a warrant—are from other couples who wanted to help me out. Did I sleep with those people? Sure did; I'm not going to deny it. But it wasn't in exchange for money. They'd be the first to tell you I'd have slept with them either way." She chuckled a bit as she continued to move her eyes between the two men across from her.

Sirena flashed him a brazen smile. "I'll tell you why your daughter has it out for me, Sheriff Abrahms."

Jessie observed the way his eyes dug into her as she stood her ground, her voice even calmer and steadier than Jessie was able to make her own voice just moments before.

"A month or two before I joined The Factory, I met Jeannette and her husband at a party down here. I ended up hanging out with them a couple weekends in a row, and she and her husband were sympathetic to my plight. What she didn't know was that he gave me $2000 in cash without telling her—at first, I mean. By the time I joined The Factory several weeks later, she had found out, and she was absolutely livid. She was even more angry that I was encroaching on her turf. She offered me $2000 more if I would never darken the door of The Factory again, but I told her no."

The sheriff shook his head, and his eyes narrowed. "I don't know why you expect me to believe a word of this nonsense. It's all absolutely ridiculous," he barked, a vein on his temple bulging with rage.

Jessie was shocked that all of this was being revealed, but she didn't want to express her surprise in front of the sheriff and her sergeant, so she just nodded her head a lot as if she had heard it all before.

"As a matter of fact, when Jessie first started following me around the club, I thought Jeannette had paid her off to get rid of me. Then Jeannette started a whole bunch of ridiculous rumors about me to try to get me thrown out. She told people I was a drug dealer, prostitute, porn star, a spy from a rival club. All kinds of bullshit, but what really made her flip her lid was when I confronted her one night just before closing."

"So what?" Sheriff Abrahms sneered.

"Well, sir, I told her I was sorry she was jealous of the fact her husband preferred sleeping with me over her, and," Sirena paused for dramatic effect, "in addition, her *own father* seemed to prefer sleeping with me over her *own mother!*"

"What the hell are you talking about?" he shouted, standing to his feet and nearly knocking over the table in the process.

The smuggest look Jessie had ever seen appeared on Sirena's face as she pulled her phone out of her bra and began scrolling through it as she continued her story. "You probably don't remember now, Sheriff, but you were a young deputy who liked to tell his wife you were working overtime when you were actually frequenting this hole in the wall pub several blocks off the boardwalk. I think it was around 1998. You know, like 20 years ago? Oh, and I was a redhead with a bigger nose and smaller tits back then."

Jessie tried to keep her jaw from dropping to the floor when Sirena held up her phone to reveal a scanned photograph, obviously several years old, of her sitting in a much younger Deputy Abrahms' lap. She had to peer closely at it, but even with a different nose, smaller breasts and red hair, it was definitely Sirena. And unmistakably Deputy Abrahms. "Bet your wife wouldn't care much for seeing this photo, would she?"

The blood drained from Sheriff Abrahms' face until he had a greenish cast about him. If Jessie wasn't mistaken, he looked as though he was about to vomit all over the table, much like she felt like doing right before Sirena showed up.

"The simple fact is, Sheriff Abrahms, you don't have any proof I've done anything wrong—because I *haven't* done anything wrong! But I could nail your daughter for slander, blackmail, and who knows what else. Not to mention the fact that somewhere in the possessions I've just cleaned out from my trailer back in Pennsylvania, there's a pretty sweet homemade sex tape featuring that same guy in the photo—remember my husband Joe filming that?"

The sheriff was so stunned, he was unable to force any words out of his mouth. He didn't even try to deny the picture or refute her accusations. He just sat frozen in his chair as though the weight of the world had just crashed down upon him.

"So maybe we can just forget this whole thing with Jeannette, and I can get back to *my* job at The Factory, and you can let my girlfriend get back to *her* job protecting the fine citizens of Ocean City. What do you say?"

He nodded his head, then lifted his chin toward Jessie. "You're free to go, Corporal Martinez. I'm sorry for your trouble."

"No trouble, sir. Thank you," she answered, working hard to conceal her glee.

Sgt. Grimes rose and shook Sheriff Abrahms' hand. "Please rest assured that everything said in this room today will be held in the strictest confidence," he promised in a deep, firm voice.

Jessie waited until she and Sirena had made it out to the parking lot where Bart was still waiting for her in his cruiser. She made a quick introduction, then leaned back against the car and raked her eyes up and down her beautiful pants-suited girlfriend. "Baby, I can't believe you just did that! That was fucking amazing!" She threw her arms around Sirena and squeezed her tightly to her chest.

"I don't think you truly realized I wasn't an outsider here in OC," she explained. "After Cap told me what was going on and about his own talk with the sheriff yesterday, it was pretty clear what I had to do."

"I never expected you to stand up for yourself like that! You were so brave and so strong!" She brushed a strand of golden hair out of Sirena's eyes that the wind had blown in her face. "I'm so proud of you."

"Do you remember what you said after you told me your story?" Sirena questioned, searching Jessie's face for recognition.

"What was that?"

"You told me you chose not to be a victim anymore," Sirena answered. "You said you chose to be a survivor. I want to be a survivor too."

Jessie pinned her beaming-with-pride gaze on Sirena, locking their eyes together in a bond of love. "You already are, babe. You already are."

Cap invited them all to his and Leah's house for a pitch-in that night. "Leah is so bored and miserable with no adult company!" he insisted. She still looked exhausted from her perch on the couch, but happy to see her friends, nonetheless.

Before dinner, he raised his glass to the crowd. "Folks, the club was nearly in jeopardy again this week, but thanks to the bravery of our newest employee, Sirena, and her girlfriend, Jessie, I think it's going to be smooth sailing from here on out! So here's to Sirena and Jessie!"

"Here here!" Calvin shouted, and everyone else raised their glasses in unison.

"I want to say something," Sirena said after the chattering of the small gathering settled down.

"Go for it!" Leah shouted from the couch. Everyone turned in her direction, surprised to hear such a loud voice resonate over the din. She laughed. "Yeah, I'm still here, guys! Go on, Sirena, I want to hear what you have to say."

Everyone shifted their attention to Sirena, who tossed her long blonde hair over her shoulder and began to open her mouth. But first she snapped her eyes to Jessie, who encouraged her with a warm smile. "Thanks for that lovely toast, Cap," she began, and he nodded. "I wanted to take a moment to thank Paisley for being such a lovely boss and being patient with me while I learn all these new-fangled social media and marketing terms I didn't know before."

Paisley laughed and nodded as Calvin put his arm around her and squeezed her tightly to her side. "I've learned a lot too just teaching you!" she joked.

Sirena continued, "I wanted to thank Cap and Leah for taking a chance on someone who didn't have anything recent on her resume, even though I do have a pretty rampant addiction to Facebook, as everyone here knows. And Instagram. Don't forget Instagram. My girl and my dog are oh-so-photogenic!" Everyone chuckled.

Jessie rolled her eyes, laughing as she remembered how many times Sirena had forced her to pose with her for a selfie so it could be uploaded to her social media accounts. She hated the fact that she knew what Instagram filters and hashtags her girlfriend preferred. *Good thing she's so amazing,* Jessie thought with a smile.

"We're very glad to have you with us," Leah said from her spot on the couch, where Lincoln had climbed aboard and was currently sitting on her lap. "And I know it means a lot to Casey to have someone taking over some of her duties."

"Ah, Casey was next on my list!" Sirena exclaimed. "Jessie, were you able to get her on FaceTime?"

Jessie nodded and held out her phone for everyone to wave hi to Casey in California. She wore a cobalt blue silk turban, and her face was exquisitely made-up. She looked amazing.

"Casey!" Sirena exclaimed. "I am so happy to see you!"

"Hey, lady!" Casey greeted her with a wave.

"So, Casey, I know you don't remember me as Leanne Grant, but we met many years ago at a party. Then later, you helped my husband and I search for properties in Ocean City, but we were never quite able to afford to move down here, much to my extreme disappointment. I was a brunette then, and I looked a little different; I was thinner and had a different nose and smaller breasts. Probably was fifteen years ago now."

"Oh my god, woman! I totally remember Leanne!" Casey shrieked. "Why the hell didn't you tell me? It's been driving me crazy trying to figure out why you seem so familiar!"

"Well," Sirena said, letting out a deep breath, "I just wasn't sure what you'd think of my new name and look. And the fact we never bought a house from you!" She giggled. "But I wanted to tell you that I have always admired you so much, and that my thoughts and prayers are with you every day."

Casey's eyes began to glisten with tears. "Thank you so much, my beautiful friend. I wouldn't have been upset at all about that! Things are going just about as well out here as can be expected. Don't worry, I'll be coming back in a month or two to visit! Make sure to hold down the fort while I'm away!"

"Oh, sure, wait till after tourist season to come visit," Cap noted, laughing.

"Hey, no one ever accused me of being dim," Casey joked.

"Finally," Sirena continued, "I want to thank my beautiful girlfriend, Jessie. I know there's a bit of an age difference between us, but I swear to god her soul is decades older than mine. She's grounded, mature, and wise beyond her years, that's for sure. She has a beautiful heart, and she's taught me so much about the kind of person I want to be. I have learned how to be strong, to stand up for myself, and most of all, that I deserve love. She didn't even know she was helping me slay my demons for the longest time, but she did, and to be honest with you—the hope I had of being with her, of being the woman she knew I could be, that is the reason I am still here today. Thank you so much, my love!"

Later that night, Jessie held Sirena close to her in bed, her favorite time of the day. She hadn't ever imagined she would get so much enjoyment from going to bed with someone and waking up next to them the following morning, but she did. It was so simple, but so magical. She pressed a soft kiss into Sirena's hair and whispered, "Thank you for the toast tonight. It was really sweet of you to say those things in front of everyone."

"Every word was true," Sirena confirmed.

Jessie stroked her fingers through Sirena's hair and brushed her lips against her cheek. "I am so incredibly lucky." She trailed more kisses down her neck. "I knew from the moment I met you that I wanted you, but I tried so damn hard not to fall for you. I just knew I was going to get my heart broken, yet I couldn't help myself. I wanted to help you."

"You helped me help myself." She returned Jessie's kisses with one of her own, stamped on Jessie's neck. "My whole life I've been trying to be someone else. I kept changing my name. I kept telling myself I deserved all the bad things that happened to me: Joe hitting me, then getting sick, his drinking, losing my family, losing our house and savings. It was just one blow after another, so I'd change my name and try to start over as someone else. It never worked."

"I'm still trying to keep track of all those aliases," Jessie laughed.

"I'm not going to run anymore," Sirena promised. "I've finally found the right place...the right name...the right woman for me."

Jessie wrapped her arms around Sirena and held her body so close that their skin nearly melted together. As their mouths met again and their hands traced each other's curves, Jessie was filled with such an overwhelming sense of peace, of rightness, that it washed over her like a tidal wave, sweeping all the old hurt and pain out to sea, while renewing her world with a vibrant hope for the future.

EPILOGUE

Cut the ending. Revise the script. The man of her dreams is a girl. — *Julie Anne Peters,* Keeping You a Secret

As they made their way across the sand, which had cooled considerably now that it was early October, Jessie looked out across the water and saw a dolphin spout before leaping into the air and crashing back down into the waves. Not surprisingly, as they always traveled together in a pod, another performed a similar maneuver just seconds later. Finally, seven or eight of them took turns surfacing and then disappearing, their sleek, charcoal gray bodies contrasting against the white crests. She reached down to grasp Sirena's hand and pull her close to her side, then pointed out to sea.

Sirena put her hand over her heart and smiled. It was an emotional day, and she carried the last vestiges of her old life in a porcelain and metal urn in her other hand. They were marching down to the shoreline where she would sprinkle a few of Joe's ashes into the pounding surf. Then they'd be heading out on Cap's charter fishing boat to spread the rest at sea.

At the moment, it was just the two of them. She wanted a few moments of privacy before rejoining their "pod" on Cap's boat. Though there was silence between them, Jessie knew that Sirena understood the family of dolphins reminded Jessie of the fact they had found their own pod to swim with. What Sirena didn't know was that Jessie had a surprise waiting for her on the boat, and she hoped it would provide some lightness to the somber mood of the day.

The skies hadn't gotten the message about the somber mood. Not at all. It was a crisp fall day, and the sun was a golden goddess taking a long, glorious bath in the radiant turquoise waters of the Atlantic. Every cloud was a perfect white feather soothing the deep, soulful blue of the sky, a blue so saturated that it nearly hurt to look at. If not for the clouds, one might lose herself in that blue.

Jessie winced when a cool wave rushed over her bare feet. "Whose idea was it to do this barefoot?" she asked. She held Georgia's leash in her other hand, accepting the reality that it was either barefoot or have Georgia drag her into the water and get her shoes wet. *Barefoot* it is, she mused.

"This feels so weird," Sirena said as she stopped right at the edge where the sand gently sloped into the water. "Weird, but right. I don't know how to describe it."

"You don't have to describe it at all," Jessie assured her. "It just is what it is."

She let out a soft chuckle. "I know that, but I do feel like I should say a few words."

"Say anything you'd like." She put her arm around her girlfriend and bowed her head as the waves continued to splash over her. It was amazing how after a few passes, the cold water didn't feel nearly as startling. But maybe it was because she was numb at that point.

"Joe, I met you when I was only twenty years old," Sirena said, her voice floating on the gentle October breeze. "That means I knew you for longer than half of my life. I thought for sure you were my knight in shining armor. But then I ended up needing another knight in shining armor to save me from you. Some days I still don't know how I survived you." She paused for a moment as she looked up, her eyes scanning the horizon. A gull swooped down to the water right in front of them, then took off again in a flash.

"I hope you're at peace now, Joe. I truly do." She carefully lifted the lid on the urn, and as if on cue, the wind carried away the top layer of particles, swirling them into the breeze before they were swallowed up by the ocean spray. Then she stood there, holding the urn in both hands while Jessie remained beside her with her arm draped around her waist.

She didn't cry. Her face didn't redden with emotion or reflect anything but a sense of relief that part of her duty was complete. She turned to Jessie and simply said, "Let's go meet Cap."

Sirena stopped in her tracks as soon as she boarded the vessel, her eyes freezing on one particular figure in the small crowd gathered on the deck. She squinted, and Jessie watched her expression morph into one of shock. She turned to Jessie with her mouth gaped open. "Is that?"

"It's your sister Elizabeth," Jessie confirmed, then, after being handed the urn for safekeeping, she witnessed her girlfriend bound across the deck till she stopped short right beside the woman who was very nearly her exact height and build, only with chin-length light brown hair.

"Terri!" she screamed, throwing her arms around Sirena and squeezing her until her breath was stolen.

"Oh my god, Lizzie, is that really you?' Sirena asked, pulling back to stroke her finger down her younger sister's face. "I'm not dreaming, right?"

"No, you're not dreaming." She beamed a grin that looked so much like Sirena's, Jessie was amazed. "I want you to meet my son." She moved away from the crowd of people to reveal a little boy who was sitting on one of the benches with an electronic gaming device in his hand. "Thomas!" she called.

Sirena clasped her hand over her chest as her eyes welled up with tears. "Thomas? That was our dad's name..."

"I know," Lizzie answered, placing her hands on the boy's shoulders as she positioned him in front of her body. "Thomas, this is your Aunt Terri. She's Mommy's big sister." Jessie heard her thick southern drawl, thicker than her sister's, drip off her words like honey from a honeycomb.

"Hi," he said shyly. He looked to be about seven or eight years old and had blond hair and green eyes. And he had the accent too, judging from just that one stretched-out syllable.

"Oh my god," Sirena gasped. "You look exactly like your mom when she was little." She looked around from Jessie to Cap, Leah, Casey, Paisley and Calvin, who were also on board, along with Sirena's brother-in-law and his wife and their two daughters. "Who made this happen? How did this—" She was so overwhelmed by emotion, she could scarcely get the words out of her mouth.

Jessie smiled. "Remember how the sheriff had investigated you so...thoroughly?"

Sirena nodded.

"Casey happens to know Sheriff Abrahms pretty well, and after I told her what happened and what kind of evidence you had about his...uh...prior indiscretions...she was able to convince him to hand over the info he had collected. Then I did some research on my own using my connections, and voila, we found an Elizabeth Burke living in Savannah, Georgia. Maiden name: Hornbeck."

"Wow!" Sirena gasped. "I'm so shocked, I don't even know what to say!" She mouthed a few words of gratitude to Casey and Jessie, then asked, "Lizzie, did you get a chance to meet Joe's brother Alan, and his wife, Rita?"

"Yes, I did, thank you," Lizzie answered. "I'm so glad Jessie got in contact with me! I had always wanted to find you, but Joe told me I would be safer if I just started over and didn't mention my family to anyone."

Any further conversation was halted when

another figure began to climb aboard Cap's boat. It was a tall woman with short, spiky dark hair and a matching complexion. "Hey, Andrea, over here!" Lizzie called. It only took the woman a few strides with her long legs to reach the rest of the assembly.

"Terri, this is my wife, Andrea," she said, gesturing toward the tall woman.

Another wave of surprise washed over Sirena's face, which gave way to delight. "Andrea, it's so wonderful to meet you," she said, reaching out to shake her hand, but then deciding to pull her in for a hug instead.

"Sorry, I had to use the ladies' room before we could shove off," Andrea laughed as she pulled away from Sirena's embrace. Jessie noticed Andrea's face was open, like she had nothing to hide, and her eyes were kind. She immediately went to stand beside her wife, her arm wrapped supportively around her shoulder.

Cap left the group to assume his position behind the wheel of the boat, and Jessie was surprised at how quiet the engine was when it started up. In no time, they were cruising through the gentle ripples of the bay, aiming for the inlet at the end of the strip of land that housed Ocean City.

"I know it's weird for us to have a family reunion on the day of Joe's memorial service, but if you really think about it, it's also not weird," Lizzie said, laughing. "Okay, let me explain." Everyone's eyes were glued to her as she carefully took the urn out of Jessie's hands and held it out in front of her.

"Joe came into Terri's life the summer I thought *my* life was ending. I still believe to this very day I probably wouldn't have made it to my seventeenth birthday if it hadn't been for Joe. That day I called you, Terri, to tell you I was pregnant, was the worst day of my life. I didn't know who I could turn to. I knew Mom wouldn't believe me. I knew she wouldn't help me. You were really my only hope.

"When you and Joe came to McDonough from Atlanta, all I could think about was how we were going to pull this off. I knew if our stepdad found out what was going on, he'd kill me. I had no doubt. I thought he would probably kill you too. But I remember Joe pulled me aside and told me not to worry. He said he was going to take care of everything."

Jessie saw Sirena's shoulders sag as the words her sister spoke sunk in. She could feel the weight of the dredged-up emotions filling her body, seeping out onto her face in the form of pursed lips and teary eyes. She knew this reunion was not going to come completely free; there would be a price. But she also wanted some closure for both women where Joe was concerned, and hoped they could embark on a new relationship, a mended one.

"Those few days I was with Joe after he sent Terri back to Atlanta were harrowing. I know you were probably unaware, Terri, but the doctor he took me to—well, as you might imagine, it was a back-alley type thing. Not a place for any woman, and especially not a scared sixteen-year-old girl who had been abused. They gave me a lot of pain medication after the procedure."

Andrea squeezed her wife tightly to her body, holding her up in her moment of pain. Sirena went to her side too, and both women supported her as she poured out the rest of her tribute to the man whose ashes she held close to her heart.

"I had a feeling I would never see you or Mom ever again," she continued. "Joe basically told me not to expect to. He kept telling me I had a new name and a fresh start, and I could be whoever I wanted to be. He left me with some friends of his, and they helped me get on my feet. It helped that my new documentation said I was 18 instead of 16.

"Terri, I want you to know something. Joe had his friend in Atlanta change my name again after I'd had the procedure. He didn't want anyone to track me down through the doctor. His friends helped me cut and dye my hair, too. By the way, Andrea knows me as Michelle. That's the name I've gone by since a few days after I got the abortion.

"Joe left money for his friends, too, so they could get me clothes and feed me. They also helped me find a job when I was a little stronger, and when I got medical insurance, they helped me find a therapist I could tell all my secrets to. He also called his friends to check on me a few times, even though I was very angry about what happened to our mom, and at the time, I didn't want to speak to him or you. But if it weren't for Joe's kindness and the kindness of his friends, I have no idea where I would be today. So, thank you, Joe, and I'm sorry I never got to tell you in person how much everything you did meant to me."

Sirena's face was red and blotchy, with tears trailing down her cheeks as she lifted the urn out of Lizzie's hands. "I don't know how much Jessie has told you about what ended up happening with Joe, but he definitely had a dark side too. He was an alcoholic, and he didn't always treat me right. The last few years I was with him, I didn't honestly know if I was going to make it out alive either. But I am so grateful he was able to save you, Lizzie—and by the way, you will always be Lizzie or Elizabeth to me, just like I'll always be Terri and not Sirena to you. So I guess I have to at least be grateful that I came out of this whole horrible ordeal stronger. And if I hadn't survived, I wouldn't have Jessie in my life—or now you and Thomas. I hope we never lose touch again."

"Me too, Sis," Lizzie echoed and pressed a soft kiss to Sirena's cheek.

Cap had stopped the boat, and the only thing they could hear were the waves rocking against the bow and the cries of gulls overhead. The horizon was a thin blue line separating earth and sea in the far-off distance, and the sun was a glowing orb of warmth shining down upon them. Sirena carried the urn to the side of the boat, bowed her head and whispered a few faint words before tossing the entire thing overboard. They all watched it sink beneath the deep blue abyss.

She turned directly into Jessie's arms and sobbed on her shoulder, until she looked up to meet Lizzie's tearful eyes. Then she wrapped her arms around her sister.

"I've had a lot of surreal days in my life, but I am pretty sure today was the surrealist," Sirena remarked. "Is that even a word?" She stroked her fingers down Jessie's back as they laid in bed facing each other.

"If it's not, it should be," Jessie agreed. "I was

hoping Lizzie would be able to get in last night so you could meet and talk about things before the service. But it just didn't work out like that. I hoped you wouldn't be mad at me for blindsiding you with it, either!"

Sirena playfully slapped her on the shoulder. "You should know me well enough by now to know that I can roll with the punches!" She laughed. "Seriously, Jessie, if anyone is adaptable, it is *moi*."

"No doubt," Jessie said, smiling. "So, I do have a little good news for you that I've been waiting to share with you..."

"Oh, yeah? What's that?" Sirena draped her arm around Jessie's waist and pulled their bodies together, then slid her leg over Jessie's hips so they formed a human pretzel.

"Close enough now?" Jessie teased her.

"Never!" Sirena shot back. "Okay, don't hold me in suspense any longer. What's your news?"

Even though it was dark in the room, Jessie could see the faint reflection of moonlight streaming in through the window and shining in her lover's eyes. "I got approved for my promotion today."

"What? Really?" Sirena gasped.

Jessie could feel the excited vibrations leave Sirena's body and race through her own.

"That's right. I'm now Sergeant Martinez!"

"Oh, honey, I'm so proud of you! You deserve this so much." She squeezed Jessie tightly to her chest and planted a kiss on her lips.

"Thank you. Bart is beside himself. He doesn't

know what he's going to do without me," Jessie said, laughing.

"I'm sure he'll manage!"

"So, I have a question for you," Jessie said, changing the subject.

"What's that?" She had a slight tremble in her voice.

"Did you think it was funny that your sister is married to a woman?" Jessie asked.

Sirena shrugged. "Not really. I thought it was pretty cool, actually. And Andrea seems like a lovely woman. She's an engineer, did you hear? That's super cool. Apparently they used a sperm donor for Thomas, but Lizzie's egg, so he's biologically her son. I thought so; the resemblance is striking..."

Jessie wasn't expecting Sirena to traipse off on a tangent. "I didn't really mean the 'being with a woman thing' as much as the 'married thing,'" she clarified.

Sirena shook her head, her long hair rustling around her shoulders. "What do you mean?"

"I guess I'm asking if you ever thought about getting married again..." Jessie let the words trail off into the darkness, scared of what might happen to them there.

She definitely didn't expect Sirena to bubble up with laughter, but she did. "Are you asking me to marry you?"

Jessie scoffed. "No—" She swallowed down the lump in her throat. "I just wondered what you thought—"

"Oh." There was a definite hint of dejection in her

voice.

"Did you want me to ask you to marry me?" Jessie asked, her tone brightening considerably.

There was a pause, one that made Jessie's heart flutter faster than she liked—especially right before she slept.

"I'd like for you to ask me someday," Sirena answered softly. "Definitely someday."

Jessie sighed. *Why do women have to be so difficult?*

"Okay, maybe sooner rather than later," Sirena changed her answer.

Jessie laughed. "Fair enough. Sooner rather than later, then," she repeated.

"I love you, Jessie," Sirena said, the last two words stretched out with a sleepy yawn. "You're going to make a wonderful wife."

Jessie nodded. "Hell, yeah, I am. Best wife you've ever had."

"No doubt," Sirena agreed, yawning again.

"I love you too, Sirena." Jessie pressed a kiss to her lover's cheek and settled her head down on the pillow. *Sooner rather than later*, she echoed in her mind. *I think sooner.*

THE END

The Eastern Shore Swingers Series will continue with Book 4, currently untitled, featuring Casey Fontaine's story with a M/M/F theme, due to arrive in Fall 2018. If you haven't read the first two books in the series, what are you waiting for? *Fisher of Men* (Cap and Leah's story) and *The Catch* (Calvin and Paisley's story) are available now!

ACKNOWLEDGMENTS

It's hard to believe as I type this that I'm about to publish my thirteenth book. It's a bit surreal, in fact. So much goes into writing a book, and there are always so many people who support you and help along the way, and this is that part where you have to try to remember to thank everyone who was part of the journey.

First off, I have to thank my husband, who is a real-life law enforcement officer, and had I not known him for the past seven years and seen the ins and outs of his day-to-day job, there's no way I would have felt comfortable making one of my main characters a cop. I am also grateful for his female shiftmates, whom I've gotten to know and who helped me wrap my mind around what Jessie might be like. Being a police officer is one of the toughest jobs I could ever imagine doing, and they simply do not get enough respect or gratitude. Not to say that all cops are good—far from it. There are good and bad people in every job. Notice the sheriff in my story is not exactly a principled man, for example. I hate it when people try to paint ALL of one category of people as good or bad. It simply isn't true, and stereotypes such as those cause so much pain, violence and misunderstanding in this world.

Secondly, I have to thank my personal assistant, Jared; my proofreader, Tina; and my beta readers and ARC readers. Early on I got some pretty critical feedback about Jessie from a beta reader, and I had a moment of wanting to ditch the entire project. I did change a few things about her, but not everything, as I felt very strongly that I didn't want her to be a stereotype. Thankfully, after I made a few tweaks, so many other beta readers fell in love with her and really with both of these women who had such painful pasts, but who are able to bond, trust, and love despite it all.

Thirdly, I have to thank Colleen at Itsy Bitsy, who has been such a wonderful friend and support to me through the years. I love the friendship we have developed, and I better get to meet you in person soon because I want to give you a HUGE hug! While I'm thanking bloggers and promoters, I always have to give a shout-out to Natasha and Read.Review.Repeat who has become such a great real-life friend of mine, and thankfully we live close enough to actually hang out in person. I love our dinners out and all the book talk, not to mention the other talk too! *wink*

I also need to give a shout out to Teresa Conner, my cover designer, because this cover is freaking gorgeous. You always have such a great vision, even when I don't know how in the hell to express what I want. Thank you for always being so patient with me.

Finally, I want to talk a little about choosing to write a F/F romance and to have a bisexual character. Though I don't consider myself to be bisexual, I do have a real heart for my bi friends because I've known so many throughout the years and know what kind of persecution they face. They are often misunderstood and have been shamed by both gay and straight people. I wanted to portray a F/F relationship in the context of a swinging lifestyle because that's what I write about. No, not everyone understands swinging or wants to do it, but it is a real, legitimate lifestyle choice, and I don't feel like anyone should be discriminated against or shamed for choosing to participate. I always try to portray the lifestyle realistically so non-participants will get a better idea of what it's really like, and will hopefully learn what it is all about without feeling the need to be so *damn judgmental*. Suffice it to say, I hate judgmental people in general (I guess you could say I judge judgy people—so sue me!) and I want to have diversity in my books, whether that's in size, age, ethnicity, race, orientation or whatever. Basically I want to write REAL people. And hopefully readers will keep wanting to read REAL people.

If you do like the whole diversity thing and the window into ethical nonmonogamy, then stay tuned, because I have some really exciting projects in the works. Thank you all for your support!

Xo,

Phoebe

ABOUT THE AUTHOR

Phoebe Alexander writes #sexpositive #bodypositive erotic romance featuring compelling plots intertwined with passionate, fiery encounters. She believes that real, relatable characters can have even steamier sex than billionaires, rock stars, and the young and lithe-bodied. She also advocates for ethical non-monogamy through her writing.

Phoebe lives on the East Coast with her husband, sons, and multiple felines. When she's not writing, she works as an editor and consultant for indie authors. She also volunteers her time running a 3000-member indie author support group. Free time is her single greatest fantasy, and if she happens to have a moment she spends it at the beach, traveling, shopping or...wait, who are we kidding? That's about all she ever gets a chance to do.

Join Phoebe's newsletter at phoebe-alexander.com or follow her on Twitter @EroticPhoebe, on Facebook at www.facebook.com/phoebealexanderauthor, or on Instagram @authorphoebealexander

ALSO BY PHOEBE ALEXANDER

Mountains Trilogy
    Mountains Wanted
    Mountains Climbed
    Mountains Loved
    Christmas in the Mountains
    The Navigator (Coming Summer 2018)

Eastern Shore Swingers Series
    Fisher of Men
    The Catch
    Siren Call
    (Currently untitled – Casey's story, Coming Fall 2018)

The Playground

Project Paradise (The Juniper Court Series)
www.junipercourtseries.com

PHOEBE ALEXANDER

Made in the USA
Middletown, DE
22 June 2018